HEATH

USA TODAY BESTSELLING AUTHORS
NIKKI ASH | K WEBSTER

Heath

DEDICATION

To Emily Brontë, for rebelling against your time and giving us a romance like no other.

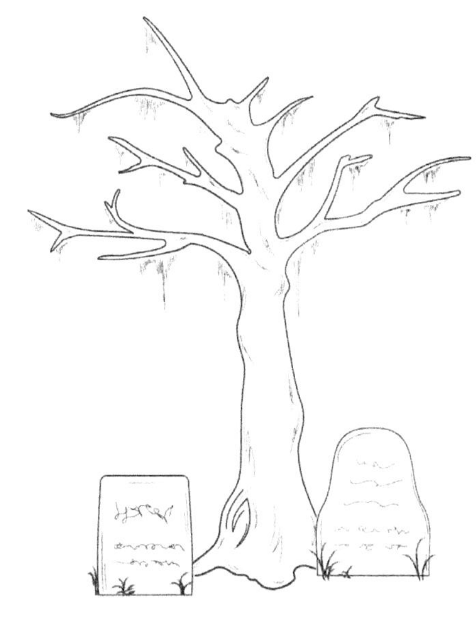

"I have not broken your heart—you have broken it; and in breaking it, you have broken mine."

Wuthering Heights —Emily Brontë

PART ONE

CHAPTER ONE

HELEN

The Present...

I STEP THROUGH THE FRONT DOOR AND TENSE, IMMEDIATELY alarmed, when a loud sob rings out through a closed door down the hallway. Miss Emily hardly ever cries. In fact, the only time I've seen her shed tears is when her horse Buckingham threw her off when she was thirteen. And that instance was more because her feelings were hurt that her horse would eject her, rather than her bruised tailbone.

Bruised hearts are far more painful.

When I reach her door, I twist the knob and enter.

Ah, sweet Emily. The apple of my eye, just like her mother.

I've never seen her look so sad in all my life. The crocodile tears spilling down her bright red cheeks could rival her grand-mother's any day.

"Oh, honey, what's wrong?" I coo as I approach her bed.

She tosses her cell phone on the pink comforter and swipes away her tears with her palms. "Everything," she says dramatically.

I sit on the edge of the bed and take her hands into mine. It's something I used to do when she was upset as a toddler. "Tell me everything."

A hiccup escapes and then another sob rings from her. "It's a boy, Nanny."

I smile at the pet name she gave to me when she was just

three. "Boys are rotten," I tell her, rubbing my thumbs along the backs of her hands.

She giggles through her tears and in this moment, I know everything will be okay. Emily is a product of two good people. That makes her better than good.

"It's Porter," she grumbles.

"The boy from your school?" I ask, a frown tugging at the corners of my mouth. "I thought Finn down the road was your boyfriend. He's nice."

Her lip curls up. "Finn and I are not boyfriend and girlfriend. We've always been just friends. He just thinks he has a say in my life." The haughty tone reminds me so much of her grandmother that I want to shake the teenage girl—shake the awful woman right out of her.

"And you have so much more in common with Porter?"

She starts crying again and for a moment, I'm at a loss.

"I just really like him and want *more* than to make out with him at the movies or in his backseat. All the girls at school want him and I know I'm not the only one he spends his time with. I want him to choose only me."

"You're eighteen, Miss Emily."

"So?"

"Porter is a teenage boy. He's a nice-looking young man playing the field. You both are too young to settle on one person."

She blinks at me, waiting for the punchline. Dear Lord, she is growing up way too fast and here all this time I thought she had her daddy in her. It looks like her grandmother's blood runs strong. "I'm eighteen. We're not too young."

"You *just* turned eighteen. He's pushing you away because he's not ready to be serious and settle down with one girl," I say with a sigh. "Because you *are* too young. You're supposed to go off to college in the city and—"

"I want to stay with him!" she cries out, throwing her arms in the air. "I want to marry him and have lots of babies. What's so wrong with that?"

So many reasons.

It's like history on repeat, destined to play over and over again.

And I am its victim—the victim history loves to haunt.

"He's not right for you," I say finally as if that explains everything.

"Why? Because he doesn't come from money? I don't care about money, you know this. I think I'm in love with him."

So stubborn, this girl.

"It's not enough. It never is. One day you'll wish for something more."

"I'm not that shallow, Nanny."

I can't say I believe her. Money talks louder than love sometimes.

"I'm not," she argues when I don't say anything. "You know I hate Finn's obnoxiously expensive car and I make fun of him for it. You've heard me. Finn and I are not a good match. I would never date some rich boy. Porter and I belong together. We have a lot more in common. I just have to make him understand."

"Let me tell you a story, darling. Scoot over," I tell her.

I kick off my shoes that make my feet ache too much these days and slide into the bed with her. We pull the comforter up to our breasts and I let out a heavy sigh.

"Love is complicated, Emily."

"No kidding."

"Love is messy."

Her phone buzzes and she has a missed text from Porter. Nosily, I read it along with her.

Porter: We can still go to the movies and hang out, but I don't have time for a relationship.

She huffs and tosses the phone back down. "What's so wrong with me?"

"It's not you," I assure her. "He's just not the one."

"I'm not giving up," she tells me, that haughty tone back in her voice.

"I was afraid you'd say that. Let's get on with this story. You may change your mind and leave the boy alone."

She curls against my side like she did when she was a youngster. "I'm pretty stubborn, Nanny. I still want to hear your story, though."

Our fingers link—her youthful ones threaded with my arthritis-ridden ones.

"This isn't my story," I tell her, letting my mind drift to the past. "No, this story is theirs. Heath and Catrina. Like the poor boy and the stubborn princess from your story."

"Oooh," she says breathily. "I can't wait."

"It's not pretty," I admit.

"I bet it ends happily."

Silly girl…happy endings are for fairy tales, not reality.

I kiss the top of her head. "I'll let you be the judge…"

CHAPTER TWO

HEATH
Twenty-Two Years Old
The Past...

"DIVERSIFICATION OF ASSETS WILL KILL US."

I lift a brow, amused. "Seems dramatic."

Mr. Crenshaw chuckles and his brown eyes flash with mischief. Just like hers. My empty heart that only ever beats for one quivers at the thought.

"I'm an old man. We're allowed to elaborate," he retorts before sucking in on his pipe. He blows out a plume of smoke that fills my lungs with toxins and familiarity. For his pipe was the very first memory I have of him. Tugging it from his grip. Banging it on the hardwood floors. Spitting out the tobacco after having a taste. Hell, my first word was probably pipe. My first everything is because of Rufus Crenshaw.

I owe him more than I could ever give him in return.

So for now, I give him my attention. I take notes. Mentally document every single word he says. The man is incredibly smart and rules C-Trades beautifully. He's a multimillionaire, one whom I spend every waking minute aspiring to be like.

"We're calling it 'elaborating.' Got it. Go on, Crenshaw. Tell me more about murderous economics."

"We're day traders, runt," he explains, his lips tugging up on one side. "Market savvy gamblers, if you will. Diversification is all about safety. Eliminating risk. Our fortune is dependent on our ability to manipulate risk. We take the leaps our clients are afraid to take. Economic cliff jumpers. You just have to know where to jump."

I chuckle and follow his gaze over to the mantle. The family portrait sits proudly, the spotlights affixed to the ceiling pointing at the picture. Crenshaw sits on a stool, a fierce expression on his normally smiling face. His eldest son, Hunter, who is my age exactly, stands behind him with his hand on his father's shoulder glaring. Typical. I'm standing beside Hunter, my dark brown hair slicked back and my deep chestnut eyes narrowed. Calculating. But it's who stands at the right of Crenshaw who makes the picture.

She fucking glows.

Catrina.

My everything.

In the portrait, she smiles as she's supposed to. Prim and proper. It's her eyes, though, that are wild. A wild I've spent my entire life chasing. Each time I think I have that wildness in my grasp, she wriggles away, taunts me some more, and the chase is back on.

I'll chase her right into eternity.

"You hear me, runt?"

Unwillingly, I drag my eyes away from her long, silky chocolate-colored tresses. Away from her pouty lips just begging for a kiss. Away, away, away. But never for long. My eyes always find their way back.

"Runt?" I chuckle. "I passed you up years ago. Around the time I turned sixteen if I recall correctly." I sit back on the leather sofa and adjust the knot on my tie. Reaching over at the side table, I pick up my tumbler of whiskey and take a swig. "Who's the runt now?"

Crenshaw cackles. The old man is always so easy to please. He loves games and I'm the only one who entertains him with them. Crenshaw plucked me from the streets of the inner city where I was homeless, without a mother, and half starved. He pulled me from a life that would have been nothing but hunger and violence and despair.

He brought me home.

He made me his.

And he gave me *her*.

Stray, stray, stray…my eyes always stray. Her green eyes snare mine so easily, and from a picture no less. The powers she has over me, at just nineteen years old, are unexplainable. Otherworldly. An intensity that doesn't die out with this lifetime, but will drag me into the next because we're linked in a way that transcends everything.

Fucking everything.

"I have a meeting next week with a fellow from Switzerland. C-Trades is about to explode. Thanks to you, son." Crenshaw regards me with fondness. Like a father. As though I *am* his son.

But his own son is lacking.

A smile tugs at my lips.

Hunter Crenshaw.

Knowing his own father sent him away to military school because he beat my ass one too many times, has satisfaction flooding through me. Crenshaw chose me over his blood. I fucking won. I always do.

"C-Trades was always meant to be a global conglomerate. This isn't the dark ages. We have technology at our fingertips, so it would behoove us to utilize it," I tell him, swirling the liquid around in my glass. I drain the alcohol, steal a glance at *her*, and then meet Crenshaw's gaze. "Branching out in other countries is wise."

He smiles at me fondly. "I knew the moment I looked into your big, soulful eyes hiding behind that shock of dirty, chocolate-colored hair that you were a smart kid. An intelligent little runt who was born at the wrong time to the wrong woman in the wrong town. God screws with the design sometimes."

I bristle at his mention of God. Often, in his old age, Crenshaw goes off on tangents like his long-time friend and church pastor, Jacob Milton. God may have created me, but he made a joke of me.

I let my gaze roam around the ornate sitting room in the massive twenty-seven-thousand-square-foot Windy Hills Estate.

Looks like the joke is on God.

I make my own way.

"Men like us have to be hard when life calls for it," Crenshaw continues, urging my attention his way. It's comical how similar he and Catrina are. Always craving the spotlight. "And we have to be soft when life whispers for it. Do you know how to be soft, runt?"

Middle of the night skinny dipping in the lake.

Affections murmured on creamy white skin under a pink, silk sheet.

Small kisses on a perfect thigh. Freckled. Quivering. Mine.

"Perhaps," I say.

He chuckles. "Don't go too soft."

"Never."

I fiddle with the handkerchief inside my pocket on my expensive suit jacket. Nothing but the best for Crenshaw's crew. I belong to that crew. The greatest tutors growing up. Fancy trips to Europe. Finest cars. Custom-made suits. Crenshaw demands the best for those around him.

Except his eldest son.

I wonder how good ol' Hunter is doing these days anyway. The fucker hasn't written or called. He's just a ghost. Cold and forgotten.

My mind drifts to the note I'd found sitting on my bed earlier before Crenshaw called for me to chat.

Come find me...

Images of Catrina taunting me with a curved finger and a wicked grin have me feeling anything but soft. It's amusing that she loves games more so than her father. Amusing and adorable. I play with her. I always have.

I love a good game of cat and mouse. It's one we play often.

"I'm the cat, naturally," she always says. "And you're the field mouse. Dirty and wild."

And then I always reply back with, "You're the kitten and I'm the monster under your bed."

Her emerald eyes always flash with a challenge.

"The monster can't find me if I'm not in my bed..." she then says.

And my response never changes. "I will always find you."

"Sir," I say as I stand, realizing the time. "I'm going to retire for the evening. I have a long day ahead of me tomorrow."

"Ah, yes. Final exams." He regards me proudly. "Soon you'll be a college graduate and when you turn twenty-three in the fall, you'll earn yourself a seat working for me. Not as my apprentice, but as a leader of my company."

"I'm looking forward to it," I tell him, straightening my spine. It's the truth. I've looked up to Crenshaw for as long as I can remember. Studying Finance, upon his guidance and on his dime. I would've graduated sooner, but I intern with him full-time. I can't keep up a full load of classes while learning from him, so I do what I can. It's taking longer than I've wished, but it's for the best because I'm getting hands-on experience. I've taken each necessary step to one day be just as successful as him. A regular rags-to-riches tale. And in this story, the big bad wolf gets the princess in the end.

"Carry on then, runt."

I give him a nod and then prowl through the dark hall-ways of the Windy Hills mansion. When Catrina and I were kids, we'd play hide and seek often. Hunter hated when we'd run through the house shouting and laughing. Bitter cunt. I'm stalking toward my room and nearly knock over the person coming out.

"My goodness, Heath! Watch where you're going!" The housemaid, Helen, huffs and picks up the soiled rag she dropped.

I smirk at her. "I wasn't the one running out of my room like my tail was on fire. Were you looking at my porn collection again?"

Her cheeks burn bright and she gapes at me. Helen, not much older than Hunter and me—and taken under Crenshaw's wing as I was—is so easily scandalized by a few choice words. Always a favorite game for Catrina and me. How far can we push Helen until she either cries, whips us with whatever she has in her hands at the moment, or utters out how we've been possessed by the devil?

"You ought to be ashamed of yourself," she hisses and swats at me with her rag. "Those porn magazines are for der-elicts and whores." She shudders and I boom with laughter.

I flash her a wicked look. "You sure do know a lot about porn mags, naughty woman."

She shoves me and stomps off. I'll get a talking to in the morning from Crenshaw because she'll no doubt tattle to him. It was worth it.

Slipping into my room, I shed my suit jacket and look about the small space. When I was a young boy and scared half out of my wits, I'd been sent to this room by Mrs. Crenshaw. Lillian Crenshaw was a frigid bitch. I know it broke the old man's heart, but he was better off the day she ran off with a younger man. She only distracted him. The moment she ran off, he poured his focus into his work and built an empire. She did him a favor.

She did me a favor as well.

By hissing hateful words and shoving me into an old sewing room—reminding me I wasn't good enough for a regular room—I'd learned at an early age that not everyone is good and eager to help poverty-stricken children in an alleyway. Some folks are spoiled as shit and don't want their pristine life tainted by the likes of a dirty little "runt." Lillian kindled a fire inside of me. To show her and those who were likeminded, that I could be better than them. That one day I would be.

I've been clawing my way to the top ever since.

Her son knows more than anyone how it feels to be on the bottom of motherfucking Heath's shoe.

Italian leather, of course, because his daddy demands the best.

"Heath…"

My name is called out sweetly from somewhere nearby. Just down the hallway outside my room. I quickly tug off my tie and pull it from my neck. She calls for me again and I all but rip my dress shirt off me. I kick off my shoes and crack my neck.

I'm coming, Catrina.

I leave my undershirt and slacks on as I slip out of the room on a hunt for her. In just my socks, I creep down the hallways quiet as the mouse she claims I am. Floorboards creak nearby and I pause mid-step. Listening. Inhaling the air. I catch a whiff of her lingering scent. Some sweet-smelling lotion I love to lick straight from her skin. My mouth salivates for a taste. Salty and sweet. Mine.

"Achoo!" A sniffle and then, "Shit!"

I rush into the room across from hers. It used to be

Hunter's room, but has since been turned into Catrina's sitting room. She likes the view of the property in this room better than hers. She had several bookshelves installed along the walls, a couple comfy reading chairs brought in, and a desk to write at put in along the long window.

"I know you're in here, my love," I say lowly from the doorway.

Now *she's* quiet as a mouse. But I can practically feel her breathing. I can practically taste her arousal.

"When I find you, I'm going to suck on your throat until you scream," I taunt.

"You can't do that. Then Daddy will know." The closet. I step over that way.

"He already knows," I counter.

"You told him?"

"I don't have to. Crenshaw's smart."

The hangers in the closet clatter together. I twist my fingers around the knob and wrench the door open. It's pitch-black in the long walk-in closet. Shuffling can be heard as she retreats deeper inside. I close the door behind me.

"Why do you always hide from me?" I ask as I run my palm along the empty hangers, letting them clack together. "Are you ashamed of me?"

"No," she grumbles, a little defensively I might add.

Irritation blooms inside of me. One day I'll prove my worth to her. I'm so close I can taste it. To all the outsiders, I'm an orphan who somehow caught the eye of a rich businessman. Unworthy. A thorn in the side of a perfect family. I don't belong. I've been told that before at church. Sanctimonious bastards. And in town, I see it in their eyes. I don't belong in their world.

Soon, though, this fucking world will be mine.

"We're in the dark, sweet Catrina. You can let your dirty little secret defile you and nobody will ever know," I growl.

She squeaks and I pounce. My palms find the silky material of her nightgown as I tackle her, and together, we fall to the carpeted closet floor, landing on a pile of old, unused pillows. She claws at my shirt, not because she wants to get away, but because she wants it off.

Little Crenshaw likes to get caught.

I nip at her jaw and her breath hitches. My cock is hard and I grind it against her thigh, reminding her just how good we are together. She moans, her fingers sliding to my gelled hair and rumpling it. Her grip tightens on my locks as she draws me to her lips.

I can't see her in the darkness, but I don't need to.

She's the most beautiful thing I've ever seen.

She's the most beautiful thing I can't see.

Hot breath tickles my lips, but I don't indulge her with a kiss. Not yet. I want to punish her a little for her earlier hesitation. One day, I'll be worthy and I'll put a ring on her finger. Then, I'll fill her over and over again with my children. If God had a plan, it didn't include us. Nothing this fiery—this intense—could come from the heavens. The flames that continually burn through us are straight from the bowels of hell.

A devil and his queen.

To rule. Together. Soon.

"Who do you love?" I ask, my lips delicately brushing over hers.

"A madman," she teases.

I suck on her bottom lip and then bite until she cries out. "Is he good-looking?"

"Hot. So hot," she breathes. "He kisses really well."

"Better than me?" I nudge her nose with mine.

"Hmm," she purrs. "Maybe you should kiss me and I'll let you know."

"Kiss you where?" I press my mouth to hers. "Here?"

"Everywhere."

I trail hot kisses from her mouth to her jaw to her throat. With eager hands, I rip at her gown, pulling the top down and exposing her bare breasts to me. "Here?"

"Y-Yes, there."

I nip at her breast and then suck the flesh between my teeth. She cries out and wraps her legs around my body. Her heels dig into my back as her fingers claw desperately at my hair.

"Tell me who you love," I murmur against her peaked nipple. "Tell me."

She moans. "You, Heath. I love you."

I suck her nipple hard and then pop off it with a loud sound. The material slides back over her breasts. I kiss down the front of her gown toward her cunt as I shove the material up her stomach. When I kiss her near her belly button, her breath hitches. Her panties are lacy and barely anything to speak of. I take joy in ripping them in two and tossing them somewhere in the closet for Helen to find. Catrina mutters my name when I wrench her thighs apart. I don't have to see her pretty pussy to know it's trimmed short, pink, and dripping with arousal. We've been intimate for years now. In secret, but the love between us grows more intense with each passing moment. Sometimes I wonder how it will be when we're old and gray. Will we combust entirely? What a beautiful fucking burn that would be.

I kiss her mound and then run my tongue up her slit. She jolts beneath me and her hips lift, seeking out the pleasures only I can offer. Sucking on her clit, I revel in the scream that will be muffled by the closet. Her taste is sweet and fucking perfect. I suck on her soft lips. Bite on her tender flesh. Inhale her scent that belongs only to me. I steal her moans and groans and curses. My fingers seek her entrance and find the places within her that also beg for attention. I play my girl like an instrument. A loud one that squawks and is out of tune, but plays beautiful music to me, nonetheless.

"Heath!" She says my name like a curse. Like when she stubs her toe or burns her fingers on her curling iron. I like that I'm the dirty and the wrong in her life. Her favorite naughty word.

I suck her clit into my mouth once more as I finger her G-spot within, loving the way she shudders with a loud, body-quaking orgasm. I don't give her time to recover. As she continues to shudder, I yank at my zipper and work my aching cock from my slacks. I give her wet cunt a slap that makes her cry out and then I push inside her. No warning. Just stab her with my need. Desperate. Hungry. Fucking now.

"Heath!" Again, I'm being chastised for being bad with good loving.

I growl and tangle my fingers in her hair. Our lips fuse together and I kiss my life. I kiss my heart. I kiss my goddamned soul. We are one, she and I. Her nails scrape down my arms and her cunt clenches around my thickness. I fuck her hard and unrelenting. I fuck her like the madman she claims me to be. I fuck her until I'm dangerously close to coming.

Slowing, I tease her mouth with mine. "I could come inside you."

She flinches. "Don't be a prick."

I lift up and grab her wrists, pinning her to the pillows beneath her. "I could do it and you'd be at my mercy."

"Is that really in your plan?" she tosses back at me, not fighting my hold on her.

Annoyed that she called my bluff, I slam into her hard

enough to make her scream again. I fuck, fuck, fuck her until my nuts seize up. With a groan, I pull out seconds before shooting my load inside her and instead come all over her perfect stomach that will one day swell with my child.

Just not yet.

I may be a madman.

But even madmen have a plan.

And plans, especially those designed by madmen, must be carefully executed.

"I love you too," I say and kiss my life, my heart, my soul's mouth.

The plan has almost come to fruition.

Soon, sweet Catrina. Soon.

CHAPTER THREE

CATRINA

"WOULD YOU CARE FOR MORE TEA?" DENISE, THE Lincolns' housemaid, asks, her thin brow quirked up as she holds the ceramic teapot in front of me while waiting for an answer. I glance toward her and realize I must've been lost in my own thoughts. It happens often, especially after spending time with Heath.

"Yes, please." I give her a slight nod and a fake smile as my thoughts go back to the way Heath made love to me last night. Lifting my teacup to my lips, I take a sip as I force myself not to let out a snicker at the mere thought of what one might think if they were to witness Heath's type of lovemaking. The way he tore my panties off my body and pushed my thighs apart. My muscles clench as I recall the way he ate my pussy like a starved man before he spread me open and fucked me like a wild animal. No, not like a wild animal. Like a madman. *My madman.*

"Catrina, you're awfully quiet," Delores Lincoln notes. "Is everything okay?"

Resisting the urge to roll my eyes over her false attempt at sounding like she gives a damn about anything other than herself, I plaster on my mastered saccharine smile, tilt my head to the side slightly, and nod once, just as I've been trained to do thanks to my many years of finishing school. "Of course, I'm just thinking about the upcoming garden party." Delores grins back then turns her attention to her daughter, Isabel, regarding her as though she's the most beautiful thing she's ever seen. Isabel *is* pretty, I guess, in a boring, innocent sort of way with her wide hazel eyes and smooth pale-blond hair.

"I recently stumbled upon the most adorable bakery while shopping with Clarissa. Sinful Delights. At first glance I was skeptical as it's located in Cobble Hill, but I must say their brownies were delicious. Clarissa ordered the rhubarb pie, and while I probably shouldn't have, I splurged and tried a piece. It was simply delectable." Her eyes widen like she's just confessed to purchasing a nine-inch dildo instead of just admitting to eating a pastry in Cobble Hill. My tea goes down the wrong way at the image of Delores with a large, thick, rubber dick, and I have to cover my mouth and fake a cough to hide my reaction.

"Mother, what in the world were you doing in Cobble Hill?" Isabel scrunches her nose up in disgust, and for the millionth time during this tea time, I force my eyes not to roll upward.

"Clarissa needed to size a woman for a wedding and unfortunately she lives over there. You know Clarissa, she'd design a wedding gown for a homeless woman if she begged her nice enough. Anyway, I was thinking we could order from them. You know, help out the less fortunate." She nods emphatically and I stifle a snort. Cobble Hill is one of the top ten wealthiest neighborhoods in New York. I know this because sometimes when Heath works from home he talks to me about his clients and what he and my father are working on to expand the business. I love that he includes me and speaks to me like I'm his equal, as opposed to treating me like I'm nothing more than a brainless bimbo—like most men treat their women.

"I think that can be arranged." I set my teacup down and

pick up a piece of biscotti. I take a bite and force myself to choke down the cardboard flavored treat, when what I really want to do is spit it out into my napkin. *That wouldn't be very ladylike, now would it?*

"Oh, Elliot!" Delores stands to greet her son, as does Isabel, and after taking a sip of tea to wash down that horrible excuse of a dessert, I do the same.

"Ladies." Elliot gives his mother a kiss on each of her cheeks before he pulls me into his arms for a hug. When he releases me, he backs up slightly and eyes me skeptically. I avert my gaze elsewhere, not able to look him in the eyes, fearful he'll be able to see what I refuse to say. That while it's all but been arranged since I was a little girl, that one day I'll become Mrs. Elliot Lincoln, my heart will never beat for him the way it pounds for the man I really love. Heath. The man whose passion burns so brightly it lights up my soul and sets my body on fire. It's Heath who pulls me out of my mundane life and into our own little fantasy world. But that's all Heath will ever be to me. A fantasy. I might be able to touch him and see him and make love to him, but the love we feel for each other will never become a reality.

"Catrina, my love, you look as beautiful as ever." Elliot smiles, but it doesn't reach his eyes and I worry he's onto me. That he knows my thoughts aren't about us. That my dreams don't include him. That even though the bastard might have my father wrapped around his wealthy little finger, he'll never truly have me. He might one day have my body, but he'll never have my heart and especially not my soul.

"Thank you, Elliot." We all have a seat and of course, he sits right next to me, his hand landing on my thigh and squeezing it softly. Everything he does is soft.

The way he kisses me.

The way he touches me.

The way he has sex with me.

Soft, soft, soft. There isn't a passionate bone in his body.

"We were just discussing the garden party, which will be taking place next month. Catrina has been such a godsend handling all the little details." Delores smiles sweetly.

"It's my pleasure." I turn to Elliot. "You're off work early. Is everything okay?"

"Never better. I was actually hoping to steal you away a little earlier than planned." He winks and I giggle at his rare playfulness. It's not often he lets loose and enjoys himself. His world revolves around the oil company he runs with his father. Everything else coming second. We've been dating for the last year since he convinced my father it was time he take me out, but I'm nothing more than arm candy for him. He doesn't really know me. He doesn't even try to understand me. Not my wants or needs or my deepest desires. He just wants me to be there to look pretty by his side.

"Only if you make it worth my while," I murmur into his ear, knowing it will embarrass him. And just as I thought, he smiles sweetly and his cheeks turn a light pink. He's so much fun to mess with.

I take another sip of my tea and silently listen as he converses with his mother and sister for a few minutes. When he laughs at something Isabel says, I notice the adorable dimple pop out on his cheek. He must feel me staring at him because he glances over at me and grins, shooting me another playful wink. While Elliot is definitely no Heath when it comes to the looks department, he's still a good-looking man, just in a more wholesome, boy-next-door sort of way. Whereas Heath is devilishly handsome with his dark brown—almost black—hair always gelled back; Elliot is softer, with his light brown hair always a mess, reminding me of a cute school boy. His eyes are chocolate brown and always bright with genuine happiness shining through, while Heath's darker, deeper brown eyes stay hardened to the outside world, only softening for me when we're alone and in our own little bubble.

"Well, we better be going," Elliot says, putting an end to our weekly tea, something we've been doing for years since I was a little girl and my mother was still around. Before she had enough of this life and escaped. Most days I want to hate her for running, but sometimes, secretly, I envy her.

The four of us stand and Isabel and Delores walk us to the door. Elliot hugs his mother and promises they'll do brunch this weekend. I spot his Mercedes in the driveway and after saying my goodbyes, head over to the vehicle. Like the gentleman he is, Elliot opens my door for me and once I'm situated, closes the door behind me. Opening his glovebox, I take my Chanel sunglasses out that I keep in here for sunny days like today and put them on. Elliot picks a station and I change it, refusing to listen to the garbage he calls music. We're almost down his driveway and to the main road when I let my mind drift to earlier.

"Finals are over," Heath murmurs, nipping at my ear with his teeth.

I love to taunt him. "Did you pass?"

"You know I did."

"We'll celebrate later tonight then," I promise.

He hugs me tight. "Dinner at Sheffield's and dessert in your bed."

"Dinner is out, but dessert can definitely be arranged."

His body stiffens and I can feel the anger radiating from him. "Other plans?"

"Nothing of importance," I tell him truthfully. "I'll come to you when your dessert is ready."

I let out a sigh and try not to think about the fact I'd

much rather be with Heath right now than Elliot. Instead, I focus my attention on where we're headed. I watch out the window as the car picks up speed and the luscious green landscapes blur together. Elliot keeps the conversation flowing the entire drive to the city. I answer the questions he asks and laugh at all the right moments, but my mind is with Heath, wishing I were at dinner with him. I glance down at Elliot's and my adjoined hands and wish it were Heath's hand I was holding. I stare out the window and wish my fantasies could somehow become a reality.

We pull up to the Grand Hyatt and Elliot stops the vehicle. He gets out before I can ask him what we're doing here. I quickly look down at my Valentino black minidress and matching pumps. When Elliot mentioned going to dinner, he didn't say where. The valet opens my door and I take my sunglasses off, throwing them into the glovebox. Then I take his proffered hand and step out of the vehicle. I locate Elliot and shoot a glare in his direction. "You didn't mention anything about going to a hotel."

He grins mischievously and my stomach drops. "I wanted to surprise you. I've made reservations at the restaurant and booked us a night in their penthouse suite." He winks, but this time I don't giggle, too annoyed.

"Well, you should've mentioned it. I'm not exactly dressed for an evening out and I-I don't even have a change of clothes or toiletries." I snub my nose in the air like I'm being put out, but on the inside I'm panicking.

"Don't worry, Catrina, the only thing you'll need tonight is yourself."

I worry about my promise to Heath to come see him later. Shit! If I'm not home tonight, Heath will burn this city ablaze in his search of me.

"I need to make a call."

"Nonsense. Your father already knows you're with me. There's nobody else who needs to know where you are." I can hear the silent meaning behind his words, but I ignore them. He extends his hand and I take it, following him into the hotel restaurant while trying to figure out a way to get ahold of Heath.

The maître d' sits us at a private table in the back corner. Elliot thanks him then turns his attention to me. "No menus?" I ask.

"No, I planned the entire evening ahead of time so we won't be interrupted." He edges his chair closer to mine and places my hands into his. "I wanted tonight to be special, my love." He leans in and places a soft kiss on my lips before backing up and smiling. "I love you, Catrina."

"I love you too," I choke out.

We go through our meal, one course at a time, beginning with the cheese stuffed mushrooms, eventually making it to our main course of Maine Lobster, and finally ending with the Strawberry Shortcake. As I take a small bite of a strawberry, I remember I'm supposed to be having dessert with Heath. Then an idea strikes me on how I might be able to get out of this, but before I can put my plan into motion, I spot Elliot getting up from his seat. I'm about to ask him where he's going when he drops to one knee while opening a teal-colored jewelry box. I tilt my chin up slightly to assess the ring and notice it's an oval platinum diamond, at least four carats. It's absolutely exquisite.

"Catrina," Elliot begins and I try to calm my beating heart. Only it's not beating out of excitement but instead in terror. I thought I would have longer. At least a few more years. "It's no secret that our engagement has been a long time coming. I've asked your father for your hand and he's given us his blessing. Will you do me the honor of becoming my wife?"

No! No! *I won't become your wife. I don't love you or want you.* I love someone else and he owns me, every piece of me. But no matter what *I* want in this life, it's not the right path. Elliot is the path I'm destined for. "Yes. Yes, I will marry you." I fight to hold back my tears as he slips the engagement ring on my ring finger, but once one tear breaks free, the rest follow in an unbroken stream. Elliot mistakes my devastation for happiness as he pulls me into his arms and kisses me softly. Always softly.

Grabbing my hand in excitement, he guides me out of the restaurant and up to our suite. "There's a bag of toiletries in the bathroom if you'd like to freshen up," he says as he removes his suit coat and hangs it in the closet. Unable to even speak, I simply nod, then I lock myself in the bathroom, my body hitting the back of the door as I fall to the cold tile in a ruined heap. Covering my mouth, I cry for everything that Heath and I will never be. For everything we can't be. Sobs silently wrack through my body as I wonder how I got to this point in my life. Loving the man I can't have and being stuck with the one I don't want. My thoughts go to my mother and how she left my father. Some would call her a fool for walking away from a life of luxury, but as I sit here in this bathroom, feeling trapped, I have to wonder if maybe choosing love over money is what saved her.

Silent tears race down my cheeks as I think about Heath. My best friend. My lover. My everything. Since the moment my father brought him into our home, we've been inseparable. There isn't a time I can recall when Heath hasn't been there. Every birthday, every holiday. But it doesn't matter that he's been raised alongside me. That he works harder to earn his money than the men who simply have it given to them.

No, life doesn't work that way. You're either born into this life or you're an outsider. And no matter what Heath does, he will always be watching from the outside while I'm trapped on the inside.

Closing my eyes, I take a deep, calming breath. Then I let out an exhale and find my resolve. I fix my makeup and freshen up. I find a silky piece of lingerie in my bag, courtesy of my new fiancé, and put it on. Then, without giving myself another glance, I exit the bathroom where I find Elliot lying in bed and waiting for me, no longer wearing his dress shirt.

"You look gorgeous," he croons, patting the top of the bed for me to join him. I climb up and crawl over next to him, and once I'm lying down, he rolls over and settles on top of me, his hands caging me in. He rakes his gaze over my face then plants a gentle kiss to my lips, his tongue delicately swirling in my mouth. I close my eyes and try to imagine he's Heath, but it's pointless. Elliot could never satisfy me in the way Heath does, at least not without my guidance. So instead of trying to wish for my fantasy, I choose to deal with my reality.

Returning Elliot's kiss, my tongue meets his as I take over. I pull his undershirt over his head and unbutton his pants, pushing them down. He's left in nothing but his boxers. I glide my hand back up and squeeze his dick through the material. He jumps slightly, startled that I'm behaving so brazenly, and breaks our kiss. With one hand still holding himself up, he uses his other hand to remove mine from his boxers and places it around his neck. I should've known he wouldn't allow me to take control. He never does. His lips meet mine once more and I can feel him guide himself into me. I'm barely wet, definitely not turned on, but he doesn't notice. He pumps into me a few times and then lets out a low groan as he comes inside me.

"I love you, Catrina. Thank you for agreeing to be my wife and making me the happiest man in the world." Then he kisses me once more, rolls off the bed, and pads to the bathroom to clean up, while I stare down at my ring and wonder how in the hell I'm going to explain this to Heath.

CHAPTER FOUR

The Present...

"N o!" Emily cries out. "This is a terrible story!"

I chuckle because she's right. The story of Heath and Catrina is awful. Wretched and wrong. Downright despicable. Certainly not a love story, in my opinion. "So I shouldn't continue then, dear?"

"Ugh," she groans in an overdramatic way. "Continue. It's like a train wreck, though, Nanny. I'm too invested in the outcome now. Nicholas Sparks wrote this story, didn't he? I bet they all die in the end. Please tell me Heath freaked the fuck out."

"Miss Emily!" I admonish. "Your mother may allow that hoodlum talk, but I certainly don't. There's a bar of soap with your name on it and I'm not afraid to use it. I don't care how old you are."

She giggles. "Sorry. Tell me he put up a fight for her. Please."

Her phone buzzes and she becomes distracted as she texts Porter.

Emily: I know you like me better than those other girls.

She stares at her phone as though she wills him to reply. He doesn't. Peeling her gaze from her phone, she looks up at me. "He put up a fight, right?"

I let out a sigh. When did Heath ever not put up a fight when it came to Miss Catrina? "It only unraveled from there. And here is where the story turns sad…"

CHAPTER FIVE

ᴴEATH
The Past…

"ᖴ**OR GOODNESS' SAKE, Hᴇᴀᴛʜ, sɪᴛ ᴀɴᴅ ᴇᴀᴛ ᴀ ʙɪᴛᴇ. Yᴏᴜ'ʀᴇ** wearing a hole in the floors," Helen snips.

I stop pacing to sit at the kitchen table and glare at the phone on the wall, willing it to ring. The plate of bacon and eggs goes ignored the moment she sets it down in front of me. My focus is on my million unanswered questions but mainly one.

Where the fuck is she?

So help me, woman, if you're not dead already, I'm going to kill you.

I don't really think she's dead somewhere. No, it's much worse than that. When she didn't call and it got late, I drove my unhappy ass down to the Low Valley Estate. Mrs. Lincoln and her prissy daughter Isabel were all too thrilled to let me know that Catrina was out with Elliot.

Fucking Elliot.

He's always been a thorn in my side. Small. Inconsequential. Not a concern. Irrelevant. Yet, recently, I'm starting to realize he's poison. Slowly infecting my sweet love. Spreading his motherfucking disease of money and power, tricking her into believing he's worthy of her.

As fucking if.

I bet his cock is laughable and he doesn't even know where to put it half the time.

"She's probably off with the young Lincoln fellow," Helen

reminds me for the ninetieth goddamned time. "They're exclusively dating after all. She doesn't have to tell her brother her every move."

I shoot Helen a withering glare that has her turning to the stove to scrub the grease from it. I'm not her brother and she damn well knows it. We're good at hiding our intimate moments from prying eyes, but the snooping maid isn't an idiot. She's been around a time or two when a playful kiss between Catrina and I has turned hot.

"Elliot Lincoln is an imbecile," I grumble.

"An imbecile with money," she retorts.

I hate money.

I hate it with every fiber of my being.

That's why I want it.

I want as much of it as I can possibly grab onto so I can manipulate it to my will. So I can fucking rule over it. I'm tired of money, or lack thereof, deciding my future—of it dictating my every move.

My love for Catrina has nothing to do with money.

And I hate that it's the very thing that tears us apart.

Which is why one day soon, after college and when old Crenshaw comes to an understanding that his daughter and I belong together, I will shed this horrible monetary curse and make my own way. A way that includes her.

There is no way without her.

The front door creaks open and I jolt from my seat with Helen on my heels. I'm just stalking into the foyer when Catrina walks in with Elliot entering behind her. My hate-filled expression is for him and him only. The pussy won't meet my stare. Instead, he exchanges pleasantries with Helen.

"Please stay for breakfast," Helen chirps, a little too fucking cheery for nine in the morning.

"The Grand Hyatt has excellent room service," he says to

her and then darts a daring look my way. "Breakfast in bed at one of the finest hotels in New York. Everyone should try it at least once." He weakens under my murderous stare and then pats Catrina on the shoulder. "Right, darling?"

She bites on her bottom lip and keeps her eyes downcast. When she tucks a strand of hair behind her ear, a big fucking diamond glitters in the light.

I growl.

"Well, if you don't mind, I need to get to the office," Elliot says lamely. "Goodbye, Catrina. I'll call you later."

Gritting my teeth with my fists clenched, I watch as he kisses *my fucking girl* on the top of her head before scurrying out the front door.

"Such a fine-looking young man," Helen murmurs.

I snap my attention her way and shake my head. "Give us a moment."

She nods and then hurries away. The moment she's gone, I prowl over to Catrina. As soon as I'm nearly touching her chest with mine, I inhale her. She smells like *him*. It makes the animal within me want to piss a goddamned circle around her, claiming her as mine. I want to drag her into the lake behind the estate and drown her until she no longer reeks of his disgusting scent.

She's mine.

And yet she wears his motherfucking ring.

"Nice ring," I hiss, my breath blowing her hair.

Her head tilts up. I'm furious and I want to throttle her. I want to drag her to some corner of this godforsaken earth and keep her there. Tie her to the fucking bed and never let her go. But the moment tears well in her big green eyes, my resolve weakens. All delightful images of cutting Elliot from throat to nut sack and watching him bleed out at my feet fall by the wayside.

A tear rolls down her rosy cheek.

My fist releases as I reach up a finger to steal her sadness. Her tears are mine. Just like her smiles and her laughter and her love are mine. All of it. Mine.

"It's just a ring," I growl. "It means nothing to me."

Her nostrils flare and more tears leak out. "Heath." My name is spoken like an apology, not a curse. Filled with shame and horror. Regret.

I pull her to me just as she crumples. Sobs rattle through her and her tears soak my dress shirt. Gently, I stroke her hair despite wanting to tug it so I can look her in the eye and demand to know why.

But I know why.

He. Has. Fucking. Money.

And I don't.

Simply put.

"I don't care if you have ten husbands," I snarl, hugging her tighter to me. "I'll always find you. I'll fuck you in their beds. I'll make you mine over and over again. You know this."

She cries harder. "I-I-I'm sorry."

"Me too," I clip out.

Her head tilts up and her fingers slide into my hair. She tries to kiss me with her tainted lips. I lean away from her. "Not with that dirty mouth. Is that the same mouth you sucked his cock with?"

She shoves me and glowers my way. "Fuck you."

"Looks like Limp Dick Lincoln already got the honors," I sneer.

Sometimes, our games aren't fun.

Sometimes, we're both losers.

Storming past me, she runs up the stairs, kicking her heels off along the way.

Chase me, she begs.

She doesn't have to say it.

I always know.

With a growl, I storm up the stairs two at a time. She barely makes it into her room before I'm prowling in after her. I kick the door shut and intercept her before she makes it to her bathroom. Her worthless fists pummel my chest and I laugh cruelly at her.

"Those fists mean nothing. The damage is already done, Catrina. Do you love to fucking hurt me?" I demand, my voice rising. "Because that's what you did."

"No! You know I don't want this!"

"Could have fooled me," I bite out, grabbing her hips and backing her into the doorframe. "You fucked him and you're wearing his ring."

"You know I sleep with him on occasion," she snaps. "Don't act all sanctimonious now. You know what we are and how this works."

I pin her body with mine and my grip finds her jaw. My forehead rests against hers as my fingers dig into her delicate flesh. Beneath his scent, I catch a whiff of *her*. Sweet and floral. Beautiful. Addictive. "I thought I could handle it when it happened, but I can't. I can't do this, love. It's too fucking hard."

She stands on her toes and I let her kiss me. Sweet and apologetic. "Since when is anything too hard for you, Heath? You're the strongest man I know."

My lips fuse to hers and then I devour her. Our tongues tangle, fighting for dominance. I always win. Today, she doesn't put up her normal fight. When we pull away, our chests heaving for air, I close my eyes. Wishing my life were different. Wishing I were born into a family like the fucking loser Lincolns. Wishing to be anything other than the runt without a last name or a past or a damn legacy.

"Hey," she murmurs, her fingers latching in my hair. "It's just a ring. Like you said. It means nothing. This is just another one of life's games. We can play by our own rules."

With a growl, I twist her away from me. My lips find her neck and I nip at her flesh as I drag the zipper down on the back of her dress. She allows me to push it from her body. It pools at her feet soundlessly. The frilly panties and bra get discarded next.

God, his scent on her disgusts me.

"You make me crazy," I hiss, my palm cupping her perfectly round bottom. "So fucking crazy."

"My madman," she breathes.

I slap her ass hard, earning a squeal from her. "I'm pissed, Catrina. I'm going to be pissed until I feel like you've been punished." My finger slips between her thighs and pushes into her pussy, causing her to moan. "I'll remain pissed until I've scrubbed every inch of that limp dick's smell off you." I slide my hand out and pop her ass again, loving the way her cheeks clench. Then, I ease my hand back to where I want and this time urge two fingers inside her. She whimpers when I fuck her with my fingers and then whines when I pull them back out to whip her again. "I'll stay pissed until I'm balls deep inside of you where I belong. Tell me you deserve what I'm about to give to you."

She groans and pushes her now red ass toward my palm. "I deserve a lot more than an ass whipping."

Slap! Slap! Slap!

I spank her ass that has been seen by another man until she's squirming and crying. When she's had enough, I tease her pussy only to whip her some more. This goes on until she's a mess. Once I think she's had enough and I can't bear to strike her anymore, I start ripping at my clothes. She stands, looking sad as fuck and remorseful as I get naked. Once I'm undressed as well, I drag *my fucking girl* into the walk-in shower with me. She screeches when I turn on the water, the icy blast a shock to her flesh, but then calms as it heats up.

Steam billows around us, trapping us in our own world. Our eyes remain glued to each other. Even as I thoroughly soap her down everywhere. She allows me to wash her until she's clean and once again all mine. His touch is a thing of the past. The moment she's rinsed off, I grab her sore ass and lift her. My cock rubs against her clit, but I don't enter her as I press her back against the cold tile wall. I tease her instead.

"Does he make you come?" I growl, nipping at her jaw near her ear.

Her body shudders in my grip. "Not even close."

"Do you think of me when he fucks you?"

"It doesn't last long enough to consider it a fuck."

Rocking my hips against hers slowly, I revel in the desperate moans as she grows closer and closer to her orgasm.

"You're not marrying him," I grind out. "I don't want to be your secret anymore."

Our eyes meet and hers are wide with surprise.

"It's not that easy," she whines. "You know that."

And I do.

I have nothing to offer her. Fucking nothing. Without Crenshaw's money, I'm just a poor kid from the ghetto. But Crenshaw loves me. He certainly loves Catrina. Maybe if we talk to him, he'd let me marry her instead of Elliot. Maybe he could loan me the money to give us our start. I know, with time, I could make her proud of me. I could be worthy and I'd pay back every cent to her father.

With new resolve, I crush my lips to hers. Kiss her violently. Desperately. I pepper unspoken promises all over her pretty mouth.

I will figure out a way for us.

We will win.

My cock slides against her in a way she loves and soon she's coming, crying out my name.

"Please," she begs, her palms cradling my cheeks. "I need you."

I grip her hips and slide her to her feet. Turning to her left hand, I kiss her palm. I wrap my palm around her wrist and kiss my way to her ring finger. With my eyes on hers, I suck her small finger into my mouth. My teeth latch around the massive diamond and I pull it off, scraping her knuckle along the way.

She doesn't fight me and when I've freed her of the abomination, I step away from her. Stalking out of the shower, I make my way over to the toilet and spit it into the bowl.

"Heath!" she admonishes as she turns off the shower.

I belt out a dark laugh before yanking her to me. Our wet bodies are slick and she almost slips from my grasp. Digging my fingers into her ass, I squat and then hoist her over my shoulder.

"Caveman!" she shrieks, beating her fists into my back.

I swat her ass again and carry her into her bedroom. She says my name again—this time like a curse word—when I toss her on the bed. But then, when I crawl over her soaking wet body, my name transforms into something that sounds more like a prayer.

Begging.

Pleading.

A desperation that matches mine.

I grip the backs of her thighs and push them against her, loving the way her tits bounce with the movement. My aching dick rubs against her slick cunt in a teasing way.

"Who do you love?" I ask, my voice low and guttural.

"Always you," she breathes.

Slowly, almost painfully so, I push into her. Her green eyes flare with love and lust and an insanity that rivals mine until I'm seated fully inside her.

"I love you. He doesn't love you like I do," I murmur, my voice cracking with emotion.

Her bottom lip wobbles. "Nobody loves me like you do."

Catrina and I fuck like rabbits, but today I stamp my very

essence on her soul. No ring or swanky hotel screw will erase me. I'm imprinting myself on her being one thrust at a time. I rub her in all the right ways until she sobs out my name. Sad. So fucking sad.

And then I pull out and mark her like the animal I am.

Seeing my cum splattered over her wet, jiggly tits and flat stomach sates my inner beast.

Mine.

"I'll make him see," I murmur, my eyes glued to her plump, pouty lips. "I'll make your father see that we're in love. That Elliot is nothing. That we can be together. Everything will be fine. I'll get a loan from him. We'll marry and I'll pay him back. Tell me you want that."

She nods. "I do. God, how I do."

"It's done then," I say and kiss her lips.

For hours we make love—or is it eternity? Time with Catrina is never enough.

I'm about to flip her over and go for more because I'll never be sated with her, when the door flings open. We scramble to yank the blanket over our naked bodies, but when I realize it's just nosy Helen, fury replaces my shock.

"What the fuck, Helen?" I roar. "Get the hell out of here!"

She squeezes her eyes shut and shakes her head. It's then I realize she's crying. "Mr. Heath," she chokes out. "Miss Catrina."

I slide from the bed and snag my slacks from the bathroom floor. Yanking them on, I then storm over to her. "For God's sake, woman, what's the matter?"

She sobs harder, so I grab her shoulders and shake some sense into her. Finally, her eyes open and she regards me with a heartbroken stare.

"He's gone."

I blink in confusion. "Who's gone?"

"Mr. Crenshaw. When I brought him his breakfast in bed

after you retired to your room, I discovered he'd passed sometime in the middle of the night. I've put off telling you long enough. He's dead."

Fuck.

Fuck.

Fuuuuuuck.

CHAPTER SIX

DEAD.

My father is dead.

This can't be real. It has to be a nightmare. I rush from the bed, pulling my robe on along the way, and race down the hall to my father's room. I swing the door open, only to find his bed is empty. The sheets are rumpled. Maybe he's using the bathroom. I cut across the room and push the door open. It's empty. Where is he? He has to be somewhere. He can't be gone. Helen is wrong. I check the closet and the sitting room. He's nowhere. I sprint down the stairs and check the living room and kitchen. He's not there.

"Where is he?" I demand. Helen mumbles incoherent things through her hands as she chokes on her sobs. "Where is he?" I repeat. When she doesn't answer me, I grab her hands and yank them from her face. "Where the hell is my father?" I shout.

"They came and got him. They picked him up."

"You should've come and got me immediately! He's my father!"

My body is shaking. This can't be happening. Not my daddy. My heart clenches in agony. I have to see him for myself. I won't believe it until I see his lifeless body with my own two eyes.

"Heath," I cry out and he wraps his comforting arms around me. "Take me to him, please."

Robotically, I get dressed while Heath does the same. When I enter the bathroom to brush my teeth, the glint of the engagement ring shines from under the water in the toilet. I let out a strangled sob as I recall Heath's words to me. He was supposed to speak to my father so we could be together. Where will that leave us now?

Plucking the ring from inside the toilet, I rinse it off using soap and water, then drop it into my vanity drawer. I brush my teeth and wash my face then meet Heath downstairs. Helen is in tears, but I ignore her cries. My only focus is on seeing my father.

Heath drives us into the city, to the hospital Helen said they brought my father to. No words are spoken between us on the way. There doesn't need to be. I know Heath is hurting as badly as I am. I stare down at our conjoined hands. We fit so perfectly together. He completes me, makes me whole. He gives me strength when I feel weak. He ignores all my flaws and loves me for not only who I am but for who I could be.

When we pull up to the entrance, I glance over at Heath, silently asking him to be with me through this. He simply nods and exits the vehicle, coming around to my side to open my door. Placing his hand back in mine, we walk through the doors of the hospital together.

My father's death is confirmed, but it's not enough for me. Despite the coroner's warnings, I demand to see his body. After several hours of waiting, we are finally called back and taken to the morgue, and it's only in that moment when I see my father's still body that I accept he's gone. I barely make it out of the room when my legs give out and I'm falling. Heath catches me, his strong arms always saving me. He holds me tight while we cry over the loss of the man we both love.

"Marry me, Heath," I blurt out. "I don't want to waste another day without being with you. Marry me and let's spend our life together."

He pulls me up with him and hoists me into his arms, my legs wrapping around his waist and my arms around his neck.

He stalks us down the hall and finds an empty room, slamming the door and locking it shut behind us. I'm not even sure what's in the room because my attention is only on Heath. His love-filled eyes and his wildly beating heart. He pushes me up against the wall, his hands gripping my ass.

"Say it again," he demands.

"Marry me," I repeat while streams of tears flow down my cheeks faster than my heartbeat. Happy and sad mixed together. I've lost my father, but I refuse to lose Heath. He's all I have left.

He studies me for a moment in an attempt to spot any untruth in my words, and once he's satisfied with what he sees, his lips brush softly against mine. I'm frozen in place at the gentleness of his touch. His mouth moves to my cheek and I feel his tongue dart out, lapping up my salty tears.

"I need you," I whisper into his ear. "Please. Make love to me." I'm aware my father is dead. I know he's never coming back. But it's that very notion that has me needing Heath even more right now. Craving that connection and closeness with him. Without saying a word, he undoes his pants and pushes my panties to the side beneath my dress. His lips once again find mine as he thrusts up inside of me. His fingers dig into my flesh as he makes love to me, giving me exactly what I need.

"Harder," I murmur against his lips, and he obeys, his thrusts turning violent. My head smacks against the back of the door, but I don't give a damn. Heath is buried inside of me, our bodies now one. I can feel him so deep his balls are smacking against my ass cheeks. My heels are digging into his back. His mouth moves to my neck as he sucks on my flesh. My hands travel from his shoulders to grip the back of his head. Pulling him closer to me. Needing every part of our bodies to be connected. I can feel our hearts pounding in rhythm against each other. Heath peppers kisses along my collarbone as he pushes into me deeper, harder, hitting that spot he knows all too well.

"Come with me," he growls, and my pussy squeezes his cock as I let go, my body shaking uncontrollably as waves of pleasure roll through me. Heath's thrusts turn frantic, his kisses turning into bites, and all too soon he's finding his own release against my lower stomach.

Silently, we clean up, and after he holds me in his arms and tells me everything is going to be okay, we make our way out of the hospital.

The drive home, we're both lost in thought and unusually quiet. When we finally pull up in the driveway, I notice an unfamiliar car parked there. I glance over at Heath, but he just shrugs. After opening my door for me, he links his hand with mine as we make our way to the front entranceway. Before he opens the front door, he stops and pulls me into his arms, his mouth crushing mine. "I love you," he murmurs against my lips. But before I can say the words back, the door swings open and standing there in the doorway is my brother, Hunter Crenshaw.

"Look what the cat dragged in. If it isn't the bastard black sheep of the family." He grins snidely.

"Hunter! Our father just died. What's wrong with you?" I shove his chest and walk inside the house, my hand still linked with Heath's.

"I'm aware," Hunter sneers. "Helen called me earlier this morning to let me know our dear old dad croaked in his sleep. Thanks for letting me know, by the way." He slams the front door and stands with his back to it, his arms crossed over his chest.

"I only found out myself earlier. We were at the hospital all day waiting to see his body. I couldn't believe it, but it's true. I saw him with my own eyes. He's gone, Hunter." I let go of Heath's hand and wrap my arms around my brother's waist. At first he's stiff against me, but then he softens, his hand coming down and patting my back. He's never been good with dealing with his emotions, but he's still my brother and the only one I have. With Mom leaving us and Dad now dead, Hunter is the only blood I have left in this world.

"I know, Catrina, but it will be okay. I'm here now and I will make sure you continue to live in your cozy little life of luxury."

I lift my head and back up. "Excuse me? What did you say?"

"You heard me. I know how spoiled Father keeps you, so to honor his wishes, I'll continue to provide for you. That is until you marry. Then it will become his problem." He turns to Heath. "You, on the other hand, are fired. I imagine in the will it'll state that you can stay living here, so unfortunately there's nothing I can do about that." Hunter rolls his eyes. "My father always did have a soft spot for you. I don't know what it is about stray dogs that people find so appealing. They're dirty and stink and most of them have rabies." He shivers dramatically. "But if you plan to stay here, things will have to change. For one"—his eyes drag over to me—"no more fucking my sister."

Heath's body moves before anyone even sees it coming and his fist connects with Hunter's face. "Motherfucker! Don't you ever speak of your sister like that."

"Heath, stop, please," I plead, my hand tugging on his arm. He allows me to pull him back, but I can see his chest is heaving in anger. Hunter's hand covers his nose, but I can still see blood trickling down from underneath. Helen, of course, comes running over and hands him a rag for him to place on his nose.

"Our father just died, Hunter. Please don't do this right now."

Hunter removes the bloodied rag from his nose and grins wickedly. "It's already been done. I contacted Father's attorney on my way here. The reading of his will is in a few minutes. Once he tells me what I already know, that the company and estate are mine, it's all over for you." He spits out some blood and it spatters in front of Heath's feet.

Once Hunter stalks out of the room, I run into Heath's arms. "He can't do this, right? He can't just take over everything. Daddy would never allow him to do that." When Heath doesn't respond, I back up so I can look him in the eyes. "Right, Heath? He wouldn't do that."

"It all depends on what he left in his will, but if what Hunter's saying is true and your father left everything to him, then fuck it. Fuck him. We don't need his money." Heath's hands frame my face. "We'll run away, Catrina. We'll find a new place, a fresh start. We'll get married. I'll make sure every dream you've ever dreamt comes true. I'll make you happy, I promise."

The creak of a door sounds and I tilt my head to the side expecting Hunter to be back for round two, but it's not my brother. It's Elliot, and while I should care that he's most likely just witnessed an intimate moment between Heath and me, I don't have it in me to give a damn.

"With what? Love?" Elliott demands and we both turn to face him. "How do you think you will pay for that new life and those dreams? With Monopoly money? Do you think you will find a job that pays like C-Trades does? Wrong. Nobody will give you the time of day. How do you even think you're going to finish your degree now that Crenshaw is gone? The best thing you can do for Catrina is to walk away now."

"Fuck you!" I shout. "The biggest mistake I ever made was agreeing to marry you. I love Heath and he loves me. My daddy would never let you get away with this." I push past him and head straight for the office. Daddy's attorney, Mr. Hendrickson, has arrived and is standing there going through the files. He looks up and grants me a sad smile.

"I'm sorry for your loss."

"Well, you must be the only one. My poor father's not even in the grave yet and my brother is trying to take over." I glare at

Hunter, who is sitting in his seat, smirking with a tissue stuffed up his nose.

"Times like these are hard and everyone handles them differently. Fortunately, your father was a savvy businessman and made sure to draw up a detailed will. I helped him do it myself."

Heath and I sit down on the loveseat and I reach for his hand. If this doesn't go as planned, I'm leaving with Heath. He's my past and my present. I can't even see a future without him in it.

"Okay, let's begin," Mr. Hendrickson says, sitting down at my father's desk. "I, Rufus Crenshaw, residing at 1531 Windy Hills Road, State of New York, declare this to be my will, and I revoke any and all wills and codicils I previously made.

"At this time, I leave my company C-Trades Enterprises, as well as my assets to my son, Hunter Crenshaw. I entrust in him to run my company and properties in my stead. I leave a trust fund to my daughter, Catrina Crenshaw, that she will receive after her five-year wedding anniversary to Elliot Lincoln. A second trust, which will be provided once she produces an heir…"

I release a shocked gasp, my hands flying up to my mouth. This doesn't make sense. Why would he do this? "Stop! When was this will created?"

Mr. Hendrickson looks up from his documents. "I would say ten years ago." I do the math in my head. It was just after my mother left and my father swore he would never allow me to end up like her. He was heartbroken and hurt. In a vulnerable state. He wasn't thinking clearly.

"There must be a newer will. This can't be the most recent one." I stand and snatch the papers from Mr. Hendrickson, reading over it and trying to make sense of all this. I feel Heath's warm touch on my back.

"Your father said after I graduated he would have his will changed. He didn't plan to die before then," Heath says, his voice filled with raw emotion. I turn into his arms and see his brown eyes flaring with devastation. "This doesn't have to change anything. It's just money, Catrina. We can still leave. You don't need that trust fund."

"That's where you're wrong," Elliot cuts in. "Lincoln Holdings is C-Trades' biggest investor. If Catrina leaves, we'll pull our funds and everything your father worked for will die right alongside him."

"Are you seriously threatening me? Threatening my father's company? You know his company was everything to him," I hiss.

"And you can save it by simply marrying me." He grins. "I'll give you until after the funeral to decide."

"There's nothing to decide," Hunter says as if I'm not in the room. "It's already done."

"He's not done reading the will." I point to Mr. Hendrickson, who is still sitting at the desk, waiting patiently.

"I've heard everything I needed to hear," Hunter retorts with a laugh, then he looks at Heath. "Guess Daddy loved me more after all. And one day my son will follow in his grandfather's and father's footsteps and everything that is now mine will become his. But you know whose it will never be? Yours."

"What?" I ask confused. The last time I heard, the doctors declared Francesca infertile and they were told they wouldn't be able to conceive children of their own.

Ignoring my question, Hunter extends his hand to Elliot, who grasps his firmly. "We'll be in touch."

CHAPTER SEVEN

"PACK A BAG," I GROWL, STORMING INTO CATRINA'S ROOM after her.

She nods and rushes over to her closet. I help her drag her eight-piece Bottega Veneta calf leather luggage—the fact that I even know what the fuck that is might be a testament as to how obsessed with this woman I am—out and onto the bed. While she sets to packing, I press a kiss to her cheek before heading to my room. I don't have much to speak of. A few nice suits that will fit into one suitcase. A box of love letters from Catrina. Some trinkets from when we were children. I also have a candid framed photo of Catrina, Crenshaw, and me not long after Hunter was sent to military school. Within minutes, my entire life is packed into a manageable suitcase.

My home isn't here.

My home is wherever Catrina is.

I slip from the old sewing room turned bedroom and carry my bag through the house. The voices from Crenshaw's office have long since dispersed. When I step inside his office, it's empty of people. The scent of tobacco and his familiar cologne flood my senses. My eyes prickle with emotion, but I grit my teeth and will it away.

Catrina has lost her father. I must be strong for her.

He was never mine.

But she is.

I walk over to his desk and stare at his open portfolio that's filled with his business contracts and client list. Crenshaw was brilliant, especially with numbers, but he wasn't good with drawing up contracts and handling the client meetings. He relied on me to assist him with all of that. We worked together as a team and ran this company like a well-oiled machine. Despite his outdated will, I know in my heart he'd want me to have this portfolio.

So, I take it.

Quickly, I shove the thick portfolio into the side of my bag and then zip it back up. I make it back to Catrina's room where she's shoving every bra, shoe, and dress she can get to fit into her bags. When she's done, she goes to her nightstand and grabs her latest journal, setting it on top. The woman goes nowhere without her book and pen. She's been writing in those journals for as far back as I can remember. There must be dozens stored away somewhere, or maybe she burns them when she's done writing in the last page. What I wouldn't give to read her innermost thoughts and feelings. To know what goes through her head. I tried once and she flipped the hell out on me. Didn't speak to me for a damn week. When she finally did, she made me promise never to read them and I agreed. The love letters she's written are mine, though. They may not reflect all of her innermost feelings, but they capture her love for me and it's something I cherish deeply.

I watch as she moves to the dresser and opens her jewelry box, taking the charm bracelet I bought for her out. She places it inside the luggage carefully as tears of frustration and sadness leak from her eyes. I'll get her to talk later, but for now, there is no time for that.

We're leaving.

As it should be.

I help her zip up one of her overstuffed bags. As she heads to the bathroom to pack up her toiletries, I sit on the bed and call a local hotel to book a room. My funds in my account aren't horrible, but they also won't get us very far. While Crenshaw didn't pay me wages for my time as most internships don't, I've worked plenty of odd jobs over the years so I could have some money in my pocket.

Thirty-eight hundred dollars.

I close my eyes and rub my temples. Fuck how I wish we weren't forced to make this decision just months before Crenshaw would have literally handed me over the keys to his fortune. It was always his plan to do so. Fuck the stupid will. It means nothing to me. I knew the old man and he was teaching me everything so I could take over when the time came.

I was so close.

My classes for this semester are over and I passed with flying colors. I only have one more semester to go. I hate that Elliot is right. Without Crenshaw's help, how am I going to finish college? I'm devastated he won't see me graduate.

I'll still make him proud.

It may take me some time to find a job, but I will. I'll use his knowledge he bestowed upon me to my advantage.

"I'm ready," Catrina says, her voice shaky.

I rise from my chair and stalk over to her. My palms cradle her cheeks as I stare intently in her emerald green eyes. "Everything will turn out okay, love. You just have to trust me."

"I trust you," she replies immediately. But the flare of her nostrils and the flicker in her gaze tells me otherwise. I'll just have to work at it to prove to her I'll provide for her. She just has to give me some time.

It takes me three trips, but I manage to get us loaded in my car. Hunter can take a lot from me, but he won't get my car. I paid for it in cash—sensible compared to Catrina's BMW—but it'll do the job. Whereas Catrina's car is in her father's name, my Honda is in mine.

"I can't believe he's gone," she says once we're on the darkened road.

I reach over and squeeze her hand. "I'm sorry."

The half-hour drive is quiet and soon we're pulling into the hotel I booked.

"What are we doing?" She wrenches her hand from mine and points at the hotel. "We're not staying here."

Frowning, I take in the building. It's not the nicest, sure, but it'll do for a place to sleep until we get our bearings straight. "It's cheap," I grit out.

Her head snaps my way and her lip curls up. "Look at it, Heath! It's a roach motel."

I bite my tongue to keep from lashing out and climb out of the car. Before I can get to her side, she scrambles out.

"Stop," she snips. "We're not staying here. They probably have bed bugs."

"It's just for the night." I stomp over to the trunk and start yanking suitcases out. "Turn down the princess dial a few degrees for just one night. Please, love."

She gasps as though my words have singed her. "Heath!"

I slam the trunk and rush over to her. Grabbing her arms, I scowl at her face that glows prettily in the moonlight. Like an angel. An angel who's frowning and fucking pouting, but an angel no less.

"Just for tonight," I grind out.

Her emotions are running high because she bursts into tears. I pull her to my chest and soothe her by stroking her silky hair.

"Everything will be okay, Catrina. Just trust me."

As Catrina sleeps on the "lumpy" bed that I caught six degrees of hell over, I sit in a desk chair by the window and scour through Crenshaw's portfolio. There were notes on his to-do list in regards to a will he'd started, but it wasn't in place yet. I found said will and sure enough, in black and white, he was handing everything over to me. His company. His trust. His fortune. He wasn't lying when he said things would change in the fall. A few short months away. He thought he had plenty of time to make the changes.

Time got the last laugh.

When I had shown the unfinished will to Catrina, she'd screamed and bounced on the bed with excitement. But the moment I explained that it had never been signed and executed, she cried herself hysterical until she passed the hell out. As much as I love her, I was glad when she succumbed to exhaustion. Without her throwing a tantrum, I can focus. I need to plan for our future.

The portfolio does provide me with the information and access I need. I spend many hours late into the night making phone calls and putting some plans in place. Sometime around dawn, once the sun has risen, I yawn and wonder what Hunter will think of my taking his father's client list.

If Hunter thought I'd roll over and take this, he's an idiot. I'm sure he's scrambling right now to have me removed from all the bank accounts. It's wasted effort, though. I took the portfolio. The information was what I was after. The money will come later.

Tired, I rise from the chair and stretch. After I shed my clothes, I slide into the bed with my girl. She sighs and then clutches onto me in her sleep. I stroke through her hair with my fingers and stare at her perfect features. So beautiful. Nothing in this world could ever be so lovely.

Unable to keep away from her any longer, I lean in and kiss her lips. I remember the first time I kissed her romantically. We'd been in her bed watching movies, something we did often.

Sure, I'd always loved her, but I wasn't sure if she felt the same. It was always Elliot this and Elliot that. She was blabbing about how when she married him one day, she'd make him build her an indoor pool and she'd insist on a private airplane. I thought she was so stunning—the way her eyes would light up when she'd talk about the things he'd buy her and how her pouty lips would purse together if she thought he might tell her no. I'd become so enamored that I couldn't help myself. I just leaned forward and kissed her. It was our first kiss. We were young, dumb teenagers and the moment our lips fused together in a kiss that had more than friendly intent behind it, it sealed our fate. A soft moan of surprise escaped her. I used that moment to enter her mouth with my tongue. The next few moments were savage and clumsy. Our heated kiss quickly turned into a dual virginity loss. The first time kind of sucked, admittedly, but then we got better. Hell, it still gets better each and every time.

"Catrina," I murmur against her mouth. "Wake up, lovely."

Her eyes flutter open and for a moment before she remembers the horrors of yesterday, delightful wickedness glitters in her eyes. I nip on her bottom lip as I slide my palm down her stomach over her gown and then push it back up. I seek out her sweet cunt with my fingers. The moment they slide along her slit, she moans in pleasure.

"Heath."

"Let me love you," I whisper as I stroke her into a frenzy. She's practically clawing at me by the time I bring her to climax. As soon as she comes down from her high, she cradles my face with one palm.

"Love me like only you can."

I spread her legs and fuck my angel right into the lumpy mattress.

Five days later...

"A lot has happened since you two have been running around doing God only knows what," Helen grumbles as she points some wait staff in the direction of the dining room. "Mr. Crenshaw would be so disappointed that Catrina would leave all the affairs to be handled by her brother. Thankfully Mr. Lincoln stepped up and saved the day. Did you see all the flowers at the service? Those were compliments of Elliot. And the casket was simply beautiful. Hand carved from Italy. I'm flabbergasted he was able to come by it so quickly. Money will buy you anything these days, I suppose."

I ignore her as I peek out the doors into the dining room. People are everywhere. The funeral was sad, as to be expected, and now we're supposed to smile like we're all the happiest goddamned people on the planet while honoring Crenshaw's memory. Hundreds of guests have shown up for a glorified after-death party. Everyone dressed in their finest black-tie wear. I'm wearing one of my few suits that I didn't have the opportunity to get pressed and an unhappy-as-fuck expression.

But this is important to Catrina.

She needs closure.

As soon as we're done with this shit, I'm going to take my girl and drive her far away from here. We'll start our life and be happy like we were always destined to be. In a few years, once I've made a name for myself, I will spoil her rotten with indoor pools and private planes. Whatever the hell she wants, I will give it to her.

I could never deny her a thing.

She comes into view looking gorgeous as ever. I notice she's put on one of her party dresses she was forced to leave behind when we left for the motel. It's black and fits her beautifully, hugging her curvy frame in all the right places. Her tits are full and nearly spilling from the top. Every asshole in here eyefucks her tits when they pass. I bide my time. No sense in throttling every guy here. I'll just wait it out and let her do her socialite duties one last time before she's relieved of them for good.

Laughter catches my attention and a growl rumbles in my throat to see Hunter having a jolly good time with Elliot. The two men, matched in size and stature, discuss whatever it is imbeciles talk about. A young woman with jet-black hair and wide blue eyes holds a baby in her arms as she feeds it a bottle. Her lips are full and painted blood red. She preens and smiles as though everyone is there to see her and the baby. I barely refrain from rolling my eyes. Hunter puts his arm around whom I'm assuming is his new wife, Francesca, and pets the infant's hair fondly.

Gag.

Elliot's sister Isabel comes to join them. She's a wee-bit lanky, her wispy blond hair pulled back in a low, elegant bun. Isabel is a little younger than Catrina, perhaps by only a few months, but they are eons apart mentally. Catrina is brilliant and clever and witty. Isabel is dumber than a box of rocks. One day she'll con some poor sap into filling her up with a kid so they can live miserable boring lives together.

Gag.

Catrina begins chatting with Isabel. Isabel holds her own and even makes Catrina giggle. The girls behave as though they're best friends, even though I know Catrina despises her. So often after their tea dates, she'd come home and gripe about how boring she is. Later, I'll get to hear all about it.

"Staring is rude," Helen snips behind me.

I turn my stare on her and glower. "Being fucking nosy is rude too."

Her face turns red and she whips me in the head with her wooden spoon. "Don't make me do that again."

I snatch her spoon, break it in two, and then toss it onto the floor. "There. I just made your job easier. Now you don't have to worry about that happening again."

Turning my attention back to the dining room, I'm irritated to see Elliot standing so close to Catrina. She's smiling—fucking smiling—at him and my blood boils. It's an act, though. My sweet love will keep her dignity until her last dying breath. Her father may be dead and her brother holds her future in his hands, yet she still prances around as though she has the winning cards.

And she does.

She has me.

Together, we will always win. I'll die making sure that happens.

Hours go by and I retreat to the old sewing room to sulk. I don't care to hang out with those people. Hunter will just cause a scene anyway. As soon as this shit is over, I'll be gone. I'll get my girl out of here and we'll take on the world together.

I end up falling asleep on my old bed and wake when I hear cheering downstairs. It's long past dusk by the time I stomp down the stairs to finally join the party. I'm stopped dead in my tracks to see Elliot with his arm around Catrina's waist and a tumbler of liquor in his other hand. He's whispering in her ear. Her cheeks turn red and she smiles at him like she does me sometimes when I'm between her thighs.

Over. My. Goddamned. Body.

I storm down the stairs, a roar of fury rushing past my lips. When I reach the bottom, all eyes are on me and the room has hushed. A snigger echoes from one corner and I recognize the bastard as Hunter.

"Time to go, Catrina," I snap as I storm over to her.

I grip her wrist and tug her to me. She lets out a choked sound. Elliot holds her tight, pulling her to him against my efforts.

"No," he says, sounding awfully ballsy with liquid courage running through his veins.

"I'm not asking you, piss ant. I'm telling my girl we're leaving," I hiss.

He chuckles. "Last I checked, she was my fiancée."

"Last week, she was for about six seconds," I seethe. "Then I threw your ring in the toilet and put my dick inside her. Keep up, Lincoln."

"Heath!" Catrina cries out. "What a horrible thing to say!"

Several people gasp in shock.

"We're leaving," I growl, tugging her arm.

This time, it's her who pulls away. She jerks her hand away, fire flaming in her emerald eyes. "No." She lifts her chin and swallows. "I've been doing some thinking…" Her gaze travels to Hunter's wife, who nods in an encouraging way. Isabel, who is beside her, smiles.

What in the ever-loving hell is happening?

Since when are Tweedledee and Tweedledumbass her backup posse?

"She's staying," Elliot says. "While you were off doing whatever poor bastards do, we were announcing to everyone our wedding date. Right, darling?"

She winces slightly but then nods. "Right."

A pain hits me hard in the chest—so sharp I think Crenshaw isn't the only person around here having a heart attack. "W-What?"

Her hand thrusts my way and his ring sparkles in the light. "I've made my decision."

I shake my head. "No. Fuck no."

"It's a done deal," she breathes.

A deal. She thinks marriage is a deal. Negotiate her pussy to the man with the most cash. Unbelievable.

Elliot winks.

I'm going to destroy him. I'm going to destroy everything he cares about.

Hunter laughs.

I will ruin that motherfucker if it's the last thing I do.

"You don't mean this," I rasp out. "Don't do this to us."

"It's the only way," she whines.

Elliot shrugs. "The only way."

I storm over to him and yank on his tie until he's inches from my face. "You will pay for this. You will fucking pay for this."

His eyes narrow. "At least we both know I can afford it."

"Get out!" Catrina cries out, choking on a sob. "You're making things harder than they should be. Just go."

"Not without you," I growl.

Strong arms snag me from behind and I'm dragged away from her. I fight my attacker, but he's caught me off guard. It isn't until I'm shoved out the door and down the stairs, falling on my ass that I realize it's Hunter.

"You're no longer welcome, stray."

The door slams and my life ends in one horrible second.

I will ruin them all.

And then get my girl back.

CHAPTER EIGHT

HELEN

The Present...

"How do you know all this anyway?" Emily asks, turning to look at me. Her wide green eyes sparkle with curiosity.

"A maid has a front-row seat into the lives of those she works for," I tell her proudly. "I've learned quite a bit. I don't have a family of my own anymore, but it was always as though I still did."

"You're family," she says and hugs me. "I love you, Helen."

I smile and hug the sweet thing back. "I love you too."

"So how do you know all about the sex stuff?" she asks as she pulls away. "Don't tell me you were watching." She snorts with laughter.

I slap her hand in admonishment. "Don't be crude, dear." I purse my lips together. "Catrina always kept her journals lying about. I tell you, Emily, she could have had an entire collection of erotic literature had she gathered them all up and published them. Terrible thing, I must say."

"But you read them," she teases. "Couldn't have been *that* terrible."

I admit that some were rather racy and brought heat to my cheeks on more than one occasion. Catrina was fond of her details. Graphic details.

"Stop your foolishness. Do you want to hear the rest of the story or do you want to fuss over how I gained such knowledge?"

Her phone buzzes and she snatches it up but then lets out a huff when she sees it's Finn.

Finn: What's your deal, Em? Are you mad at me?

Emily: I'm busy.

Finn: Too busy for dinner?

Emily: You know I hate the fancy places you always want to go to.

"I'm more of a burger and fries kind of girl," she says to me.

Finn: So we'll go where you want to go. Stop ignoring me. I miss you.

Emily: You know I'm seeing Porter and I don't think he'd like it if we were out having dinner together.

Finn: Porter is a dick.

"Ugh, whatever. I'm so done with him." She chucks her phone into her lap, ignoring it when it buzzes again. "He's so annoying. Okay, fine, continue. I won't question your sources," she says with a laugh. "But I'm glad *I* don't have a journal."

I don't remind her that her phone is like a journal. And on more than one occasion, I've caught up on Miss Emily by reading through her texts and emails. The Porter and Finn saga is one I'm well versed in.

I'll save *that* story for another time.

"Do you want to answer him back?" I ask.

"Nope, I want to hear the story."

"Well, all right then. Where were we?"

"Catrina chose Elliot. I don't know why but she did. Did Heath come back for her? Did they run off into the sunset?" she asks excitedly. "Tell me what happened next."

"Ahhh," I say. "Let's fast forward several weeks. Catrina and Elliot's wedding day. Catrina's journals certainly detailed that day quite vividly…"

CHAPTER NINE

Catrina

The Past…

Dear Diary,

Today is my wedding day. I shouldn't be thinking about Heath, but I am. He just doesn't get it. He never has. The money. The power. The social class. Heath needs money to survive while I need it to thrive. Yes, I love him. My body and soul crave him, ache for him. But how could he expect me to give up everything to be with him? My father's business, who Heath helped run, would go under. I would lose my trust fund, leaving me penniless. I'm devastated that my father didn't change his will. When Heath showed me the new one, the one that should've been in place, I thought I'd be able to have it all. Heath. The money. The power. The status. But then he told me it wasn't signed, and in that moment I knew I would have to choose: love or money. Love doesn't pay for homes or vacations or cars. It doesn't buy food or clothes. Anybody who tells you they would choose love over money is either full of shit or has never enjoyed the comforts and luxuries money can buy.

It broke my heart to watch Heath get pulled from our home and escorted off our property the day of Daddy's funeral. Even several weeks later, when I think about that day, I feel such pity for Heath and what he must've been going through. He loved my father and losing him was hard on us all. My heart aches knowing we can never be together. But

the truth is we were never supposed to be together. He was a sneaky kiss in my bed, a dirty fuck in my closet. He was a craving, a guilty pleasure, but he was never supposed to be my forever. Feelings got involved and ideas got twisted and suddenly he was asking me to give up my life to be with him. If Heath truly loved me, he would've never asked that of me. He would understand why I need to marry Elliot. If Heath truly loved me, he would want what's best for me.

-CC

I close my journal and place it into my purse, the one I will be taking with me on my honeymoon. Then I head into the dressing room to finish getting ready.

"Catrina, that dress looks exquisite on you," Delores coos, and I turn in my ivory Oscar de la Renta wedding gown to look at myself in the mirror. My makeup is professionally done to perfection. My chocolate brown hair is down in perfect waves, topped with a Swarovski crystal bridal tiara. My attire is complete with Manolo Blahnik crystal suede point toe pumps. I swallow thickly, refusing to regret my decision. This is the life I was meant to live, not slumming it in some Motel 8 where I could catch a disease simply from using the shower there.

"Thank you, Delores." I watch myself in the mirror as I tilt my head to the side slightly and smile wide.

"Are you sure you don't want Hunter or Elliot's father to walk you down the aisle? I can imagine how hard it must be to get married without your father being here to give you away."

"I'm sure. This is something I need to do on my own."

"Okay." She leans in and gives me an air-kiss to each cheek. "I'm going to find my seat and we'll see you at the end of the altar." She closes the door behind her and I turn back to the mirror. When I see not only my reflection in the mirror but someone else's I let out a screech, but it's quickly muffled with a pair of large, rough hands.

Heath.

He spins me around to face him, and before I can scream, his lips crash into mine. Instantly, my body melts into his as his tongue finds its way into my mouth, lashing and laving with my own.

When he breaks our kiss, his chocolate eyes meet mine and the glare burning in his gaze sends shivers down my spine. Betrayal. Devastation. Heartache. All because of me. Before I can speak, try to explain, he whips me back around and my hands hit the couch cushion. He flips my dress up and rips my panties off my body. They're part of my La Perla bridal lingerie. I should scream. Beg him to stop. I know what's coming next. But I don't do anything. I can't. I can never deny this man my body.

His hand comes down and smacks my butt cheek. I squeal too loud and he hushes me before smacking my bottom again.

Smack. Smack. Smack.

My ass smarts in pain from his smacks, but my pussy clenches in anticipation. I should stop this. I should stop him. Instead, when his hand comes down again, this time the hardest of all, I let out a needy echo. I wait for another smack, but when it doesn't come, I glance back to find him scowling at me. Anger blazing in his eyes. I open my mouth to apologize, but no words come out. I'm not sorry and he knows I'm not. It would just be a lie.

Instead I turn my head back around and lower it to the couch, ready and willing to take whatever it is he gives me. His fingers slide underneath me and fill my pussy. I'm drenched. He pumps them in and out of me, working me up into a frenzy, forcing me to once again forget the world around us. I'm about to come when he pulls them out. I let out an unsatisfied whine, but he just chuckles darkly. And that's when it hits me. He's here to punish me. The spanking and denying me of my orgasm. He's hurt and he's going to try to hurt me the only way he knows how. Sexually. Damn this man.

"Please," I beg, but he ignores me. His fingers reenter my pussy and I breathe a sigh of relief, but then they're gone again. A few seconds later, I can feel them a few inches higher as he pushes into my forbidden hole. We've only attempted to do this once before when he begged me. It hurt and we didn't finish. Of course he would do it now. He's taken me every other way possible. I should demand him to stop. I'm in my wedding dress, for God's sake, about to say 'I do' to another man. But when he pushes his fingers deep into my ass, I let out a guttural groan and I know my body will never be able to tell him no. I need him to claim this last part of me before I walk down the aisle and give myself over to another man. The burn from his thick fingers is strong but after a few times, the pain turns into pleasure and before I know it, I'm writhing against his fingers, needing more.

I hear the sound of his pants unzip and I startle. He wouldn't do what I think he's going to do, would he? I sneak a glance back and watch him as he strokes his dick a few times. Then he enters me from behind, once again filling my pussy so deliciously. I moan out in pleasure as he simultaneously fucks my ass and pussy. Another orgasm builds. It feels so good. I need this release. I can feel it building higher and higher, and just as I'm about to explode around his cock, he pulls both his fingers and his cock out. I look back, confused, just in time to watch him press his thick cock against my ass. He pushes into me slowly and my forehead drops to the couch as I gasp. A mixture of pain and pleasure once again hitting me. I don't know whether to scream or cry. Once he's completely seated in me, he starts to thrust in and out of me. His hands gripping my hips to the point of pain. I can feel him losing control, his fingers digging into my flesh. I try to reach under me to find my clit, to seek out my own pleasure, but he growls and smacks my hand away.

"Please," I plead, but he ignores me as he continues to savagely fuck my ass. The burning sensation serving as a reminder that I've hurt this man and deserve to be without pleasure. His movements turn frantic. His breathing heavy. He thrusts harder, deeper into my ass. It hurts, yet it also in some strange way feels good. And then he stills inside of me and I feel his warm seed shoot into me. Wordlessly, he pulls out, breaking our connection. He doesn't kiss me or hold me or comfort me like he always does after we make love.

Flipping my gown back down, I stand and can feel his cum dribble out of my ass. I turn around to face him, furious that he's treated me this way.

"What the hell is wrong with you?" I demand, my head held high. Heath grips my chin and growls.

"If you do this, Catrina. If you marry this cocksucker, it's over between us. Do you understand me? Don't you dare come crying back to me when he doesn't satisfy you like I do."

"Satisfy me?" I huff. "You didn't satisfy me just now!" I scream into his face, not even caring that there are several hundred people on the other side of the door waiting for me to walk out and marry Elliot.

Heath grabs my hips and pushes me onto the couch. He flips my dress back up and before I can ask what he's doing, he disappears underneath. Seconds later, his tongue is plunging into my wet folds. He licks and laves at my juices, working me up into a frenzy. He sucks on my clit and I lose it. My orgasm hits me hard and my body quivers in pleasure. My hand falls over my eyes as I try to control my breathing. I don't even know how I'm going to walk down the aisle with my legs feeling like jelly.

"Heath," I whisper his name. I can't believe I let this happen. When he doesn't answer me, I open my eyes, only to find myself alone in the room. Who the hell does he think he is to leave me with an ultimatum?

The room is silent, only the sound of my heels click-clacking against the tile as I make my way to the bathroom to clean up. Once I'm presentable, I open the door and head to the entryway to the church aisle. I hear the wedding procession playing and I breathe in a deep sigh of relief that I'm not too late.

Fuck Heath and his ultimatums. I'm about to become Mrs. Elliot Lincoln.

The wedding was beautiful and the reception was everything I expected it to be, complete with a five-course sit-down dinner and ending with the seven-tier wedding cake made with ivory fondant that matched my dress, with strings of diamonds draped along the edges that matched my tiara. Elliot made sure every one of my requests were met. He's accommodating that way. We say our goodbyes to our guests and make our way up to our suite. We're staying at The Plaza New York, which is also the same hotel where our reception took place. Heath could learn a thing or two from Elliot when it comes to picking hotels. He might be able to make my body sing, but he has no idea what it takes to satisfy my other needs.

Once the elevator reaches the top floor and we get out, Elliot guides me into the luxurious bedroom. Turning me around, he begins to undo the buttons on my dress. "You looked absolutely breathtaking," he murmurs into my ear before he places a chaste kiss to my neck. Because my dress is strapless, it falls in a heap onto the floor. I'm left standing here in nothing but my ivory bra and heels. He doesn't comment on the fact I'm not wearing any panties. Instead, he lifts me into his arms and settles me down on the bed. I'm lying on my back and he's kneeling over me as he rains soft kisses along my collarbone and all over my breasts while whispering sweet and loving words to me. His hand comes up and massages my breast, and I let out a groan he mistakes for pleasure and not annoyance.

"Elliot, pinch my nipples," I murmur, jutting out my breasts.

His brows furrow in confusion. "I don't want to hurt you." His words remind me of the way Heath claimed me just a few short hours ago. The way he unapologetically took my ass, leaving me in such pleasurable pain.

"I want you to hurt me," I insist sweetly. "Pinch my nipples. Bite them. Suck on them, please."

Elliot's frown deepens. "I don't know what's gotten into you, but you're my wife and I'm not hurting you." His voice tells me he's done with this conversation, so I don't bother to reply. He spreads my legs and enters me. I flinch slightly at the intrusion, still deliciously sore from earlier, and I'm thankful in this moment that Elliot never lasts long.

He makes love to me, continuing to kiss my breasts and my neck, and once he comes, he rolls to his side and says, "Maybe tonight we made a baby." He grins. "One that will be half of each of us. I've seen you doting on Francesca's baby. Would you like one of your own?"

I'm shocked still at his words. Have I ever considered having a baby of my own? Surely not. I am only nineteen years old. I'm too young to be weighed down by a baby. Sure, my sister-in-law's son is quite adorable, but that's only because once he starts crying I can give him back. However, my mind goes back to the will, the one that stated in order to receive a second trust, I must produce an heir.

"I suppose so," I answer slowly, "but I would need Helen with me to help. I wouldn't know the slightest thing about taking care of a baby."

Elliot beams, happy that I've told him what he wants to hear. "This, I can do."

"She may not come willingly," I warn. "She can be a cranky witch when she wants to be."

"Don't you worry about a thing. I'll make it happen. Helen will come to live with us at Low Valley Estate. Thank you, Catrina, for once again making me happy."

CHAPTER TEN

One Year Later...

A YEAR IS A LONG TIME, BUT WHEN YOU'RE LIVING THE KIND OF life I've been blessed with, it goes by in the blink of an eye. They say marriage is bliss. I can't argue with that. My marriage has been the gift that keeps on giving. And I do love my gifts.

Helen and I moved to Low Valley Estate right after my exquisite wedding to Elliot. Of course she put up a fight like I knew she would, but just as Elliot promised, he made sure she made the move with me. I would never admit it to her, but having her here with me has helped get me through feeling homesick. I know that Low Valley Estate is only down the road from my family's estate, but it still felt like I was moving across the country. Not only did I lose my father, but I lost all the comforts of home he provided. Elliot has done everything in his power to make the transition as smooth as possible—including giving me access to his Black card so I can spend my days with Isabel and his mother, shopping. And while shopping—as well as hosting our weekly teas and attending brunches at the country club—keep me busy, I still can't help but miss my old life.

Don't get me wrong, I'm happy with Elliot. He spoils me silly with trips to the city, expensive jewelry, and dinners out. It's clear through his actions he loves me and will make sure I'm given the best this world can offer, and I will admit I care for him as well to a certain extent, but that doesn't stop me from missing Heath. What Elliot doesn't understand is that no matter what he does in an attempt to win over my heart—whether it's purchasing that beautiful new BMW for me that I told him I had to have, or gifting me my favorite prized thoroughbred from the breeders—it's not mine to give. Heath stole it long ago and never gave it back. And if I know him like I think I do, he has no intention of ever doing so. Heath, that sadistic bastard, would rather smash my heart to smithereens before he would hand it back over to me so I could give it to another man.

Not that it really matters at this point. No matter how much I've tried to get Heath out of my head, I can't. He follows me everywhere I go. When Elliot touches me far too softly, I recall all the times Heath would push my limits. Bruising and punishing. When Elliot refuses to talk business to me, I can't help but think back to when Heath would ask for my opinion. When Elliot brings me home meaningless trinkets, I try to block out every thoughtful gift Heath has given me: from the first edition of *Wuthering Heights* that he saved up and purchased for my birthday one year because he knows how much I love British literature, to the charm bracelet he gave me for Christmas, promising each year to add another charm. I glance down at my unfinished bracelet, with only three charms linked on: a book to symbolize my love of reading, a yellow taxi cab that he purchased after he made me take my first ride in one through the city, and a heart with a key hanging on it, which he gave me on Valentine's Day. He told me I hold the key to his heart.

Speaking of hearts, mine is aching. I have all the things money can buy, yet here I am longing for the one thing it can't. Damn Heath! I hate the hold he has over me.

"We're here," Elliot says, and I push my thoughts of Heath to the side. The driver opens my door for me to get out, and when I step outside and take in my surroundings, I see we're standing on Madison Avenue, adjacent to the Morgan Library, and directly in front of us is a food truck. My heart picks up speed as a flashback to a couple months before my father passed away hits me in full force—back to a time when my world felt complete.

I have just gotten home from my weekly tea with Delores and Isabel Lincoln and I'm not even through the foyer when Heath appears out of nowhere and announces we're going on a surprise trip. Refusing to give me any details, he hoists me over his shoulder with a slap to my ass and carries me outside to the car where he deposits me into the passenger seat before walking around to the driver's side and getting in. He starts up the car and presses the button to lower the top of my convertible BMW.

When I give him a curious look, he simply grants me a boyish grin and says, "It's too nice of a day out not to enjoy the breeze." With his hand in mine, he puts the car in drive and peels out, the dirt from the driveway kicking up behind us.

"Heath! Where are we going?" I laugh, my hair whipping around my face from the wind, as we drive down the windy road.

"It's a surprise! Now pick something good to listen to and enjoy the ride." He smiles my way and I let out a happy giggle. I love when Heath is carefree. When he lets his guard down and simply enjoys life.

"I'd rather enjoy you." I rub my hand flirtatiously along his crotch and he hits me with a warning glare.

"Woman, don't start something you can't finish."

"And who says I can't finish?" I bite down on my bottom lip seductively while undoing his pants.

"Your track record for refusing to give me head speaks for itself," he points out.

"There's a first time for everything." Taking his dick into my hand, I stroke it a few times to get it hard. Heath glances down and I feel the car swerve.

"Heath! Watch the road." I laugh.

"I can't help it. You're touching my dick."

"Well, help it. I don't want to die giving you a blow job," I scold. Heath chuckles and I go back to giving his now hard cock attention. Dipping my head down, my lips wrap around his hard length as I take him all the way in. I start off slow, getting used to him in my mouth, wetting him with my saliva. Once he's hard as steel, I start to bob my head up and down over his shaft. I have no clue what I'm doing, but Heath must be enjoying it, because the more I suck, the louder he groans. His fingers grip my hair and I think he's going to force me farther down, but he doesn't. Then the thought of him forcing me has me squirming in my seat. He slaps my ass and I take him deeper, the tip of his dick hitting the back of my throat.

"Fuck, woman, I'm going to come," he moans out as a warning. Wanting to make it good for him, I don't heed his warning, and a second later, he's coming down my throat. I choke on his salty seed and gag, lifting off him and coughing loudly.

Of course Heath finds this amusing, throwing his head back with an animated laugh. "I warned you!"

Grabbing a napkin from my glovebox, I spit out what I hadn't swallowed. "Well, how was I to know your cum would taste like the ocean mixed with urine?" I pout, embarrassed.

"Hey, don't get upset. You give great head." Heath winks at me. "And I might even let you do it again on the drive home."

I roll my eyes, trying to think of something to say, but when I look around at our surroundings, I recognize where we are. "Heath!" I exclaim. "You brought me to the Morgan Library!"

"You said you wanted to see the British Literature Exhibition, didn't you?" He grins, and I throw my arms around his neck, planting a big wet kiss on his cheek.

"Thank you."

We spend the entire afternoon walking around the library. I know Heath doesn't care about eighteenth century literature in the slightest, but he pretends to by asking me questions and pointing out things from every exhibit. And only when we've seen it all twice and the library *makes their announcement that they'll be closing soon, does he take my hand in his and walk us out of the library and down Madison Avenue. When my stomach rumbles and I tell him I'm hungry, Heath grins mischievously and walks us over to a food truck that's parked along the side of the road.*

"No way!" I withdraw my hand from his. "I was thinking more along the lines of the Madison Café."

Heath snorts out a laugh and snatches my hand back up in his. "Yes, way. Today you're going to eat like the common folk." His eyes shine playfully, so I don't argue further. When he steps up to the truck, he orders for the both of us and makes me promise to at least try it.

Once our order is ready, he hands me my food and explains that it's Russian dumplings. Taking a hesitant bite, I'm shocked by how flavorful it is. The dumplings are juicy, tasting of beef, onions, and potatoes, and I wonder if I can get Helen to make this dish at home.

"Good, huh?" Heath asks knowingly.

"It is," I concede, taking another bite.

"Sometimes slumming it isn't so bad," he murmurs.

"Catrina, are you okay?" Elliot asks, shaking me out of my thoughts.

"Yes, I was just thinking we could try out that food truck over there." I point to the truck parked along the edge of the road. It isn't the same one Heath and I ate at, but the aching pain in my heart over missing Heath has me wanting to try it anyway in hopes of feeling close to him again, even for just a moment.

"I'm almost positive that food truck would fail over a hundred safety and health inspections. Don't be ridiculous, I've brought you to the Madison Café, your favorite."

"Well, this is where I want to eat!" I point to the food truck and Elliot glares at me.

"Are you buying?" he asks incredulously and I shoot daggers his way.

Who the hell does he think he is?

"No, you are." My arms cross over my chest defiantly. I scowl at him, refusing to move toward the café. For a long moment, Elliot and I stare at one another in a silent standoff, but I know I've won when he finally relents with an annoyed sigh and walks us over to the food truck. The Asian food isn't half as good as the Russian cuisine Heath got for me, but I don't tell Elliot that. I eat my entire plate of food with a smile plastered on my face, hiding a snicker when he complains he's going to get food poisoning from eating this food, or sick from my forcing him to sit on the city bench. Unfortunately, it was a wasted effort on my part, as I don't feel any closer to Heath, but again, I don't mention that to Elliot.

Once we're done eating and have disposed of our trash—and Elliot insists we don't have time to check out the library today—we head back home. The moment we arrive, he tells me he has some work to do, so I make my way outside to take a walk down to the stables. One of the perks of living with Elliot are the horses. While my father felt they were too much of a hassle to maintain, Elliot's family has an entire horse ranch complete with stable hands.

I walk down the middle of the barn and find my favorite American Quarter horse Elliot bought me. She pops her head out when she sees me coming and lets out a neigh. Grabbing a carrot from the bucket, I feed it to her while I rub her beautiful brown nose. "Gerald, I would like to ride Copper," I request to one of the stable hands that I find mucking the stalls. He scurries off to get her ready, and once she is, he helps me up, and with a click of my heel, Copper takes off in a trot.

The path leads us down to the large lake that separates my family's estate and the Lincolns'. My thoughts go back to all the times Heath and I would go swimming in these very waters during the hot summers. Elliot would come down on his horse with Isabel by his side and scold me for swimming in the dirty water. Then of course he would tattle on me to Helen. Heath loved when I would get punished. It just meant hours of time spent in my room without anybody bothering us.

My heart constricts as I think about Heath. Next week will be Elliot's and my one-year wedding anniversary. It will also make one year since the last time I saw or heard from Heath.

Bored of riding and sad from reminiscing, I make my way back to the stables and hand Copper back over to Gerald. Elliot is still in his office working, so I look for Helen and find her in the kitchen, making my favorite blackened shrimp salad.

"What's the matter, dear?" Helen asks without even looking up from what she's doing.

"Nothing." I sigh. "Just bored."

"How could you possibly be bored? You have the entire world at your fingertips."

Yeah, the entire world minus one broody, sexy-as-sin man who I miss more than I care to admit.

"I just am," I snap, which has Helen glancing up and assessing me.

"Want to know a rumor I heard?" she taunts, focusing her attention back on the cucumber she's slicing.

"I suppose." I feign indifference.

"I heard Mr. Heath is back in town." Her eyes dart up and I force myself not to react as my thoughts go back to the last time I saw Heath. *My wedding day.* The way he ruthlessly took me right there in my wedding gown. The way he claimed my ass, punishing me for choosing Elliot over him.

Before I can respond to what she's said, I hear the doorbell ring. I sit frozen in place. It can't be, can it? He wouldn't show up here. Not after all this time. Not after I chose Elliot over him. And then I hear *his* voice and it has me shooting out of my seat and scurrying into the foyer.

Heath. In an expensive navy blue three-piece suit, he stands in the foyer with a devious smirk splayed across his face. He looks just like he did the last time I saw him, yet different. I can't quite put my finger on it, but he appears to be more refined, more worldly. His hair is gelled back like it always was when he worked for my father, but now he's sporting some scruff that's been neatly trimmed into a distinguished goatee. Usually I prefer a clean-shaven man, but as his finger and thumb come up to rub his new facial hair, I imagine how it would feel between my thighs. His eyes meet mine and the muscles between my legs clench in excitement. His gaze drags down my body and his tongue darts out to wet his lips. The same tongue that was sucking on my clit the last time I saw him. The last time I was fully pleasured by a man.

"And to what do we owe this pleasure?" Elliot says, sarcasm dripping with each word, as he walks up next to me and wraps an arm around my waist.

"Didn't you hear? I'm living at Windy Hills."

CHAPTER ELEVEN

Heath

Oɴᴇ ʏᴇᴀʀ I'ᴠᴇ ᴡᴀɪᴛᴇᴅ. Bɪᴅɪɴɢ ᴍʏ ᴛɪᴍᴇ. Wᴏʀᴋɪɴɢ ᴍʏ fucking ass off. It's a hard world out there, but I've learned that if you look and act the part, most people just go with it. And that's what I've been doing. Getting people to just go with it.

Little by little, day by day.

Each second I was away from her, I was able to think. Really think about my situation and how I got there. Most importantly, who was to blame. A man with an idle mind and time on his hands will create a cleverly dangerous agenda.

I'm pleased that the Lincolns are stunned by my surprise appearance. Helen mutters her displeasure nearby and my grin widens. Elliot gapes at me, his mouth opening and closing as though he wants to say something to me. While he gapes like a fish, I pounce on his wife.

"Don't I get a hug?"

Catrina seems to shake away her daze and a screech of excitement echoes from her. My heart clenches when she throws herself into my arms. After having been denied her scent, her touch, her voice for so long, I greedily indulge in her.

"You just disappeared!" she exclaims against my neck, her hot breath speaking straight to my neglected dick. "I was worried sick!"

Good. Exactly what I'd hoped. It fucking killed me when

she chose him over me. But I know my Catrina. She thinks she wants one thing, but her heart has another idea. Her heart always wanted me. Now, it's time to remind her of that.

"I'm back now," I assure her, squeezing her. "Come on. Let's get the hell out of here and catch up."

Elliot clears his throat. "Darling." His tone is shrill and feminine. As though his nuts are shriveling up in fear—fear that I'll walk right out that door with his wife sitting on my dick. The thought is tempting. "Catrina." This time it's harsher.

She unwillingly peels herself away from me, but I lock my arms around her waist. Our faces are inches apart. I could just kiss her now. Elliot Lincoln would have to watch.

I could.

But I won't.

Not yet, anyway.

"I'll get my purse," she breathes. "There's a cute little French restaurant down the—"

"Catrina," Elliot snips. "Don't be ridiculous. Helen will make some refreshments and we'll entertain Mr. Heath."

Helen scurries away to do his bidding.

I bite back a laugh. Fucking pussy. He doesn't trust me alone with his wife. And he shouldn't. The moment I get her alone, I'm going to defile her and stain her with me.

Catrina's green eyes flicker with disappointment. Poor girl's probably been half-dead with boredom. She thought I'd lick her back to life.

In due time, love.

"Fine," she huffs, placating her whiney husband. "But I want to hear every detail, Heath."

She grabs my hand and guides me over to a loveseat. I sit, pulling her down beside me. Elliot glowers at me but takes a seat in a nearby chair. He blabbers on, but I'm not interested in what that prick has to say. I'm too busy admiring her. Her cheeks have rounded out some. They must feed her well here. It looks good on her, but I'm smart enough not to bring up the fact she's gained some weight. I'd like to keep my balls. Her husband already lost his and she keeps them in her purse. Our hands remain conjoined and I run my thumbs across the tops of her hands. So smooth.

"I missed you, my love," she mutters.

Elliot goes silent.

"My best friend," she amends, flashing Elliot a polite smile.

I laugh, earning a warning glare from Catrina.

"Anyway, tell me where you've been." She bats her lashes and bites on her bottom lip. Gives me those pretty *fuck me* eyes like she used to. This bored housewife is ready for some excitement.

"I've been in London."

"London?" she gasps. "Why? What's in London? How did you get there?"

Without money she means.

"I have my ways," I say, winking at her. "Tell me how married life is treating you. Are you satisfied with this new life?"

Her nostrils flare and a blush creeps up her throat. I wonder if she's remembering the one time I fucked her in the lake with swimmers nearby. Or the time I fingered her in the movie theater. Perhaps she's recalling the time I licked on her pussy while she talked to her father on the phone when he was away on business.

"Elliot provides well," she says primly and flashes him one of her beauty queen smiles.

He grunts and then thanks Helen when she sets down a tray of cookies and lemonade.

"Lovely," I tell Catrina, once again laughing. I wonder if she ever regrets her decision. Was an indoor pool worth a year of no orgasms? "Sounds like the perfect life."

I turn away from Catrina to pick up a glass of lemonade. Elliot shoots laser glares at me, but I ignore him. Catrina leans into me, her head resting on my shoulder.

"You smell good. New cologne? Is this Armani?" Her fingers run along my jacket lapel. "It's new. Where did you get a new Armani suit? I have so many questions," Catrina chatters on.

"I have my ways," I say again. Then, I turn to Elliot. "How is Isabel these days?" I don't care about her, but I want to rattle him. A vein pulses in his throat at the mention of his little sister.

"Isabel is fine," he clips out. "She is—"

"Right here," Isabel chirps from the doorway and then prances into the room, batting her lashes. "I'm right here."

So pathetic. The whole lot of them.

"Good afternoon, Isa." I wink at her.

Her cheeks burn bright red and she looks away. "Good afternoon, Mr. Heath."

Catrina squeezes my shoulder. "I think you're bigger. Have you been working out?" She looks up at me with her seductive eyes and flashes me the look she always gave me when she wanted my undivided attention. Naturally, Catrina doesn't like sharing my attention with Isabel. *Noted, darling.*

"I've been doing a lot of things," I assure her. My eyes drop to her lips. She licks them and I grin.

"Catrina," Elliot grunts. "You're being overly welcoming to Mr. Heath. Perhaps give him some space to breathe."

Her nostrils flare and annoyance flickers across her features. "I've missed him. He's my best friend. It feels like a decade, not a year. Right, Heath?"

"Feels like a lifetime indeed," I agree. "But I'm back for the time being. There will be plenty of time to catch up. We'll pick right back up where we left off."

She fights a smile. The last time I saw her, my dick was inside her ass on her wedding day to another man. Picking up where we left off would be very naughty. Catrina never was a good girl.

"And if Catrina is too busy to entertain you, I'm available," Isabel pipes up, smiling at me.

I stare at her. Small tits. Thin and willowy. Nothing in the looks department that even compares to Catrina's voluptuous body. The fact that she considers herself an equal to my love is laughable. Still, I toy with her.

"I may take you up on that. A man has to eat and no man wants to eat alone," I say, flashing her a polite smile.

"Isabel, you should run along," Elliot snaps. "The adults are talking."

I snort and Catrina slaps my thigh. I capture her hand with mine and bring it to my lips to kiss her knuckles.

"I am an adult," Isabel hisses. "Don't be an asshole."

Helen gasps from nearby. This time, I let loose a boisterous laugh.

"She certainly has an adult mouth on her," I taunt.

Elliot rises from his chair and points at his sister. "Please leave, Isabel. I have some matters to discuss with Mr. Heath. Alone. Go on, now."

Isabel—the fragile fucking girl—stares at him as though he's struck her. Her bottom lip wobbles as she stands. When her eyes seek out mine, I wink at her again.

"Now," Elliot reminds her.

With a huff, she rushes from the room. Five bucks says she's in the hallway bawling her eyes out. "You had matters to discuss?" I ask, my interest piqued.

Elliot sits once again. "Do tell us how you've come to live at Windy Hills. Last I heard, Hunter and Francesca were living there. All was well."

Francesca. I nearly shudder. I can't stand that woman.

"It seems Catrina's brother has welcomed me back." Because I highlighted the goddamned will and shoved it in his face. Crenshaw made sure I had a home there, stating that as long as Hunter owns the home, I have the right to reside in it. "Time heals all wounds, I suppose." I lean in and whisper to Catrina, "Time stopped while I was gone. Time was frozen as I tried to memorize every detail of you, my love. The soft sound of your laughter. The breathy way you say my name. The exact shade of pink your skin would turn when you'd come."

She gasps. "Heath…"

"I can almost still taste you on my tongue. Sweet," I murmur before kissing her temple. "Or is that the lemonade I still taste?"

When I pull away, Elliot's face is nearly purple. He grips the arms of the chair as he grinds his teeth together.

That's right, motherfucker. You never really had her. She was always mine.

"Heath," he grinds out. "If you'll excuse us, my wife and I have plans this evening that we must get ready for." He stands and holds out his hand, waiting for me to shake it.

"No, we don't," Catrina blurts out.

I twirl a lock of her hair around my finger and tug. "Don't worry, love, we have all the time in the world."

She groans when I stand and I have to pull my other hand from her death grip. I don't shake Elliot's hand and walk past him. Catrina starts after me, but Elliot snags her by the wrist and hauls her to him. I won't stick around for his sad attempt at being macho.

"We'd love to have you for dinner at the Windy Hills Estate, Catrina. Any day, you're more than welcome." I flash her a suggestive smile before stalking out of the sitting room.

I whistle a jovial tune as I exit their impressive home and stalk toward my brand-new Bentley Mulsanne. The car is like my old Honda, but a helluva lot more expensive. I admire my vehicle as I approach. When I sit down inside, I'm shocked to find Isabel sitting in the passenger seat. All attempts at behaving with any sort of decorum have flown out the window. I'm no longer playing a fair game with Elliot and Catrina. No, all bets are off now. The gentleman has taken a seat and the beast is ready to play.

"May I help you?" I sneer, my tone condescending as hell.

Her hazel eyes widen as though she didn't expect that sort of greeting. "I, uh, I like you."

I lift a brow that says, *And your fucking point?*

"And I thought maybe we could go out or something," she rushes out, her face burning crimson once more.

"Hmmm. *Or something?* Elaborate on the something."

She bites on her thin bottom lip. This poor girl is simple and boring. I wonder if she compares herself to the beauty who resides inside her home. What a horrible life to always be second best.

Boldly, Isabel leans forward. "We could kiss," she breathes.

"Have you kissed anyone before?" I ask, arching a brow.

"Nobody that matters."

"I shouldn't matter to you," I growl. "I take and take. I never give. Not to someone like you."

Her brows furl together and her eyes water like she might cry. *I would gobble you up in a second, Goldilocks.*

"I could surprise you," she says.

"You can't handle anything about me," I warn. "Much less surprise me."

Boldly, she climbs across the center console and straddles my lap. I won't admit it, but this *does* surprise me. Her body is bony and awkward, but it gives me ideas. Wicked ones.

Fuck you, Elliot.

I grab the front of Isa's dress and yank it down, exposing her small tits to me. With a critical eye, I inspect them. One is slightly bigger than the other. Imperfect.

"I'm a monster." I look up at her. "Do you understand? I would destroy you."

She cups my cheeks with her hands. "Maybe I want to be destroyed," she murmurs breathlessly.

A low, evil chuckle rumbles from me. "So you'd let me fingerfuck you right here? In the driveway with your brother close by?"

Panic flashes in her eyes, but she squeaks out a yes.

"I don't think you deserve to come," I sneer.

She runs her fingers into my hair, messing up the gelled style. "Okay."

Okay.

Ha!

"Okay," I mimic, taunting her. "We'll see."

She gasps when I shove her dress up her thighs, seeking her panties. I easily tear them from her tiny body and shove them in the cup holder. Then, I slide my fingers past her golden snatch and push my longest finger deep inside her. She's wet—dirty little girl—and she's not a virgin.

"Yes," she whimpers. "More."

"More fingers?" I challenge.

She doesn't answer, so I work another finger into her tight channel. Her body clenches around my fingers and worry flickers in her gaze.

"I'm rough. Sweet little girls like you can't be with men like me."

"Why not?" she asks, pouting.

"Because I'll fucking hurt you," I snarl.

She cries out when I grab a handful of her hair and draw her to my mouth. I don't kiss her but bypass her mouth instead and latch my mouth to her neck. I fuck her needy cunt hard with my fingers, but I don't let her come. She moans, faking her pleasure. Liar. I bite her goddamned neck until she screams and tries to get away.

As she scrambles into the passenger seat, I watch her. She cries and adjusts her dress but doesn't climb out of the car. Stupid girl. Wiggling my wet fingers, I get her attention.

"Do you taste good?" I ask her.

Tears roll down her cheeks and she shrugs. "I don't know."

"I don't know either," I tell her simply. "And I don't care."

She gapes at me.

"I'll purchase you some new underwear next time I'm in the city. Now if you'll run along, I have business that needs tending to at home." I give her a polite smile, dismissing her.

Her fingers clumsily fumble for the door handle as she climbs out of the car. I watch her run back to the house, pushing past Helen, who watches me in horror.

I wave to Helen with my fingers that are still wet from Elliot's little whore sister.

Helen turns on her heel and disappears.

Good riddance.

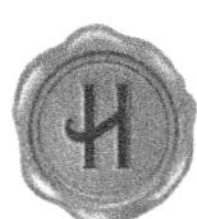

After a shower, cleaning any residue of the slutty girl off my person, I exit the bathroom with my towel tied around my waist. I've taken up residence in my old room at Windy Hills. For now. Soon, I'll make some changes.

"Up."

The sound of a young voice steals my attention. Hunter's child—Harrison is his name I've learned—toddles along the hallway, his chubby arms reaching up for me.

I glare at him. "What, boy?"

"Up," he says again. "Up."

The hallway is empty, but his nursery room door is ajar. Can't these half-wits watch their kid?

"Go to your room," I bark out.

He blinks at me, unfazed by my outburst and tone, with wide blue eyes but doesn't budge. "Up." He lifts his arms for me to pick him up.

"Were you born stupid, boy? I said go to your room." My voice thunders in the hallway.

"Harrison?" Francesca calls out in a singsong voice as she exits the bedroom. When she sees me, she flinches. "Mr. Heath."

I lift a brow, waiting for her to approach. "I'm about to do some work and I don't need a baby interrupting me," I snap. "Go on. Take him away."

She's frozen in place, worrying her bottom lip between her teeth.

"Up," Harrison says again, tugging at the bottom of my towel.

I grumble and fist his overalls at his back. He lets out a squeal of delight as I pick him up as though he's a fucking puppy trying to piss all over my floor. I stalk down the hallway past her and into his nursery.

"Stay here," I order as I deposit him into his crib.

"Noooo!" he cries out.

Francesca, finally having found her wits, rushes past me to collect her son. I leave without a backward glance. Stalking down the hallway, I make my way to my room and push inside. I've just closed the door behind me when I realize I'm not alone.

"Did you fuck her?" Catrina asks, her nostrils flaring with fury.

I frown in confusion. "Francesca? Hell no."

She swallows and shakes her head, pointing out the window toward her new home at Low Valley Estate. "Not her. Isabel."

I laugh. "Is that what she told you?"

"Don't laugh at me, Heath! This is serious. That is my husband's sister. You don't get to just fuck her to piss me off!"

Raising a brow, I take her in. Her cheeks are flushed from anger and her hands are shaking. The dress she's put on is a simple one that I could get into quickly if I chose to do so. I drop my towel, loving the way her angry eyes turn to lust as she admires my impressive physique. Turns out, working out is a great channel for aggression. I wonder if my countable abs and perfect oblique muscles reflect *my* anger.

She brings her hand to her mouth as her gaze settles on my cock. It's flaccid at the moment, but thoughts of Catrina bouncing on my dick has it thickening between us.

"Put some clothes on," she mutters.

"Nothing you haven't seen before," I challenge.

She nervously twists her massive diamond around her ring finger. "Focus. You fucked Isabel and I won't let you change the topic."

I prowl closer to her, but she doesn't retreat. Once my cock is pressed against her stomach, I run my fingers through her silky tresses. "I didn't fuck her."

"But Helen said she was straddling you in your car and—"

"Helen makes shit up," I snap. "Nosy bitch."

"So you didn't do anything with Isabel?"

I press my thumb to her pouty bottom lip, missing the way it feels against my flesh. "I didn't say that."

Her lashes blink rapidly at me. "What?"

"She came on to me. I fingered her. Poor thing couldn't handle a love bite so she ran off crying," I say with an evil grin.

Catrina growls and slaps me. "You asshole!"

When she starts to slap me again, I grab a handful of her hair, pulling her close to my face. "I'm an asshole because you care so much about her virtue or because you don't want me with anyone else?"

She tries to look away, but I tighten my grip in her hair.

"Tell me," I hiss, my mouth close to hers. "Tell me. Are you jealous, Catrina?" I brush my lips across hers. "Because I'm fucking blind with rage over the fact Elliot Motherfucking Lincoln gets to stick his mediocre dick in you whenever he wants to."

Tears well in her eyes. "I don't love him."

"No, you love *me*, which makes all of this so fucked up."

"I do love you," she agrees. "We can be together. Like old times. He doesn't have to know." She starts to unzip her dress and I shake my head.

Catrina loves her secrets.

"Get on your knees."

Fire blazes in her eyes. "What? No."

"Now, love."

She softens and allows me to ease her to the floor. My cock bobs in her face. Her gaze is challenging as she looks up at me. I simply lift a brow and silently say, *If you love me like you say, suck my fucking dick, love.*

Her left hand wraps around my thick cock and her

diamond glimmers in the light. Satisfaction trickles through me. There's no sweeter revenge than being able to take the very thing your enemy adores the most and bend it to your fucking will.

"Suck my dick and tell me you could never love him like you love me," I sneer, never letting up the death grip I have on her hair.

Her tongue darts out and she licks my tip, sending shivers of pleasure rippling through me. "Always you, Heath."

She slides her juicy lips around my hardness and eases down as far as she can go. I let out a groan of pleasure. The tip of my dick teases the back of her throat, but my practiced whore doesn't gag.

"Do you suck his dick?" I demand but keep her head stationed over my cock.

Tears well in her eyes as she tries to shake her head. I push forward into her throat and my eyes fall shut. Fuck, I've missed this—missed us.

"Good girl," I hiss out.

She gurgles and slobbers but otherwise takes my cock like she has long since perfected how to do. When I'm about to come, I pull out and stare down at her beautiful face. My fist rubs up and down my length until I explode. White ribbons of cum splatter on her smooth flesh. Her eyes flutter shut as more cum clings to her thick black lashes. I love that I've just defiled what legally belongs to Elliot Lincoln, and I've done it in that motherfucker Hunter Crenshaw's house.

Oh, how easy it is.

When I'm finished, I step away and pick up the discarded towel before tossing it at her. She swipes away my mess and then stands quickly.

"I don't want you seeing Isabel," she bites out.

I bypass her to grab some boxers from a drawer. Once

I've put them on, I stroke my fingers through her hair. "You're not allowed to be jealous, Catrina. You're married, remember?"

"Heath..."

"I have some work to do. You know the way out."

CHAPTER TWELVE

HELEN

The Present...

"UGH, HE'S BEING DIFFICULT," EMILY GROANS. "HE'S TOYING with her."

"That's Mr. Heath for you," I agree.

Her phone buzzes and she sighs.

Finn: You can't ignore me forever.

"I can and I will," Emily says, huffing. Instead of replying to Finn, she texts Porter.

Emily: You can't ignore me forever.

I want to add my two cents, but I bite my tongue instead. I've meddled enough in this lifetime to know it doesn't matter. Love does what it wants in the end.

"Okay, continue," she instructs. "This is getting juicy. Don't leave any detail out."

"Very well."

CHAPTER THIRTEEN

CATRINA

The Past...

"THAT BASTARD!" I SLAM THE FRONT DOOR OF THE ESTATE and stalk up to Isabel's bedroom, swinging her door open.

"What the hell were you thinking?" I cut across the room, and grabbing a handful of her hair, I drag her out of her bed and onto the floor. "He's not yours! He doesn't even want you. Don't you ever touch him again." I climb onto Isabel, who is crying like the damn baby she is and, winding my hand back, I slap her right across her face.

"Catrina!" Helen shouts, running into the room and pulling me off Isabel before I can slap her again. "What has gotten into you?" she admonishes, but I ignore her, shooting daggers at Isabel. Helen reaches down and helps her up, moving her hand from her face to check out the damage. Such a whiny little girl. It was just a slap. I watch her cry crocodile tears to Helen.

"Oh for God's sake." I roll my eyes at her dramatics. "It won't even bruise." She should've thought about the consequences of her actions before she threw herself at Heath.

"What is going on here?" Elliot enters the room, his eyes taking in the situation.

"Catrina attacked me," Isabel cries.

"Why would she attack you?" Elliot asks, confused.

"Because..." she begins. My eyes meet Isabel's and my brows rise, silently daring her to tell Elliot she let Heath finger her. When she cries harder, not answering, I hide my grin. *That's right, skank, you wouldn't dare tell your dear old brother the truth. We both know you don't have the guts.*

"She borrowed my dress and didn't give it back," I say and Helen shoots me a shrewd look. *Fuck off, witch.*

"A new dress can be purchased. Right now I need to speak to my wife in our room, please." Elliot grasps hold of my elbow and guides me down the hall to our bedroom and into our sitting room. Once we're inside, he closes the door and gives me a knowing glance.

"Want to tell me what's really going on?" he questions.

"I already told you," I snap. "If you don't believe me, that's on you."

Elliot cuts across the room and backs me up against the wall. "Don't you fucking lie to me, *wife*! Helen saw you follow after Heath! Did you fuck him?" His nose finds its way to my neck and he sniffs me like a dog.

"No! And even if I did, so what?" I push his chest and he stumbles back a couple of steps. "I chose *you*, didn't I?"

"So what?" he barks. "So fucking what? You're my wife! I don't need you behaving like a goddamn whore!"

"I'm a whore?" I snigger. "Your sister was the one getting fingered by him in the car!"

Elliot's eyes widen in shock and horror. "Is that why you attacked her? You were jealous?" He snorts. "Jealous of her being with that flea-ridden mutt?"

"Heath is not a mutt!" I shout. "He's my best friend and I love him. You're the one who's jealous because no matter how much money you spend on me, I'll never love you the way I love Heath. You'll never satisfy me the way he satisfies me. Every time we have boring sex, I wish it were him. Wish it were him fucking me. You know why?" I taunt. "Because unlike you,

Heath fucks me like a man is supposed to fuck a woman. Hard and rough."

Elliot's palm cracks against my cheek and my face whips to the side, but unlike his cunt of a sister, I don't shed a single tear. No. Instead I look Elliot dead in the eye and cackle loudly.

"While I love to be slapped, I prefer it to be on my ass as Heath is fucking me from behind." I raise my brows and lift my chin high in defiance. "But you wouldn't know anything about that since the only position you're familiar with is missionary."

I watch as metaphorical smoke comes shooting from Elliot's ears. "Catrina, that's enough! You are my wife. Or have you changed your mind?" Elliot's nostrils flare and he sneers at me. "We could divorce," he taunts. "Then you'll be left with nothing. Is that what you want, *love*? To void your father's will and be penniless?"

Feeling backed against the wall, I let out a shriek and slam the door that separates our bedroom from the sitting room and lock it. Then I go to the other door and lock it as well. Then just to ensure the asshole can't get in, I grab the chairs from the corner of the room and push them against each door.

"Catrina!" Elliot bangs on the door. "Will you just let me in?" *Bang. Bang. Bang.* "Stop behaving like a child, please." *Bang. Bang.* "We both said things we didn't mean. Come out and we can talk."

What a pussy! Well, fuck him! I pick up the lamp and chuck it across the room, watching it smash into pieces. Fuck him with a goddamned ten-inch dildo. He knows he has me. He knows I'm not going anywhere. It doesn't matter that my body, heart, and soul belong to Heath. I'll never divorce Elliot. It would destroy my father's company, his legacy. It would void my trust funds, leaving me with no money. Not able to hold in my heartbreak any longer, I fall to the floor in a disheveled heap as my grief pours out in a flood of uncontrollable tears.

I hate this. I hate the hold Elliot has over me. I hate my father for not changing his will sooner. And I hate Heath for letting Isabel touch him. He knows he's mine. All he would have to do is accept that I have no choice but to remain married to Elliot. We could still *be* together.

Why does it have to be all or nothing with that man? Damn him! Lying down in bed, I snuggle into my pillow and cry myself to sleep, wishing for a solution that doesn't involve me losing everything.

I wake the next morning, tired and groggy, from a restless sleep. I use the bathroom and notice my eyes are puffy from crying. After showering and getting dressed, I find dozens of notes that were slipped under the door from Elliot, begging me for forgiveness and to open the door. I crumple them all up and throw them into the trash can. Then I call Windy Hills.

"Crenshaw residence," Francesca answers.

"Francesca, it's Catrina. How are you?"

"Oh, I'm good, dear. And you?"

"Just fine. Is Heath home?"

The line goes silent for a moment and then she says, "He is, unfortunately."

Ignoring her rude comment, I ask if I can please speak with him. I hear shuffling and then Heath's voice comes over the phone.

"Catrina, did you have a good night, love?" Smug bastard.

"You know I didn't, Heath." I try and fail not to whine. "Elliot is being mean to me and I locked myself in my room."

Heath lets out an amused chuckle. "Would you like me to come and get you?"

"Would you?" I ask, hopeful.

"Are you ready to divorce and leave him for good?"

"You know I can't!" I shout through the phone. "I love you, Heath. Please."

"No."

"Please," I plead. "If you would just see reason—" Before I can finish my sentence, my stomach begins to contract so violently that I find myself bolting to the bathroom. I don't make it in time, though, and I end up vomiting all over the tiled floor. The smell has me gagging as I try to catch my breath and get my body under control. And just when I think my stomach and heart have calmed, I feel the pain in my stomach building again and I drop to my knees over the toilet seat just in time to release whatever is left in me.

"Catrina!" I hear Helen shout through the door. I wait until I know I'm not going to puke again, then, moving the chair from the door, I open it to let her in.

"Oh, dear, are you okay?" she coos, placing her hand up to my forehead. "You don't have a fever."

"I don't know what came over me. I was just fine and then I wasn't." Remembering I left Heath on the phone, I make my way back into the bedroom and pick it back up.

"Are you there?"

"I'm here," he says, his voice full of concern. "What happened?"

"I threw up," I admit, "a few times."

"Get off the phone, so you can rinse off and I can clean up the mess," Helen instructs.

"I have to call you back." I hit end before he can say goodbye, still pissed off over everything.

"Come on. Go shower." Helen takes the cordless phone from my hand and places it on its base before leading me into the bathroom where a warm shower is waiting for me. I remain in the shower until the water turns cold, and once I get out, I see the bathroom is back to its pristine condition. Grabbing a fluffy towel from the rack, I dry off and wrap myself up in my robe. Taking my brush from the drawer, I begin to brush my wet strands when my eyes land on a white and blue box. Dropping the brush to the floor, I stare down at the box for several beats, my heart beating erratically. Then, with shaky hands, I snatch it up and read the label: Pregnancy test. Helen must've left this here. But when did she buy it? Did she notice something I didn't?

This can't be happening. *But isn't this what I wanted? To get married to Elliot and have his baby so I could receive the money I deserve?*

With shaky hands, I tear the box open and read the instructions. I do as it says and when I'm done, I begin pacing back and forth across the bathroom—impatiently waiting for the results. I'm not sure what I want the outcome to be. If I'm pregnant, will Heath and I be over for good? Of course we will! I'll be having another man's child. If I'm not pregnant, is this a sign to leave Elliot and choose Heath? But then I'll lose everything.

I wait and wait and wait for what feels like hours, pacing back and forth, back and forth. Confused. Scared. Nervous. When I check the clock for the millionth time, I see it's time.

I stop in front of the test and count the number of pink lines. One. Two.

I'm pregnant.

With Elliot's child.

Heath will never forgive me.

I remain in bed for the next few days, refusing to see anyone except for Helen, who brings me soup and holds my hair back while I throw up. I write in my journal every emotion I'm feeling. My thoughts are a jumbled mess but writing them out always helps. Elliot begs to see me, but I refuse him access. Helen tells me I'm behaving like a child but I don't care. The things he said to me were vile. And then when he slapped me. Him being exiled from our bedroom is the least he deserves.

"Is it true?" A familiar baritone voice has me sitting up. "Is it true, Catrina?" Heath stalks across the room to the side of the bed. I know what he's asking, but I can't say the words out loud. It will mean admitting everything is about to change—again.

He sits on the edge of the bed and I slide up into a sitting position. His hand cups the side of my face. I avert my eyes, not wanting to see what's going through his head, but when his thumb and forefinger grip my chin and jerk my face to the side, he forces me to look at him. And there it is, written all over his face like permanent marker scribbled all over the wall.

Disappointment.

Heartbreak.

Disgust.

Love.

He stares intently into my eyes and I blink back the tears that are threatening to fall. "I'm so sorry," I finally whisper, my words coming out hoarse from the giant ball of emotion stuck in my throat.

"No, you aren't," he replies, his voice devoid of all emotion. "Don't go soft on me now, love." He leans in and places a chaste kiss to my lips. "Run away with me. We can leave it all behind. I'll raise this baby like he or she is my own." His eyes plead with hope even though he already knows my answer.

"Stay," I beg. "I only have to stay married to him for four more years and then we can have it all."

"We can have it all now, Catrina. You and me, that's all we need to be happy. You've been surrounded by wealth and luxury for the last twelve months. Did it make you happy?"

My lips begin to tremble as a single tear falls down my cheek. "It's too much money, Heath. You have to understand. And it's not just me. My father's business could fail. We'll lose everything. The estate, our inheritance. You're asking me for the impossible. It's not fair."

"Then you've made your decision." Heath stands and I reach my hand out for him.

"No, you're making it for me," I cry. "Don't make me choose, please."

' "Don't you dare blame this on me," he growls, his jaw clenching with fury. "This is your doing."

"No." Gut-wrenching sobs wrack my body as Heath backs up, the distance between us growing. "You have my heart, Heath." I stumble from the bed in an attempt to bridge the gap between us. "You own me, body and soul."

"Yet you refuse to give me *all* of you," he hisses.

"I'm giving you every part of me that I can." My eyes plead for him to understand.

"I want it *all!*" he booms. "Every goddamned piece of you. I can't share you." He steps toward me and kneels down at my level. "Can you give me *all* of you?"

And I know in this moment I'm about to lose my best friend. My lover. My soul is about to become detached from my body because I am nothing without Heath, yet I can't be what he needs me to be.

"I didn't think so." And with those parting words, Heath walks out of my bedroom and out of my life.

The next several days go by in a blur. I continue to remain in bed, still refusing to leave the room. Elliot is no longer exiled, but he hasn't come to see me. I don't know if it's because he's mad at me for the way I behaved or if he's embarrassed for the way he behaved. Either way I welcome the quiet. Then one afternoon I hear shouting from downstairs. Too curious not to go down and listen, I pull my robe on and tiptoe down the hall to the top of the stairs. I can see Elliot pacing back and forth in the foyer with the cordless phone glued to his ear. His face is bright red with anger and the hand not holding the phone is clenched into a tight fist.

"You made your choice, Isabel, and you shall live with it! As of this moment you are no longer a Lincoln. You are dead to this family, and when you wake up one day with regret for leaving with that low-life bottom feeder, and you will...do not even think about coming home because as of now you no longer have a home here."

My hands come up to my mouth to muffle my gasp. *Isabel left with Heath...this can't be true.* Elliot slams the phone against the wall then darts his eyes over to mine.

"Did you hear that, *wife*? It seems my sister has given up everything to run away with Heath. She chose him over this family. I guess your choice has been made for you." Then, without waiting for my response, he stalks out of the foyer and into his study, slamming the door behind him.

CHAPTER FOURTEEN

ĤEATH

Five months later...

"**P**LEASE JUST TALK TO HIM," ISABEL WHINES FROM THE OTHER side of the door. "I've learned my lesson, Mother."

Delores's voice can be heard yapping from the other end of the phone, but I can't make out the words.

"I know how the Lincoln men are. Stubborn." Isabel sighs heavily when her mom yaps some more. "I know I chose this path. You guys gave me everything, but I denied it to run off and marry *him*."

I grin at the mention of myself.

Her mother bitches some more and then Isabel groans. "Surely you can convince Elliot to let me come home. You have to try, Mother. Father agrees with him now, but he can be persuaded too."

She's quiet as her mom babbles some more.

"I can't just put on a brilliant smile and fake it until my brother and father soften," Isabel whines. "I can't. And you're wrong, it is as bad as I say. Money isn't everything. Just because he's found some money somewhere doesn't suddenly make him tolerable."

Some.

Ha.

Isabel, the crybaby of the fucking century, sobs to her mother. "Please. I can barely function here. He's not nice to me." Then she screams out in frustration. "I know Heath was never nice to anyone, Mother. But I thought it would be different with me. I thought I could change him."

Fucking liar.

She wanted to make Catrina jealous.

And I wanted something in return.

We both had our agendas and we must deal with the consequences.

Her mom must say something that sends Isabel into a panic because she turns to begging. "If they're coming for dinner tonight, plead for me. Beg of my brother to allow me to come home. Please."

She sniffles. "I love you too." Then, she makes a kissing sound before hanging up.

I wait a moment before pushing through the bedroom door of our swanky London flat to find her sitting on the edge of the bed with her face in her palms. She looks terrible. All she does is cry, secretly smoke on the balcony as if I don't know about it, and nearly starve herself. And all it does is make me angry. She has everything she could ever want. It's not like I'm abusing her. Isn't that what these motherfuckers want? Money? Isn't that the answer to all their goddamned problems?

"It's late," she mutters before lifting her head and staring at me with pitiful hazel eyes that are red from crying. "Where were you?"

Nearly every other day she accuses me of cheating on her. The only cunt I put my cock into is hers. It's getting to be annoying that it's this she chooses to fight with me about every day.

"Her name was Lola. She tasted fucking divine," I lie just to watch her lose her shit.

She stands from the bed and throws the cordless phone at me. It hits the floor with a crack and slides under a chair. Her skinny body launches at mine and she pummels her useless fists into my chest. I let her throw her tantrum for all of thirty seconds before I lay down the law.

Grabbing a handful of her hair, I draw her to my face. "I only fuck *you*, my wife." Unfortunately.

Her nostrils flare, but the fight leaves her. I walk her backward to the nearest wall. She may not be my Catrina, but she *is* my wife. When her ass hits the wall, I rip at her gown and send it careening to the floor. She cries out when I push her panties down her thighs. I grab her hips and twist her away from me. Her fingers dig into the plaster walls as I unzip my slacks to pull out my aching cock.

Upon my first attempt, she's too dry. My cock can't go in, not without hurting her. But this wife of mine is easy to manipulate. She gets off on sweetness.

"Why aren't you wet for me?" I demand, my mouth at her ear as I rub my dick along the crack of her ass.

"Because I hate you," she mutters.

I kiss her ear and then the side of her neck. A small moan escapes her when I suck on the flesh. "I hate you too, but we both like to come."

My hand wraps around to her front and I massage her clit. She whimpers and pushes her ass into me. With my other hand, I tease her slit that's growing with wetness.

"When are we going to make a baby?" I coo, loving the way she shudders.

So. Fucking. Easy.

"I don't know," she breathes.

Slowly, I ease the tip of my dick inside her cunt. "Maybe if you weren't so miserable all the time, your body would accept what I have to give you. I thought you liked gifts."

She cries out when I slam into her hard. Her body thumps against the wall. Her bony hips will no doubt be bruised. I rub her pussy until she's writhing and giving up the bitch act for now. I know the moment we come, it'll be back to business as usual.

"Beg for me to come inside you," I snarl, my free hand sliding into her hair to fist it. "Beg to be defiled like a whore."

"Ah," she hisses. "Please."

When she unravels with a ragged orgasm, I grunt out my release. I wait until my cock stops throbbing to let go of her hair. My lips find her shoulder and I kiss her. It's the only way to make her compliant when I want something. As my cock softens and slides out of her, she relaxes. I turn her to face me. My fingers, still wet from where I massaged her, dig into her dainty jaw as I lift her gaze to mine.

"Isabel, my fragile and lonely wife?"

She blinks at me as tears well in her eyes. "Yes?"

"I want you to throw out the birth control pills. I'm going to give you a baby."

Her expression turns into one of horror. This isn't her decision. It's necessary. She'll bear my child and that is the fucking end of it.

"What if I'm not ready?" she challenges.

I could fight her. Yell in her face and tell her how it's going to be. But this little girl isn't played that way. With her, it's simple.

"Sweetheart," I coo, my voice soft and caring, "*I'm* ready." I kiss her mouth gently at first and then I devour her. Desperate to be loved and for any sort of attention, she throws her arms around my neck, kissing me back.

Isabel is no Catrina.

She'll never compare.

But she's the woman I have right now and I'll be damned if I don't use that to my advantage. I'm a man, after all. Grabbing her bony ass, I lift her and carry her over to our bed. I toss her onto it before quickly shedding the rest of my clothes. Her eyes are wide and unsure as I prowl over her. I capture her mouth again. My dick is already hard again, eager for this new step in my plan.

"Look how wonderful you are when you comply," I praise as I pepper kisses all over her mouth. "So sweet and lovely. I wonder if our child will have your eyes or mine. Are you imagining the sounds of laughter as our children run through these halls? I would buy them all ponies and when they are older whatever they want. We will spoil them."

She feeds on my lies as though they are her sustenance. "I want to have your baby," she chokes out, surprising us both.

I'm gentle as I make love to her. If I close my eyes, I can almost pretend it's one of the tender moments I shared with Catrina. With Catrina on my mind, I whisper the words the girl so desperately needs to hear. "I love you."

She comes.

And then I do too.

Tomorrow we'll throw out the pills and I'll fuck her until she's carrying my child.

"Oh, Heath, can we go back to New York for a visit?" Isabel pleads from her chair by the window. "I miss my brother and his wife. My parents too. Please."

I have too much work to do before I can go back.

Soon.

Just not yet.

"Perhaps at Christmas," I lie as I stalk past her to my closet. I hang up my suit jacket and pull off my tie. Once I've kicked off my shoes, I unbutton the cuffs to my shirt and roll the sleeves up. When I emerge, Isabel still has a book open in her lap and is staring out the window.

I walk over to her and follow her stare. A little boy stands on the street corner with his mother. They're homeless. His face is dirty and she's begging for change. When his big brown eyes look our way, I nearly shudder.

That child doesn't have a Mr. Crenshaw to save the day.

No, he'll probably grow up to be some shitty criminal because his mother won't go get a goddamned job.

"Do you think he's hungry?" Isabel asks.

I know he is.

I don't remember my days before Crenshaw, but when I first came to live with him, I'd have nightmares about a gnawing hunger in my gut.

"He's not of your concern." I grab her wrist and pull her to her feet. Today she wears overalls over a tank top and her blond hair is twisted into a messy bun. She's a far cry from the debutante she once was. To be fair, she's much prettier when she's with me. "I like how you look lately," I admit. "You're eating more."

Her cheeks burn red and she bites on her bottom lip. "I gave up smoking too."

It's been two weeks since I told her we were going to have a baby and she's really gotten on board. Eating right. Exercising. Doing her part to help me around the house whenever I need something. Who knew being nice could yield such fruitful results?

Too bad being nice is eating me alive.

So often I have to bite my tongue and not compare her or taunt her.

I may be an asshole, but I'm not stupid.

And at the moment, I manipulate her to my advantage.

"Have you taken a test?" I ask.

She laughs. I haven't heard the sound in ages. "It doesn't

work like that. These things take time. I'm not due for my period for a couple more weeks."

"So we just fuck and fuck and fuck and hope for the best?"

Her head bobs up and down. "Yep."

My hand lifts and I run my knuckle along her throat. Her eyes close and she leans into my touch. As I slowly undress her and then myself, I let my mind wander to work this afternoon. I spent the entire day with a big client. One I have been working on for months. He handed over the proverbial keys to his kingdom this morning, and I showed him exactly how rich I could make him. I'm flying high on success. It's almost time.

"Bend over," I murmur as I guide her over to the bench in the window. She places her palms on the seat and bares her ass at me. I slap her ass with my dick before pushing inside her heat. Always so wet and accommodating these days. "Touch yourself and make yourself come," I demand. "Don't make me do all the fucking work." Luckily, my harsh words when we fuck turn her on. Her cunt clenches around me as she touches herself.

I push forward until we're both kneeling on the bench. I smash her tits against the cold glass and drive into her relentlessly. My teeth nip at her shoulder as I stare out the window. The homeless woman holds the child to her breast, shielding him from our show, and glowers at me.

A good man would move away from the window.

A good man would finish fucking his wife and then send her down to give the poor duo some food.

A good man would scoop that boy up and give him a home, money, an education, and a future.

I'm a bad man.

I stare down at the dirty woman as I fuck Isabel so hard her head hits the glass with a loud thud. When Isabel cries out in pleasure, I wrap my arm around her waist and pull us back. She knows the drill. Her body falls forward and she rests on her elbows. I stand and keep her ass prone to me. A few more pounds into her and I grunt out my release. I fill my wife up with cum and hope this time does the trick.

And for the next fifteen minutes, I keep her just like this with her ass in the air.

One can never be too sure, and I don't want a drop of me to escape from her until it's done its fucking job.

"I need more money," he says over the line, shame in his tone. His child cries out in the background. I can even hear his wife bitching at him. "Please. Just a small loan. The property taxes are due and I…"

Gambled away what he had.

Exhilaration burns through me. "How much?"

"Not much this time."

Last time was fifty thousand. As was the ten times before that.

"I'll wire you the money after you sign the loan agreement," I tell him. Same as always. "Watch in the mail for it. I'll have my attorney draw it up straight away."

"Thank you, Heath. You don't have to do this and yet…"

I smile. "Don't think anything of it. You know why I do it."

But he doesn't really—he only thinks he knows.

"Thank you," he says again, his voice happier in tone.

I hang up and lift my gaze to see Isabel standing in the doorway of my office. While I like to fuck, I'm growing bored of this baby making shit. I just want it to stick and then we can be on our way.

"Helen says everyone is doing well," she chirps as she prances into the office.

Fuck Helen.

"Lovely," I deadpan.

"I told her you're not always a bitter scoundrel," she says and flashes me a bright smile.

"Then you lied," I growl as I grab her waist when she nears and pull her to me.

She's all giggles as she straddles my lap. I work her panties to the side as she unfastens my pants. My cock gets pulled into her grip and then she's easing herself down over my length.

Her mouth fuses to mine, but I can hardly keep my dick up. I'm bored of these games. If she doesn't get pregnant soon, I'll lose my fucking mind. This time, I check out mentally. My mind drifts to late night romps under the sheets with *her*.

My true love.

The one *he* stole.

Elliot fucking Lincoln doesn't deserve what he has. Catrina always was and always will be mine. Soon, everything will fall into place. I can swoop in, rescue my beautiful princess, and we can ride off and have the life we always wanted.

"Ow," Isabel whimpers. "You're hurting me."

I blink away my daze. I'm sucking hard on her little tit like I used to do with Catrina while gripping her ass painfully. Irritation blooms inside of me. No sense in pretending. Isabel will never be her. She can't handle a rough fuck. She can't handle anything.

Pulling away from her breast, I look up at her. I shove my middle finger past my wife's lips and watch her eyes widen in shock. Once it's good and wet, I pull it back out and bring it around to her back. When I push into her tight ass, she screeches and begins to cry. The way her pussy clenches around my cock has me throwing my head back and groaning with my release. She tries to wriggle away, but the moment my seed spurts inside her, she freezes.

She knows the drill.

Stay fucking still and give me a goddamned baby.

She sobs and her fingers gingerly touch my chest as if she's unsure what to do. I grit my teeth, bothered by the fact I almost scared away my frightened little kitten, and look up at her.

"I didn't mean to hurt you." Lies. I slide my finger out of her ass. My cum leaks out of her, soaking my slacks. "I got carried away. For one moment, it felt like it did when I was with *her*." Not a lie. But it's a morsel that my desperate wife needs.

Her wet lashes blink several times in confusion. "*I* can give you more. *I* can be like her," she breathes. "*I* can be better."

Never.

Not even close.

Not at all.

"Perhaps it means I'm finally letting go," I utter. I'll never let her go.

"Oh, Heath," she breathes and kisses me deeply. "I swear I can be better. It just caught me off guard. We can try those things if you really want to. I want to make you happy."

"I'm feeling happier…" I say, because it's true. Because everything I ever wanted is nearly within my grasp. "And when you get pregnant one day, I'll be fucking thrilled."

She hugs me tight and buries her face against my neck. "It *will* happen. I promise."

I pat her bony ass because affection is what makes her compliant.

It better happen because it's all part of the plan.

CHAPTER FIFTEEN

HELEN

The Present...

"Oh no," Emily whines.

"What is it, dear?"

"Isabel is going to get pregnant and Heath's going to fall in love with her. Ugh," she groans. "I can't take it. She's not his lobster. I don't want him to love her."

I shake my head. "Heath never loved anyone but himself and Catrina. Don't fret, my dear." I let out a heavy sigh. "It's almost as if you're rooting for them. I already told you this wasn't a happy story."

Her phone buzzes and she picks it up. There are several missed texts from Finn and one from Porter.

Finn: We need to talk.

Finn: I'm tired of this bullshit, Emily.

Finn: He's nothing but trash.

Porter: I'm not ignoring you. Some plans fell through. We can hang out later if you want.

Her fingers fly like the dickens as she types out a response to Finn.

Emily: Grow up, Finn Browning! You're a bully when you don't get your way.

Then, she taps out a reply to Porter.

Emily: Like we could go to dinner?

Her phone buzzes and buzzes and buzzes.

Finn: HE'S FUCKING USING YOU!

Porter: I could pick you up. We could take a drive and just park someplace quiet.

Finn: So help me, Emily, don't make me drive my Maserati over there and strangle you. I will, angel, I so fucking will.

"Ugh, dick."

"Language," I huff. But I do tend to agree with her about Finn Browning's attitude. While his intentions are good, he has a horrible way of going about it. "Ever think maybe he's reacting that way because he cares?"

"I guess," Emily admits reluctantly.

Porter: I was thinking about that picture you sent me. I'd like more like that.

Emily sighs. "He's so romantic."

I purse my lips in displeasure. "Not what I'd call it, young lady."

Finn: That's it. I'm done with this shit.

"Ughhhh," she grumbles. "Get me out of this real-life drama. I want to go back to the love story. It's clearly much more entertaining than mine." Despite her words, she exits her texts and starts flipping through selfies she's taken with Finn. I'm not sure what she has against the boy. Whenever they're together, they laugh and flirt. He stares at her as though she's his entire world. I'd like to intervene, but I don't. Love has a way of getting through the thickest skulls and making them see sense eventually.

"Look at how cute you two are," I say when she stops at a picture.

In the picture Finn is biting her jaw and you can tell she's screaming. From an outsider looking in, they're in love. Too bad Miss Emily hasn't come to that conclusion.

"Perhaps we should stop," I mutter. "This is where the story takes a turn for the worse. Are you sure you want to continue?"

"A turn for the worse? Why?" Emily exclaims. "I thought

you said he didn't love Isabel and he only loved Catrina. That's all that matters!"

"Catrina got ill during her pregnancy. She was bed-ridden. I worried it was her heart poisoning her." I frown. "I reached out to Mr. Heath and asked him to come home."

"Awww," Emily says, hugging me. "You did well, Nanny. She was heartsick and you wanted to heal her."

If only it were that simple.

"Hold your tongue, darling. I simply stirred the pot and made things worse, I fear. On a dreadful, stormy night, Mr. Heath showed up. At the worst possible time, mind you. That was a part of his character, I think. Always showing up when nobody wanted him…"

"I think it's romantic he always fought for her."

CHAPTER SIXTEEN

Catrina

The Past...

"Helen! Helen, can you hear me?" I scream out and wait to hear if she's coming up the stairs. When she doesn't answer and I don't hear any movement, I yell out my husband's name. Of course he doesn't answer either. Huffing my annoyance, I close my journal and place it along with my pen in my nightstand before I flip the covers off me. Then, throwing my legs to the side of the bed, I plant my hand on the nightstand to help pull myself off the bed. When I'm finally standing and the dizziness has passed, I waddle down the stairs. Not spotting anyone in the reading room or sitting room, I make my way to the kitchen, where I find both Helen and Elliot, as well as his parents.

"Good morning, Delores. William." I give each an air kiss.

"Catrina, how are you feeling? I thought you were supposed to remain in bed as much as possible with your condition," Delores coos. "From what we've heard your condition is quite serious."

"It is serious, however, staying in bed is impossible when Helen and Elliot choose to ignore me, forcing me to get out of bed. I'm starving and parched and apparently both of them have more important matters to handle than to take care of me." I pluck a bottle of water from the fridge and slam the door.

"Catrina, don't be a brat," Elliot scolds and I shoot him a deadly scowl. "My parents are leaving to Florida before the storm gets much worse and Helen and I were seeing them off." I forgot today is the day they're leaving. Having decided that it's time to retire, William has handed over the company to Elliot and purchased a home in Florida they plan to make their permanent residence.

"Elliot, be nice," Delores admonishes. "She's pregnant and on bed rest with your child."

"That's okay," I snip. "I expect nothing less from my husband. Will you be returning for the birth of your grandchild in a couple of months?"

"We might not make it back for the birth, but we will definitely plan a trip for soon after." Delores smiles sweetly.

"From what I've heard from Isabel, she and Heath are trying for a baby as well," Helen adds. "Maybe you will have two grandbabies close in age." At her words, my water bottle drops to the floor, water spilling everywhere. Helen rushes around to pick it up and starts cleaning the wet mess.

"Isabel is no longer part of this family, therefore, any *child* they create will not be a part of this family either," Elliot sneers.

"Agreed," William adds. "It's such a shame she chose that riff-raff over our family."

"I still feel you two are being too harsh on her." Delores frowns. "She's a young woman who feels she is in love." In love! Ha! That may be so on her end, but *my* Heath would never love her. He only has room for one love in his heart and that's me.

"Sometimes the necessary lessons must be given through tough love," William replies, completely devoid of emotion. The intercom buzzes, announcing someone has arrived. "Our car is here, Delores. Time to go." He gives Elliott a hug with a pat on the back. "Do me proud, son. Our company is in your hands."

"I will do you more than proud, Father." Elliot grins wide and I roll my eyes. Helen catches my reaction and raises her brows up, her lips pursing together in admonishment. I swear the damn woman has eyes everywhere.

"Helen, I'm hungry. Please make me a bowl of chicken noodle soup. Extra carrots and only white meat. I'll be in the library." I give Delores and William a hug. "Safe travels."

"Was your soup to your liking, dear?" Helen asks, placing my bowl and cup onto the tray.

"It was a bit salty," I reply without looking up from my book.

"That's odd. I only added a pinch," she says, lifting the tray. "Is there anything else I can get you?"

"A glass of water. Clearly, your idea of a pinch of salt differs significantly from mine, and now I'm feeling dehydrated. You know too much salt can raise my blood pressure. Are you trying to kill me, Helen?"

Before she can answer me, the house phone rings and she sets the tray down to answer it.

"Lincoln residence." Helen pauses for a moment. "Oh, Isabel, it's so nice to hear from you," Helen coos and my ears perk up.

"What wonderful news…Of course I will visit." Visit? Is Heath coming home? It's been nearly eight months since I found out I was pregnant and he took off with Isabel. My heart pitter-patters at the idea of seeing my Heath again. *Oh, how I miss him so!*

She listens to whatever that bitch is saying, her face lighting up. "Yes, sweet girl, I will even make your favorite Shephard's pie." I roll my eyes. Her skinny ass needs to eat several dozen Shephard's pies to put some meat on her bones. Ugh! I can't believe Heath actually has sex with her. It's probably the equivalent of fucking a skeleton.

"Don't worry, Isabel, sometimes conceiving a baby takes time. It doesn't happen right away for everyone. Don't let Heath upset you, please." Conceiving a baby? So what Helen said earlier was true. Heath and Isabel are *trying* to have a baby?

Why would they be trying?

That would have to mean they want a baby together.

Surely not.

Absolutely fucking not. Not Heath. Helen is mistaken.

My foot kicks out in front of me in anger and the tray of food crashes to the floor. Helen huffs and tells Isabel to call soon, that she has a mess to clean up.

"Why must you be so difficult, Catrina?" Helen sighs, bending down to pick up the shattered pieces of ceramic.

"It was an accident. Why must you still talk to Isabel?" I scoff. "You know Elliot doesn't approve of you continuing to keep in touch with her."

"And is your concern about me speaking to Isabel or your jealousy that she and Mr. Heath are happily in love?"

"It won't work," I snap. "Trying to make me jealous. I am a happily married woman. My only concern is over the fact you're choosing to speak to her, knowing the man who pays your bills prohibits it."

"My job is the last thing you should be—"

Hearing a muffled moan, I cut off Helen. "Shh, do you hear that?"

"Oh, yeah. That's what I'm talking about." My eyes dart around at my surroundings.

"Hear what?" she questions, standing with the tray in her hands.

Am I hearing things? Then I hear it again. *"Mmhmm, yes!"*

Throwing my book aside, I stand and make my way out of

the library and into the hallway, Helen following right behind. *Is somebody having sex in this house?* I listen some more. *"Oh God, yes!"* What the hell is going on? The only other person left in this house is Elliot. Tiptoeing over to Elliot's office, I see his door is closed. He wouldn't dare! Putting my ear to the door, I hear another moan and then a grunt. That cheating bastard!

"Catrina…" Helen begins, but my warning glare quickly shuts her up.

Hoping to catch Elliot in the act, I swing the door open and find him sitting at his desk alone. His eyes widen in shock and he shuffles quickly to zip his pants. "What are you doing?" I step farther into the room, toward his desk, slamming his office door closed behind me. He quickly sits up and scurries to turn off what he's watching on the television, but I'm quicker and I make it around his desk before he can get shut it off. And right there on the television are two people fucking like rabbits.

"You sick bastard!" I let out a loud shriek, pushing him backward in his chair. He rolls back slightly and I'm able to get a good look at the muted screen. The woman is on her hands and knees with her legs spread open and her ass in the air, getting fucked from behind. Is this guy serious?

"Your wife is pregnant and has pre-eclampsia, a life-threatening condition! And here you are, jerking off to some trashy bleached blond bimbo getting fucked in the ass!" My anger multiplies by the second and I can feel my blood pressure rising. How dare he get to find pleasure while I'm stuck being miserable! My fist comes out and pushes the heavy TV to the floor. It hits the ground and smashes into pieces. Then I swipe everything off his desk. Various papers fly all over the place.

"I hate you!" I shout, and he stands up out of his chair, his hands turned up in a placating motion. I can still see his dick is hard in his pants and it makes me furious to know he was seeking pleasure from someone else. "I'm your wife! You haven't fucked me in months, yet you're fucking yourself to the sight of another woman. How dare you!" I snatch up a picture frame from the shelf and fling it at him. He ducks and it crashes to the floor.

"Catrina, calm down please. You know it's not good for you or the baby to get worked up." Elliot approaches me slowly like I'm some feral animal. Well, fuck him! Fuck him and fuck Heath and Isabel! Fuck them all! I hope they all rot in hell!

"Don't you want me?" I let out a sob. "Is it because I'm fat and ugly now?" I swipe away my tears as I picture Heath fucking Isabel's skinny ass. "I can please you, Elliot." I move closer to him, my hand rubbing along his hard bulge. I bet Isabel doesn't satisfy Heath the way I did. "Do you want me to please you?"

Without waiting for his response, I undo his pants and pull his dick out. It's not hard anymore, but I can get it there. Spitting on my hand, I stroke his shaft up and down. Elliot lets out a low moan. I feel his pre-cum dripping from his tip and I still my hand. His gaze darts down to me. "I was close," he whines.

"Why should you be the only one to get pleasure? If you want to come, you can do it after you've made me come first." Backing up, I slowly lower my body onto the couch, my swollen baby bump protruding out. "Make me come, Elliot," I demand. He follows me over to the couch and kneeling in front of me, he pulls my panties down then spreads my legs. His fingers find my clit and he massages my nub. I'm too dry and it does nothing for me.

"You have to get me wet!" I snap. "Use your mouth." Elliot gapes at me. He's never eaten pussy before. Well, it's time he starts. If he can jack off to porn, surely he can lick his wife's pussy. "Now," I demand.

He dips his head and his tongue dances across my seam. "Slow down," I instruct. "This isn't a race. Slowly, lick my clit." He does as I say and my fingers come up and pinch my nipples.

My eyes close and I imagine Elliot is Heath as he laves at my juices.

"Yes," I moan out. "Right there. Harder." Heath's licks get rougher as my orgasm builds higher. "Oh God, yes! Stick your fingers in me." He pushes a finger into my tight channel, but it's not enough. "More!" Another one. "More!" Heath fucks me with three fingers while sucking on my clit and I fall over the edge, my orgasm ripping through my entire body. When I open my eyes, I see Elliot standing in front of me, wiping his mouth off with the back of his hand, and my heart drops that it's not Heath.

"I don't feel well," I mutter.

"What about me?" His eyes drop down to his hard cock.

"Fine, but hurry, please."

I'm lying across the chaise lounge in my bedroom, staring out the window at the torrential downpour. The news said several areas are prone to flooding and we could be looking at some power outages if the storm doesn't weaken. But inside, it's relaxing to watch. I could lie here for hours with my hand rubbing across my swollen belly, feeling my baby kick. I could've found out if it was a boy or a girl but chose not to. It will be a nice surprise once I give birth in a few weeks.

"Looks like I might have to find the candles in case the storm gets any worse," Helen says, changing the sheets on my bed.

"I suppose." I sigh then take a sip of my tea.

"And what is wrong with Catrina today?"

I watch her from the corner of my eye as she moves from making the bed to dusting the lamps. "Can't you do that when I'm not in here?" I snip, my eyes going back to the falling rain.

My mind goes back to the days when Heath and I would play in the rain. We would run through the puddles, splashing each other for hours, until our lips were blue and our teeth would chatter.

"Then it wouldn't get done," Helen says. "You haven't left your bedroom in months, dear, and with the baby due in a few weeks I'm trying to get everything ready."

"Where's my husband?" I ask, turning my attention to her. She's now placing my folded clothes into my drawer.

"In his office." Of course he is. He spends more time than not in there, using the excuse that he has double the work to do since his father handed over the reins to him. I call bullshit. We both know he's just hiding away like a little bitch because he can't handle me pregnant. Like it's my fault I've fallen ill with pre-eclampsia. It's my fault my blood pressure rises too high at times. He wanted me pregnant and now he acts like I'm a damn burden. Whatever, it's probably for the best anyway. I can't stand to be around him most of the time.

The chime of the doorbell rings out through the house, and Helen announces she'll get it. It's probably just another delivery for the nursery. I take another sip of my tea, my eyes going back to the rising lake. Then picking up my journal, I open it to a blank page and write the date.

Dear Diary, I begin.

"Catrina." My head whips around and I see *him* standing in the doorway.

"Heath," I gasp, closing my journal and dropping it onto the ground. I knew he'd be back to see me. He could never stay away too long.

CHAPTER SEVENTEEN

HELEN OPENS HER MOUTH AND I WAVE HER OFF AS I TOSS MY umbrella onto the floor. "Leave us."

She grumbles but obeys, leaving us alone. I stalk over to where Catrina sits on the sofa and kneel on the floor beside her. Her lips are plump and parted in surprise. So beautiful.

Our eyes lock and hers become glassy with tears. I reach up and brush a stray lock of hair from her face, tucking it behind her ear. Her cheeks are full and flushed, a light shade of pink.

"You're beautiful," I murmur.

She chokes on a teary laugh. "I'm fat."

Sure, I notice she's thicker and her belly is big, but she's still the same Catrina I've been in love with since the first day I laid eyes on her. "You're not fat." I grab one of her swollen hands and bring it to my lips. I kiss each knuckle until I reach the one with the giant diamond. It cuts into her flesh and seems uncomfortable. When I slide it from her finger, tugging to free it, it has nothing to do with fucking over Elliot and claiming what's mine, but everything to do with giving her comfort. I drop the ring to the floor and it clinks.

"You're swollen," I say with a frown, rubbing the indented flesh. "Are you feeling okay?"

She beams at me, brighter than any sun or star in the sky. "I'm feeling wonderful now."

"Fuck how I've missed you," I mutter before resting my head

on her giant belly. "You smell like life and love and every single thing I've craved since the day I no longer had you in my arms."

"Oh, Heath," she sobs, her fingers sliding into my hair. Her fingernails scratch along my scalp as she strokes me. "I missed you too."

I press kisses on her stomach through her gown and kiss my way up her chest to her throat. She sighs happily when I pepper more kisses along her flesh. When I reach her jaw, I open my mouth to kiss her skin. I suck her salty flesh between my lips to taste what I've been yearning so long for. My lips trail up until our mouths are a breath apart.

"I've come to rescue you, my princess," I breathe.

Her lips press to mine and we kiss sweetly. Like our first kiss when we were teens. And just as we did back then, the kiss becomes ravenous and desperate. Our mouths mate like our bodies have so long been denied.

She tugs on my hair and pulls me away. Her eyes are wild, darting all over my features as though she tries to memorize everything about me—as though I may disappear at any moment.

I'm not going anywhere.

I'm here to stay.

"I'll love you forever," I tell her. A vow stronger than any silly wedding promise. The vows our hearts made when we were younger have always stayed true. Our flesh may have temporarily belonged to another, but our hearts—our motherfucking souls—only ever belonged to each other.

"You've come to tease and torment me." Her bottom lip quivers and tears stream down her red cheeks.

I cradle her face with my palms and swipe away the wetness with my thumbs. "I've come to make everything better. Windy Hills is mine now, love."

"I don't understand." She blinks in confusion.

"Your brother didn't have the wits about him to keep it. It's mine and soon we can finally be together."

"What about Elliot?" she asks and then her tone turns bitter. "What about Isabel?"

A growl rumbles from me. "Fuck them. They are nothing. We are everything."

"I'm ready," she tells me. "I can't stay here any longer. I'm so tired of being unhappy. I miss you. I miss us. This was all a horrible mistake. How will you ever forgive me?"

"Forgive you for tossing my heart into the floor and fucking stomping on it?" I taunt.

"Yes," she groans.

"Forgive you for choosing that weak pussy over me?"

"Yes." A sniffle.

"Forgive you for being blind to the suffocating love all around you?"

"I've been destroyed since the moment I made that terrible decision."

"My heart was broken, I'll admit," I say with a frown. "I wanted to ruin every motherfucker who lured you away and kept you away from me."

"And me. You wanted to ruin me."

"No, my love." I kiss her sweet lips. "My revenge was never with you. It was always for you. I never wanted to ruin you. Just wanted to ruin the world around you so we were the only two left standing. The only two who mattered."

"Oh, Heath. I'm so sorry. I'll pack a bag. Straight away. We'll leave. Drive to Canada. Anywhere but here," she says sobbing. "I want to leave it all behind."

I grab her hands in mine and squeeze. "So we will. There are some affairs that need sorting back at Windy Hills and you need your rest. Call me if you need me. In the morning, I'll come for you. Have Helen pack your things. Then we'll go. We'll run far away from our mistakes and into our future."

She throws her arms around my neck and hugs me. Her breath tickles my ear as she whispers the words I always felt deep into the marrow of my bones. "I love you, Heath. I always have. It was always you."

I kiss her hair and neck. "I love you too, Catrina. You are my existence."

The ride in my Bentley back to Windy Hills in the pouring rain is lonely. Leaving Catrina as she bawled like a baby was heart-wrenching. But it gave me new resolve. Reminded me what all this hard work was for.

Her.

It was always for her.

Working tirelessly to start my own company. Reaching out to Crenshaw's old clients and schmoozing potential investors. I used what Crenshaw taught me, conned some people to take a leap of faith, and I hit the ground running. I was able to take W. Heights Investments and evolve it into an international power-house. And Hunter, that stupid fuck, couldn't keep his father's gold mine from drowning. Slowly, little by little, not only did I poach on his clientele thanks to the contact list I'd procured from Crenshaw's portfolio, but I also made that fuck reliant on me. He wasn't educated or cunning enough to keep C-Trades from sinking. Hunter was robbing Peter to pay Paul. And whom did he run to when he needed help?

The same motherfucker he threw out on his ass without a dime to his name.

A brother would help out a brother.

Loan after loan, I injected money into his dying legacy. I tied each loan up with balloon payments and astronomical interest rates. I made a knot of his debt and pretended as though his increasing debt didn't worry me. It didn't. I was biding my time. In fact, right before I left Isabel at Windy Hills to go see Catrina, I dropped all the notes on his desk and told him it was time to pay the fucking piper.

I'm grinning like a loon as I drive through the heavy downpour. The roads are nearly impassable in parts as water touches the edges. I hope this shit blows over soon because as soon as I wrap up my affairs, I'm getting out of here with Catrina.

I pull up near the front door at Windy Hills and climb out. I may be chilled as fuck from the rain soaking me to my bones, but my heart is on fire. I'm burning with exhilaration.

"Heath!" Isabel cries out when I burst through the door. Her brows are furrowed together and she is frowning. "Where were you?"

Earlier, I'd been in such a hurry to see Catrina after I dropped the bomb on Hunter, that I blew out of here without so much as a goodbye.

"I went to see your brother's wife," I tell her, my voice turning hard. "I went to see Catrina."

Her throat bobs and fat crocodile tears well in her hazel eyes. "W-What? Why?"

"You know why," I sneer.

She shakes her head. "No."

Walking past her, I shed my soaked coat and fumble with the coffee maker. I manage to get a pot brewing before turning to face her.

"Yes, Isa."

"But we're…you and I—"

"Things have changed. My heart always belonged to Catrina. You knew this."

She lets out an enraged scream. "No! You fell in love with *me*! *We* fell in love! We were going to start a family!"

I stare at her, emotionless. "It would have helped me further my agenda, yes, but things have changed. Catrina and I are leaving together. My attorney will handle our divorce, Isabel. You'll be set up with a handsome alimony check each month. There is nothing to worry about."

"I don't want your money!" she cries out. "It was never about your money!"

"Well, you'll get it anyway," I snarl. "Stay here. Move in with your brother. I don't give a fuck, Isa, but we're done. You were there when I needed to get my dick wet until I came back for her."

She freezes and gapes at me. "You're a cruel, miserable man."

"And you tried to paint me otherwise."

The tiny thing stomps over to me and I close my eyes, expecting the blow to my cheek. Instead, her lips press to my still-wet cheek and she whispers, "Cruel."

When I open my eyes, she's already rushing from the room. I don't go after her. Instead, I pour two cups of coffee and carry them into Hunter's study. The moment I walk inside, I see that it's been ransacked. He's a disheveled mess and the room reeks of whiskey.

"Done throwing a tantrum?" I ask and set down a mug for him on the desk.

He staggers over to the desk drawer and pulls out a fifth of Jack. His hate-filled eyes are on mine as he unscrews the lid and chugs it.

"Suit yourself," I say coldly. "You'll need a clear head, though, to sort your business. Well, what remains."

"She left me," he hisses. "She fucking left me."

I'm not surprised. Being married to a gambling drunk would

take a toll on anyone. It was the smartest move to leave him when she did. Her child deserves better than his father.

"Your father would—"

"Don't you dare mention my father," he roars, kicking the desk. His untouched coffee sloshes out and splatters the mahogany.

I raise an eyebrow. "He would have wanted you to have a place to stay."

This catches him off guard. "You'd allow us to stay here?"

"Francesca already left, I thought."

"She didn't take Harrison."

Irritation rises in my chest. "I own you now, Hunter Crenshaw. You can begin paying back your mountain of debt by keeping the property up to my standards and doing my bidding."

He grits his teeth before knocking back another swallow of the alcohol. "I hate you," he sneers.

"Hate doesn't pay the bills. I suggest you find something that does. Make yourself useful. Sober the fuck up. And stay under my thumb where you belong."

Riiiiing!

Riiiiing!

Riiiiing!

Absently, I pick up my desk phone and grunt out a hello.

"Heath," Catrina hisses into the phone. "He's being ridiculous!"

My heart rate spikes and I snap my portfolio folder closed. "Why? Did you tell him you were divorcing him? What's wrong?"

She sobs. "I told him I was leaving. He forbade me to go!

I'm no one's to control!" She screams out a slew of obscenities at him.

"You're mine," I growl in agreement. "Tell him to go the fuck away."

"Is that him?" I hear Elliot shout. "Are you fucking him? Did you fuck him under my roof?"

"Let me talk to him," I snarl.

"No," she snaps. "He's going to go the hell back to his office where he can whack off to his double-jointed porn whores! We're over and he knows it!"

They struggle and I nearly crack the phone in my grip. "Catrina," I bark.

"Let go of me, you whiney bastard!" she yells at him.

"Stop being a bitch!"

Slap!

"You scratched my eye!" Elliot wails. "I'll be blind because of you!"

"I'll carve them out and feed them to you if you dare lay your hands on me again!"

"Catrina…" I growl.

"I can't take another second with this poor excuse for a man. Please come get me, Heath. I don't care if we have to sleep in the car!" she cries out.

I glance out the window and groan. The rain is coming down so hard and has been for hours. I'll have a helluva time getting out if the roads are flooded over. While she bitches more at Elliot, I run my fingers through my hair in frustration.

"It's awful out," I grumble.

"I don't care! Just get me out of here!"

When she screams again and the line goes dead, I hang up the phone and burst from my office, my heart in my throat.

I yank a coat on by the door and step outside. The wind is howling and fierce. Stinging pellets of rain assault my face. I look beyond the driveway at the road that leads to Low Valley Estate and groan. My fucking car will never make it past the rising water that's now covering the road.

Her screams are on repeat in my head.

So help me if that motherfucker touches her again, I'll scalp him. I'll cut him from ear to ear. I'll beat his goddamned face to a bloody pulp and stomp on it until he's dead. Nobody fucks with my girl. Nobody.

I make it over to the barn, winded and already soaked as fuck. The horse Francesca bought for Harrison resides in the barn. My horse now. Everything is mine now.

Including Catrina.

And I'm going to get her once and for all.

CHAPTER EIGHTEEN

CATRINA

"WE'RE HAVING A GODDAMNED BABY TOGETHER!" Elliot shouts as I pull article after article of clothing off their hangers and shove them into my suitcase while Helen quietly handles my drawers. She knows better than to say a damn word. Her look earlier made her opinion known and I made mine known as well. I. Don't. Care.

"You're a heartless asshole and I don't love you. I never loved you!" I zip my suitcase closed and drop it to the ground, popping the handle up. "Helen, grab this one as well." I leave the suitcase behind and scamper down the stairs, ignoring the growing pain in my back.

"And you love that peasant? He's married to my sister!" he shouts after me. "And in case you haven't been paying attention, she's been begging to come home for nearly a year!"

"I don't care." I grab a bottle of water from the fridge and gulp it down, trying to tamper down the dizziness I'm feeling.

Elliot steps directly in front of me, this time being smart and not touching me. "I've given you everything, Catrina. Everything. You want to leave? Fine. But wait until after you have our baby."

"So you can try to keep it from me?" I hiss. "Not a chance." My palms come down onto the kitchen island and my head drops as I try to take a calming breath. My eyes close and I wish away the now searing pain that's radiating through my body. I just need Heath. Once he's here and takes me away from this place, everything will be okay. I hear the sound of a door slamming shut and I lift my head, the room spinning. My body sways slightly and I will it to stop. Then I stumble to the foyer, stopping just in front of him.

My Heath.

My love.

All mine.

He's going to take the pain away.

Make everything better.

His presence comes in like the growing storm outside. Fierce, impenetrable, harsh. And I love it. I want to get swept up in him. To lose myself along with him and never return. When his intense gaze bores into me, I nearly collapse. The relief is almost too much to bear.

"Take me away from here now!" I beg, throwing my arms around him. My oversized bump prevents us from getting as close as I crave. His wet hand grips my chin and tilts my face up to meet his hardened eyes. His cheeks are wet from the rain and he's visibly shivering because he's completely soaked. I run my palms up and down his drenched jacket and realize water has pooled at his feet on the floor.

"My love, you need to calm down. The weather is horrendous outside. I was forced to come by horse because the roads are flooded." The lights flicker and my gaze shoots up to the crystal chandelier above us. "We'll never make it out of the drive."

"No," I cry. "We have to leave now." My head falls to Heath's chest as angry tears stream down my face.

"You will not be going anywhere," Elliot demands, making his presence known. I feel Heath's hands, which are now holding me, tighten before he releases me from his hold and moves toward Elliot.

"The lady has made her choice, now I suggest you accept it and run back into whatever cave you've crawled out of. You are not wanted nor needed." Heath's tone is calm and devoid of all emotion. He steps even closer to Elliot, his voice now merely a whisper. "I would hate to have to take everything from you the same way I did from Hunter." He chuckles darkly. "Oh, who am I kidding? I would love to. Just give me a reason."

Elliot's eyes widen in shock, his face turning beet red. "Get out of my house now!" His voice is trembling, his eyes refusing to meet mine.

"Gladly, as soon as this storm passes." I can't see Heath's face with his back to me, but I can hear the grin in his words. "Helen, why don't you make yourself useful and put on a pot of coffee for me…for old times' sake?" The lights flicker again. "It's going to be a helluva storm. I hope you've checked your generator and supplies," he says to Elliot, who is visibly shaking in anger.

Then he turns his attention to me. "C'mon, love. Let's find a cozy corner in this place so we can discuss where we'll travel first. You mentioned Canada. But I know you've always wanted to go to Paris. I'm thinking we can do one better and experience all of Europe."

"She's not going anywhere!" Elliot hisses, but Heath ignores him. Wrapping his arm around my waist, Heath guides us into the sitting room. Just as we're sitting down, the pain in my back becomes so unbearable I let out a cry.

"Catrina, what's the matter?" Heath edges closer to me, his arms wrapping around my back and waist, the rain from his jacket soaking through my clothes. His hand covers a small portion of my belly.

I try to speak but the pain increases and I'm left feeling breathless. My eyes close and I groan in agony. "My-my back," I choke out.

"Oh shit," I hear Elliot whisper. My eyes shoot open and follow his gaze down my body to see what he's looking at.

"What is it?" I ask, not understanding why his face has turned pale. When Elliot doesn't answer, but instead stays standing in front of me, frozen in place, I lose my patience with him. "What's wrong?" I demand. "Fucking tell me!"

But before Elliot can answer, Heath yells, "Catrina! You're bleeding. Helen! Get in here now."

I look down over my large belly and see Heath is right. Blood is trickling down my thighs. My stomach tightens, and I double over in pain.

"Heath, something's wrong," I whimper, my hands wrapping around my stomach. "My baby."

"It's okay, my love. Breathe for me." Heath lifts my legs onto the couch and I lie back against the pillows. The pain increases by the minute.

"What should we do?" Elliot asks worriedly.

"How about you make yourself useful and go get some goddamned towels!" Heath barks, and Elliot scurries away down the hall.

"It hurts," I sob. "I need to go to the doctor."

"I called for an ambulance," Helen announces, "but the entire town is flooded. The roads aren't safe. They said it could be hours before they can even attempt it." My stomach tightens again, and I scream out in distress from the blinding pain.

"There's no time," I hiss. "I think the baby is coming now." The pain hits again in full force and this time I feel a pressure in my groin that has me needing to pee.

"Her water broke!" Helen says. Her voice is shaky, but my lids are too heavy to look at her. I'm tired and the pain is too much, too all-consuming. I feel an ice-cold hand come across my forehead. Oh, it feels so good. I didn't realize how hot I am.

"Heath," I mutter. "I'm not feeling too well." My heart is pounding against my chest.

"Shh, it's okay, my love. Everything is going to be okay."

"We have to get this baby out of her," Helen cries. I can

feel hands between my legs, but I can't pry my eyes open. I'm just so tired.

"Catrina, you have to push, dear," I hear Helen say, but I'm too exhausted.

"Heath, I'm…tired."

"Push," he growls.

I try so hard until I black out. When I'm shaken back awake, I can hear Helen sobbing about all the blood. But they can see the head. They can see the baby's head.

"Come on," Heath urges. "Almost there."

I notice Elliot standing in the corner watching. Fear shining in his features. This is nothing new, though. He's always worried about something. But then I look over at Heath and see the concern around his eyes. The frown marring his beautiful lips. Heath is never scared. He fears nothing, no one. But right now, I can see it. He's frightened and that has me scared.

I put every ounce of energy I have left into pushing. This time, I don't black out, but I feel as though my soul is leaking from my body. I don't know how to pull it back in. At least it's in his hands. He's always taken care of every part of me.

"No! Catrina, stay the fuck awake!" This time it's Heath speaking or maybe he's yelling. He sounds so far away. "You need to meet your baby girl, goddammit!"

My baby. A sweet baby girl. I have a little girl…

"Open your eyes and stay with me. Please, love," Heath begs, but I can't. My eyes won't open. My chest is heavy, but the pain is finally gone. "I love you."

And it's the last words I hear before the blackness takes over my body and I succumb to the darkness.

I love you too.

CHAPTER NINETEEN

"Don't just fucking stand there!" I roar at both Elliot and Helen, who wear matching stares of horror. "Do something about this baby!"

The child—a girl covered in blood—squawks in my arms, but I'm not concerned about her. She's chubby and flailing. Safe and alive. It's my motherfucking soul that's in jeopardy here. My Catrina is pale and unmoving.

She's not dying.

Not on my fucking watch.

Helen and Elliot both seem to snap to attention. They take the baby and tend to her while I shove towels between Catrina's thighs in hope to staunch the bleeding. Elliot manages to cut the cord with his pocket knife and then they move away. Everything blots out except for her and me.

"Sweet love, listen to me," I beg. "Stay with me. Do you hear her crying? You did that. That's your little girl. You have to stay awake to hold her."

Warm heat floods around my hand and it's then I realize blood has completely soaked through the towel.

No.

Fucking no.

She's dying.

My love, my life, my goddamned soulmate is draining away second by punishing second.

"No," I croak. "Please no."

Hot rivers of devastation run down my cheeks and splash on her pale face as I kiss, kiss, kiss her all over. Not enough kisses. All the kisses in the world still won't be enough.

Nooooooo!

My bloody palms cradle her cool cheeks, streaking the pasty white flesh crimson.

"I love you!" I wail, almost as though I am cursing her. "I love you and you can't leave me!"

I swear her lips move.

I love you too.

I blink, blink, blink away the blur and rain more kisses on her. So many to give and not enough time. I want her to have them all. So long we were denied the time for kisses and sweet caresses. I'll give them to her now.

Kiss. Kiss. Kiss.

I try desperately to give her what she deserves in her last moment. I want her to know my love for her won't be snuffed out the moment her heart takes its last beat. Our hearts are one. Mine will continue beating for her. Always for her. Never-ending for her.

Goddammit!

I clunk my forehead to hers and nuzzle my nose against her cold one. Kiss. Kiss. Kiss. Those lips are so chilled. I have to fucking warm them up. Someone cries. Ugly and heart-wrenching and gutting.

It's me.

It's me.

It's me.

All alone without her.

Please don't go.

I plead with my heart, hoping somewhere, somehow, she still feels me. That since we share the sweet beats she will feel my desperation and cling to it.

The sobbing gets worse and everything is dark around me as I bury my face in her hair. The scent is one I remember from when we were children. My safety net, this woman. My solace. My motherfucking peace.

She's taking it all away from me.

Stealing it so she can have something to hold onto in the afterlife. A memory of us.

I'm left all alone.

Fucking alone.

I want the memories back. I want her heart beating. I want us, goddammit!

Shaking her, I try frantically to get her to wake back up. But can you wake the dead? I'll sure as fuck try. I shake, shake, shake my heart, praying to force it to beat.

This is war.

I'll fight for this tooth and nail.

Fight against her eager escape into death.

We are life. We are now. We are here.

Not separate. Never separate. We cannot exist apart.

She knows this and yet she leaves me anyway.

She fucking leaves me!

Voices and crying and a baby sighing.

Fuck them all.

Fuck their motherfucking beating hearts.

I just want hers.

I'd give up my own for her.

God, take the stuttering part of my heart because you already stole the other half!

Her body is limp and grows stiff. Lights flicker. Time doesn't exist. Hours go by. Hours and hours. I don't fucking care. I hold her. I cry for her. I smell her sweet, sweet hair.

I have her pinned on the sofa, stroking the soft locks of her silky hair that is sticky with drying blood. I kiss, kiss, kiss her neck and whisper how I love her. I promise her I will never leave her.

I'll hold her forever.

You cannot let go of part of your soul!

It's fucking impossible!

Those sobs. Loud. Horrible. Mine.

The other three beating hearts in this home have left me to my unbearable grief.

It's just the one that doesn't thump and the one that is nothing without the other.

Dead.

I may as well be dead too.

I am dead.

She fucking killed me the moment she sucked in her last breath.

Oh, God.

"Catrina, my love," I whisper. "Why did you leave? How will I ever find you again?"

My body shudders as a chill sets in. In my bones. In my soul. So cold.

Clackclackclackclackclack.

My teeth chatter together and the never-ending tears on my cheeks are icy rivulets.

Clackclackclackclackclack.

I could sleep. Just close my eyes and let death steal me too. It's so cold in here. My love is frozen stiff now. Or is that death that has turned her into a beautiful statue? If only—if only I could keep her this way. Rather than burying her in the cold earth, I'd love to keep her like this. In my arms. Prone to my continuous kisses.

Sleep.

Sleep.

I'll be gone soon too.

Death, take me to her, motherfucker!

Clackclackclackclackclack.

The chill is warming. It invites me in. I close my eyes.

In the dark, dark darkness I hunt for her. It's so fucking cold here. I will find her.

"Catrina!" I wail. "Catrina!"

In the dark, dark darkness she hides. I can sense her. A stifled giggle. Her scent lingering in the air. That overwhelming presence whenever she is near.

Searching and searching.

I follow my heart and come up empty.

Why is life so cruel?

My body is shaking. From the cold? No, someone is doing it for me. They steal me. They take me away from the most important hunt of my existence.

Clackclackclackclackclack.

"You're so cold," Helen rasps. "Heath, come and stand by the fire so you don't catch pneumonia. At least change out of those wet clothes."

I cannot stand. I will not leave my love. Squeezing my stiff, beautiful love in my arms, I snarl at the prying woman. "Go the fuck away from me!"

She jerks her hand back and affixes me with a distraught stare. Finally, the woman leaves, but it's only to add logs to the fire in the fireplace. I stare at Catrina's perfect blue lips with the red flames reflecting off her pale, bloody skin giving her the deception of life behind those dull features. The room warms, but my heart stays frozen. It's dying. A broken heart is real and it's a killer.

Oh, God, how it fucking hurts!

A warm blanket is draped over me and I want to push it away. I want to freeze to death. I want to die. But I'm too weak to do anything.

All I can do is hold her.

Hold mine.

My Catrina.

Scraaaape!

The sound of metal on metal has me cracking my lids in protest. Bright light shines in from a window. Helen stands by the window where she's recently dragged the curtains open.

"Leave, woman," I growl, my voice a bitter croak.

"I will not, Mr. Heath." She waves a hand at me. "You've not moved in two days. I'm sorry to say this but…" she trails off and holds her nose. "The body is starting to stink."

I glower at her. "Leave, you meddling bitch!"

She purses her lips and walks forward but not too close. Her nose crinkles. "The electricity is still down, but I could run you a warm bath. We have candles galore. You need to eat and drink a little something. I'm afraid you've fallen ill with pneumonia."

"I'll stay," I hiss.

The smell makes my nostrils flare, but I ignore it. Stale blood isn't pleasant. But know what's worse? Losing your mother-fucking soul. That's worse. I clutch Catrina's hard body tighter.

"She'd have a fit, you know," Helen says softly. "Knowing you let her stay in such a state. Ruined."

I wince at her words. "She can't speak against it, now can she?"

She huffs. "But if she could, she'd want to be cleaned up at once. Please take a bath and allow me to clean her up some. We can plan her burial. You can see the baby—"

"I don't care about the baby!" I roar, my body trembling with fury. "The only thing I've ever cared about is gone! Gone,

Helen! How can you stand there so unfeeling? You loved her too."

"Dear Lord, Heath, of course I loved her," she exclaims. "And because I loved her, I know what she would have wanted. She wouldn't want this…"

I lift up, my body weak and shaky, to stare down at Catrina. Without her life burning through her, she is a cold husk. Simply a body. Bile rises in my throat. I'm hugging a corpse. Her heart is gone. Her laugh and wit are erased from this world. So what in the fuck am I still clinging to? Decaying flesh?

Shuddering, I pull away, disentangling my limbs from her stiffened ones. Our clothes are nearly fused together from the blood and I peel myself from my other half. I stare at her body, my heart tearing in two all over again.

Heat leaks down my cheeks.

A man has never cried as much as me, this I am certain of.

I'll never be able to turn it off.

"Come now," Helen urges, wrapping my blanket back over my shoulders.

I stand on wobbly legs and the room spins. A pang in my stomach outmatches that of my heart. All I feel is pain. All I'll ever know is pain. This is my future. My past—God, I loved her beautiful smile—has dictated this for me.

We slowly make our way from the room and the scent of candles—fruits and home baked goods—assault me as we enter the hallway. It no longer smells like death and despondence. Carefully we step up the stairway. One, two, three. We go and go until we're at the top. She guides me along the hall until I hear it.

A sound.

Tiny little whimper.

I stop in a doorway to find Elliot in a rocking chair holding a bundle to his chest. He creaks and creaks as he pats the bundle with his palm in attempt to soothe the wiggling beast.

"Mr. Heath," Helen whispers.

Ignoring her, I stalk into the room, fury, a match to my soul. I'm on fire. I want to burn everything. When I tower over them, he finally looks up at me. His eyes are swollen from crying, but he's not crying now. His cheeks are not soaked like mine. His soul is not wrecked.

He is sad.

I am ruined.

"Do you want to hold her?" he asks huskily.

With a curl of my lip, I stare down at the child, who waves a mighty fist at me. The little mother murderer. She lets out a wail and he produces a bottle. Greedily, the abomination suckles from the rubber nipple as if she always preferred fake to the perfection only a mother could provide.

"I want her buried beneath her favorite willow," I snarl, my glare never leaving the baby. "You know the one."

"Catrina?" he asks in confusion.

"She's the only corpse in the house," I snap. "But trust me, Elliot, I'd love nothing more than to change that."

He holds his baby to him, terror flickering in his eyes.

But I'm talking about me.

If someone handed me a rope right now, I'd gladly hang myself this instant.

"Don't be silly, Heath," he says, his voice tight. "We have plots in the cemetery because she is my wife—"

"SHE IS YOUR NOTHING!" I scream so loudly the baby starts screaming too.

Helen tugs at the back of my jacket and tries to pull me from the room. "Oh, honey, you need to get ahold of yourself."

I allow her to pull me to the doorway, but I grab the frame before she can steal me away.

"You will pay," I threaten. "You will all pay for this."

Elliott's eyes go wide. "It wasn't my fault," he whines. "I didn't want her to die."

"You will bury her as she would have wanted," I seethe, my eyes burning into him. "You will do it. I want your word now."

"Okay," he mutters. "We'll see. Just leave me and my daughter alone."

I give him a hellish, evil smile. "I'm afraid that's something I can't promise."

This time, Helen yanks and I go.

To wash away the worst moment of my life.

The blood may run clean from my skin, but I'll never be able to fill the gaping, horrible hole in the middle of my chest. That wound will bleed until I take my last breath.

CHAPTER TWENTY

I THOUGHT IT WOULD BE MORE DIFFICULT WATCHING THEM TAKE her body to prepare it for burial, but there was no warmth left. No smiles for me. No laughter for my ears. Fucking nothing. I watched the coroner cover her with a sheet and roll her out of Elliot's home. The baby screamed, and a tiny curl of satisfaction wove itself inside my heart at seeing Elliot struggle to calm her. Helen fussed and fawned over the child.

And I left.

I find my horse in their barn and tip my head in thanks to their ranch hand Titus, who's taken care of my horse in my absence.

Absence.

I checked out for days.

Helen said I clutched onto Catrina for two days and then I spent another day holed up in a spare room. I paced the floor until I was sure I'd worn a hole in the carpet. The baby's cries were maddening.

Cat.

Her real name is exactly her mother's, but I was relieved to hear Helen take to calling her a shortened version. I'm not sure if it was for my sake or the fact the child sounded like a fussy kitten. Either way, I'm glad I don't have to hear my love's name spoken in a way as though she is alive.

She is gone.

I close my eyes for a brief moment before reopening

them and mounting my horse. The storm has long passed, but smooth flooded waters cover the earth in some areas along my path. Undisturbed and perfect. I want to ruin it. I want to ruin everything.

"Hyah!" I holler to my animal and take off out of the barn. I run my horse as fast as he will go through the waters, destroying the calm as we plow through it. A numbness has begun to settle in my bones. Nothing to do with temperature. Something of the permanent sort.

Our hearts are the same, therefore now that hers does not beat, mine has gone into a permanent coma. It'll never wake.

The wind stings my flesh as the horse runs, but I ignore it. Quickly, I do my best to harden every part of me. My time for being soft faded the moment my love died in my arms.

I fly across the flooded landscape, sometimes sinking so deep in some areas that I wonder if we'll go all the way under, when I swear I see a flash of dark hair. My memories haunt me. Times when we were children—when we'd run through the puddled fields laughing and screaming.

All gone.

The trip home goes quicker than I'd hoped. It takes me a bit to settle the horse in the barn since Newton is missing. He normally cares for the horses. He'll be fired the moment he shows back up. *If* he shows back up.

There's a new sheriff in town. Hunter Crenshaw handed over the keys to an empire when he decided to indebt himself to me. New rules around here. And the first rule is when I send Newton packing, Hunter will have a new job.

Ranch hand.

Unpaid.

This cold rage that fuels me feels familiar in my veins. I welcome it so it will chill the burning in my chest. My revenge has been in the shadow of my lover. Lurking and waiting.

Ever-present. A moving, throbbing entity just waiting to be fully unleashed.

Time to be free, my beast of hate.

Go forward and cause massive destruction in every single one of their lives.

An evil smile tugs at my lips as I walk into the home and kick off my rain-soaked shoes. The first thing I notice is the silence. And the electricity is out.

That motherfucker left.

Weak. He's weak as shit. I'll still break him. I'll find him and break him slowly.

I hear a sound within the home and I cock my head listening. Poor, pampered Isabel is probably frantic as a starved mouse. She hasn't worked a day in her life. If Hunter and the boy left, then that means she's all alone probably wasting away waiting for someone to wash her clothes and cook her food.

She'll pay for her part in this too. I wasted too many months with her when I could have been with Catrina. My hands fist as fury burns through me. I haven't thought up what her penance will be, but it will come to me. If she thinks I'll send her off to her brother now, she has another thing coming. She's my wife, goddammit.

I storm through the living room and take the stairs two at a time, calling out her name. When I make it to our room, the drawers have been pulled open and emptied. The closet is bare as well.

The bitch left.

Everyone leaves.

I hear another sound downstairs and I exit my room. I'm slower as I walk back down the hallway, which is how I notice the stench this time. Alcohol. So much of it. When I step into Hunter's office, I find him passed out in his chair. But as I near the desk, I see the empty bottle of pills.

Weak. Ass. Motherfucker.

I check his pulse and he's as cold as his goddamn sister.

She was taken from me and he ran away like the pussy he is.

Fatigue wears on me. Running on fumes and lack of sleep for days on end wears on you. I stifle a yawn and decide I'll call the coroner in the morning and hope the water has receded on our road enough for them to come get him. Sleep is more important. I'm headed for my bed when I hear it again.

Silently, I stalk the sound out in case my wife is playing some stupid fucking game. I sneak into the kitchen and the sound comes from the pantry that stands ajar. Rustling. Crunching. Grunting. Well, that's the biggest damn mouse I've ever heard. It sounds like it's ransacking the pantry. Maybe it's a coon.

I grab the knob and pull the door open. What I find has me gritting my teeth.

"Momma," the orphan whines.

My heart is cold and empty as I stare at him. This boy. Left behind by both his parents.

"Orphan," I grumble, "your asshole parents left you with me."

He starts to cry. Hell, I would too.

While he sobs and toddles around me, clutching onto my pants, I cut an apple into slices and make a peanut butter sand-wich. I set it on the table and watch as the half-starved boy nearly inhales the food.

"Milk," he whines.

I watch him with narrowed eyes. He's filthy and smells like shit. The stench of alcohol clings to him. He no doubt tried to get his weak father to wake from his death. I feel pity for the thing.

"Everything in the fridge is shit," I tell him. "Electricity is out."

"Shit?" he questions.

I bark out a harsh laugh and he smiles at me. "Yep, shit. Want some fucking water instead?"

The toddler orphan babbles what I assume is an effort to parrot yet another curse word. It satisfies me that Hunter left his only legacy with me. Mine to ruin. I'm going to ruin everything.

"I'll ruin you too," I explain to the boy as I fill a cup with water but leave it running, turned to warm. I squat and my nostrils flare when I get a whiff of his shitty ass. "Here. Drink."

I have to help him, but he guzzles the whole glass. His eyes are droopy and he looks as sleepy as I feel. Once he finishes, I set the glass on the counter and plug the sink drain. The sink fills with warm water and I pour in some dish soap to be safe.

"You stink, orphan," I grunt as I bend to start shucking off his clothes. He wiggles and cries, but I'm stronger. I take off his soiled diaper that is coming up both his front and back and toss it in the trash. Then, I snag the filthy runt and toss him in the sink. He screams and squirms, but then he gives up. His curious blue eyes stare up at me. I scrub him with the dish sponge and vow to throw it in the dumpster later. Once he's clean, I wrap him in a dish towel and hold him to me as I make my way through the house.

"Momma," he cries when we pass his parents' room.

"Nope," I grunt as I bypass the room to go to his nursery. It takes some wrangling but I manage to put a diaper back on him because I don't want that fucker shitting all over the place. I find him some zip up pajamas and grab his stuffed zebra. "Let's go."

He clings to me and sucks his thumb, falling asleep before I've even left the room. I'm half tempted to throw him in his bed, but then he'd probably start hollering the moment I close my eyes. Not happening.

I find my room and close the door behind me. Then, I kick out of my wet pants and socks before crawling into my empty bed with the orphan. I settle on my back and pull the covers over us. The kid may not be something I want to deal with right now, but he's warm.

As soon as my eyes close, I see her. Her smile. Her twinkling eyes. Her soft brown hair blowing in the wind. A severe ache tears through my chest again.

She's dead.

There's no bringing her back. That's out of my control.

But there *are* things in my control.

And those things will be handled tomorrow.

Today, I sleep away the pain and invite numb hatred into my heart.

Tomorrow, I get my revenge.

CHAPTER TWENTY-ONE

The Present...

"T HAT'S IT?" EMILY DEMANDS, SOBBING. "IT CAN'T BE IT! What an awful story, Nanny!"

She slides from the bed, her phone still in her grip, and runs to the bathroom. A few minutes later, she comes out and dabs at her eyes with a tissue. Sweet Emily is so pretty. Just like her mother. I scoot to the edge of the bed and pat the blanket beside me. She flops down very unladylike.

"I can't believe that's the end," she says sadly.

I hug her from the side and kiss her head like I used to do when she was a little girl. "Oh, sweetheart, it's not the end. Not the end at all. I'm afraid the story's just getting started."

"But she died," she moans. "Their love is dead."

I purse my lips. "I never claimed Mr. Heath's story to be one of romance. You conjured that in your head all by yourself."

"It's a tragedy," she grumbles.

Her phone buzzes and she stares down at it. Of course I peek too.

Mom: Dad and I are bringing pizza on the way home. We've missed you.

Normally, she blows off her Mom's texts, but she's especially fragile after that part of the story.

Emily: I miss you too. Nanny's telling me about Heath.

I swat her. "Tattletale."

Mom: Nanny doesn't know the whole story.

Emily looks up at me in question.

"I know enough," I say with a huff.

Emily: You want to fill in the gaps?

Mom: After dinner we'll go sit on the porch swing. Some stories need to come straight from the horse's mouth. No exaggeration. Just cold, hard truth.

"I don't exaggerate," I snip at Emily.

Emily laughs. "Sometimes you do."

Her phone buzzes again, but it's not her mother.

Finn: When I get there, we're going to talk.

Emily lets out a furious growl.

Emily: I'm sick. Nanny is taking care of me. We can talk tomorrow.

"Persistent boy," I mutter.

Finn: Are you okay? Do you need anything? I can bring you soup and hold you.

Emily lets out a shuddering breath that makes it sound as though she really is ill even though he can't hear her.

Emily: I just need rest. Alone.

Then, she taps out a text to Porter.

Emily: Come hang out with me at my house.

She waits a long five minutes where Porter doesn't respond. Finn sends her a few selfies of himself that makes her smile despite her stubbornness.

"Okay, let's hear the rest of the story," she says finally.

"It's not an exaggeration," I snip out. "Let's get to it before your mom comes in and gives you the quick, boring version."

PART TWO

CHAPTER TWENTY-TWO

CAT

Eighteen years after her mother's death...

THE SUN IS SHINING BRIGHTLY UP IN THE CLOUDLESS SKY. I HAVen't checked the heat index, but I wouldn't doubt if it's hitting some kind of record high. The summers in New York get hot, but this heat is almost unbearable. Needing to rinse off the stickiness my sweat has created, I remove my Chanel glasses—a gift from my dad last Christmas—and place them on the table next to my lounge chair. I walk over to the deep end of the pool, and raising my arms, dive in. The cold water immediately cools my body temperature down several degrees. Putting to use my years of swim lessons, I swim to the other end, and staying under the water, flip off the wall and swim back to the deep end. When I come up for air, I look toward the chairs and see Theo is missing.

"Theo?" I call out, turning every which way, not seeing him anywhere. He was just sitting next to me a minute ago. Where could he have gone? "Theo!" I call out again. That's when I feel something grip my ankle. I let out a loud shriek, kicking my foot out to force whatever is holding my leg hostage to let go.

Looking down, I see it's Theo under the water. He swims to the top and shakes his curly dirty blond hair out like a damn dog. Water spraying everywhere.

"Seriously?" I laugh and splash two handfuls of water his way to get him back.

"Jesus, Cat!" Theo groans. "You kicked me straight in the chest." He pouts like a little boy, and I laugh harder.

"Serves you right!" I scold. "That'll teach you not to scare a woman in the water."

"We're in the pool, not the ocean!" He chuckles with a shake of his head. "What did you think was grabbing hold of your leg?"

"I don't know." I shrug, not bothering to say my first thought was that it was indeed a shark. I'm aware it's impossible, but it didn't stop me from thinking it. "I just felt something grab my leg and I reacted."

Theo swims closer and backs me up against the pool wall, his arms bracketing my body.

"Were you afraid it was the Loch Ness monster?" He grins wide.

"No." I roll my eyes and attempt to break free of the confines of his arms, but when I do, he only cages me in tighter. His knee separates my thighs and rubs up against my sex. I stifle a moan. *This isn't right...*

"Does that feel good?" he asks, his brown eyes locking with my green ones.

"Theo." His name releases from my lips with a squeak.

"We've been dancing around each other all summer, Cat. Don't fight this." His knee continues to move back and forth, hitting my clit oh-so perfectly. I need to stop this. Stop him. His lips are now close to mine. Too close. And I swallow thickly, praying he doesn't do what I think he's going to do.

"Theo, please." And even to my own ears, the words are breathless, like even though I'm trying to tell him to stop, I really want him to keep going. And in a way I do. I've never had an orgasm before. I want to know how it feels. But not with *him*.

When Theo first arrived straight from boarding school at the beginning of the summer I was excited to finally meet my aunt Isabel's son. After all, she was my father's only sister. It was sad when she died last year from cancer. Even though we weren't close, she and Theo were the only family we had left. My grandparents both died several years ago. Now it's just my dad, Theo, and me.

Theo and I became fast friends and have spent the entire summer together. His flirting at first was innocent enough. I chalked it up to his personality. Maybe it's a European thing. He is from Paris. But lately, his flirting has become *anything* but innocent. Little touches here and there, sexual innuendos that he laughs off but still have me wondering if he's serious. But right now, this is the boldest he's ever been.

"The—" I begin to say his name again, stronger and more determined to stop him. But before I can finish, his mouth crashes against mine, his tongue pushing through the seam of my lips. My hands come up to his chest to push him away, but he's too strong. I can feel something inside of me building. I need to stop him. I can't do this. We can't do this. If we do, there's no going back.

Instead of attempting to push at his chest, my hand goes into the water. I grip his knee and push it away from my body. He tries to grab my hand, but I bite down on his lip and he pulls back in shock.

Before he can say a word, my hand comes up and my palm meets his cheek with a loud smack.

"What the hell, Cat!" His tongue runs along his bottom lip, swiping at the blood dripping from where my teeth connected with his flesh.

"I told you to stop."

"No, you said, 'Theo, please.'"

"You know what I meant!" I push against his chest, and this time he backs up, allowing me to swim away. "We can't do this." I shake my head and step out of the water. "It's wrong."

"It doesn't feel wrong," he insists, following me out of the pool.

I grab my towel and wrap it around my body.

"Your mother is my father's—"

Theo cuts me off. "Who cares!" He throws his arms up in the air. "Our parents haven't seen each other in years. Hell, they've only spoken a handful of times since I was born."

"It doesn't change the facts." I step toward Theo, who now has his towel wrapped around his waist. "You've become one of my best friends. Please don't ruin our friendship," I beg. "That's all that will happen. I'm not in any place to be with *anyone*. We're about to start our senior year. I need to focus on my grades, so I can get a scholarship. My dream is to go to Yale, and even if I get in, I can't afford the tuition without them offering to pay."

"Okay." Theo's palms come up in a placating gesture. "I'm sorry."

"Thank you." I grab my glasses and put them back on to block out the sun. "I think I'm going to shower and go for a ride on Copper." Copper is an American Quarter horse my father had purchased for my mother when she was still alive. He's too old to be ridden often, but every once in a while I like to take him for a ride. It helps me feel closer to my mom. Because she died when giving birth to me, I never got to meet her.

"I'll join you," Theo says.

"Are you sure?" I ask. I know how much he hates to ride, which is why I mentioned it. I was hoping to have some time to myself.

"I'm sure."

"Fine," I agree. "Meet me in the barn in twenty minutes."

Twenty minutes later, we're both showered and dressed. Titus, the ranch hand, has Copper and Shorty—my five-year-old Thoroughbred my father bought for me for my thirteenth birthday—ready to go. I prefer to ride bareback, but Theo requires a saddle. He's scared he'll fall off, again. I laugh to myself at the memory of the first time we went riding. Shorty started to trot and Theo wasn't ready. He slid right off, falling to the ground. Now, he insists on only riding with a saddle in place.

We ride along the trail in silence. The only sound coming from the horses' hooves as they clack against the hard ground. When we make our way around the lake, I pull back on Copper's reins to stop him.

"We need to turn around," I say to Theo as Shorty steps up next to my horse.

"Let's keep going." He nods in front of us. "Check out what's on the other side of the lake."

"I already know what's on the other side. It's the Windy Hills Estate." Since as far as I can remember, my father's only rule when riding is that I'm not allowed to go any farther than halfway around the lake. The other half is owned by an angry asshole, and while my father won't say much about him, it's obvious the two of them don't get along.

"What is it, like haunted or something?" He chuckles.

"What are you, ten?" I roll my eyes. "Of course it's not haunted."

"Then let's go check it out."

"I'm not allowed. I'll get in trouble if my father finds out."

Theo throws my words back in my face. "What are you, ten? Let's go! I'm bored. Plus, he's not going to find out." Before I can argue, he kicks the side of Shorty's belly and takes off in a gallop toward the other side.

"This is a bad idea!" I yell, tapping the side of Copper, who takes off after Shorty. We make it to the other side of the lake in less than five minutes. There's a barn similar to ours. But that's all we can see. If there's a house there, it's not visible through the overgrown shrubs and trees lining the property.

"Okay, you've seen the other side. Can we head back now?"

"Yeah, okay," Theo says, but he keeps riding closer to the barn.

I'm about to yell at him when I hear a rustling of the trees and a few seconds later, an older woman who is riding along the trail in a golf cart, in what looks like a maid's outfit, makes her presence known.

"May I help you?" she asks.

"I'm sorry," I say, "we were riding around the lake and didn't realize how far we went." I shoot a glare at Theo, who just grins.

"Oh, dear." The woman eyes us up and down. "Are you… are you Catrina Lincoln?" She steps out of her golf cart, so to be polite, I jump off Copper, so we're at eye level and extend my hand.

"I am." The woman takes my hand in hers and delicately shakes it. "And this here, is Theo Lincoln, my cousin."

At my words, the woman's face whips around to look at Theo, who drops down off Shorty and makes his way over to us.

"Nice to meet you," he says to her.

"Yo-you're Theo Lincoln." Her hand stays in Theo's for a beat too long, and he shoots me a *what the hell* look before pulling his hand back.

"I am, and you are?"

"My name is Helen. I'm the housekeeper for Mr. Heath and Mr. Harrison."

"Mr. Heath?" Theo questions. His brows are furrowed in confusion.

"What's wrong?" I ask him.

"Nothing. I've just heard my mother mention that name before."

"And who is your mother?" Helen asks.

"Was. She passed away last year, but she grew up across the lake over at Low Valley Estate," Lincoln says. "Have you worked for Mr. Heath for long?"

I could be wrong, but Helen looks as if she's been spooked. Maybe the house *is* haunted… It takes her a few seconds to answer, but she finally does. "I'm so sorry to hear that. I've worked at the Windy Hills Estate since I was a young girl." Her eyes shift away and I wonder if there's more she isn't telling us.

"Maybe you knew her then," I say. "Isabel Lincoln. She's my father's sister."

"I did know her. I also knew your mother." She smiles softly.

"Really?" I ask. "I don't know anyone who knew my mother besides my father, and he'll barely speak about her." My heart clenches in my chest. "She was the love of his life, but she died giving birth to me."

"I knew your mother well," Helen admits. "I was the housemaid for her family and her for many years. I was actually there the night you were born." Tears fill her lids, but she quickly swipes them away. "I'm sorry. That night was…emotional. You look just like her, you know: brown hair, green eyes, beautiful."

"Thank you. I've only seen a couple photos of her. My father said he doesn't have any."

"No, he probably doesn't. She grew up here." Helen points back toward Windy Hills Estate. "Would you like to see some pictures?"

My heart picks up speed at the thought of finally being able to learn about my mother, but then I remember my father. "I would love to, but I would have to ask my father first."

"Of course, dear. Any time. It's an open invitation."

"Helen!" a masculine voice calls out. "Helen!"

"Over here," Helen yells back, and a minute later, a gentleman appears—if he can even be called that.

My eyes rake down his body starting with his shaved head, making their way farther to his shirtless front, which is dripping in sweat. I watch as the droplets of water run down his tattooed chest and over his six pack of abs, which are also inked, continuing their descent through a thick trail of hair that leads toward his…

"Ahem." My eyes dart back up to his face and lock with his piercing blue eyes. "My eyes are up here, sweetheart." His hand runs over his shaved head and I wonder what it would feel like. Is it smooth or maybe prickly? He smirks mischievously like he knows exactly where my mind was going, and my cheeks heat up.

Needing to break our stare down, I avert my eyes back over to Helen, who is grinning widely.

"This is Harrison," she says. "Harrison, this is Catrina and her cousin, Theo Lincoln."

"I go by Cat," I say.

"You're Catrina's daughter?" Harrison confirms.

"I am. Did you know my mother too?" I ask curiously

"No, I've just heard of her." Harrison's gaze shoots over to Helen, who is no longer smiling.

Okay then…

"We really should be going," I say to no one in particular. "We've been gone for a while, and my father might be looking for me. It was nice to meet you both." I walk back toward my horse and, pulling myself up, climb onto his back.

"It was nice to meet you too," Helen says. "And my offer stands. Please come over any time."

"Thank you. School starts next week, so I imagine it will be hectic, but I'll ask my dad if maybe I can come by this week-end." My attention turns to Harrison. "Will you be attending Heights Academy?"

Harrison snorts. "The stuck-up snobby high school in town? No."

"Okay…you don't have to be so rude. Does that mean you go to public school?"

"I don't go to school." He glares daggers my way. "I work

at Heights Automotive." His hand comes up and rubs the side of his neck, and that's when I notice the tattoos cover *all* of his body, not just his chest and torso. Both of his arms and even part of his neck are also covered in ink. Before seeing him, I would've said that many tattoos on a single person's body is uncalled for, maybe even trashy. But as I take in the art all over his body, I can't help but think it looks beautiful. It's almost as if it belongs on him, like without the tattoos, his body isn't complete.

"Up here, sweetheart," Harrison says dryly, once again catching me checking out his body.

"Sorry." I shake my head to calm myself. What is going on with me? I've never been this affected by the sight of a guy before… "It was nice to meet you."

"I believe you already said that." Harrison laughs.

"Be nice," Helen scolds.

"Right, okay…well, bye," I say, and I'm about to take off when I remember Theo is with me. I look over at him and if looks could kill, Harrison would be dead. "Theo, you ready?" I ask.

"Yeah, let's go." And it doesn't go unnoticed he doesn't even bother to say goodbye to Helen or Harrison before taking off.

CHAPTER TWENTY-THREE

"DEAR HEAVENS," HELEN SAYS, HER VOICE SHAKING. I'm not paying much attention to her because I'm watching Cat. Cat Lincoln. The wind blows her wet hair free from the bun she was wearing and her chocolate-colored locks bounce behind her as her horse runs. Her idiot cousin struggles to stay on his horse. He looks sorely out of place.

But her?

She looks free. One with the wild. Beautiful.

With a sigh, I tear my gaze from her. People like her don't date people like me. Heath likes to remind me of that shit daily. Bitterness creeps up inside me, but I swallow it down. If I let it bother me, he'll sniff it out. The fucker will play with my annoyance like a kid with a ball. He'll pound it into my forehead until I'm ready to scream with rage. So, I'll tuck my little attraction away and keep it for later. Something to jerk my dick off to.

"We have to tell him," Helen utters, killing all fantasies of Cat naked in bed with me.

"What the fuck?" I groan.

She swats my arm. "Language, young man."

I tower over this older woman, but I don't correct her. Once, when I was around ten, I thought I could smart off to her. Called her every dirty name in the book. While Heath laughed and encouraged my bad behavior, Helen dragged me over to the sink and washed my mouth out with soap. It was disgusting as hell.

And later that night, when I cried all alone, it was Helen who came to me and stroked my hair. She's the closest thing I've had to a mother, so I try not to piss her off if I can help it.

"Why do we have to tell him?" I ask, turning to regard her, giving her my best puppy dog eyes that used to get me cookies before dinner.

She purses her lips together. "He needs to know."

"That we met a beautiful girl and her goofy-ass cousin from down the road?" I rub at the back of my neck and groan. "Hardly seems like Heath would care." But even as I say the words, I know that's not exactly true. According to the dozens of journals I found years ago hidden in a closet, Catrina and Heath were in love. Telling him we ran into her daughter—the baby she had with the man she chose over him—will only serve to piss him off. He's going to care, but not in a good way.

The only things Heath truly cares about in this world is his stupid company and making money. Money he keeps greedily squandered away. Money he refuses to use to update the house we all live in. Money he doesn't touch even though the barn is falling apart. Money that would have been useful when I begged him to loan it to me for college.

"You earn your own money, orphan. I've given you a home, food, and a place to rest your head. More than your weak, useless parents did. Don't forget that. And you'll always be in my debt."

His words always repeat in my head. He's right. When I was just three, my mother abandoned me and my father took the easy way out, overdosing on a bottle of pills. I'd nearly starved to death, but it was Heath who rescued me and took me in. He's hardly a father figure, but I've never gone hungry again, and for that I am thankful. I have Helen and she's like a mother. From what I've heard, not long after Heath found me in that pantry, Helen left her previous employer to come here. Heath offered to double her pay to come work for him and look after me. She agreed and has stuck around ever since. The moment I turned eighteen, I worried Heath would kick me out on my ass. It was then I begged for a loan for college. I was denied but was told I could continue to stay in the home as long as I kept the property in order and cared for the livestock. I'd had to take a second job at Heights Automotive so I could have extra money. I'm saving up to get my own place one day. Until then, I endure him and all his stupid games. One day, I'll leave and never come back.

"He'll care," she hisses, grabbing my forearm. "Come on."

She drags me into the house and as soon as we step inside, I immediately cool off. Heath's house, no matter how fucking hot it is outside, is cold. It's almost as though the home itself is a ghost. When I was a kid, I'd have nightmares and cry to Heath. He'd tell me to grow a pair of balls, toss me back in my room, and shut the door.

"Mr. Heath!" Helen calls out.

An annoyed grunt resounds from the kitchen. I allow her to drag me into one of his favorite places to dwell. Close to the coffee maker. He sits perched at the head of the table with his reading glasses sitting on the end of his nose. His perpetual scowl is present as he taps away on his laptop. A fresh cup of coffee steams from beside him as he works. Upon realizing our staring, he lets out an exasperated huff, lifts a dark brow, and pins us both with a *what the hell do you want* glare.

Helen releases me to pace the kitchen. I saunter over to the pantry that is kept full and try not to linger on a memory I have—one of my earliest—of scrounging for food. Now, I grab an apple from a bag and then set to rinsing it off. I lean my ass against the counter and take a bite, watching Helen as she frets. Heath, never a patient man, grits his teeth and clenches his jaw as he waits for whatever it is she has to say. Something tells me he won't be as impacted by what she has to tell him as she thinks. She's pretty damn dramatic when she wants to be.

"Out with it, woman," Heath barks.

She lets out a garbled sound and stops her pacing. "I think he's your boy."

Because I'm the only other male in the room, Heath darts his gaze my way. Cold and hateful. Like always. I smirk at him.

"Not me," I say before biting into my apple again as I quickly connect the dots. Helen isn't telling him about Catrina's daughter. She's telling him about Isabel's son. *His* son. It makes sense. Catrina dedicated several pages in her journals to bitching about Heath and Isabel trying to have a baby. Guess they succeeded…

"No, not Harrison," she huffs. "Mr. Lincoln."

Heath frowns, confusion marring his normally calculating features. "Elliot? You're not making any goddamned sense, Helen."

"No, not Elliot. Theo. He has a darker shade of her blond hair and her thin lips." She nervously swipes her palms on her uniform. "Isabel."

Heath stiffens and glowers at her. "Impossible."

"Hear me out," she utters. "We just saw him with Mr. Lincoln's daughter. He looked like a male version of your ex-wife, but that's not all. He has your eyes, Mr. Heath. Same color brown."

"If she had conceived my child, she would've asked for money. I would've found out from Elliot. This is impossible," he snaps, but his tone indicates he's unsure.

"Yeah, I don't know, Helen," I interject, swallowing some apple remnants. "The kid was a preppy pussy. Looked soft as fuck. I don't really see an ounce of Heath in him."

Helen doesn't bitch at me for my language this time but shoots me an unimpressed stare. "He was raised by his mother. If you had known her, you'd know she was soft." She turns back to Heath. "But he has your eyes." As if this is all the proof she needs.

"Why are you telling me this?" Heath seethes. "If he's my son…" he trails off and slams his fist down on the table, sloshing the coffee out onto the surface. "That bitch! She knew she was pregnant and kept this from me. That's why she ran and refused to take any money from me. She severed all ties so she could hide my kid from me. If this shit is true, I'll make her pay!"

Helen grabs a towel and sets to cleaning up the mess. Her voice is soft and shaky when she utters, "She's dead, Mr. Heath."

His features grow stony. For one moment, you might confuse his reaction to grief or regret or sadness. But I know him better than anyone. He's thinking. Planning. Figuring out how this news benefits him and his agenda. With Heath, there's always an agenda.

"Elliot, that weak snake, kept this from me," Heath says, his voice icy. "He's done."

"You're going to kill him?" I ask, nearly dropping my apple core.

Heath rolls his eyes and rises from his seat. "No, dumb boy. I'm not going to kill him. I'm going to bury the proverbial dagger in his chest. Quick deaths are for movies and old classic tales. I prefer long, agonizing, torturous ones that bleed my victims dry of everything that makes them who they are."

"Oh, dear Lord," Helen cries out. "I thought you'd be happy to learn you had a son! I thought it'd make you less bitter. Here you are babbling about more revenge! Never mind. Forget you heard anything. The boy is happy. Just leave him be."

Yeah fucking right.

"He's my son," Heath says, his lips quirking into a devilish grin. "Now that I know he exists, I can't in good conscience not bring him home to me."

"Mr. Heath," she pleads.

"Prepare a room. My son is coming home. Thanks for the

intel, Helen. Your meddling comes in handy sometimes," he says, smirking at her.

I don't like the pussy kid, so taking him away from his pretty cousin sends curls of satisfaction twisting inside me. And maybe she'll come visit him, which means in turn, I'll get to see her.

As Heath passes me, he narrows his eyes as he regards me. "Don't look so excited. He's not your brother. Remember your place here. You're the orphan. I own you."

I bite back a derisive laugh and give him the nod he's looking for.

He pats my head. "Good dog."

I'm shoveling shit in the barn when someone whistles. I toss the shovel down and regard Heath with a questioning stare. He's dressed in one of his expensive suits he reserves for going into town in. I think he likes waving around the fact he's rich as fuck. When he's at home, though, he doesn't care. It's always for everyone else's benefit, not his own. I think, deep down, he doesn't even like money. To him it's another one of his games. Something to win and use over others.

"Yeah?" I ask as I saunter his way.

"We're going into town. Shower and do it quickly. You'll always be that shitshow that crawled out of that pantry all those years ago. But today I need more from you. Drive me to town. I may need to use excessive force and I want to be prepared," he tells me coldly.

I let his insults slide and give him a clipped nod. Once I'm showered and dressed in a pair of black jeans and black T-shirt, I climb into his brand-new S-Class Cabriolet Mercedes. It's midnight blue and a convertible. I know the asshole won't let us take the top down, but I enjoy the purr of the engine. The cars I get to drive at the shop are all shitty clunkers. He doesn't ask me to drive him often, but when he does, I jump at the chance to drive around in luxury.

"Where are we headed?" I ask as I gun it onto the road.

He fists his hand but doesn't get onto me about my speed. "W. Heights Investments."

"You hardly ever go to the office and when you do, you drive yourself. Why am I suddenly needed?" I mutter mostly to myself.

He scoffs. "Because I *might* need your muscle, orphan."

Heath is such a prick, but he raised me. I'm used to his snide comments. It's not like he woke up one day and started being an asshole. He's been an asshole for as long as I can remember. At least he never put his hands on me growing up. His vicious tongue was his favorite weapon and when I was young its cruelty was almost too hard to take. But as I grew older, my skin thickened and I became immune. If he ever did try to touch me, I'd stomp his old ass into the ground.

"So whose ass are we *maybe* kicking?" I ask as we pull into the parking lot after a lengthy drive filled with brooding silence.

"Elliot Lincoln."

I jerk my head to look at him. "Here?"

His nostrils flare and he smiles. Cold and hateful. "Well, he works for me. Here. I own him like I own you. Where else would we find him?"

My brows shoot up. "I thought you hated him."

"I do."

"So why did you give him a job?"

"I didn't give him anything. He was in no position to take. His company was failing, so I invested in it. Eventually, it failed altogether. He needed a job, so I took him in." He climbs out of the vehicle and stares up at the massive building with pride.

There are no labels or markings that indicate the company name. Just a big building.

"Wow, so generous," I utter. Heath is anything but generous.

"Come," he grumbles, ignoring my comment.

I follow him into the building. It's quiet aside from a few people working in offices. We find one at the end and it's larger than the rest. The placard on the wall says: E. Lincoln.

"Where's your office?" I ask.

He smirks and motions with his head. "I let him use mine."

I frown because nothing about this seems legit. I know Heath too well. He does nothing out of the niceness of his heart. It means he has this man by his balls.

Twisting the knob, he saunters right into the room. A man, slender and with similar features to that dickhead Theo I met, stares back at us with his thin lips parted in surprise. His brown hair is graying and thinned out on top. He stares at Heath, but my attention falls to the pictures on his back credenza. Pictures of her. Cat. A smile tugs at my lips as I glance at each picture from when she was young to her senior pictures. She's so fucking pretty.

"Good afternoon, Elliot," Heath says in a cold tone.

"W-What are you doing here?" Elliot demands, his hands shaking.

Heath strolls into the room and sits in the chair opposite of him. "In case you've forgotten, this building is mine. This office is mine. Everything in it is mine."

Elliot freezes and looks down at his lap. "I've done everything as asked."

"Hmmm," Heath mutters. "I suppose. I check up on your work and you do a decent enough job."

"So why are you here?" Elliot rasps out.

"I'm here to talk about my son," Heath snaps.

The room falls deadly silent as Elliot flinches in horror. "Well, we don't know for certain and—"

"He has my eyes," Heath snarls.

Despite him never having seen Theo, he uses this tidbit of information against Elliot. I have to agree, they do have the same eyes.

"But I wasn't sure…" Elliot trails off.

"We both know he's mine."

Elliot's head hangs, defeated. "Just leave him be," he pleads.

"Absolutely not," Heath growls. "I was denied knowing his existence all these years. But you knew. You knew and you kept it from me. Tell me, Elliot, was the money you borrowed the past couple of years to help take care of *my* boy?"

"I, uh," Elliot utters.

"Or maybe you used the trust you were left when Catrina died. Is that what you did? Did you use the money she received for giving you that baby to hide mine?"

"Heath, please…"

"I want you out by the end of the week," Heath snaps. "You're done."

"What?" Elliot bellows.

"I want you out of my house," Heath seethes. "I want you out of my building. I want you off my payroll. I want you out of my life. Give me my motherfucking kid, pack your shit, and go."

"You own Cat's house?" I ask, dumfounded.

Heath doesn't humor me with an answer, but Elliot's trembling gives me what I need to know. Irritation swells up inside me. He's just going to kick them out over this?

"Heath, maybe it's not that big of a deal—" I start, but Heath pins me with a murderous glare.

"Let the adults talk, orphan." He makes an irritated sound and snaps his fingers before pointing to the door.

Like the trained dog I am, I grumble and huff from the

room. I stalk along the hallways and burst out the doors, eager to go kick a fucking tree or something. I hate Heath. When I slam into someone, they bounce off me and hit the pavement with a thump.

"Ah!" a familiar, feminine voice cries out.

When I glance down, I realize I've smashed into *her*.

Cat Lincoln.

She no longer looks wild and free like when I'd seen her earlier today. No, she's taken the time to fix her hair and apply makeup. Her dress is fancy and expensive, but what has my dick growing hard is the way it's pushed up her hips, exposing a silky flash of pink panties between her creamy thighs. I stare for a beat too long before I look into her green eyes that are glassy with tears. Her bottom lip, pink and glossed up, trembles.

I kneel in front of her and pull her dress down over her thighs to cover her up, our eyes locked in a heated battle. "You okay?"

She swallows thickly and nods. "I think I skinned my hand." She holds one of her hands up.

Without hesitation, I grab her wrist and pull it to me. A little scrape with a few tiny beads of blood colors her pink palm. So tiny and soft. Such a stark contrast to my massive, rough, and tanned one. Now that I'm so close, I get a whiff of her sweet floral scent and it makes my dick lurch in my jeans again. Fuck, she smells good.

"You need thicker skin," I tell her, smirking.

The tears that were threatening in her eyes get blinked away and she glowers at me. "You pushed me down. You're a big freaking giant. It has nothing to do with thick skin. Maybe if you weren't so thick-headed."

I grin at her as she struggles to free her wrist from my grip. Because I'm stronger, I pull her toward me and inhale her tender skin on her hand. "My apologies," I murmur. "What are you doing here?"

She glances past me. "I came to see my dad. I wanted to talk to him about my mother." She bites on her bottom lip. "Are there really pictures of her at your house?"

In the closet along with the journals are several boxes of Catrina's stuff, including tons of photos.

"Yeah," I say, my voice husky.

"Was she pretty?"

Not as pretty as you.

"She was okay," I grunt out.

She frowns as though my words offend her. "I want to see her."

"Come over and I'll show you."

I rise to my feet and pull her to hers. Still, I don't release her wrist. The wind blows and ruffles her silky hair. Without thinking, I tuck a strand behind her ear with my free hand, not wanting her face to be obstructed. Her cheeks blush furiously and it does nothing for the state of my dick.

"How old are you?" she asks, her voice small and shy.

My gaze falls to her lips that are way too tempting. "Too old for you."

She lets out an exasperated huff. "I wasn't asking like that."

I lift a brow. "You're jailbait, though, right?"

Her cheeks grow impossibly redder. "I'm seventeen. I'll be eighteen soon."

"When you turn eighteen, come over and I'll show you lots of things."

She gapes at me. "I just want to see pictures of my mother. I don't know what you're insinuating."

I pull her palm to my mouth once more, but this time, I lick her sweaty flesh, loving the gasp that escapes her. "I think you know exactly what I'm insinuating."

She yanks her hand away and glowers at me with a fiery glare that does nothing to calm my hard cock. I knew the second I laid eyes on her that I'd been attracted to her. She already starred in one shower cock-fisting fantasy today. Now that I've licked her salty skin, I'm going to be thinking of her a lot more until I get her in my bed.

"You're a pig," she huffs.

"Wrong animal," I tell her with a grin. "The ladies usually prefer the word 'stallion.'"

"I'm not your typical lady, *pig*," she retorts before storming up the steps.

The wind blows and her dress lifts, giving me a nice view of her ass in her pink panties. As if she knows I'm checking her out, she turns and flips me the bird.

"Soon, Cat. You can fuck me soon."

Her squeal of frustration is the last thing I hear before the door closes behind her. With a wide grin on my face, I saunter back over to the Mercedes and climb inside. I turn on the engine to get the AC going but then push the button to let the top down. While I wait for my evil master to ruin his minion, I thread my fingers behind my head and close my eyes. Every thought is filled with her. Full, pouty lips. Wild, fiery green eyes. And pink panties.

Soon, Cat.

CHAPTER TWENTY-FOUR

CAT

MY ALARM CLOCK GOES OFF, INDICATING IT'S TIME TO GET up. Letting out an annoyed huff, I hit snooze and throw my pillow over my face, wishing I could rewind the clock and sleep for another week. I should be excited for today. Hell, I should be ecstatic! For one, today is my birthday. The big one-eight. It's also the first day of my senior year, which means I'm not only nine months away from graduating, but I'm that much closer to hopefully getting into the college of my dreams—Yale. On top of that, I've been named captain of the cheer squad this year, something I've been looking forward to since my freshman year when I joined, and our first practice is today. So like I said, I should be ecstatic…but I'm not. Because while all of this positivity is happening in my life, I can't help but feel like there's a dark storm threatening to destroy my beautiful sunshine. It's as if it's looming over me and waiting to cover my bright rays with black clouds and nasty rain. My thoughts go back to last week after I ran into that delicious asshole Harrison at my dad's office—well, what I *thought* was my dad's office—only to learn everything I ever thought to be true was a lie.

I walk down the hall, past Sheila, my dad's sweet receptionist. She doesn't notice me because she's in the middle of a phone call and typing away on her computer, but I know she won't mind me walking back to his office. He's always had an open door policy when it comes to me.

Noticing his door is closed, I raise my fist to knock, when I hear shouting. Instead of knocking, I place my ear to the door to listen. My dad never yells—not at me, and certainly not at his clients or employees.

"I said I'm done!" a masculine voice that isn't my father's booms through the wooden door. "I won't say it again. Pack. Your. Shit!"

"Please, Heath. My daughter only has one year left of school. Don't do this to me—to her. How will I help pay for her college? I need this job." This time I recognize the voice as my father's and my heart sinks. What's going on here? Packing up to go where? And why? This doesn't make any sense. My father is the boss of W. Heights Investments. Why would someone be commanding him to pack up and leave?

Needing answers, I place my hand to the knob to open the door and am about to turn it, when the door swings open, pulling me with it. I fall forward and into the arms of someone. With my head in his chest, I can't see him, but I can smell him. All masculine with a hint of musk. When I look up, it's Mr. Heath, the other asshole who lives at Windy Hills. I've never formally met him, but I've seen him a few times in town. My father made me promise to stay away from him.

"I'm sorry," I blurt out when he glares in my direction.

"Sorry for what?" Mr. Heath sneers. "Eavesdropping and getting caught, or falling into my arms?" He backs up slightly, and his dark brown eyes slowly peruse my body. If I didn't know better, I would think this man was undressing me with his eyes alone. Suddenly feeling exposed—which is ridiculous since I'm fully dressed—I swallow thickly and bring my arms up to cover my breasts. He smirks devilishly at me and steps closer. So close, I can feel the heat radiating off his body. With an evil chuckle that sends shivers down my spine, he leans in and says, "You look just like your mother. Same perfect dick sucking lips, same perky breasts, same thick creamy thighs. I wonder if your cunt is just as sweet as hers was."

My body goes stiff at his words, and my eyes dart to my father, who is standing behind his desk glowering at Mr. Heath. He's too far away, though, so he couldn't have heard what he just said.

"Heath, leave," my dad demands in a tone I've never heard him use before.

Mr. Heath's smirk transforms into a wide grin at my dad's words, but he doesn't back up or make any attempt to leave. Instead he once again speaks softly into my ear, so only I can hear. "Your father just lost everything, but maybe you could convince me to give a little bit back to him. You know where to find me." And with a salacious wink, he pushes past me out the door.

It was after he left, my father told me the truth. He lost the family company to Mr. Heath years ago and now works for Heath's company. Not only does he own my father's job, but he also owns our home. And because Mr. Heath is pissed at my father for something—he wouldn't say what—he's taking it out on my father by firing him and forcing us to move out of the only home I've ever known. So like I said, while I should be excited for everything that is to come, it's all being overshadowed by the thoughts of my father becoming unemployed and us becoming homeless.

My alarm goes off once again. This time I turn it off and get up. There's no point in avoiding the inevitable. After showering, doing my hair and makeup, and getting dressed in my school uniform, which consists of a white ruffled button-down top, a blue, yellow, and white plaid tie, a matching plaid skirt, and my favorite pair of yellow Chucks, I head downstairs for breakfast.

Theo and my dad are already sitting at the table silently eating waffles my father made. When they spot me enter the kitchen, they both look up with a smile. While Theo's is wide and flirty because he has no clue we're all being kicked out of our home, my father's is forced. I take a closer look at my dad and notice how much older he seems. There are stress lines marring his once smooth forehead. Crow's feet have appeared in the corners of his eyes. His once light brown hair is now sprinkled with gray. He looks like a man who's carrying the weight of the world on his shoulders.

"Good morning, honey." My dad stands and comes over to make me a plate of food. "Happy Birthday." He gives me a kiss to my temple. "I was thinking we could have dinner here tonight to celebrate your birthday. I'll even pick up a cake from the bakery in town you love."

I don't point out that our yearly tradition has always been to have dinner with my friends at Madison Café, my favorite French restaurant. All of their entrees are delicious, and they have the most delectable Crème Brûlée. While the restaurant is expensive and my father isn't the kind of man to eat at extravagant restaurants, ever since he told me Madison Café was one of my mother's favorite restaurants, we've never missed a birthday dinner there. The fact we're not going there this year tells me just how bad it is for my father—for us.

"Sounds good, Dad." No longer hungry, but also not wanting to offend my dad since he did make these for my birthday, I sit down and cut up my waffle.

"Happy Birthday," Theo says. "Do you feel older?"

"A little bit." I laugh softly, but even to my own ears, it sounds strained. Theo gives me a concerned look, but I avert my eyes to my food, stabbing a piece of my waffle with my fork and shoving it into my mouth. Usually the waffles taste sweet and delicious, but today, they taste bitter and depressing.

After we're both done eating and say goodbye to my father, we head to the garage to my car. It was a gift from my father for my sixteenth birthday. A Ford Mustang GT. It's not a BMW or Mercedes like most of my friends drive, but it's the car I wanted. It's black on black with a convertible top and a V6 engine. She's sexy and I love her…and I wonder if I'll have to give her up now that my father has lost his job.

Pushing my negative thoughts aside, I click the garage door

opener and wait for it to go up. Once it does, I back out of the drive and then peel out down the dirt road, dust kicking up behind us.

"Everything okay?" Theo asks. After my father told me about our situation, he asked that I not tell Theo. He wants to speak to him himself.

"Everything's fine."

"Doesn't seem like it. The past week you've spent your time in your room playing angry music. Is it something I did? Our kiss?"

I glance at him quickly then back to the road. "No, but that does need to stop. Everybody at school knows you're my cousin. If they find out you've kissed me, they will destroy both of us. I don't know how it was at your boarding school, but here at Heights Academy, you're either in or you're out. I'm in, and it needs to stay that way." I'm already about to lose everything else. I can't lose my reputation at school as well.

"Who said anything about them finding out?" Theo's hand lands on my bare thigh and moves up my leg. "I can keep a secret." His fingers reach the apex of my thighs and ghost across the top of my panties.

I swat his hand away. "Stop or you'll be walking to school."

He chuckles but doesn't argue.

School is school. I thought it would feel different being my last year, but it's all the same. Same kids I've gone to school with my entire life. Same friends. Same teachers. My first period is Calculus, which flies by, followed by English. Then it's lunch. After getting a turkey wrap and a soda, I sit down at my usual table, where two of my close friends and cheer mates, Anne and Charlotte, are already eating and gossiping over whatever they've heard in the rumor mill. We're only back to school for three hours and from the sound of it, two girls are knocked up, one of our friends was cheated on, and some sophomore guy had an affair with one of the teachers. Same shit, different year. At least this will be my final year here, and then I will be off to Yale. *If you can afford it.*

Once a few of our other friends join us, Anne tells everyone all about her summer in Italy, and Charlotte brags about how she almost lost her virginity to an older guy while she was in Europe.

"Guess who I had first period with? Theo Lincoln." Anne's brows waggle up and down. "That guy is fine. Is he single?"

"Ewww! That's my cousin," I say, pretending to gag. "And yes, he's single."

"I call dibs!" She tilts her head to the side and shrugs with a smirk.

"Whatever," Charlotte says with an eye roll, "I'm not about to waste my time with the boys here, now that I've experienced a real man."

"You mean *almost* experienced a real man," Kelsie, another friend of ours who is also on the cheer squad, says, and everyone but Charlotte snickers.

"Cheer practice is still happening after school, right?" Anne asks.

"Of course," I say, "Why wouldn't it?"

"Well, it is your birthday, so I thought maybe your dad would be taking everyone to Madison Café like he does every year." The girls all look at me, waiting for the invite they usually get.

"Madison Café is so last year." I roll my eyes, trying to play it off. "I'm eighteen now. I don't want some big spectacle for my birthday like a child," I scoff. Thankfully, the bell for third period rings before anyone can say anything.

The next two periods fly by and then it's time for cheer practice. We go over several of our routines and discuss some new ones. Next Friday night is the first football game of the season, so everyone is excited. Since Theo is on the football team, he meets me by my car after both of our practices are over, and we head home.

I'm not even through the foyer when I stumble over several boxes in the doorway. One of them reads Cat's closet and tears prick my eyes. This is really happening. We're really being evicted.

"What's going on?" Theo asks, opening one of the boxes that has his name scrawled across the side.

"We're moving," my father says, making his presence known. "I'm sorry, Cat." He gives me a chaste kiss to my forehead. "I was hoping to prolong this until after your birthday, but Heath has demanded we leave in two days."

"Heath? The guy that the maid mentioned by the lake?" Theo shoots me a confused look, and my dad's eyes go wide.

"Cat, tell me you didn't go over there."

"I'm so sorry, Dad," I say as my dad's fist comes down onto the box in anger.

"It's my fault," Theo cuts in. "Cat told me she wasn't allowed, but I insisted. If anyone is to blame, it's me. I'm sorry."

"Dammit, you two." My dad's fingers come up to his hair and he pulls on the strands in frustration. "That explains how he found out."

"Found out what?" Theo asks, his eyes bouncing from me to my dad. I watch as my dad struggles with what to say, how to answer Theo. He lets out an exasperated sigh, as if he's finally given up.

"Heath is your father." My dad closes his eyes and shakes his head.

My eyes dart to Theo, whose mouth drops down in shock. He doesn't say anything for a minute, almost as if he's trying to process what my father just told him. His mouth opens and closes a few times, but words don't come out. My dad and I stay quiet, waiting for Theo to speak. I can't even imagine just finding out that my parent really is alive. Too bad soon he'll learn his dad is an asshole.

When Theo finally speaks, his words come out in a disgusted hiss. "Are you fucking serious? She told me she didn't know who my father was." He swipes his box of belongings onto the floor. "She fucking lied?"

My dad shakes his head and sighs, ignoring Theo's outburst and remaining calm. "Your mom did what was best for you. She left him when she found out she was pregnant."

"So this entire time, I could've had a father? I could've been getting to know him. Who the hell did she think she was to make the decision as to whether my father should be in my life?" Theo kicks the box of his stuff that he knocked onto the floor, and it flies across the room and hits the wall.

"He's not a good guy, Theo," my dad says. "As parents, we try to make the best decisions we can for our children, and your mom felt it was best to raise you on her own. It's why she never came to visit over the years. She didn't want to take a chance of him finding out about you." My dad moves slowly toward Theo in an attempt to comfort him, but Theo raises his hands up and my dad stops in his tracks.

"I thought you said she disgraced the family and so she was cut off?" I ask, confused. Ever since I was old enough to know we had long-distance family, I was told my aunt Isabel never visited because she wasn't welcome. We would take trips to Florida to visit my grandma and grandpa, and they would refuse to even discuss her. It was as if she was no longer a member of our family. That was until she passed away last year and my dad became Theo's guardian. He was away at boarding school, so aside from meeting him once for his mother's funeral, I didn't see him again until he moved in with us for his senior year.

"She did," my dad says, answering my question. "She took

off with Heath and married him after knowing what a terrible person he was…still is." He places emphasis on the last two words, looking Theo right in the eye. "We warned her, but she wouldn't listen, and she was cut off. It only took a short time of being married to him before she was begging to come home, but we felt she needed to learn her lesson. Then she got pregnant." Dad frowns with a soft sigh.

"I shouldn't have cut her off. I felt so guilty when I found out she was pregnant. Not that I don't love you, Theo. I do. You're my nephew. But you have to understand, I never wanted that for my sister." Dad steps closer to Theo, and this time, Theo lets him. He places his hand on Theo's shoulder. "You don't know Heath like I do. He would've destroyed your mother. I blamed myself for not convincing my father to take her back before she got pregnant and did the only thing I could do. I gave her enough money to leave."

"And now he knows about me?" Theo questions.

"He does, and he's not happy that I've kept you from him. He's fired me and is kicking us out of the house. He's insisted you go and live with him."

"Like hell!" Theo hisses. "I don't even know this man, and if what you're saying is true, that my mother ran away to keep him from knowing about me, why the hell would I want to live with him? And what about Cat?" Theo's gaze meets mine momentarily, concern evident in his eyes, before he turns back to my father. "Where is she going to live?"

"I've found an apartment to rent in town. It's not much, but if I sell my vehicle and Cat's, it will be enough for us to get by until I find another job."

My car…I knew this was coming, but it still hurts. Not because I'm losing my car, but because we're losing our life. Our home, our cars, everything is being taken and all that will be left are our memories.

"There has to be something we can do," Theo says.

"I wish there was, but knowing Heath, his mind is already made up. The only thing we have in our favor is that you're still seventeen and I'm your guardian. I'm hoping that will hold him off for a little while, giving you time to turn eighteen and be able to make your own decision as to where you want to live."

"I'll talk to him," Theo insists, but my dad holds his hand up to stop him.

"You will do no such thing. Heath is not a man you make deals with. He's worse than the devil himself."

Just then, Mr. Heath's words come back to me: *"...maybe you could convince me to give a little bit back to him. You know where to find me."*

"I just remembered I left my textbook at school. I need to get it before the janitor locks up." Not wanting to chance either of them catching me in my lie, I head straight for the door.

"I'll come with you," Theo says, following behind me before I can make it out the door.

"No!" I shout. When I glance at my father, I see his brow is raised in concern. *Shit!* "No," I say again, this time softer, more controlled. "I need to go by Anne's house as well, and her mother doesn't like boys over."

"What about dinner and birthday cake?" my dad asks.

"As soon as I get back, we'll celebrate my birthday."

And hopefully we'll have more to celebrate.

When I arrive to Windy Hills, the gate is open, so I drive right in and park next to another vehicle. The house is huge like ours and just as beautiful. Only while ours is more modern with white walls and black shutters, this home screams classic beauty with its old wooden shutters and wrought iron window boxes. It's obvious the home needs to be updated, but for some reason, it only adds to its charm.

I knock on the massive, mahogany door and notice my hands are shaking. *What am I doing here?* I know what he wants… well, what he insinuated anyway. *Can I give him that?* I have to. If it means my father will be able to keep his job and our home. If it means Theo won't be forced to live with this man—Theo might drive me crazy at times, but he's still family—I have to at least try.

I hear someone yell, but it's muffled, and then the door creak opens and standing in the doorway is none other than Mr. Heath himself.

"Well, well, look who it is. Little Catrina. Come to make a deal?" His devious smirk causes me to visibly shudder. *I can do this*, I chant to myself.

"It's Cat. Can we talk, please?" My voice comes out as nothing more than a whisper. Dammit, I need to grow some lady balls if I plan to deal with this man.

"Sure thing, *Cat.*" Mr. Heath opens the door wider and moves to the side, allowing me access. I walk in and the door slams closed behind me. I jump at the sound, and he sniggers humorously. *Get control of yourself, Cat…*

I follow Mr. Heath through the living room and into what looks like an office. "Have a seat," he murmurs as he shuts the door. There is a massive wood desk with two chairs in the corner—one behind the desk and one for a guest—and a coffee-colored leather couch against the wall with a wood coffee table in front of it. When I go for the chair, his hand grips my wrist tightly.

"Let's get comfortable." He pulls me onto the couch and sits next to me, leaving only a few inches between us. "So, what can I do for you?" he asks with a small, knowing smirk splayed upon his lips.

As I think about how to word what I want, I take a moment to look at Mr. Heath. With his chocolate brown hair and just as dark eyes, I can now see the similarities between him and Theo. They both have the same sharp nose and square jawline. The other day when I saw Heath, he was dressed impeccably in a three-piece suit, which screamed money and power, but today he's in simple gray lounge pants and a white T-shirt. For some reason, seeing him dressed like this makes him seem more approachable.

I take a deep breath and raise my chin, hoping it will give me some more confidence—or at least make it *look* like I'm confident. "I want you to give my father back his job and our home, and I want you to leave Theo alone."

Mr. Heath stares at me for a long beat, his smirk now gone and his face devoid of all emotion. And then slowly his smile comes back, and he throws his head back with a boisterous laugh.

"Is that all?" He laughs some more. "Why don't you ask for a million dollars while you're at it?" He grins like a damn Cheshire cat and stands. He walks over to the liquor bar in the corner I didn't notice before and opens a canister. With a pair of tongs, he drops a few ice cubes into a tumbler and then pours himself several fingers' worth of what looks like whiskey.

"I don't need a million dollars," I grind out. "I just need my home and for my father to be employed."

Mr. Heath holds a glass up, silently offering to make me a drink as well, but I shake my head. The last thing I need is to be drunk while dealing with this man.

He shrugs and walks back over to the couch, sitting down next to me. We're so close his knee rubs against mine. He takes a sip of his drink, sets it down on the table, then finally speaks. "And for me to leave *my* son, who was kept from me, alone."

"Yes." I nod with fake conviction.

"And what do I get?" he asks slowly. His fingers brush up my arm, and my traitorous body reacts with goose bumps covering my skin.

When he sees my reaction, he laughs cruelly. "Your mother used to act the same way to my touch."

"You were with my mother?" I ask softly, confused by his words. I'm trying to stay focused, but as his fingers continue their trail up my arm and across my collarbone, it's getting harder to keep my mind straight.

His eyes lock with mine, and he nods once. "Before *and* after your father." His lips curl up into a sneer, and his eyes leave mine as he one-handedly undoes several buttons on my school blouse. I watch his fingers as they move the material to the side, exposing my white-laced bra. A trickle of fear washes over me because I'm in unchartered territory with a man I don't even know. His fingers now run a line down the swell of my left breast and over to my nipple. My nipple hardens against my will, and my cheeks heat up. *I should not be turned on by this man's touch!* A tremor ripples through me at how easily he plays my body. At how I just sit here and take it. I'm immobilized and I'm not sure what is holding me prisoner. Maybe not fear, but certainly nervousness.

"Just like your mother," he murmurs. "Do you like it rough too?" he asks, his gaze never leaving my breasts. "Your mother, she loved it rough. Something your father could never give her."

His words are like ice being poured onto my overly heated body. I swat his hand away and back up slightly. "He loved her, and she loved him."

"He was a fucking pussy." He edges closer. "I bet he's already packed up his shit and is ready to move. Am I right?" he asks, and I nod because he is right.

His hand goes to my thigh and pushes my legs open. Then, without wasting any time, he moves his hand upward and under my skirt, and unlike when Theo did the same thing to me in the car and it did nothing for me, Mr. Heath's touch has my body feeling like it's being lit on fire. "Like I said, he's a pussy. He doesn't know you're here, does he?"

I shake my head, refusing to speak. I can see my chest rising and falling heavily, and I'm afraid if I talk, my voice will come out just as labored.

"Just like your mother," he murmurs. "She would do anything it took to get what she wanted." I want to push his hand away, but I know what he's getting at with his statement. If I want my father to keep his job, if I want to keep our home and for Theo to be left alone, I need to be willing to do anything.

He moves my panties to the side and spreads my folds open, then he gently strokes my clit. I hold back my sigh of pleasure, refusing to give this man anything, and try to focus on something else. The art hanging up on the walls. The various bottles of liquor. His fingers leave my clit and I wonder if he's done. Did he just want a little touch? But then I hear a clanking sound and my eyes dart to his hand just in time to see a piece of ice between his two fingers.

"Wha-what are you doing?" I ask. He couldn't possibly be planning to put that ice…

"Shh…" he murmurs as he moves my panties to the side once again and pushes the cold object up against my clit, causing me to let out a loud squeak. My hand flies up to cover my mouth, but I'm too late. He's already heard me react to what he's doing to me. He nods slowly with a cruel smirk splayed upon his lips as he rubs my clit up and down with the piece of ice. I feel it start to melt as the cold liquid drips down my seam, cooling down my overheated and turned on body. He uses the ice to work me up into a frenzy, but it's not enough to set me off. I want to scream for him to just get me off already, but I bite my tongue, not wanting to give him anything more. Once the ice is completely melted and I can feel only his finger against my skin, he stops stroking my clit.

I take a deep breath of relief. Maybe he's done. Maybe that's all he wanted to do. Tease me—

Only before I can finish my thought, he barely pushes a single warm finger into me, telling me he isn't done with me yet. "Just like your fucking mother. Dripping wet."

In the quiet room, I can hear myself panting loudly. I need to control myself. This man is bad. I don't want this. I'm only doing this so he'll give us back our lives. "Are you going to let my father keep his job?" I ask breathlessly.

"Maybe." He smirks as he eases his finger in and out of me, barely reaching his knuckle. My vagina clenches around his finger and he chuckles darkly. "Does that feel good? My finger inside you?"

"I need to know if my father will remain employed," I demand. There's no way I'm allowing this to happen without him confirming our deal. My hand wraps around his wrist, stopping his intrusion. Only when I stop him, his finger is still inside me and I can feel it wiggling against my vaginal walls. I stifle a moan, and his shoulders shake with silent laughter.

"This is my deal, little Catrina. I make the rules. Either move your hand from my wrist, or any deal I *might* make is off."

"You're a cruel bastard," I snap, but obey.

"Your mother preferred me that way. It turned her on. And from the way your tight cunt is sucking in my finger, virgin girl, I'm thinking the poisoned apple doesn't fall far from the tree." He pulls his finger almost all the way out then pushes it back in slightly, and my traitor legs spread wider, wanting more. This time I can't stifle my moan, and when it hits Mr. Heath's ears, he lets out a low growl. Not able to look at him any longer, I let my head fall backward and close my eyes. Maybe if I pretend it's someone else who's fingering me, I won't feel so dirty. The first guy who pops into my head is Harrison. He might be an arrogant asshole, but he's still a sexy arrogant asshole.

I pretend it's him who's fingering me.

A hand grazes across my breast and I pretend it's Harrison's hand.

My bra cup is pulled down and wet lips land on my nipple, sucking and biting on it. I pretend those lips are Harrison's. Another finger lands on my clit and begins to rub circles. I pretend the finger is Harrison's and I wish he'd push it all the way in. My body is getting worked up. I've never experienced an orgasm before, but the feeling is a lot like what Theo was doing to me in the pool.

"Relax, sweet Catrina. Come for me."

I pretend it's Harrison's voice speaking to me, and I relax my body, allowing the impending orgasm to build. The sooner I come, the sooner this all ends. Maybe he won't want to have sex with me. Maybe he just wants this one orgasm.

Just as my legs begin to tremble and my clit begins to pulse, and I'm almost positive I'm about to experience my first orgasm, I hear the door swing open, and a voice bark out a, "What the fuck!"

My eyes shoot open and my legs close with Mr. Heath's finger still inside me.

CHAPTER TWENTY-FIVE

AFTER CAT WALKED OUT THE DOOR, UNCLE ELLIOT apologized to me some more. He told me once again he wished he would've been there for my mom instead of turning his back on her. His apology sounded sincere, and I told him I forgive him, but that doesn't stop me from wondering about my father. And with my mom gone, I can't go back and ask her what she was thinking or why she made the choices she did.

Growing up, it was always just my mom and me, and maybe it was because of that fact we were close. I always wondered why we never visited our family in New York, but I didn't think too much of it. She used to give various reasons such as money was tight, or she needed to work and couldn't take off. For as far back as I can remember, my mom worked part-time at a small bakery in town a few days a week. She would go in after she saw me off to school and she would make sure she was off before I got out. Now that I'm able to see the entire picture with more of the facts, there's no way we could've afforded to live in our two-bedroom flat and her send me to private school on her small income.

Then when I turned fourteen and all my friends were attending boarding school, she allowed me to go. Looking back, at that point, she wasn't even working at the bakery any longer. She had said she was taking some time off. It wasn't until she passed away that I realized she wanted me to go, so I wouldn't see her sick. All these years it was my uncle who was sending her money to take care of me.

I want to trust that what Uncle Elliot said is the truth. That my mom kept me from my father because she felt it was best for me, that he was sending her money so she could hide from Heath, but at the same time, I feel like it's something I need to see for myself.

I want to be pissed that he fired Uncle Elliot and evicted him and Cat from their home, but I can also see where Heath is coming from. He just found out he has a son. He has every right to be pissed. And the fact that he's pissed has me questioning if he's really as bad as everyone is making him out to be. If he was that bad of a guy, wouldn't he not care that he has a son?

Needing to get some answers, I wait until Uncle Elliot excuses himself to continue packing, then I slip out the back and head down the trail along the lake. It's not a long walk, but it does give me time to think. I'm not going to assume the worst in Heath. I'm going to speak to him myself and make my own judgements. Maybe I can convince him to let Uncle Elliot keep his job and home, and I can come to live with him so we can get to know each other.

When I make it to Windy Hills Estate, I spot a couple ranch hands who are too busy working to notice me. I walk around the side of the house to the front to knock on the door, and that's when I see Cat's Mustang.

When she said she had to go get her textbook from school and then visit her friend, I didn't believe her, but I assumed she was upset over having to move and needed some space. I figured she wanted to go vent to her friend or take a drive by herself, but I never thought when she walked out the door, she was going to Heath's house.

I knock on the door once but nobody answers, and my

mind immediately goes to Cat's safety. What if she came here to confront Heath and something has happened? What if he is a bad guy like Uncle Elliot said? Turning the knob, the door creaks open. I step inside and the place is quiet.

"Hello?" I call out, but nobody answers. That's when I hear a loud moan coming from the room off to the side. Without thinking twice, I cut across the room and swing the door open. And what I see in front of me has me wanting to kill someone.

Cat, with her legs spread open and her bare pink pussy on display, has her head tilted back as she moans loudly in pleasure as some guy who looks to be the same age as my uncle fingers her while sucking on her perfect tits.

"What the fuck!" I yell, and Cat's head pops up, her shocked eyes landing on mine. The guy sitting next to her slowly removes his finger from between her thighs and his lips from around her nipple and grins up at me like he doesn't give a fuck that he was just caught getting her off.

"Theo." Cat jumps up from the couch, and my gaze goes to her exposed breast. She looks down and immediately pulls her bra up and starts buttoning her shirt. When she's done, she pats the front of her skirt to make sure nothing else is showing and then she looks up at me. Her cheeks are tinted pink from embarrassment—or maybe from being turned on—and normally I would find it cute, but right now I'm too pissed.

"Who the fuck are you?" I approach the piece of shit who has the nerve to be laying his hands on the woman I want. His grin grows wider as he takes the finger he just had inside of Cat and sucks on it before standing and taking a sip of the drink on the table.

"Heath." He holds out the offending hand to shake mine with a knowing fucking smirk. And when I glare down at it, refusing to shake his hand, he sneers. "I'm your father."

Father?

My father?

Quickly assessing this smug asshole's features, I notice that while he's clearly older, it's almost as if I'm looking at a mirror of what I'm going to look like twenty years from now: same height, same build, same goddamned brown eyes. My hair is a few shades lighter than his, a perfect mixture of him and my mom. My gaze continues downward, and I spot a birth mark on the inside of his forearm. My eyes go to my forearm where I have a similar one. *Jesus, this man really is my father, which means…*

"You have something going on with my fucking dad?" This can't be happening.

"No." Cat shakes her head emphatically as she steps away from Heath and toward me. "I came over here to make a deal with him."

"You did what?" I yell, and Cat cowers. I turn my gaze back to Heath, who still has that fucking smirk on his face. "What the fuck is going on? I find out you're my father and when I come over here to meet you, I see you're halfway to fucking my girl."

"*Your* girl?" Heath questions with a grin at the same time Cat yells, "I'm not your girl."

"Well, you're not his either, but I don't see that stopping you from spreading your legs for him!" I shout, and Cat glares.

"Fuck you!" she hisses.

Heath laughs once then walks over to his desk, sets his tumbler down, and pulls open the drawer. "It seems to me you're upset that little Cat here was willing to go further with me than you." He shrugs, squirting some hand sanitizer into his palms and rubbing them together. "Don't be jealous, son. She was only doing it so her pussy father would keep his job and their home."

"You thought seducing my father would get your dad his house back?" I ask Cat, who doesn't look the least bit apologetic or ashamed.

"Like mother, like daughter." Heath snickers.

"Fuck you both!" Cat yells. Then she walks over to me and jabs her finger into my chest. "I didn't come over here to seduce anyone. Your *father* came on to me at my dad's office and told me he would be willing to make a deal with me. So, I came by here to see what he wanted."

"And what?" I sneer. "Your legs fell open and his finger slipped in?"

Heath lets out a derisive snort, and Cat's eyes water.

"I just—I just wanted to help. He said he would give my dad back his job and let us keep the house. He said he would leave you alone. My dad told you he's a bad guy." Tears slide down her face, and I feel like a piece of shit for being so cruel to her.

"Ahh, so Elliot's been talking shit about me, has he?" Heath swallows back what's left of his drink and slams the glass down onto the desk. "Did he also tell you that your bitch of a mother kept you from me?"

Moving Cat to the side, I cut across the room and get right into Heath's face. "Don't you ever call my mother a bitch!"

"Just calling it like I see it." He shrugs nonchalantly. "She kept my own flesh and blood from me for seventeen goddamned years. That's something a bitch would do."

"I've known you for thirty seconds and in that time you've called my mother a bitch and blackmailed Cat into letting you finger her to save her family. I came over here to give you the benefit of the doubt, but I can see my mother and uncle weren't wrong." I turn my back on Heath and walk over to Cat, taking her by the arm. "Let's go."

Her glassy eyes widen, but she nods. We don't make it out

of the door before Heath speaks. "The two of you move in here with me, and I'll allow Elliot to keep his job." We both freeze in place, then turn around to face Heath, who's not showing any emotion.

"What about our house?" Cat asks before I can. "Can he stay living there?"

"House is mine."

"He sold it to you?" Cat questions, taking a step back into the room.

"I *took* it from him years ago." Heath grins wickedly. "It's my house. I allowed you to live there."

Cat gasps in shock while Heath pushes his chair out and drops into it, tossing his feet up onto his desk like he doesn't have a fucking care in the world. Like he hasn't just turned *her* world upside down.

"None of this makes any sense," Cat whispers so low I'm not sure if she's speaking to one of us or to herself. I place my hand against the small of her back in an attempt to comfort her, but she moves forward, stepping away from my touch and closer to Heath.

"Can he stay living there?" she pleads with a tone that screams desperation.

"No," he answers without any hesitation, his face still devoid of all emotion. "He kept my son from me. He deserves to lose his life."

"But—" Cat begins to argue, but Heath holds his hand up.

"Your father's job in exchange for you both moving in here. That's the deal." He raises his brows at me. "What will it be?"

"Cat?" I ask her, because she's the one whose life will be changing the most. When she doesn't answer me, I bridge the gap between us, so I can see where her head is at. Her eyes are cast down, and I can see she's worrying her bottom lip.

"Cat," I say again, this time lifting her chin slightly, so she's forced to make eye contact with me. "What do you want to do?" I drop my fingers from her face to give her the space I know she needs.

She stays silent for another moment, then turns to Heath.

"What about my horses?" she whispers softly.

"Not my problem," Heath scoffs.

"Yes, they are," I say.

"Fine," he relents. "You can keep your horses here. You have until this weekend to move your shit in here, or the deal is off."

After we're shown out, Cat offers to drive me back home. The short drive is done in silence, both of us with a helluva lot on our minds. For me, I'm still in shock that the first time I met my father was with him fingering the one girl I care about. How could she let him do that to her, yet she won't even give me a chance? I thought it was because she was shy. She mentioned she's never had sex before, so I thought she was just nervous. But then she opened herself up to him with no problem. She did say he was the one who came on to her...fuck! My father better not become my fucking competition once we're living under the same roof. He and I are going to need to have a serious chat.

When we pull up, Cat doesn't make any attempt to get out of the car. "You okay?" I ask.

"I have to tell my dad that I'm going to live with the one man he despises the most in the world. What do you think?"

"I think it's a shitty situation, but at least he will have his job back."

She groans. "Somehow, I don't think he will see it that way. Plus, after all that, he still has to move and now, not only are you being forced to live with Heath, but so am I."

Taking her hand in mine, I bring it up to my lips for a kiss. "I don't agree with what you did, but I know your heart was in the right place. Thank you for trying."

"Theo." She gives me her usual warning glare, but this time I refuse to let her go. If Cat had it her way, I would give up on us without a fight. But after what she did for me today—going to my dad with the intention of doing whatever it was he wanted just so I wouldn't have to move in with him—proves that she has feelings for me as well.

"I can't help how I feel about you," I tell her honestly, taking both of her hands into mine.

"We can't go there," she chides, pulling out of my grasp and getting out of the car. I get out as well and come around the front, blocking her from going inside. When she tries to walk around me, my hands grip her hips to stop her.

"We could," I insist, pulling her closer to me and willing her to feel what I feel.

"Theo, you're hurting me." Her brows furrow, and when I look down, I see my fingers are gripping her tightly.

Reluctantly, I release her. "I'm sorry. I just wish you would give us a chance."

"You have to stop this," she snaps. "Whatever you think you feel for me isn't real, and even if it is, it's not okay."

I let out a frustrated sigh, wishing I could find a way for her to understand that the love I feel for her trumps whatever society deems acceptable. That when I look at her, I don't see my cousin. I see a beautiful, smart, caring young woman. Maybe if we had grown up together I wouldn't feel this way, but we didn't, and I want her. And if she would stop giving a shit about what other people think, she would realize the chemistry we have is worth exploring.

"Just please promise me, you won't go there with my dad again," I plead. I couldn't take it if she gave my father any more of what she won't give me.

Father. Dad. My own flesh.

As much as I want to be excited that I know my father now, I can't. Not after what I just witnessed.

"I promise."

The moment we step into the house and close the door behind us, Uncle Elliot comes running out. "Tell me you didn't go over there!" he yells. "Tell me the two of you didn't go see Heath after I told you not to! Please! Tell me!" he begs, but it's clear from the fear in his tone he already knows we did.

We both stare at him, our silence enough to answer him. His face crumples and he scrubs his face with his palms in frustration. "No," he says bitterly.

"We did," Cat says softly. "But he's giving you back your job."

Uncle Elliot snaps his head up, dropping his hands, and stares wildly at us, his eyes darting back and forth. "In exchange for what?"

Her shoulders hunch as she murmurs, "Theo and me going to live with him."

I watch as Cat's head lowers and her eyes stay trained on the floor. When I look back up, Uncle Elliot's face is twisted up like he's in pain.

"No. No. No. Please, no. Please, Cat. Please tell me you didn't make a deal with him." Uncle Elliot's knees drop to the floor in front of Cat, and she raises her head so she can look at him.

"I'm so sorry, Daddy." She drops to the floor so she's

eye level with her father. "I'll still come to visit you on the weekends."

"He's letting me stay living here?"

"No." She shakes her head. "But now that you have your job we won't have to sell our cars, so I can drive into town and see you."

"Oh, Cat, you have no idea what you've done." Uncle Elliot takes Cat into his arms and hugs her like she's his lifeline. "I should've run just like my sister. Taken you far away from here. Now it's too late."

"It's going to be okay," Cat whispers. "I'm going to be okay."

While still holding his daughter in his arms, Uncle Elliot looks up at me and a single teardrop falls from his eye. "He's done it," he whispers. "He's gotten his revenge."

CHAPTER TWENTY-SIX

The Present...

I'M GOING CRAZY. NANNY LEAVES ME AT A CRUCIAL PART IN HER story so we can have dinner. Mom and Dad were happily discussing a new barn she wants built for the horses, so I don't interrupt to demand more of the story. But when Nanny excuses herself to go home and my parents are playfully bickering over whether or not barns are supposed to be red, I nearly scream in frustration.

"What's going on?" Mom asks, her brows pulled together in concern.

"Boy problems." Not a total lie.

"Something I can take care of?" Dad questions, flexing his bicep muscle and fisting his hand.

I let out a giggle and shake my head. "I can handle it myself."

"That's my girl," he says with a grin. He flashes Mom a knowing look that I don't interpret well. "I'm going to watch the game I DVR'd. Leave you two to your girl talk."

He pulls Mom in for a hug and gives her a sweet kiss before ruffling my hair and leaving us alone in the dining room.

I want what they have. The way Dad's eyes track my mother whenever she's in a room. How her eyes light up and she always smiles for him. It's as though they share a secret bond and I want one. They bicker and give each other hell a lot, but they always make up. Love is present in every argument.

Finn and I argue.

But he's like the rich assholes from Mom and Nanny's story. Further proof that I don't belong with someone like him.

"I'll get this cleaned up," Mom says. "Why don't you grab some Moscato and meet me on the porch swing?"

"Don't tell Dad you're letting me drink," I tease.

"Your secret is safe with me."

While she cleans up from supper, I grab a couple of glasses and the bottle of wine before heading outside. Tonight, the air is crisp. It's a starless night with all the clouds out, so I can't see far beyond the porch.

I set the wine and glasses down to check my phone.

Finn: It's taking everything in me not to come to you. You're not really sick, are you?

My heart aches that Porter hasn't responded. Sometimes, he gets busy and doesn't look at his phone. Not like Finn, who is clearly obsessed with his.

And me.

Me: Oh, I'm sick.

Sick of him.

Finn: Emily, I'm sorry.

I frown as I read his words over and over again.

Me: For what?

Finn: That I make you angry.

I let out a satisfied grunt. He's right. He pisses me off all the time.

Well, not all the time…

Don't think about how his intense stare burns you right to your core. Don't think about the way you feel on fire and light up whenever he's near—like you might blow off like a flaming ember whisking off from a bonfire. He's your best friend and you're not a good fit. Don't think about the way his hand fits perfectly in yours. Don't think about how when you're down, he crawls into your bed, feeds you snacks, and tickles you until you cry. Don't think about how he sometimes brushes your hair behind your ear and lingers his fingers there as though he can't bear to stop touching you.

Don't. Think. About. It.

Finn: But you make me crazy.

"The nerve!" I growl, furious that I was thinking nice things about him.

Finn: You're the only girl who can make me crazy.

My stomach flutters at his words. His stupid words. That was not romantic or sweet. He called me crazy. Asshole.

Me: You're the crazy one!

Possessive, beastly brat.

My mind drifts to the way my skin shivers when he lazily runs his fingers along my bare skin when we watch movies. How he sometimes buries his nose in my hair and inhales me as though I smell good to him. The way he signs his initials F.B. on everything he comes in contact with—notepads, my bare skin, any dust Mom misses when she cleans.

Finn: It sounds like we have more in common than you like to admit.

I hate when he's right. He gets this dumb gorgeous smug grin that I want to wipe right off his face. Sometimes I wonder if it'd melt away if I kissed him. A shiver of delight ripples through me.

Me: I'm not crazy.

My thumping heart begs to differ.

Finn: You're the craziest girl I know.

Me: Go find someone else to bug.

Finn: But you're my favorite.

My heart does a dramatic flop in my chest.

But you're my favorite.

Ignoring him and his stupidly sweet words, I text Porter again. He didn't respond to my last text and I didn't really expect him too. I text him what I know will get a reply.

Me: Want to pick me up and take that drive tonight?

He never comes to my house, aside from picking me up. Sometimes I wish he'd take the time to formally meet my family and hang out, maybe watch a movie or something here. Like Finn. Instead, Porter likes to get me alone. Which, I like too, but sometimes I want more than that. Until he gets on board and wants more too, I have to go with what works. And us going off together alone is what gets me his undivided attention.

Porter: Will you be wearing panties?

I let out a groan, my neck heating. Just once, I wish he were into me for more than a fun time. I keep holding out and it gets me nowhere. I stare at my phone and can't bring myself to reply.

Do I really want to be someone's backup plan? Someone who only becomes important when the other has time?

Finn always has time.

Again, I think about his crooked grin and strong, athletic body. The way he'll chase me around the kitchen island with peanut butter on his hands, taunting me. How it feels when he pins me, swipes it on my cheek, and then dramatically licks it off, making me scream.

Me: Why do you like hanging out with me?

I send the text to Finn, rather than replying to Porter, before I can second-guess myself. With Porter, it's because we fool around. He's a guy and he makes his needs known. But why does Finn hang around? It's not like I satisfy any of his needs.

Finn: I think you know the answer to that question,

angel. You're funny and crazy and beautiful. I like when you fall asleep during the movie and drool all over my shirt. I like when you wake up and your green eyes are soft as you stare at me wordlessly. It's times like those, I want to show you how you make me feel. I'm not looking to cop a feel in the backseat of my car, Emily. With you, I'm looking for a lot more. You deserve a lot more.

My heart catches in my throat as I read his words over and over again. He's right. I do deserve a lot more. A lot more than Porter gives me.

Mom comes out wearing an unusual smile and carrying a blanket. I'm dying to hear the rest of this story, but I'm also freaking out about Finn and his texts. I want to reply, but I need a minute to get a handle on my emotions. I toss my phone on the table and cuddle up beside Mom when she sits down on the swing with me.

But you're my favorite.

Another tug at my heartstrings.

"Want to talk about the boy problems?" Mom asks as she pours us our wine and nods at my phone. She could always sense my mood. I'm guessing I'm that obvious.

I grab my glass and sit back, shaking my head. "No, I want you to tell me about your boy problems. It seemed like everything turned out like it was supposed to in the end. Everyone got their happily ever afters. I need hope."

Hope that I can navigate my feelings. I want to be smart, but my heart is confused. It's doing erratic little flops at the idea of Finn and me in an actual relationship. One that's not just friendly flirting and arguing over silly things. But more. So much more.

And that scares me. Because in all the months I've been hanging out with Porter, my heart has never flip-flopped for him the way it is right now for Finn.

Mom chuckles. "Well, it didn't come easy, that's for sure."

"I'm ready. Give it to me straight."

"Where did Helen leave off?"

"Somewhere around the time when a deal was made with the devil and you had to go live at Windy Hills," I say.

"Ah, it was just getting ugly then."

My phone buzzes, and I ignore it despite the thundering inside my chest. "I can handle some ugly."

It's better than thinking of Finn and his stupid pretty smile and his stupid sweet words.

But you're my favorite.

CHAPTER TWENTY-SEVEN

WHAT THE FUCK?

I look up from where I'm changing the tire on my bike to see Heath pulling into the driveway. In a new car. A fucking Porsche 911 Turbo S with tricked out chrome wheels. I stand and let out a whistle of appreciation. It's metallic black with flecks of silver in the paint that catch the afternoon sun.

Holy shit, it's gorgeous.

He slams the door a little too hard for my liking—because a car that beautiful deserves to be coddled and adored—and tosses the keys my way. I catch them before they hit the ground. My chest tightens, but I don't dare give into hope that it's mine. Heath isn't kind and generous. He's a dick. Usually a dick with a plan. I'm sure this is part of said plan.

"Make sure it's gassed up and then I want you to teach him how to drive it," he says, without looking my way as he strides up to the house.

I fist the keys and stalk after him. "Who?"

He stops and turns to regard me with narrowed eyes. "My son. Who the hell do you think I was talking about?"

Gritting my teeth, I swallow down the urge to throttle the fucker. "So he's really coming to live with us?"

His nostrils flare. "He's. My. Son," he says, punctuating each word as though that explains everything. He motions at the house and the car. "Of course he's coming to live here. This is all his."

I refrain from rolling my eyes. "When will he get here?"

"After school I presume." His expression turns cold. "If they're not here in the next hour, I'll hunt them down myself."

Them?

I frown at him. "His uncle is coming too?"

The cold, calculating smile he wears like a fucking uniform spreads across his face. "No. My son and his pretty little cousin."

Cat.

She's a bit of a diva and kind of a brat, but she can't come live here. Heath would eat her alive.

"Why?" I demand, the word coming out harsher than I intend.

He studies me with curiosity. "Because she made a deal with me. She stays here and her daddy can keep his job."

"You're not going to…" I trail off and run my palm over my sweaty neck. *Fuck her?*

I don't have to say the rest of my question because he knows exactly what I mean. His brown eyes gleam wickedly, making a flash of anger burn through me.

"As tempting as that sounds because she's quite a delicious little girl, I have other plans for her." He stares off down the road where a car is approaching, kicking up dust. "I always have plans."

"What plans?" I ask. Normally I don't care what the fuck Heath does. Now? I fucking care. Him messing with Cat doesn't sit right with me.

"She's going to marry my son," he says blandly. "I'm going to fuck over Elliot once and for all."

"Her cousin?" I bark out, laughing coldly.

He shrugs. "Yeah. So?"

"She can't marry her cousin. It's against the law."

Stalking over to me, he pokes my bare chest. I'm sweaty as fuck from working on my bike, so his finger slips away, his nail scraping me in the process. I hiss at the flare of pain.

"Money says she can marry whoever the fuck she wants," he snaps. "And lucky for me, I have lots of it. That means, she'll do as I fucking say."

I'm ready to press the issue, but Theo and Cat pull up in her black Mustang. As soon as they park, Theo climbs out and throws me a hateful look that matches his lovely father's. The apple didn't fall far from the goddamn tree.

"My son," Heath says in a bored tone. "Harrison will show you how to drive your car."

Theo stops dead in his tracks, losing his glare. He grins like a stupid moron. "This is my car? A Porsche?"

"Happy early birthday," Heath grumbles. "Have Helen show you to your room. I have some work to do."

With those words, Heath storms in the house.

I toss Theo the keys and then walk over to where Cat still sits in the driver's seat of her car. She stares straight ahead at the house, as if she's about to walk right into the boughs of hell. If she only knew.

Theo climbs in his car that probably set Heath back nearly two hundred grand and fires up the engine. Immediately, it sputters as he kills it. Dumbass.

Smirking, I rap on Cat's window with my knuckle. "Hey. Better close that mouth before you catch bugs."

She snaps her mouth shut and pushes on the door, shoving me out of the way. "Don't talk to me, pig."

I snort with laughter. "Stallion, remember? Why are you mad, jailbait? I thought you'd be happy to see me." I waggle my brows at her and flash her a panty-melting grin.

Her fury melts away as she boldly stares down my bare chest. When her eyes make it to my lower stomach, she swallows and darts her eyes back to mine. "I'm legal. I had my birthday a couple of days ago."

Stepping toward her, I cock my head. "I missed your birthday?"

Her bottom lip wobbles and she looks down at her feet. A tear streaks down her cheek. I'd enjoyed fucking with her, but she's upset. I'm not a total dick. Reaching forward, I run my knuckle across the wetness on her skin.

"Don't worry," I murmur, "I'll make it up to you."

She lifts her chin and regards me with watery eyes. "It better be good because this was the worst birthday ever."

I smirk at her. "I hear a challenge." My eyes drift over to where Theo is killing the engine again. "And I'm very competitive, mustang girl."

A smile tugs at her lips. "Mustang girl and stallion?"

Throwing my head back, I boom with laughter. "So you admit I'm a stallion?"

She gives me a shove and sticks her tongue out. "I prefer pig."

I follow her around to the trunk and help her pull out some suitcases. Theo curses and climbs out of his Porsche.

"Show me how to drive this thing," he grumbles. "I think it's defective."

The only thing defective around here is him.

"Later," I grunt. "I'm busy."

He sees me trying to grab all of Cat's luggage and seems to snap out of brat mode. He strides over and hugs Cat.

"Everything is going to be okay," he vows to her. "I'll protect you from him." He shoots me a withering glare.

She doesn't need protecting from me. Ignoring him, I start carrying her shit into the house. Something good smelling wafts from the kitchen and my stomach grumbles.

"She takes my old room," Heath calls out from his office. "And I expect everyone for a family dinner."

Family dinner?

Since fucking when?

Rolling my eyes, I stomp up the stairs and take her stuff to the room that's long since been abandoned. It's a small room that used to be for sewing according to Helen. A simple double bed sits on one corner against a wall of bookshelves. Beside the bed is a small table and lamp. In the corner, there's an armoire. A window overlooks the barn and beyond that the lake. In the far distance you can see Low Valley Estate.

Fucking Heath.

Forcing her to look at her house.

"Whatever," I grumble under my breath as I drop her suitcases to the floor.

Voices resound from the hallway. Heath's voice is booming with excitement as he speaks to Theo.

"Let me show you to your room, son," he says.

Cat stands in the doorway as the footsteps fade down the hallway. Her lips are pressed together as she takes in the space.

"It has a nice view," I grunt as though that will make everything okay.

She swallows and nods. "Thanks."

I look past her out the hallway and then tug her inside. She lets out a squeak when I close the door, shutting us in the small room. Taking her hand, I give it a squeeze. It's clammy in my grip. I walk her over to the window but don't let go.

"If you need anything, come find me. Heath is a dick, but he's not the biggest dick around here. I'll knock his crazy ass out if I need to," I tell her with a growl.

Her features soften as she regards me. "He hates my dad."

"I know," I say, shaking my head. "It's all I ever hear about.

I think it was his favorite bedtime story to tell me growing up." And what he left out, the journals filled me in.

She shudders. "I would have run away if I were you."

I frown and squeeze her hand again. "But *you* ran *here*, mustang girl. Out of the field and into the burning barn. Stupid. So very stupid."

Her nostrils flare as she tries to jerk her hand back. "You're an ass just like him."

I arch a brow at her. "Do you really believe that?"

"No," she admits with a huff. "God, I hate him."

"Join the club. I'm acting president of the Heath Hate Club. We're looking for a new VP."

She lets out a giggle, and I decide I'm going to do whatever it takes to get her to do that more often. This house is a miserable place. Her laughter just lightened it up.

"I'm scared," she whispers when her giggles fade.

I release her hand to cup her cheek. She doesn't shy away from my touch. Staring into her pretty green eyes, I inhale her scent and try to provide some comfort. Truth is, she may be spoiled, but she's about to get a taste of the shitty life. I know firsthand what that life tastes like.

It's cold and lonely.

"You won't be alone," I blurt out. "I'll be here."

Instead of scoffing that she barely knows me, she nods. As though my words soothe her. My chest expands with pride.

We stare at each other for a long moment. The air seems to crackle with electricity. I find that my stare settles on her plump, juicy lips. Lips I'd love to suck on. She darts out her pink tongue and wets her bottom lip. I have to suppress a groan.

"You won't be alone," I say again, my voice barely a whisper.

She tilts her head up and bites on her bottom lip, her eyes burning with intensity. I could kiss her. I want to kiss her. As I lower my head, giving in to the urge, the door flies open.

"Cat," Theo barks out.

She jerks away from me and crosses her arms over her chest. "Yeah?"

"Are you okay?" he demands as he strides in. He glowers at me as he pulls her against his chest.

I smirk at him. "She looks okay to me."

All humor fades when I notice Heath watching from the doorway. His eyes are narrowed as he takes in the scene.

"Go wash your filth, orphan. You're stinking up my house," Heath says coldly.

Theo snorts, and I flip him off.

I shoulder past Heath but don't say anything as I head down the hallway to my room to shower. His eyes bore into the back of my head, but I don't let it show it affects me.

Truth is, I'm pissed.

Whatever game he's playing has just gone to another level. I thought I knew Heath, but apparently, he's got his hands back in his bag of tricks and is ready to play with more people. And fuck if it doesn't piss me off something fierce that Cat is one of those people.

You're not alone, Cat.

And for once, I'm not either.

"This is good, Helen," Cat says softly. "Thank you. How did you know it was my favorite?"

Heath, from the head of the table, lets out a mocking laugh. "We know everything about you, girl."

She bristles and shoots me a panicked look. I wink at her. Her shoulders relax and she pokes around at her food. I've only been around this girl for a minute and I can already tell she's nothing like her mother—at least the one from the journals. Whereas Cat is sweet and soft-spoken, her mother was a raging bitch. Reading her journals, I often wondered if maybe the woman had something psychologically wrong with her with as hot and cold as she was.

"How did you and Mom meet?" Theo asks Heath around a mouthful of food. His arm is over the back of Cat's chair, and it irks me how possessive he is over her.

"She wanted my dick and I gave it to her," Heath says, shrugging.

Helen lets out a huff. "Mr. Heath!"

"He asked," Heath grunts.

Theo's cheeks have turned red either from embarrassment or anger. Judging by the way he fists his hand around his fork, I'm going to go with anger.

"It looks like Heath just gives his dick to everyone around these parts," Cat snips, her eyes on her plate.

Heath laughs. "I'll give it to you too if you ask nicely."

Theo and I both rise to our feet. My chair knocks back and hits the floor with a loud clank.

"Don't be an asshole or we'll leave," Theo growls. "Consequences be damned."

Cat tugs at his arm. "Theo, it's fine."

He glowers down at her. "It's not fine. He can't talk to you like that."

Heath sips his wine and motions for Theo to sit. "Calm down, son, I'm just joking. Apparently Cat is the only one who knows that." He shoots me a satisfied smirk.

I yank my chair up from the floor and settle back in it. Helen pats my shoulder, but it does nothing to calm me.

Theo takes his seat, but he's stiff and no longer eating. I shovel in the rest of my food to keep from knocking my fist through Heath's pearly white teeth.

"So, Theo," Heath says, changing the subject. "What are your plans for after high school?"

Theo relaxes and smiles at Cat. "We're going to go to Yale together."

Heath snorts. "Oh really? Cat, you have a hidden college fund I don't know about? Do I need to make your dad forfeit that as well?"

Theo gapes at Heath in horror. Fuck, he has so much to learn about his dad.

Heath grins. "Kidding, son."

Theo's jaw clenches, but he continues as though he actually believes Heath. First thing to know about Heath is he doesn't joke about anything. He's Mr. Fucking Serious about everything, especially when it comes to revenge.

"We're going to go to Yale and then we thought about traveling abroad," Theo says. "I grew up in Paris. I'd love to take Cat there one day."

She gives him a fake-ass smile and he seems satisfied by it. While he prattles along about their plans, I watch her. Her silky brown hair is pulled into a neat ponytail and her makeup has been scrubbed clean. So young and innocent. It maddens me that she's in the lion's den. Succulent and mouthwatering. I know it will only be a matter of time before Heath tries to take a bite.

I turn my glare on Heath, who watches me with interest. My jaw clenches as I give him my best, *You touch her and I'll fuck you up, old man* look.

He seems to interpret it because his brown eyes gleam with challenge. Heath may have more money than God, but I have something money doesn't buy.

And that's a mean right hook.

Once I'm sure everyone is asleep, I sneak into Cat's room. When I kneel down, I slide my palm over her mouth.

"Wake up, mustang girl."

She starts to scream but thankfully I have her mouth covered.

"Shhh," I murmur. "I want to show you something."

Her head nods and I slowly pull my hand away. It's dark, but the moonlight shines in through her window, lighting up her sleepy eyes.

"Where are we going?" she asks, her voice a breathy whisper.

"I owe you a birthday present."

Her teeth flash in the moonlight as she grins. "Really?"

"Really," I grunt as I grab her hands and pull her to her feet. "Now come on and be quiet."

I keep one of her hands in my grip as I guide her from the room and down the hallway. We pass my room, then Theo's, and finally Heath's. The last door at the end always remains locked, but I have a key. Pulling the key from the chain around my neck, I unlock the door and slip inside with her. I quietly push it closed and then carefully take her around the covered furniture to a closet. It's pitch-black in the closet, but I know it like the back of my hand. I pull her inside and close the door behind us.

"This way," I whisper as I guide her deeper into the long walk-in closet. It's an L-shape and when we reach the corner and turn, we are in my favorite place in the whole house. My spot. "Sit."

"There are pillows," she murmurs.

"I used to hide out in here when I was a kid. Heath never looked for me here," I tell her. I pull the chain from my neck and then reach for her in the dark. My palm brushes against her hair, but she doesn't pull away. I manage to slide the chain around her neck. "Now you can hide here too if you want."

She's quiet for a moment and then she reaches for my hand. "Thank you."

I lean past her and push on a small LED light I stuck on the wall. The small space glows faintly in a bluish white light. Her face is shadowed to me, but when she turns to look at the light, I can see her profile and she's smiling.

"I like this place," she says, looking at all the pillows strewn about. She reaches over and grabs a plush blanket and pulls it into her lap. "Maybe I'll never leave."

"Stay as long as you want."

She turns to look at me once more, but I can't see her features in the shadows. "Why are you being so nice to me?"

I frown and lean back against the wall, releasing her hand. "Do I have to have a reason?"

"Most people do."

"I'm not like most people," I grumble.

She moves to sit beside me, leaning her back against the wall too. Our legs are outstretched in front of us but hers are covered with the blanket. I tug some of the covers over my bare legs and when my leg slides against her smooth one, my dick hardens.

"I did it for my dad," she says softly. "I couldn't bear to see him lose everything."

"So you sacrificed yourself?"

She starts to cry and I feel guilty. Wrapping my arm around her, I pull her to my side and kiss the top of her head. Her hand fists the front of my T-shirt as she cries against me. We're quiet as she sobs and eventually her tears dry up.

"Got that out of your system?" I tease.

She lets out a breathy giggle. "For now."

"Good, because I wanted to give you your present."

"I thought this place was my present."

"Part of it," I tell her as I lean over to pull the plastic tub my way. "I think this room was your mom's sitting room of some sort. Maybe her own private library or reading room. I'm not sure. Heath keeps some pictures in her old room but most of them are in here."

"Pictures of my mom?"

"Yeah."

She scrambles for the lid and pulls it off. Her hand dives into the box and she pulls out a handful of pictures. The light is dim, but it's obvious she looks just like her mother. Her mother was always smiling, but in the pictures with *him*, her smile was the widest.

"I hate him," she says, running her thumb over Heath's face. In this particular picture, they're probably around thirteen or fourteen. He stares at her as though she's his everything. I've never seen him look that way in real life. Only in pictures. Only with her.

"He's a dick," I agree.

She thumbs through many photos before turning to me. "How could she love someone like him? No wonder she married my dad. He's good and gentle and kind. Heath is a monster."

"Yeah," I say as I reach into the tub. "She didn't think so." I hand her one of the many journals that belonged to her mother when she lived here as a girl.

Cat takes the offered journal and starts reading. She scoffs and snorts, obviously in disagreement over how wonderful Heath is. I've read them all. Some just detail out the things she and Heath did for the day. Some entries are love notes to him. Other entries are explicit recollections of their lovemaking in their teenage years.

"This is my dad," I tell her, pointing to another picture I find. My chest does a squeeze, but I ignore the bite of pain. I don't remember him. Not really. My earliest memories were of Heath and Helen. I have glimpses of what my dad looked like. The pictures fill in the blanks.

"What's his name?" she asks.

"Hunter Crenshaw. He's dead."

"That's my mom's brother," she says softly. "You don't look like him."

"I was adopted," I grumble. "Guess my mom didn't want to keep me."

She snaps her gaze to mine. "She left you with Heath?"

"She left me with my dad, but he overdosed on pills and died. It was actually the same night your mom died. Heath said he looked for my mom because 'she owed him,' but he never found her. I don't think she ever wanted to be found." I shrug as though it doesn't bother me. But it fucking bothers me. If it weren't for Heath, I would've starved to death.

"I'm sorry," Cat says, patting my thigh over the blanket, "that's tragic." She doesn't remove her hand.

"Life deals us a shitty hand, but if I've learned anything from that asshole, it's that you have to play the hand you're dealt. And play it well."

I slide my hand over hers and thread my fingers with hers. "You're not alone here."

She turns and presses a kiss to my lips, surprising me. Her other palm finds my cheek and she runs her thumb along my scruff. When her mouth parts, I lean in and brush my lips along hers. My tongue swipes out, tasting hers, and a low, hungry growl rumbles through me. I'm about to grab hold of her and kiss her until we're both desperate for air, but then we hear it.

"Cat?"

We both freeze and her wide eyes meet mine.

"It's Theo," I grumble. "Better get out of here before he finds our spot."

She grins at me and gives me another chaste kiss. "Thank you. This was the best birthday present."

The blanket slides away and I get a glimpse of her long, smooth legs before she scampers off and disappears around the corner. I pick up the picture of her mother and stare at her smiling face.

I can certainly see how she drove Heath crazy.

Cat's been here barely a day and I can't fucking think straight.

But I'll be goddamned if I turn into him.

CHAPTER TWENTY-EIGHT

Cat

It's Friday night lights, and just like every year, the first game of the football season is Heights Academy versus Windfall public, the only other high school in town. The game is always held here at Heights because our stadium is state-of-the-art whereas Windfall's field looks like a dirty patch of grass with some rusted bleachers on each side of the field.

On one side of the stadium—where I'm currently standing on the sidelines—are the wealthy families dressed in their Armani and Prada, who drive around in their Beemers and Benzes and can afford the five-figure monthly fee to send their kids to Heights. On the other side are the families who wish they were on this side. They're the families who shop at the local mall or Walmart, drive around in a Honda mini-van, and can barely afford for their kids to go on the end-of-the-year field trip at their public school.

For my entire life I thought I was part of the family who belonged on this side of the field, but now as I look around, it hits me that looks can be deceiving. Sure, my father drives an expensive car, and we used to live in an expensive home. We dress the part, look the part, hell, we even speak the part. But it is all a farce.

We're not rich, we're owned.

I'm only able to go to school here because Mr. Heath allows me to. My father is able to drive the car he drives because Mr. Heath allows him to. My clothes, my car, my education. It's all because Mr. Health allows for it to happen. And with one snap of his fingers, he was able to take whatever he wanted away. My father is now living in a tiny one-bedroom apartment in town. Our home is empty. Our lives turned upside down. And I don't doubt for a second, everything Mr. Heath has done is because he begrudges my father for being with my mother when he feels she should've been with him instead.

The more I think about everything I've learned the last couple weeks, the more I feel like a fraud. Knowing my life has been one big lie has me itching to get out of this cheer outfit, away from this school, and go where I belong. I guess the question is, where exactly do I belong? Right now, I haven't the slightest clue. I used to think I belonged wherever my father was, but now I can't even be around him without feeling resentment toward the lies he's chosen to shove down my throat my entire life.

I let my mind drift back to several of the entries I read from my mom's journals. Where she admitted she was in love with Heath but couldn't stand the idea of being poor. Her entries are what led me to ask my dad how things managed to change so much from what my mom wrote.

Without being able to look me in the eyes, he shook his head and frowned and said his love for my mom was his biggest downfall. He was so blinded by his love for her, he didn't see Heath coming. And before he knew it, he lost just about everything. It was clear my father never read her journals, and I didn't have it in me to tell him the truth of what they entailed.

With the journals messing with my head and heart, and forcing me to question everything, I decided to pay her grave a visit. I think I was hoping by being close to her, I would find the answers I was looking for. I found my answers, but it wasn't my mom who gave them to me.

I should be at school, but I'm not. I've never skipped before, but I just couldn't bring myself to be around other people today. My heart is hurting and I don't know how to handle it. Normally, when I have a problem, I go to my father. But this isn't something I can go to him about. I could, but then he would be hurting as well. And the last thing I want to do is hurt my father. He's already been through enough. So, instead, I took the day off school to visit the person who is the reason for my heartache.

My mother.

Luckily, living with Mr. Heath is nothing like living with my father. For one, he doesn't care where I go or what I do. He won't even notice that after I dropped Theo off, I left campus and came straight here. To my mother's grave. I don't visit her often. She's located in our family cemetery, and while it's pretty in a creepy sort of way, with big shade trees and tons of flowers everywhere, I never bought into needing to be here to feel close to her.

But right now, I'm desperate.

Ever since Harrison showed me my mother's journals I've been reading through them, and with each entry, I'm wishing he'd never shown them to me. Growing up, the only parent I ever had was my father, and he wasn't just my father. He was my best friend. He's always been there: for every school play, recital, sports event… I couldn't ask for a more loving, hands-on dad. I never knew my mom, but every milestone, my dad would say things like, "Your mother would've been so proud of you" or "She would've loved to be here." And I always believed him. I believed, had she been alive, we would've been a happy family.

But now, as I read her journals, I'm hit with the cold realization that the picture my father painted of my mother all these years was drawn while being blinded by his one-sided love for her. Meanwhile, I've yet to find a single entry that says she loved my father or that she wanted to be a mother. Her younger years were sweet and wistful. It's evident she loved Mr. Heath very much. Just not enough to put him above her love for money. But her later years leading up to her death, I'm not sure she loved anybody, not even herself.

I turn the page of the current journal I'm reading.

Dear Diary,

My heart has been shattered into a million pieces. It's hard to breathe. Heath finally returned and what happens? I find out I'm pregnant. Damn, Elliot! Now, Heath is gone once again. Only this time he's left me for another woman. For Isabel Lincoln, no less! How could he do this to me? He is supposed to love me! You don't leave someone you love! It's not my fault I fell pregnant. He should've returned sooner! He should've never left. I hate him! I hate him for leaving. I hate Elliot for getting me pregnant! I hate my father for writing that stupid will. I hate him for dying before changing it! I hate my brother for firing Heath. I want Heath back. I want to NOT be pregnant. Every day I wake up and wish for it all to be a nightmare. That I will go to the doctor and he will tell me it's all a mistake and I am in fact not pregnant. Elliot is so excited to become a father. I can't even stand to be in the same room as him. I just want Heath back. I want him to pull me into his arms and tell me everything will be okay. But he's gone. And I'm afraid this time, he might not come back.

My eyes close and a single tear hits the page. The wetness causes the ink to run down the paper and blur several of the words. Not only did she not love my father, but she wished I was never born.

"What are you doing here?" The masculine voice has my head shooting up in surprise. I've been here for several hours and nobody has come by. "Shouldn't you be at school?"

My eyes land on Mr. Heath. He's standing above me, dressed impeccably in his three-piece suit with a scowl marring his face.

"I'm visiting my mom," I tell him, wiping the tears from my lids. "Is that why you're here?" I ask dumbly. Why else would he be here at my family's burial plot? Surely, he doesn't have any family here.

"She wasn't supposed to be buried here," he says with a look of disgust. "But your father, like the fraud he is, buried her here anyway."

"Where was she supposed to be buried?"

"Under her favorite willow." When he speaks now, his lips almost upturn into a small smile. Then his eyes land on the journal in my hands. "Snooping through my closet, I see."

"How did you get her journals anyway?" I ask curiously. When she passed away, she was living with my father at Low Valley Estate.

"I took them," he states matter-of-factly. "Just like everything else I took that your father didn't deserve."

I simply nod. I can't argue with him there. It's obvious this man takes and takes and takes without considering for even a second the consequences of his actions.

"So, are you enjoying the book?" he asks with a devilish smirk, and I know he's read them. They are filled with recounts of many nights she and Mr. Heath made love. Some in vivid detail. My cheeks heat up and Mr. Heath laughs.

"Don't worry about coming across any sex scenes with your father. You won't find any in there. He was dull and nothing they experienced together was worth writing about." Once again, I can't argue with him. Based on what I've read, it's clear my mother wasn't exactly attracted to my father.

"I was actually reading the journal of her pregnancy." I don't know why I tell him this. Maybe I'm hoping he will say something that contradicts her words in this journal. That maybe she turned to these books when she was down and out, but in real life, she was actually content and happy…and wanted me.

Mr. Heath stares at me for a moment and when he doesn't say anything, I add, "I don't think she wanted me." I hold my breath, waiting for him to speak. I've only known Mr. Heath a short while, but in that time, I've only known him to be blunt, honest, straight to the point. He doesn't sugarcoat anything.

"She didn't," he confirms in a cold tone. "If she hadn't died, she would have left you with your father and started a life with me. You were a mistake. A deadly one." His gaze holds my own and I will *the tears not to spill. I don't doubt he's telling the truth, but I'm not about to let him see how much that truth hurts. Instead, I stand and step away from the grave.*

"She's all yours," I whisper as I walk away.

That picture my father painted was definitely skewed.

After reading her journals, I've concluded that either my father really was blinded by love, or he chose to believe the lies, not wanting to deal with the truths. In the end, he was so lost in those lies, he didn't see what Mr. Heath was plotting and planning. When my father lost it all, instead of acknowledging that and finding his way back, he allowed for a vindictive evil man to pin him up against the wall by his throat. And because of the choices he made and the lies he told himself, now I'm in the same situation. Living in the devil's lair and allowing him to call all the shots. Every night I spend at Windy Hills feels like Mr. Heath's fingers are little by little being tightened around my neck. I'm slowly suffocating, and soon all the oxygen will be forced from my body and all the life I once felt inside of me will be completely sucked out of me, leaving me dead inside.

"Cat," Anne yells, "Theo is going for the touchdown."

I take a deep breath and remember where I am. Raising my pom-poms, I call out the next cheer. "End zone, and go!"

The squad immediately begins to cheer in unison. "The end zone is what we're looking for! So come on, Heights! Take that ball and score!" Our arms fly straight up into an H just as Theo catches the ball and runs toward the end zone. When his feet make it over the line, the crowd screams and claps.

"Touchdown!" we all shout, shaking our pom-poms in front of us. The buzzer rings out, indicating the game is over and Heights Academy has won: 28-14.

"Party at my house!" Charlotte announces as we all climb into our vehicles. Because Theo still hasn't gotten the hang of how to drive a clutch yet—and refuses to ask Harrison again for help—he's been catching a ride with me to school every day. He jumps into the passenger seat, freshly showered, and grins wide.

"Did you see that shit?" he asks, clearly still pumped from their win.

"I did! You were on fire!" I smile back, thankful he's stopped pressing me for more, and our friendship seems to be back on track. I don't think I could handle having our relationship on the rocks on top of everything else. I might not feel the way Theo *thinks* he feels about me, but I do care about him. He's become an important person in my life, and our friendship means a lot to me. He's also the only person who knows the truth about our living situation. Everyone else thinks we're having our home renovated and staying with Theo's dad until the renovations are complete.

We arrive at Charlotte's house and I park along the road, not wanting my vehicle to get blocked in. Charlotte's parents go out of town at least one week a month and every time they leave, she throws a massive party complete with alcohol, weed, and God knows what other recreational drugs. My dad would kill me if I let hundreds of kids get trashed under his roof while he's not home.

Not that I would ever throw a party under my dad's roof, especially since his current home can barely fit the three of us in it, let alone the entire student body. My thoughts travel to *my* current home: Windy Hills Estate. I giggle as I imagine the fit Mr. Heath would throw if I threw a party. I've been walking on eggshells around his place, afraid of what he'll do to me if I upset him. Thankfully, he hasn't tried anything since I've moved in, but once in a while when our paths cross, whether it's at the table for dinner or when I get up in the middle of the night to get a drink of water, he makes it a point to stare at me a beat too long, to run his gaze over my body a little too slowly, almost as if he's trying to taunt me. I try not to let it get to me, but every time his tongue darts out to wet his bottom lip, my vagina clenches as if it has a mind of its own and remembers his finger inside of me while his tongue licked my hardened nipple. The biggest mistake I made that day was pretending it was Harrison. It allowed my walls to come down and enjoy everything he did to me.

Now, instead of feeling disgust toward Mr. Heath, I'm left feeling turned-on. And it doesn't help that Harrison kissed me in the closet, leaving me wanting more. Wondering if given the chance, he could bring me the same kind of pleasure Mr. Heath *almost* brought me to.

Of course, the chances of that happening are slim since Harrison hasn't given me the time of day since that night in the closet, whereas I experienced the most memorable kiss of my life. Obviously, he didn't feel the same way, though, because since that night, he's barely even acknowledged I exist. Honestly, if I didn't remember the kiss so vividly, I would think I imagined the entire thing. I've gone back to our secret spot a few times, hoping he would follow me in and we could maybe pick up where we left off, but no such luck. When he's not at work, he's at home in the garage. And when he's not in the garage, he's in his room with the door shut.

Dammit! I need to stop thinking about these damn men! What I need to focus on is using my living situation to my advantage. I might be stuck living under Mr. Heath's roof to keep my father employed, but that doesn't mean I have to allow him to control me. He thinks he's won this game, but maybe it's time I show him I'm a worthy opponent. Starting with a house party. What's the worst he can do? Ground me? Take away my car? I scoff at the thought. Then an idea hits me…

If he took my car, maybe I could convince Harrison to take me to school on his motorcycle. The thought has a river of heat flooding through me. My friends would have a fit if they saw me pull up on the back of his bike. Sure, he's not on the same rung of their social ladder, but not even my rich friends can deny how hot Harrison is.

I'm reminded once again of our kiss. The gentle yet possessive way his lips consumed mine and—

"What's got you looking so happy?" Theo asks, stealing me from my thoughts of Harrison. When I look up, I see he's standing next to me with the driver side door open. I didn't even notice him get out. He extends his hand for me and I take it, stepping out of my car. He closes the door behind me and keeping my hand in his, guides us up the sidewalk.

"I was just thinking how much fun it would be to throw a party at Mr. Heath's."

Theo stops in his tracks and turns around to face me.

"Will you please drop the mister? We live with him and he's my dad. He's not exactly a stranger anymore."

"Sorry." I shrug. "It's habit. So what do you think?"

"About throwing a party there?"

"Yeah." I nod. "It's not like he's going to kick us out, and you know everyone has always wondered what the inside of his monstrous mansion looks like." I internally roll my eyes as I remember when I told my friends we were living there temporarily. They all wanted to know what it's like to live with the illustrious brooding and wealthy Mr. Heath. What his home looks like. What he eats. Does he ever smile?

"You barely even come out of your room when you're home. Now you want to throw a party?" Theo questions.

No, I want to piss off Heath. But I don't tell him that. Ever since we've moved in there, Theo has been all about trying to get to know his father. He even invited him to come and watch him play tonight. Of course the asshole just cackled and told him recreational sports are for pussies. For a brief moment after he said that, I was almost positive Theo considered quitting the team. But before he could give it too much thought, I grabbed him by the arm and told him we needed to get going.

"Maybe it will help me feel more comfortable. You know…like a housewarming party." I bat my lashes and Theo smiles warmly at me.

"Okay, I'll talk to him."

"Or we could just throw it." I giggle, imagining the shocked look on Heath's face when he sees hundreds of teenagers all over his house, playing beer pong, drinking his expensive liquor, fucking on his couches. "Please!"

"Fine!" Theo relents. "We can throw a party if it will make you happy. Now, can we please go inside and celebrate this win?" He lets go of my hand and pulls me into him, tickling my sides.

"Yes!" I squeal. "Tonight, we celebrate!"

"Have you seen Theo?" I ask Clifton, one of Theo's friends and the quarterback of the football team. The moment we stepped foot into the house, Theo was pulled in one direction by his fellow teammates for a game of beer pong, and I was pulled in the opposite direction by Charlotte so she could tell me all about a new guy she met and has the hots for. Several hours later, and I'm exhausted and ready to go home. Being the good friend that I am—and not wanting to be stuck here overnight—I agreed to be the designated driver, so Theo could celebrate the win. Now it's after midnight and I'm over hanging out with everyone else who is trashed and making fools out of themselves while I'm still sober.

Clifton bounces the ping-pong ball against the kitchen table—that is doubling as their beer pong table—into a cup of beer and everyone cheers. "I think I saw him upstairs with Anne earlier."

"Thanks!"

I climb the stairs and head down the hallway, opening each door, but not finding Theo or Anne. I do find several couples getting their freak on, though. When I get to the last door, which is Charlotte's room, I open the door quietly in case there's another couple going at it. And what I find has me frozen in place.

Sitting on the edge of the bed with his head thrown back and his eyes closed is Theo. Anne, like Clifton said, is in here as well, on her knees with her lips wrapped around Theo's dick. His fist is tangled in her hair and he's pushing her head up and down while she slurps and gags loudly. But that's not what has me frozen in place. It's what he's murmuring while she's slurping and gagging.

"Fuck yes, Kitty Cat. Suck me good." Holy shit! Please tell me that's the pet name he's given her. Please, please don't let it be my name he's calling out.

I'm about to back out of the room when he moans again. "Fuck, Cat." Bile rises up my throat at the thought of my cousin imagining it's me giving him head.

Just as I'm about to leave, he lifts his head and locks eyes with me. It must dawn on him that I just heard him call out my name because he pushes Anne off him, completely disregarding her, and stands, coming straight toward me. I glance down at his dick, which is still hard and hanging out, and wonder why in the world Anne was gagging. It doesn't seem like it's big enough to cause someone to gag…but then again, I've never had one in my mouth…or in any of my holes for that matter.

Following my gaze, Theo's eyes go wide before he quickly tucks himself back into his pants and zips them up.

"Tell me I misunderstood," I say, and he at least has the decency to look at me sheepishly.

"Dammit, Theo!" I thought he had gotten past his feelings for me, or at least understood nothing was going to happen between us. He's been such a good friend these last couple weeks. He hasn't tried anything. I thought we were on the same page.

"Let me explain," he begs, and that's when I remember Anne is still in the room. She's now standing and watching our entire interaction, and she doesn't look the least bit confused or upset that the guy she was giving a blow job to was *not* calling out her name.

Feeling ridiculously embarrassed and not wanting to have this conversation in front of one of my best friends, I turn my back on Theo and run down the hallway. I hear him bellow my name as I descend the stairs and run out the front door, but I don't stop or acknowledge him. When I reach my car, I jump in and drive away. I chance a glance in my rearview mirror and see Theo standing there with his head hanging down, his body bent at the waist, and his hands resting on his knees. A minute later, my phone vibrates in my pocket, but I don't check it. I know it's him.

Turning the music up, I try to get lost in the lyrics, wanting to forget about what just happened, but I can't stop replaying the way Theo moaned out my name. The look on his face when he realized I heard him. He wasn't mad or upset. He was embarrassed. All this time, I thought he had some weird crush on me that would go away in time, but now I'm beginning to see it's more than that to him.

The first tear pricks my eye as the realization hits that this isn't something we can just bounce back from. This wasn't him trying to cop a feel or sneak a kiss. This was my cousin moaning out my damn name while getting his dick sucked by another girl, who seemed all too okay with everything. I'm almost back to Windy Hills when my phone goes off for the millionth time and I lose it. How am I supposed to look at Theo after this? How am I supposed to live and sleep under the same roof as him? He promised to be there for me. Now I'm just supposed to what, act like it didn't happen? Pretend like he doesn't have some weird infatuation with me? Am I supposed to just take him to school like everything is okay? Oh my God! School! What if Anne tells everyone what happened?

With my eyes filled with tears of embarrassment, I pull my still-vibrating phone out of my pocket and chuck it across my car. It hits the window and falls to the floor, continuing to vibrate.

"Are you fucking kidding me?" I yell out as my cries get harder. Not able to take another second of the taunting vibration, I lean over to snatch the phone off the floor, so I can turn it off.

When I extend my arm and see it's still out of my grasp, I look back up at the road, and after confirming nobody else is on this road but me, I unlock my seatbelt, so I can extend my reach. I've almost gotten it when I feel something hit the bottom of my car and I'm jerked forward. Momentarily forgetting about the cell phone, I put both hands back on the wheel as my car continues to drive up onto the median. In fear of my car flipping over, I grip the steering wheel tighter and try to gain back control of my car. But it's too late. The car grinds up against the middle of the median and bottoms out. I press my brake pedal and the car comes to an abrupt stop.

"Dammit!" I pound my fist against my steering wheel. I put the car in reverse and slowly back up off the median, flinching when I hear a loud screeching sound coming from under my car.

"It's okay," I say to calm myself. "That's just the bottom of the car. It's low to the ground and the median is kind of high." I continue in reverse until my car is back, safely on the road.

"All right." I take a breath of relief and put the car in drive. I press my foot against the gas pedal and drive forward a few feet. The screeching noise has now added a grinding sound to the mix, but it seems to be driving okay. Figuring I'm only a few miles from home, I continue to drive slowly down the dark road, the ear-piercing noise getting louder the farther I drive. And that's when I hear the rumbling of a motorcycle behind me. Briefly, closing my eyes, I send a quick prayer up to God that it's anyone but Harrison on that bike. I look behind me, but I can't make out who it is.

He's wearing a black helmet over his head, so I can't see his face, and suddenly I'm nervous. If this isn't Harrison and I'm on this deserted road alone with a broken car and this stranger following me, there's a good chance I'm about to become one of those people on a milk carton. I pick up my speed—my car now completely shaking under me—but the guy on the bike is obviously able to keep up.

I drive for another half a mile when I reach one of the few streetlights on this road. Of course, it's red. I consider running through it, afraid if I stop, I'm going to become another statistic. Instead, I lightly tap my brake and let my car coast slowly, praying the light will change quickly.

When I glance back and don't see the bike behind me, my heart begins to race. *Where the hell did he go?* Still hearing the rumbling of his bike, I look to my left and see he's now next to me—in the wrong lane! The streetlight shines brightly over the both of us, and I'm finally able to get a better look at the man on the bike.

And I would recognize that body anywhere. His neck, a collection of thick, manly tendons that are connected to his powerful shoulders—which are covered in beautiful art that extend down his muscular biceps all the way to his thick forearms ending at his wrists.

"Pull over!" Harrison yells, knocking me out of my drool fest and confirming what I already know—that it is in fact him on the bike.

Can this night get any worse?

"Pull over!" he shouts again, and I do as he says. After crossing through the four-way stop, I pull my broken Mustang over onto the shoulder of the road, then turn it off and get out. Harrison pulls up in front of my car and cuts his ignition. He pulls his helmet off, revealing his familiar buzzed haircut, and I stifle a moan, still wishing for the opportunity to run my fingers across the top and see what it feels like.

His hand smacks down on my hood and he bends at the waist to check out the underside of my car. I use the moment to check out his ass. Unlike the boys at school who either wear khakis or baggy ripped jeans, Harrison is always in jeans that fit his perfect ass and muscular thighs just right. He stands back up, and reluctantly I force myself to focus on his face and not check out the front of him.

"What the hell happened?" Harrison snaps.

"I think I broke my tire." I shrug, unsure.

"You think you broke your tire," he repeats my words slowly.

"Yeah." I nod. "I was driving and my tire hit the median." I don't bother to tell him it was actually the entire underside of my car that hit it. Semantics.

Letting out a loud sigh of frustration, Harrison's eyes close and his head tilts up to the sky like he's praying to God to give him some patience. His hands come up to scrub the front of his face, and that's when I lose the internal battle within myself to not check him out. My eyes leave his face and land on the delicious six pack of abs that are peeking out from the bottom of his fitted shirt.

Why does this man have to be so damn sexy?

"Hey, mustang girl, eyes up here!" He snaps his fingers in my face, breaking me out of my trance. I guess he's done praying. "Are you sure just your tire hit the curb? Because it looks like your axel is hanging from under your car."

"Isn't the axel part of the tire?" I ask. Harrison's hand reaches back and scratches the back of his scalp, and I will myself not to see if his shirt is riding up again. But then when his head falls forward and his hand rubs along his nape as he lets out what sounds like a growl, I can't help myself. My eyes dart back down, and sure enough, I'm able to get another glimpse of the bottom two tight abs, which are peeking out from between the bottom of his T-shirt and the top of his jeans.

"All right, let's go," he says, and my eyes jump back up to meet his.

"Huh?"

"Let's go. I'll give you a ride home on my bike."

"What about my car?"

"Did you not hear everything I just said?" He glares at me. "The axel looks like it's broken. Your car isn't drivable. I'm going to have to get a tow truck out here to pick it up…" His words trail off, and he goes silent, his eyes locking on my body for a brief moment.

"What the hell is that?" he asks, motioning at me, as if he's just now noticed the outfit I've been wearing this entire time.

"My cheerleading uniform." I tilt my head to the side in confusion.

"Please tell me that's not what you wear to the football games."

"What's wrong with what I'm wearing?" I look down at my royal blue and white top. Sure, it dips down low, showing a bit of my cleavage, but it's not inappropriate. There's a white capital H directly underneath my chest and the top stops just above my belly button, revealing the belly ring I got done for my sixteenth birthday. My skirt is the same color blue with a single white diagonal stripe across the front and two thin slits that go up the sides to allow movement in the otherwise skintight outfit. And finishing off the outfit are my white Chucks.

I stand in place, waiting for him to answer me, but instead, he remains silent as his eyes slowly rake down my body. He's more than a couple feet away, but it feels as if every inch of my skin is being heated from just his gaze alone. And when his eyes stop on my legs and he lets out a low groan, I bite down on my bottom lip to stifle my own. How is it possible to be so completely turned on just from the way he's looking at me?

Squeezing my thighs together, I attempt to relieve the

ache between my legs, but it does nothing to tamper down my sudden need to find my release. I've never thought about getting myself off before, but right now, the only thing on my mind is getting home, shutting my door, and touching myself to the image of Harrison and the way he's eyefucking me right here on the side of the road.

"Jesus, let's go." He steps toward his bike.

I remember my cell phone and purse are still in my car. "Let me grab my stuff." I climb back inside my car and toss my phone and keys in my purse before getting back out. Harrison takes my purse from me and throws it in a bag on the side of his bike, his eyes never leaving me.

"Here, put this on." He hands me his helmet. It's so big and heavy I almost drop it. Not wanting to argue, I do as he says and place it over my head. The thing must weigh a good thirty pounds! My head falls to the side and I force it back up, only to have it fall the other way. Harrison notices and for the first time allows a small smile to grace his lips.

"You look like a bobble head," he says before he lifts me up and sets me on the back of his bike. Not expecting that, I let out a squeal, which has him laughing. And my goodness, his laugh is just as beautiful as his looks.

He lifts his leg over the bike and sits down. "Hold on tight, mustang girl," he yells as he presses his foot down and revs the engine to start the bike. It roars to life, and just before he takes off, I wrap my arms around his hard body and dig my fingers into his rock hard abs, holding on for dear life.

The ride home is only a couple miles, but as I sit on Harrison's bike with my body wrapped around his, I wish we lived farther away. I consider asking him to take me for a longer ride, but before I can get up the nerve to, he pulls up the driveway and parks the bike. He gets off first, then helps me off. I pull the helmet off my head and begrudgingly hand it to him.

"Thanks for the ride."

"First time on a bike?" he asks.

"Yeah," I admit. *And I hope it's not my last…*

"What'd you think?" His top teeth drag along his bottom lip, almost as if he's nervous to hear my answer. And that has me smiling on the inside, that I can make a man like him nervous.

"I think I would rather be back on your bike than standing here about to go inside there." I nod toward the house.

"Where's your sidekick?"

"Who?" I ask, confused by his sudden change in tone.

"Theo." He raises his brows like I should already know who he's talking about. "The guy is practically stuck to your side like glue," he scoffs.

I pause for a moment, trying to figure out where this attitude is coming from. He can't seriously be jealous. That thought is laughable. While Theo is cute, in a little brother sort of way, he doesn't hold a candle to Harrison. The man is beyond gorgeous.

"We, umm…we had a little falling out tonight. He's still at the party." I brace myself as I wait for him to ask what happened, but instead he just nods.

"I'm off tomorrow. I was thinking about taking a ride. Wanna go with me?" His eyes sear into mine, and the butterflies I felt when we kissed come back.

But then I remember he's ignored me for the past two weeks, and my guard is back up. "Why?"

"Why what?" he asks, confused.

"Why are you asking me to go for a ride with you? You've pretty much acted like I don't exist the last couple weeks. What's changed?"

His lips twist into a grimace as if he's contemplating how to answer my question. Finally, he lets out a frustrated sigh and says, "You being here complicates shit, and I don't like complications."

I flinch at his words. "Excuse me? You act like I *want* to be here."

"I'm not saying you do, but you asked why I've been avoiding you. The minute Heath sees me give you any attention, you'll become a game to him."

I let out an unladylike snort. "I'm already a fucking game to him! Hence me living here."

"Nah," he says, shaking his head. "You haven't seen what that man is capable of. I have plans to one day get out of here, and I don't need you and your *sidekick* complicating shit for me."

Wow! Who is this guy? I step closer to him, but he takes a step back. "So, let me get this straight, you don't want to deal with my complications, yet you showed me the secret closet filled with my mom's stuff, gave me the best kiss of my life, and now you're asking me to go with you for a ride on your bike?"

I see it when his face softens and he steps toward me. "The best kiss of your life, huh?" He grins teasingly, and I groan. I can't believe I just said that.

"It was okay." I shrug.

"No, you just said it was the best kiss of your life. You can't take that back now." His grin widens, and I roll my eyes.

"Yes, I can, and I do."

"Say it again," he taunts.

"No." I take a step back. "I already took it back."

"Say it." He edges closer, and my back hits the brick wall.

"Fine!" I huff. "It was the best kiss of my life, meanwhile I'm just a stupid complication to you. Happy?"

I turn my face away, not wanting to look at him. I'm acting like an emotional little girl. Damn him!

Pressing his palm to my cheek, he forces me to look at him. "Look, I'm sorry. What I was trying to say…it came out wrong." His fingers push a wayward hair out of my face. "I enjoyed our kiss in the closet, too." He smirks playfully. "I asked you to go for a ride with me because I want to spend time with you. But that doesn't change the fact that us spending time together will complicate shit for both of us."

"I can handle it. I'm tougher than I look."

"I'm beginning to see that." His eyes dart to my mouth, then he presses his lips to mine. It's soft and sweet and ends way too quickly.

"Yes," I say, answering his original question.

"What?" he asks, confused.

"Yes, I'll go for a ride with you."

He smiles wide, looking all too beautiful under the moonlight. "Well, okay then."

"Okay then," I parrot, feeling stupid. I suppress a groan because I'm so lame when it comes to guys and saying the right thing. Luckily, he seems pleased by what he sees because his grin widens.

"Cat," he says, his brows furrowing as he grows serious. "We'll do this again tomorrow." His voice grows husky. "But we'll take our time."

I start to head toward the front door when I remember he said he would tow my car for me. "Hey, Harrison," I call out and he stops in his tracks, turning around. "Will you still be able to tow my car to the shop tomorrow?"

"I'll text my boss, Damian, and tell him to do it in the morning." His boss? Shit! That will mean I'm going to have to pay. I had assumed Harrison was just going to do it himself.

"Oh, umm…thanks, but I don't have any money."

"It's all good," he says. "He owes me a favor." His lips curve into a beautiful smile.

"Thank you."

We both stand here for a long beat, neither of us making the first move to leave. I don't know what I'm waiting for or what exactly it is I want to happen. It's not like he's going to throw me over his bike and make love to me right here in the driveway.

"I need to put my bike away," he finally says with a small smile.

"Oh, yeah, okay. I better go in and get changed. I'll see you in the morning."

"Bright and early."

"Okay, good night." I lift my hand and give him a small five-finger wave before I turn and head inside without looking back. The house is quiet and I'm too tired to shower, so I change out of my uniform and throw on a soft long T-shirt and climb into bed. My fingers make their way down to my panties but stop before they make contact with my vagina. I want to experience an orgasm now more than ever, but not with my own fingers. No, that won't do. I want my first orgasm to be at the hands of Harrison. If he could turn me on the way he did tonight without even touching me, I can just imagine what he could do to me if he actually put his hands on me.

CHAPTER TWENTY-NINE

Harrison

After my morning shower, I run my palm across my buzzed head to swipe away the wetness, and then throw on a pair of jeans, my black Doc Marten boots, and a T-shirt. I snag my gray hoodie and am pulling it on when I hear arguing from down the hallway. Walking down the hall, I see that Cat's door is ajar and I can hear Theo's whiney voice begging for her to forgive him. Forgive him for what? Both irritation at him doing something to piss her off and satisfaction that she's mad at him are warring inside me.

"Now the whole school will know you want to fuck your cousin," she snaps grumpily.

I bite on my fist to keep a laugh from bubbling out. Asshole is on her shit list.

"Anne won't tell anyone," he assures her. "It was a mistake."

"A mistake that could cost us our reputations. If anyone finds out that you called out my name while—"

"No one will find out," he stresses. "She promised me. I told her it was a kinky thing. It wasn't real."

They both are quiet for a moment.

"We're cousins," she reminds him.

"It's stupid," he remarks. The floorboards creak and I imagine he's pacing the floor, upset that he can't fuck his cousin.

"Is that all?" she asks. "I need to get ready."

"I'm sorry," he says lamely.

"So you've said."

I love that she doesn't roll over and let the brat get his way. If he's anything like his dickhead father, he's used to getting his way. To be told no must drive him insane.

"Cat," he murmurs.

I step in the doorway and take in his sulking frame. She sits up in bed, her dark hair in disarray, with the blanket wrapped around her. Her frown melts away when she sees me and I'm rewarded a breathtaking smile. A smile I'd love to kiss once more.

"You ready?" I ask.

Theo jerks around and glares at me. He's standing in a pair of boxers and nothing else. It annoys me that he's in here half dressed, begging her to forgive him. Did he think she'd invite him into her bed and they could fuck away their problems? My hands fist at my sides.

Cat nods happily and climbs out of the bed, abandoning her blanket. Both Theo and I rake our gazes down her body. She's wearing a T-shirt and not much else. I can see her nipples through her shirt and it makes me want to give them a little bite. Theo lets out a pained groan and adjusts his cock in his boxers, then leaves his hands in front of him, hiding his erection.

"Where do you think you're going?" he demands.

She stops and puts her hands on her hips to scowl at him. Of course she'd look hot as hell doing it too. Cat Lincoln is prettiest when she's fired up and angry. "I'm going out."

"With him?" he sneers, gesturing with one of his hands at me.

Her head turns my way and I love the way she takes in my appearance in an appreciative way. She lets her eyes roam up my body to my lips. When I smile, she mirrors my grin. "With him," she says breathily.

Take that, motherfucker.

Theo lets out a sound of disbelief before storming from her room, clipping my shoulder on the way out the door. He stomps back to his room and the door slams shut. I prowl over to Cat and finger a strand of her hair while looking down at her.

"It's cool out today. Wear something warm."

Her cheeks blaze crimson and she bites on her bottom lip, nodding. "Okay."

I hold her gaze and stare at her smattering of freckles on her nose and cheeks. Usually, she wears makeup and hides them. They're cute and I like that I'm finally getting to see them.

"I'm sorry your cousin wants to fuck you," I say, grinning.

She rolls her eyes and goes to shove me away, but I grip both her wrists. Leaning in, I brush my lips over the shell of her ear over her hair.

"Harrison," she breathes, her voice sounding slightly strained.

"I can't say I blame him," I murmur before pulling away.

She flutters her lashes at me and smiles shyly. Shy is cute on her too. I release her hands and step back.

"Make it quick. Don't bother fixing your hair because the wind will fuck it all up. You look good the way you are too, so forget about the makeup," I grunt.

Her green eyes light up at my words. "Yeah?"

"Fuck yeah," I say and then turn on my heel. "I'll meet you out front in half an hour."

I leave her room and head back to mine to grab my wallet and keys. When I glance toward Theo's room, the door is open and he's no longer in it. I grab my stuff and head downstairs.

The house smells like bacon and my stomach grumbles. I'm just about to go grab something to eat when I hear voices coming from Heath's office. Curious, I walk over to the door that stands wide-open but don't let my presence be known.

"Dad, I want her."

Fucking Theo.

"Of course you do," Heath says coolly. As though that's the order of the world.

Theo lets out a frustrated huff. "I want her to be mine. Not as my cousin, but as my girl."

"I already told you she was yours," Heath bites out. "You need it in writing too?"

Theo grumbles. "You're saying she's mine and yet she keeps telling me we can't be together."

I clench my jaw, remembering how Heath blandly told me that Theo was going to marry Cat. All part of his stupid revenge plan. This is ridiculous. She's a fucking woman who can make her own goddamn decisions. I hate that that fucker lives like he's some evil king and can control every single person around him.

He doesn't control me.

And, clearly, he can't control Cat either, no matter how much he wants to.

"Theo," Heath says in a bored tone. "She is yours. She will come to learn this. Even if I have to tie her to a chair in the basement and keep her there. Understood?"

Theo laughs and I grind my teeth to dust. Theo thinks Heath is joking. That fucker never jokes about anything.

"But," Theo says, his humor fading. "She's going on a date with *him*." The way he refers to me has my stomach hollowing out. As though I'm the fucking filth under his feet.

"Who?" Heath sneers.

I step into the doorway and lock eyes with Heath. He

blinks rapidly for a moment as he connects the dots. Then, his upper lip curls in distaste.

"The orphan," Heath bites out, narrowing his eyes at me. He snaps his gaze to his son. "Cat is a Lincoln. The Lincolns only care about one thing. Money. And you, my dear boy, have lots of it. Upon your eighteenth birthday, you'll be granted access to millions. What you do with it is up to you. If you want to lavish the spoiled vixen with cars and homes and trips to fucking France, so be it. Until then, you know where my checkbook is. Do what you have to do. If anyone knows, it's me. Money buys anything. *Especially* the girl."

I swallow and cross my arms over my chest. My features remain impassive. I refuse to let these rich fuckers intimidate me.

"Cat's not some captive," I say lowly.

Theo winces at my words. Heath simply shrugs.

"The Lincolns were always a slave to money." Heath's features are icy. "You know nothing, orphan. Go scamper back to your pantry and eat the breadcrumbs I've allowed you to have."

I try not to let his comment affect me. When my stomach growls, Theo laughs. Ignoring them, I storm out of the room and head straight for the kitchen. Helen is fussing over the waffle iron. I steal a handful of bacon and an apple before heading out the door. After I inhale the bacon, I pocket the apple and call my boss. Once I make arrangements to have him pick up Cat's Mustang, I mess around with my bike to take my mind off Heath and his dickhead son.

Leave.

I could. I should. I will.

Hell, I'd been ready to. I've saved enough to stay someplace cheap and just have my job with Damian at the shop. But then *she* showed up. And now, I don't want to leave her alone with them. I'll stay until Heath forces me out. It's only a matter of time.

As if my thoughts of her have summoned her, she exits the house. Her sleek brown hair has been pulled into a low ponytail at her nape. I can see she's added some mascara and lip gloss to her pretty face, but other than that, she's still the fresh-faced girl who rolled out of bed not long ago. She dons a royal blue Heights Academy hoodie and a pair of skinny jeans that hug her slender legs. I'm happy to see she wears practical shoes—a pair of black Chucks.

"Did you eat?" I ask.

"I'm not hungry," she says, shrugging.

I pull the apple from my pocket and toss it to her. Despite not being hungry, she starts munching on it while I pick up the helmet and place it on her head. This time, her head doesn't wobble as much and she seems pleased, grinning at me. I find myself staring and have to look away.

"Where do you want to go?" I ask, looking off down the road in the distance.

"The lake, maybe," she says through a mouthful of apple bits. "The city. I don't know. Where do you want to go?"

Someplace far, far away from here.

"I know of a place," I tell her, straddling my bike and turning over the engine. The loud, rumbling blast cuts through the quiet morning and I love it.

She tosses the half-eaten apple to the ground and climbs on behind me. The heat of her slight body warms me. It's as though her body was meant to mold against mine because with her tits pressed against my back, she feels good there. When her hands slide inside my hoodie pocket and settle on my lower abs, I chuckle because she seems like she's a fan of me too.

"Hold on," I tell her, revving the engine before taking off, kicking up gravel behind us.

She squeals, but it's the delightful, happy kind of sound that makes my heart clench in my chest. She squeezes my middle and hugs her thighs against the outside of mine. I reach down and give her a pat on her thigh before gassing it.

We ride through the hilly countryside for hours. I point out places of interest along the way. She's all smiles, even when I take her to a shitty diner for lunch. It's nearing late afternoon and the clouds are becoming ominous, so I decide to take her to my favorite place so we can rest for a bit. We turn off the main road and I drive along a tree-lined gravel road called The Moors, going slow as not to fishtail. It opens up to a marshy bog. I like it here because there's a lot of tree cover and it's quiet.

After shutting off the bike, the sounds of nature take over. Frogs croaking. Crickets chirping. Birds squawking. The soft pattering of the occasional raindrop on the leaves around us.

"Wow," she says as she pulls off the helmet and hands it to me. "It's pretty out here."

The bog is covered in a bright green layer of algae. Not a place you want to swim, but it's pretty to look out at. Something disturbs the water and Cat shivers.

"Alligator?" she asks.

I laugh. "This far north? I doubt it. Probably a snake."

"Ew," she groans, clearly not happy with that answer either.

I grab her cold hand and guide her through some trees to a spot I like to sit at. It's under a canopy of trees, but the giant rocks covering the ground are mossy and smooth. In my boots, I'm sure-footed, but she slips upon stepping on a rock, and I have to pull her to me to keep her from falling.

Her cheeks turn pink as she looks up at me, her smile never waning.

"I like this smile," I tell her softly. "You don't smile much and I like it when you do."

She looks away and the smile fades. "I'm not speaking to my father because of the lies he told and the secrets he kept from me. My cousin wants to bone me. And I live with a psycho hell-bent on making my life a living nightmare. Not much to smile about."

I slide my palms to her cold cheeks and turn her to look up at me. "But you smile for me."

Her grin returns. Perfect and fucking beautiful. "I do."

"I like that," I grunt. "Know what else I like?"

She bites on her bottom lip and shakes her head.

"You."

Dipping down, I nuzzle her cold nose with mine until she lets out a breathy gasp, freeing her lip. Then, I press my mouth to hers, eager to taste her again. She parts her lips, allowing my tongue to sweep out and brush against hers. The small, needy moan she gives me is all the encouragement I need. I slip one palm to her ass and pull her against me, squeezing her ass cheek. Her hands fist the front of my hoodie as she kisses me frantically. Our sweet kiss quickly becomes not so sweet at all.

"Harrison," she murmurs against my mouth. She pulls away and my eyes fall to her red, swollen lips.

"Yeah?" My voice is husky and raw.

"Are you going to blow me off after this kiss and avoid me?" Pain flashes in her eyes, sending a flare of guilt ravaging through me.

I groan and pull her tighter to me. "No. I can't stay away from you for some fucking reason. You get under my skin, mustang girl. And I kind of like it." I smirk at her playfully.

She smiles again and stands on her toes, bringing her closer to my height. "Good, I kind of like it too." Her kiss is soft and quick this time.

I release her to sit on my favorite rock that hangs over a ledge, overlooking the marshy bog. My legs dangle over the side and I pat my lap. Her gaze darts past me to the green waters and panic flares in her eyes.

"I'll keep you safe," I vow.

My words have her relaxing. She starts to sit in my lap with her back to me, but I manhandle her until she's straddling me. I stare at her up close. So fucking pretty. Reaching up, I wind a strand of her dark hair in her ponytail around my finger. When I tug it slightly, she giggles.

"I like looking at you," I admit with a crooked grin.

Her tense body turns to liquid in my arms as she melts against me. She scratches her fingernails along my buzzed scalp as she explores me closely. When her lips press to my nose, I let out a contented sigh.

For so many years, I've drifted along not really feeling connected to this world. But right here, right now, with her in my arms, I feel tethered. Every soft drop of rain against the treetop canopy, every whisper of wind, each croaking frog—it all feels more real. As though I've woken up from a foggy dream. Everything's so clear.

Her eyes flutter closed as her cold hands settle on my jaw. She leans forward and kisses my mouth sweetly. I let her control the pace. My palms roam her ass and when they slide beneath her hoodie under her shirt, she lets out a hiss.

"Cold hands," she groans, arching closer to me. Her tits are pressed against my chest and I want to spend days sucking on them. Not here, though. Here, I settle for what we have.

"Thanks for keeping them warm," I tease, stealing another kiss.

Once she gets used to my hands on her bare back, she cuddles closer. Our kissing is slow and unrushed. Nipping and sucking. Tasting and teasing. My dick is hard as stone. And she's so innocent, she doesn't do anything to taunt me. She is simply happy with just kissing.

I've been with many women over the years. It's always a quick tearing of clothes and savage fucking. Nothing this sweet. Even after I emptied my dick into those condoms, I felt cold and alone, despite the warm naked body I'd been with.

But this?

She's real and she makes my chest ache.

"I like you," I mutter, nipping at her bottom lip. "You make me feel not so alone."

As though my words have shocked her, she pulls away to regard me with sad eyes. "You feel alone too?"

"Not right now. Right now, I'm fucking happy."

Her smile is breathtaking. "I'm happy too."

With my gaze smoldering into her, I slide my palm slowly to her front, between us. Her nostrils flare, but she doesn't stop me. I trail her flesh with my fingertips, loving the way she wiggles.

"That tickles," she rasps, her cheeks bright red.

"My bad," I say and then slide my palm to cup her over her bra.

She blinks at me rapidly and her breathing is heavier. I could have her right now if I wanted. She'd probably let me strip her down and fuck her on the cold, mossy rock. But then would she become one of the nameless others? I sure as hell don't want that. If taking it slow means I get to keep her longer, that's what I'll do.

I pull my palm away and she lets out a growl.

"Harrison," she complains.

Chuckling, I slide the eager hand back to her spine and caress the flesh there. "Yeah, babe?"

"You're teasing me on purpose." Her bottom lip juts out and her green eyes flare with annoyance.

I laugh at how adorable she is. "I like teasing you."

Her palms find my shoulders and she grinds against my aching dick, making me growl. My fingers bite into the flesh on her back as our hot stares burn into each other.

"It's not nice, is it?" she asks breathily.

When she grinds on me again, I close my eyes and tilt my head back. "Feels fucking nice to me."

She giggles and stops her torture to kiss my mouth again. I lie back on the rock, pulling her with me. We kiss and rub and tease until it starts to grow dark. We're both wet from the rain droplets that have snuck their way past the canopy of trees. I reach up and tug her hood over her head. She mimics my action with mine and then kisses me again. With our hoods over our heads, it's like we're in our own little world.

"Can we stay here forever?" she asks. I don't think she's joking.

"I wish," I mutter.

It's getting dark and I don't want to drive her around in the woods at night. I pat her ass with both hands.

"We better go, Cat."

She groans but stands up. I get to my feet and wrap an arm around her waist to keep her from sliding off the ledge and into the water. We make it out of the immediate cover of the trees and the rain comes down harder on us. She shivers and her teeth chatter.

I hate how fucking sad she looks.

"Time to go home," she utters bitterly.

I grip her hips and turn her to face me. Staring down at

her, I memorize her pretty features. Widest green eyes I've ever seen. Plump pink lips. Perfect nose.

"We'll do this again soon," I promise. "I'll distract you until you graduate. Then, you won't have to deal with that asshole."

She kisses me hard and desperately. If she keeps it up, judging by the state of my throbbing dick, I might never take her home. I might just fuck her against the nearest tree and keep her.

Eventually she pulls away, a frown marring her beautiful face. "I'm ready."

I'm not.

And yet I let out a sigh and hand her the helmet.

I run my knuckles over her chilled cheekbone as I make a promise to her. "Things will get better."

I'll make sure of it.

I'm graced with one of her sweet smiles.

And she believes me.

CHAPTER THIRTY

WE ARRIVE BACK TO THE HOUSE, AND AFTER PARKING HIS bike, Harrison takes the helmet from me and hangs it up in the garage next to his. We enter the house through the mud room. The lights are all off and it's unusually quiet. Not that the house is usually hopping, but at the very least there's usually a kitchen light or television on. Taking my hand in his, Harrison guides us through the kitchen toward the stairs. My stomach sinks at the thought that our day is over. We've spent the last twelve hours together, yet it doesn't feel like enough. I've never felt this way about anyone before. Sure, I've had boyfriends, but nothing serious, and nobody I spent hours with and at the end of the day craved more.

Just as we're about to ascend the stairs, someone clears their throat and we turn in our place to see who it is. Leaning against the kitchen door is Helen with a huge knowing smirk splayed across her lips. She's in a long robe and holding a tea cup in her hands. Feeling like we've just been caught doing something bad, my face heats up in embarrassment. It's weird having a mother figure around, but at the same time it feels like this is a rite of passage. The mom who catches her daughter sneaking in late.

"I hope you two are behaving," she murmurs, raising one brow.

Harrison nods and mumbles out a, "Yes, ma'am," which causes me to let out a giggle. I love how he can be such a hard ass, and then one word from Helen and he crumples.

"Good night, Helen," I whisper, and she gives me a playful wink.

"Good night, dear."

Harrison pulls me up the stairs and when we get to my door, we both stop in our place. Our hands remain linked together.

"I had a nice time today," I tell him honestly.

"Me too." He smiles a boyish grin that has me wanting to beg him to come into my room with me so we can continue our day. As if he can hear my thoughts, he groans softly and shakes his head. He dips down slightly and gives me a gentle kiss to my lips. Then one to my nose. When my face scrunches up at his sweet gesture, he laughs softly and the sound reverberates through my body.

"Sweet dreams, mustang girl," he murmurs. Then he reaches past me and turns the knob to my door, opening it for me. For a second I think maybe he's going to come in, but then he backs up, and with one curt nod turns his back on me, walking down the hall to his room without looking back.

The sun shines through my window, telling me it's late into the morning and time to get up, but my exhausted brain and body are telling me I need more sleep. Pulling my blanket over my shoulders, I snuggle into my pillow and close my eyes when my phone begins to ring.

"Ugh!" I groan out loud as I grab the offending device. When I see it's my dad calling, I sit up. It's been over two weeks since I've seen him. I tried to go over to his new apartment last weekend, but he told me he needed to work. I don't understand why he's pushing me away. He's the one who lied and caused this entire situation, yet he's acting like I'm in the wrong.

I hit answer. "Dad."

"Baby girl." My heart expands at his nickname for me. I hate that we're living separately my last year of school.

"How are you?" I ask, willing the tears that are threatening to fall to stay put.

"I was wondering if maybe you wanted to come over for lunch. I miss you, Cat."

"Oh, Daddy." I choke out a sob, allowing the tears to spill over. "I miss you too."

"Don't cry, sweetie," he begs. "What time can you come over?"

"I'll get ready now." I throw my covers off me and scamper off the bed. "I'll be there in an hour."

We hang up, and I quickly jump into the shower then get dressed, throwing on a pair of skinny jeans and an off the shoulder top. I find my UGG boots in the back of my closet and pull them on as well. Not wanting to waste a minute I could be with my dad, I throw my damp hair up into a messy bun and run down the stairs. I'm sending a text to my dad to let him know I'm on my way when my feet hit the hardwood floor and I crash into a warm body. I look up to find Theo glaring daggers at me.

"Going somewhere?" He crosses his arms over his chest and I stifle a giggle at how ridiculous he looks in this position compared to Harrison. Unlike Harrison's muscular and strong biceps and forearms, Theo's are lanky and long-limbed.

"Actually, I'm going to see my dad," I say, pushing past him.

"I looked for you yesterday, but you were gone all day without your phone."

"Yeah, I went riding with Harrison. Sorry."

He tenses and his eyes search mine. A mixture of fury and hurt. I hate that he's upset with my being with Harrison, but it's not like Theo can date me anyway. His mother is my father's sister. At the end of the day, we just can't be. I always knew it, but he still seems to have trouble understanding that concept.

"We need to talk about Friday night," he says, following behind me into the kitchen. I grab a peach, rinse it off, and take a bite into the juicy goodness.

"I don't have time." I shrug. "Tonight?"

Theo groans, but nods okay. Taking another bite of my fruit, I head out the garage door when I remember I have no car. Damn it!

I spot Harrison kneeling next to his bike and an idea sparks.

Coming around the side of his bike, I press my elbows into the seat. "Hey there, biker boy." Harrison's fiery gaze meets mine and then his eyes dart to my cleavage. When I look down, I see in this position, my breasts are spilling out of my shirt. I've never been one to flaunt my assets, but when he looks at me like he wants to devour me, it has me wanting to walk around naked just so he'll keep looking at me like he is right now.

Hungry.

Feral.

Like he's about to strike.

Maybe I'd let him bite me…

"You got the biker part right." He smirks devilishly. "But the boy part…you're way off there. All fucking man here." He bites on his bottom lip as he rakes his gaze over me appreciatively.

"That's yet to be proven," I taunt.

"I'm pretty sure it was yesterday when you were grinding your hot cunt against my *manly* dick."

His words cause heat to flood through me. "Could've been a sock." I shrug with a breathy laugh.

Harrison's gaze turns smoldering. "That sounds like a challenge."

"Kind of hard to prove anything when you won't even step foot in my room." I raise an irritated brow.

"I was trying to be a gentleman," he says.

"Maybe I'd prefer you to not be one."

"Be careful what you wish for, mustang girl." Harrison grins wickedly as he stands, wiping his greasy hands on a rag. I throw my leg over the side of his bike and sit, my hands holding on to the handlebars.

"And to what do I owe the pleasure of a pretty girl sitting on my bike?"

"I need a ride."

His blue eyes are blazing with lust and become predatory as he steps closer, his legs hugging the front tire of his bike. His hands rest on top of mine. "Oh, I can give you a ride," he whispers. Chills run up my spine and I visibly shiver.

"To my dad's," I add with a grin, and his eyes dance with laughter.

"Sure, let me just wash my hands and then we can go."

Twenty minutes later, we pull up to my dad's apartment complex, and after five minutes of begging Harrison to join me, he agrees and parks his bike.

"Baby girl!" My dad pulls me into a tight hug and kisses me on my cheek. It's when we step inside and close the door, he realizes I'm not alone. He takes a long look at Harrison and smiles softly.

"You must be Harrison." He puts his hand out to shake Harrison's hand. "I'm Elliot." Harrison shakes his hand.

"I'm sorry," Harrison says, his brows furrowing together in confusion, "but I don't think we've met."

"No, you wouldn't remember me. You must've been no more than three when your father passed away. Many years too late, but I am sorry for your loss. I lost my Catrina the same night."

"You knew my dad?" Harrison asks. "Did you know my mom?"

"I did. I grew up with Catrina and Hunter. I only met Francesca a few times, but I could tell she loved you very much."

"Yeah, so much she left me." Harrison snorts in disbelief. His features remain cool and impassive, as though he doesn't care about his mother. But the tick in his jaw and the way his dark brows pull together tells me it does bother him. Dad may say that Francesca loved him, but Harrison clearly doesn't believe it. It's plain to see that he's still hurting, all these years later, from being left by his mother.

"It was a tough time. Heath had just come back and taken the company from your father. We all lost a lot, some more than others."

Harrison's eyes go wide in shock. "The company Heath runs was my dad's?"

"No." Dad shakes his head with a frown. "He took it and dismantled it."

"Why would he do that?" I ask. "Wouldn't he want to use the company he took to turn a profit?"

If possible, his features become even more crestfallen. "Heath's entire life is about one thing: revenge." He smiles sadly at the two of us, then says, "Enough about Heath. Come sit and tell me how you've been. How's school and cheerleading?"

Dad sits on the couch and Harrison and I sit across from him on the love seat. "School and cheer are both good. Just taking it one day at a time, I guess. It's weird living in a new place."

"I know. I'm so sorry, Cat. I hate that I've failed you."

"You didn't fail me, Dad," I insist.

"Yes, I did. I made horrible choices that led us to lose our company. I have no savings left. I can't even afford to pay for your college."

Standing, I walk over to my father and sit next to him. "Listen to me, please." I take his hands in mine. "I don't care if we're rich or poor. I don't care what I drive or where I live or if you can afford my college. All I want is for you to be happy and for us to be a family again. Find another job, Dad, please. I'll defer from college a year and work too. We can live here together. Don't allow Heath to control us."

Dad looks me in the eyes and tears trickle down his face. "How did I get so lucky to end up with such an amazing daughter?" He wraps his arms around me and kisses my forehead. "I love you, baby girl. I promise. I will get out."

The rest of the visit goes smoothly. We focus on the positive, which means Heath isn't mentioned again. We order in Chinese for lunch and the three of us watch a movie. When it's dinner time, Helen sends a text asking if we will be home for dinner.

"How is Helen?" Dad asks. "I haven't seen her since your mom passed away."

"She's really sweet," I tell him. "She makes it more bearable to be there."

Dad smiles. "I bet, and she can cook like no other." We all laugh. Then Dad turns his attention to Harrison. "Are you close with her?"

"I am. She might as well have raised me." I see the fondness in his eyes when he speaks of Helen. So different from the way my mom used to describe her in her journals. I don't think there were many people my mom actually liked or could stand to be around.

"Good. That makes me happy. After Catrina passed away, Helen offered to stay on to help raise Cat, but when we found out your father had died and Heath was going to keep you, we felt it was best for her to work for Heath. He offered to pay her double what she was already getting paid, so that helped." He chuckles.

"I don't know." Harrison laughs. "I don't think you could pay me ten times the amount to willingly work for Heath."

"Well, Helen is an angel, that's for sure. And if there's any-one who can deal with Heath's shit, it's Helen."

After we talk for a few more minutes, Dad says he has work to get done before tomorrow, so I text Helen to let her know we will be there for dinner and then we say our goodbyes. My dad makes Harrison promise to come back with me the next time I visit.

Dinner is enjoyable since Heath is out of town on business and Theo isn't home. It's just Helen, Harrison, and me.

"This roast was delicious," I tell Helen when I bring the dishes to the sink.

"Thank you, dear," she says with a soft smile. "If you'd like, I can show you how to make it next time."

"I would love that!" I fill up the sink with hot, soapy water and begin to rinse the dishes off. "You know, I went to see my father today."

"Did you have a good visit?" Helen asks, taking the dishes from me and placing them into the dishwasher.

"I did. He said he misses you and your cooking."

Helen smiles sweetly, her cheeks turning a light shade of pink. "Well, the next time you go over, I'll send you with some of his favorites."

"Or you can join me." I shrug nonchalantly.

"Maybe," she says softly.

"Are you playing matchmaker?" Harrison whispers into my ear, and I giggle.

"Shh…" I say, handing him the sponge. "Make yourself use-ful and wipe down the table."

"Yes, ma'am," he replies. And with a swat of his hand to my backside, he walks away, laughing out loud.

I notice Helen watching us. "What?" I ask shyly.

"Nothing, dear. Just nice to see you both smiling."

Once the dishes are done and the table has been wiped

down, Harrison excuses himself to shower. Needing to rinse off as well, I follow him up the stairs.

"You know, we could shower together," I say when we're standing in front of my door, once again. "Save the water and all that."

Harrison laughs, his blue eyes glimmering with delight. "If I got you naked in the shower, we would waste even more water because I wouldn't let you out until I fucked you against every damn wall and in every position possible."

He grips my ass cheeks and pulls me into him for a kiss. "Think of me while you're scrubbing down this sexy body," he murmurs against my lips.

"Only if you promise to think of me."

"That's a fucking given."

CHAPTER THIRTY-ONE

"ALL I'M SAYING IS YOU DON'T KNOW THIS GUY. HE COULD'VE taken you into the woods somewhere and raped you, and because you didn't have your phone on you, you wouldn't have been able to call for help."

I close my eyes and take a deep, cleansing breath, chanting to myself not to kill Theo as he drones on for the millionth time this morning about me not being reachable all day Saturday or Sunday.

"What if something happened and—"

"Enough!" I snap. "My God! I am here and breathing and nobody raped me!" I push him out of the bathroom. "I need to get ready for school."

"But—" he whines.

"Uh-uh." I shake my head and hold my hands out, needing him to stop talking right this second. "Out!" I push him once more and then slam the door in his face, so I can finish getting ready for school. I apply a single coat of mascara, a thin layer of lip gloss, and brush my hair one last time.

Grabbing my backpack off the back of my chair, I close my bedroom door behind me and fly down the stairs. Helen, the sweet woman she is, has my breakfast sandwich wrapped and ready to go, wishing me a good day at school.

"Thank you, Helen!" I yell as I run out the front door. I've never had a mother before, but I imagine the way Helen dotes on me about eating and doing my homework is what it would be like. I'm looking forward to her showing me how to cook and bake. One day I would love to have a family of my own, and while it's nice to have someone like Helen around, I would like to be able to take care of my family myself.

I make my way down the sidewalk and onto the driveway when it hits me my car is still out of commission. Damn it! I spot Theo sitting in the driver seat of his Porsche. The window is rolled down and he's grinning. Damn boys and their toys. I jump into the car and turn to Theo.

"Good thing your new daddy bought you a car because I have no clue how long mine is going to be stuck at the shop."

His brows furrow as he turns the starter and the car roars to life. "You never did tell me what happened."

"I hit the median." I shrug. "Harrison had it towed to the shop in town as a favor, but I have no clue when I will have the money to get it fixed. Even with my insurance, I'll still have to pay the deductible."

Theo's hand comes across the center console and rests on my leg. "Don't worry, Cat. I'll take care of it for you." His fingers rub circles into my thigh, and it has me feeling uneasy. He promised he would stop this, but once again here we are.

"Theo," I warn, and he moves his hand, placing it on the stick shift.

"Sorry." He gives me a weak smile. "I'll go by the shop after school and pay whatever they need." Well, that's interesting, since the last time I checked he was just as broke as I am. He pulls on the stick shift, but it doesn't budge. I glance at the clock. We're about to be late for first period.

"We gotta go," I point out.

"I know, I'm trying." He groans, pulling harder on the stick shift, which doesn't budge at all.

"Please tell me you know how to drive this car." Damn it! We're going to be so late!

"Nope, he doesn't." My eyes fly to the side to find Harrison leaning into the passenger side window. His face is only inches from mine and he's sporting a sexy grin. He's so close, I can smell his body wash: clean and woodsy. I inhale to get another whiff and he chuckles. My face heats up at having been caught sniffing him, but he doesn't call me out on it. Instead he leans in farther and presses his lips to mine. What I think will be a chaste kiss quickly turns into more when his tongue slips into my mouth. When the kiss ends, Harrison pulls back slightly and grants me the most adorable grin.

"Good morning," he whispers.

"Morning," I say back with a smile. Using my top teeth, I pull my bottom lip into my mouth and can taste him on me. It's fresh and minty. His eyes light up and one side of his mouth pulls up into a smirk. Forgetting where we are, our eyes stay trained on each other, neither one of us wanting to look away first. That is, until Theo reminds us we're not alone.

"If you're done molesting Cat, we need to get to school."

I whip my head around and glare at him. "I wouldn't go there if I were you," I warn and Harrison laughs. "But he's right." I turn back to Harrison. "We do need to get to school."

"Well, don't let me keep you." Harrison gives me one more chaste kiss before backing away and standing next to the car. He's in his usual attire. A white T-shirt, fitted jeans, and boots. His muscular arms cross over his chest and I remember what it felt like when he used those same strong arms to pick me up and place me in his lap. His biceps naturally flex as he chuckles softly and I make a mental note to make him take his shirt off for me later and show me all of his tattoos.

But right now, we need to get to school. Then it hits me what Harrison said when he walked over here. "You can't drive this car?" I hiss.

"He was supposed to show me how!" Theo whines and glares toward Harrison.

"Great!" I unlock my seatbelt with more force than necessary and push the door open, stepping out of the car and swinging my backpack over my shoulder. "How are we supposed to get to school, Theo?" I shout.

He shuts the car off and gets out. "I'll ask my dad if I can use his other car." He nods toward the BMW sitting in the garage that I've yet to see driven.

Harrison throws his head back with a laugh and I glare his way. "What's so funny?"

"That car is a stick shift too!" He snorts. "Real men can drive a stick." His shoulders shake with laughter.

"Okay, *real* man," I hiss and walk over to him, then jab my finger in his chest. He stops laughing when he sees how pissed off I am, wiping the amusement off his face. "Can you take us to school, please?"

"I can take *you* to school." He grins, walking over to his bike and grabbing two helmets. I glance over at Theo, who's shooting daggers at Harrison. The last thing I need is these guys at each other's throats.

"In the car," I clarify. "Theo needs to go to school too." He might be acting like an ass lately, but he's still my cousin and friend, and I can't just leave him here.

Harrison opens his mouth to argue, but when he sees I'm not playing around, he rolls his eyes and groans. "Fine, let's go."

The ride to school is quiet, and once we arrive—a good thirty minutes late—Theo makes it a point not to get out of the car until I do.

"I'll see you later," Harrison murmurs against my lips. I should be yelling at him for rubbing us in Theo's face, but every time his lips touch mine, I turn into a puddle of goo.

"I have practice after school till four."

"I'll be here to get you." He gives me another kiss then turns around to face Theo. "See you after school, honey." He grins wide and Theo growls.

"I'll find my own way home." He pushes the door open and slams it closed.

"Even better." Harrison shrugs. "See you later." He shoots me a wink.

Theo is waiting for me on the sidewalk, and when I get out and Harrison takes off, he immediately starts in on me. "The guy is an uneducated grease monkey."

"Don't start." I roll my eyes and walk ahead of him toward the main doors.

"Are you fucking him?" Theo asks.

"It's none of your business what I'm doing with him," I yell over my shoulder, picking up my pace. If his goal is to see how far he can go before I beat his ass, he's about to reach the finish line. The front office secretary gives us our late passes with a warning and then we both head to class without saying another word to each other.

The day drags by slowly. At lunch, Anne won't even make eye contact with me, but at least, from what I can tell, she hasn't said anything about what happened Friday night to anyone. Finally the last bell of the day rings out, and after grabbing my stuff from my locker and changing into my practice outfit, I head out to the field. Once all the girls are there, we begin going over each of the cheers for Friday night.

"All right, ladies, let's do *Dynamite* one last time and then we're done for the day." *Dynamite* is a new cheer I showed them for the first time today. It has a couple complicated lifts, but everyone seems to be quickly picking it up.

"Ready, okay." I clap four times as I chant the beginning of the song. "We're dynamite. We're dynamite."

I turn around to face my squad, continuing the moves, but

also watching to make sure everyone has it down, when I first notice Charlotte's moves falter. Next, Anne messes up. They both attempt to save the cheer as Kelsie grins at something behind me, her motions becoming sloppy.

"Stop!" I command and everyone pauses. "What's going on?" My gaze follows several of the girls. And that's when I see him. Harrison, still in the same clothes he was wearing this morning, is perched like a damn model against the picnic table, his hands pressed against the top of the table and his legs crossed in front of him. When our eyes meet, he shoots me a panty-melting wink.

"My God, that man is sexy," Charlotte says. I ignore her, turning back around to get my squad in order.

"Yes, he is," Kelsey agrees in a sing-songy voice that has me wanting to bitch-slap the melody right out of her.

"I've seen him in town," Elena, another cheerleader, adds. "He drives a motorcycle and works at the auto shop."

I open my mouth to tell them to shut up and focus when Anne says, "Same. My sister said she hooked up with him a while back. Said he's an animal in bed." And I'm pretty sure I just vomited a little bit in my mouth.

"I heard he's a fuck-and-run kind of guy," Darby says with a pout.

What the hell is going on here?

"Oh yeah," Anne agrees. "But I bet that one time would be worth it. It's not like he's husband material." Everyone laughs, and my stomach knots at the realization of how judgmental my friends are.

"Oh no." Charlotte shakes her head in disgust. "I heard he never—"

"Enough!" I yell. "Practice is over." I swipe my pom-poms off the ground and stuff them into my gym bag. Then, I throw my bag over my shoulder. When I turn around to leave, I notice ten pairs of eyes all staring at me.

Anne is the first one to speak. "Is he here for you?" Her condescending tone has my blood boiling.

"And if he is?" I volley back.

"Cat, you're not like dating him, are you?" Kelsey asks. Okay, forget bitch-slapping, if I don't get out of here, I'm going to end up suspended for beating one of these judgmental bitches' asses.

"Actually I am." I shoot her a fake grin, daring her to say something back. When everyone stays quiet, I snatch up my backpack and turn back toward them one last time.

"The next time any of you talk shit about my man, I will make you regret it." My eyes land on Anne first. "The last time I checked, every guy you've slept with is either taken or is into someone else."

My glare goes to Charlotte. "And your father wouldn't know what the word faithful means if it smacked him in the face."

I glower at everyone else. "Keep Harrison's name out of your mouth." With their jaws left hanging open, I walk away, straight over to Harrison. Dropping my gym bag and backpack, I wrap my arms around his neck and pull him into me for a searing kiss. Without missing a beat, his hands find my ass and he picks me up, twirling us around and setting me onto the table top, his lips never leaving mine. I should regret what I said to my friends. Apologize to them so I don't ruffle any fragile feathers. Anne knows shit she could use to make my life a living hell. But for some reason, when it comes to the man currently fusing his lips against mine like I'm his lifeline, I lose all logic.

When our kiss ends, he pulls back slightly and smiles.

"Hey," he murmurs. "Miss me?"

"That depends. Just how many women have you fucked and dumped in this town?"

His eyes widen and his jaw drops open in shock for several

seconds before he picks it back up and speaks. "Cat," he begins, and I can tell by the grimace he's sporting, whatever he's about to say isn't going to be good.

"Never mind." I shake my head. "I don't want to know." I continue to shake my head, unsure of what to think or how to feel. I avert my eyes over to the school building as I try to stop the hot tears that are burning my lids from falling.

"Hey, look," Harrison says, "I don't know what those girls said to you, but I can tell you right now, I have no intention of fucking and dumping you." I look at him and his eyes are pleading for me to believe him.

"Okay," I whisper. "I'm sorry. They all just started talking about you and all the women you've had sex with and I freaked out."

"I can't change my past." He frowns. "Hell, I'm struggling to get control of my future." His brows are furled together and his blue eyes are imploring me to understand. I don't really understand, but I can sense his sincerity. And because I like him, I let it go.

"Can we just get out of here?" I ask, and he nods in agreement.

"Hell yeah," he says. "Where do you want to go?"

"Anywhere, I don't care. Just away from here."

"You got it." He grips my hips and sets me onto the ground, then bends and grabs my bags for me. Taking my hand in his, he pulls me over to his bike and hands me a helmet. After tying my bags onto the back of the bike, he lifts me onto the back seat and throws his leg over the side and gets on, revving the engine.

"Hold on tight," he yells over the rumbling noise. I wrap my arms around his waist, my head resting against his back as he takes off. When he hits the main road, he speeds up, and the cool afternoon air sends a chill through my barely clothed body. As the comments and accusations my friends made run on replay in my head, I find myself holding on to Harrison tighter, afraid to let go. Terrified that whatever is going on between us isn't going to last. I'm already falling too quickly, and I'm trusting that Harrison will be there at the bottom, waiting to catch me. But what if he isn't? My fingers make their way under his shirt, needing to feel his skin. His hand lands on my bare thigh and he gives it a gentle squeeze. No, I refuse to believe he won't be there to catch me. Until he proves otherwise, I'm going to trust him.

When we pull up to the road that leads to Windy Hills, I frown. When I said anywhere, here was not exactly what I had in mind. But instead of turning down the driveway, Harrison keeps going. Eventually we come to a dirt road that if you weren't looking for it, you would miss. He slows the bike down and turns onto the road. Trees that look to be hundreds of years old line both sides of the path, the tops coming together and forming a canopy of sorts. When we get to the end, the dirt and trees both end, and in front of us is the backside of the large lake that connects our two estates to each other. But from here, you can't see either home.

Harrison parks the bike and helps me off. He opens his bike bag and pulls out a blanket. He shakes it out and lays it on the grass before he plops down and pulls me with him.

"Ask me anything," he says. "Whatever it is you want to know, I'll tell you." I think about the questions I could ask him: how many women has he slept with? Did any of them mean anything to him? How many times was he with each woman? But anything he says won't change how I feel about him. He's here with me now, and that's the only thing that matters.

So, instead I ask him the only question that matters to me. "Will you hold me?"

CHAPTER THIRTY-TWO

Harrison

Her hair smells like apples. And I really love apples. It feels right with this girl tucked under my arm as we watch several geese splash in and out of the lake water. If the guys at the shop saw me right now, they'd give me so much shit. I already caught nine kinds of hell this morning after I dropped Cat off at school. I'm never late so when Damian gave me the third degree, I admitted it was because I had to take my girl to school. Frank and Lou wouldn't shut the hell up after that. Damian simply smirked. I suppose it's strange. I've never dated before. I fuck, but never date.

With Cat?

I'm doing it all backward and I don't even care. I like it. I like that we haven't fucked. I like that I'm taking the time to notice what her hair smells like and the way her laugh sounds. It feels like I've been drifting through this life and I'm finally starting to see what's around me.

All I see is her.

Everyfuckingwhere.

And I love it.

My life was dark and dismal and fucking drab.

Cat is laughter and smiles and big, innocent eyes. She distracts me from everything else with her sweetness. Something I didn't know I had a taste for, but now I can't kick this craving.

"It's pretty out here," she says, her palm splaying over my

chest. "I've seen it from the other side of the lake, but not this side."

She lets out a heavy sigh. Since seeing her dad yesterday, she seems lighter. A weight has been lifted from the poor girl's shoulders.

"I used to come out here when Heath was being unbearable," I tell her, running my fingers through her sweet apple hair.

"Which is always," she says, huffing.

I bite back a grin. "Pretty much. But sometimes, especially when I got older, I wanted to fucking throttle him. To keep from losing my cool and beating him to a bloody pulp, I just slipped out and came here."

"Another spot," she whispers. "You have so many. The closet, the swamp, here."

"When you don't own your life, you have to find ways to make it yours. Small acts of rebellion. These places don't mean shit to Heath. He couldn't care less if I hid out in a closet. To him, it was a stupid, childish thing to do. To me, it was everything. It was something I could control," I admit softly.

She sits up and turns to look at me. Her cute nose is scrunched as her green eyes regard me curiously. "Why do you stay?"

"I'm not sure," I mutter. "Something always kept me tethered. Sometimes I thought it was my father's memory. Other times I think I held out hope that Heath would change and treat me like a real son. And then other times, I'd look at Helen and realize I'd miss her if I left. Every time I got ready to scrounge up the money I had and take a leap, something stopped me." I lean forward and press my forehead to hers. "This time, it's you."

She smiles. "I'm glad you're here."

"Me too."

I lie back on the blanket and pull her to me. She traces letters or pictures on my abs over my shirt and each time she dips low on my stomach, my cock aches. Little tease.

"The other girls you dated…" she trails off. "Did you take them to your spots?"

"No," I say with a harsh laugh. "Not at all."

"How come?"

"Because I didn't like them."

"But you had sex with them?"

It sounds dirty and wrong just laid out in the open. "These spots…my small acts of rebellion…" I sigh and close my eyes. "It's the same thing with women. Just another escape."

Her lips press to mine. "Am I an escape?"

Sliding my fingers into her hair, I hold her to me and kiss her sweet mouth. Once I've had my fill, I release her and stroke her face. I squint against the sun to look at her. "You're not an escape. You're different."

She beams at me. "How come?"

"You know all those journals that belonged to your mom?"

She nods.

"Well, I read them as you know, but what I didn't tell you is that I was obsessed with some of them."

"Why?"

"Because she humanized him. She made me like him in the way she described him: noble and fierce. He loved her so unconditionally." I swallow and admire Cat's supple lips. "I don't know…it just made me wish for something like that. To want someone so deeply and fully that you'd do anything to make them yours."

"So you're telling me you're a romantic," she teases as she straddles my lap. "The big, bad motorcycle man with tattoos has a bleeding heart for a good love story."

I flip her quickly and pin her with my body, loving the way her squeal echoes across the lake. "I loved the erotic parts too."

She grins at me in a devilish way. "What sort of erotic things?" I know she's read them herself, but I'll play along.

I grip her wrists and push them to the blanket. Staring down at her, I rock my hips against her. Her lips part and her green eyes flash with heat.

"When they were teens, before they took the dive and fucked, they would do stuff like this," I tell her lowly.

My dick is hard and aching as I rub it against her sweet spot. She squirms and lets out a moan. Her cheeks burn crimson. So beautiful.

"Can I orgasm this way?" she asks, her voice breathy.

"You've never had one?" My voice is husky and raw. I feel like a fucking teenager all over again with this girl.

"Well..." she trails off. "Oh...Oh...."

I rock against her, rolling my hips, and attack the side of her throat. Her skin tastes sweet and I suck her flesh between my teeth, no doubt marking her. She moans louder and squirms beneath me.

"Feel how turned on you make me, Cat?" I growl.

She whimpers, but I don't release her wrists. I love her pinned and at my mercy. When I rub at her in just the right way, she jolts. So I make sure to do it over and over again until she cries out in pleasure. Her eyes flutter closed and her cheeks turn pink. She's so pretty when she comes.

I release her wrists so I can touch her hair and kiss her sweet mouth. Then, I lift up and grin at her, ignoring the way my dick begs for its own release. "Does that answer your question? I can get you off a million different ways without you even having to take your clothes off."

"Wow, that was way better than I expected." She bites on her bottom lip as she stares at me with a reverent stare. It makes my heart rate speed up. I love the intense way she looks at me. Nobody has ever looked at me this way. Sure, I've had women practically throw their panties at me. Because they wanted me to fuck them.

But Cat?

She wants a lot more than my dick, although I know she'll be happy to finally get that too. Cat wants my stories and my kisses and my caresses. She wants all of me.

"That was your first orgasm?" I ask.

Her eyes leave mine and she looks away, as though she's shy. "I almost got off once, but…"

"Theo?" I hate the way my voice sounds strained and jealous.

"Worse."

I grip her jaw and pull her attention to me. "Who?"

"Heath."

Disgust ripples through me. "What?"

"Don't look at me that way," she says, her voice cracking. "I didn't want it."

As though her words burn me, I jerk away from her and rise to my feet. "He forced you? What the fuck, Cat?"

"N-No, I mean, at first I didn't want it. But the next thing I knew, it felt good. Oh, God." She bursts into tears. "I was try-ing to help my dad."

I pull her into my arms and hug her. "I'm going to kill him."

She shakes her head and looks up at me. "Don't. He caught me at a weak moment. I was confused and it felt good. But…"

My palms slide to her cheeks and I swipe at her tears with my thumbs. "But what?"

"That, just now, was real. It was better than good. It was amazing."

Pressing my lips to hers, I will the anger to simmer down. "You tell me if he so much as looks at you funny and so help me, Cat, I will knock his teeth through his skull."

She smiles at me. "Why? Because you like me?"

I snort and grab her ass with both hands, pulling her against my chest. "Because you're mine."

"You can't claim me," she says playfully. "I'm not some thing to own, caveman."

"I do what I want, mustang girl. You're mine and you might as well get used to it."

She pretends to pout, but her green eyes flare with pleasure. Like me, Cat is lonely and the idea of someone wanting to keep you all to themselves is pretty fucking enticing.

"Fine, then you're mine too," she tells me with narrowed eyes.

"Good."

"Good."

I smirk and she smiles.

I'm so fucked with this girl.

I'm sitting in the dark in the closet when I hear footsteps. Soon, the door opens and then she makes her way to our spot. When the dim light suddenly fills the space, she lets out a squeak of surprise.

"Harrison!" she hisses. "You scared the crap out of me!"

She looks hot as hell in her little sheer nightgown with her hands on her hips. When her eyes roam down my bare chest, she bites on her bottom lip and loses some of her anger at my scaring her.

I reach up and take her hand before pulling her into my lap. She melts against me, her legs straddling my thighs.

"Did you miss me?" I tease, running my fingertips along her back.

She giggles quietly. "I just saw you like an hour ago. Remember, after dinner when you made out with me in the hallway?"

"I missed you too," I deadpan.

She giggles and swats at my chest. "You're ridiculous."

I slide my palm under her hair and curl it around the back of her neck. Her lips part when I pull her close. I swallow a small moan that escapes her the moment our lips fuse together. We kiss slowly as we take the time to taste and enjoy each other. I'm fucking addicted to this girl. I can't stop thinking about her and I like spending time with her. She's funny and sweet and adorable as hell.

"Someone wants another orgasm," I rumble against her lips when I realize she's grinding against me.

"Maybe," she purrs.

My dick jolts in response. "You're such a tease."

Our lips meet again and the kiss gets more heated. My fingers bite into her hips as I help her rock against me. I'm only wearing a pair of boxers, so I can feel every bit of her much easier than earlier today through my jeans.

"You feel so good," I praise against her mouth. "Like if you keep it up, I won't be able to behave, baby."

"Nobody's asking you to behave," she breathes.

"I'm not going to fuck you on the closet floor," I groan.

"Why not?" she pouts.

"For one, I don't have a condom. And two, you deserve a special spot."

Her body tenses as though I've rejected her. That couldn't be further from the truth.

"But even though I'm not going to fuck you," I growl. "I'm going to need to see your perfect tits."

She lets out a gasp when I start pulling her gown up over her head. A shiver runs through her when my gaze lands on her young, bouncy breasts. I grab them both and lean down to taste them. So sweet. What's even sweeter is the way she whimpers in pleasure. Her nails scratch along my scalp and her hips flex as she seeks pleasure elsewhere.

"This is so sexy," I groan as my thumb runs along her bellybutton ring. "Everything about you is so fucking sexy."

She grins at me and kisses me hard. I slide my palm lower and run my fingers along her slit over her silky panties.

"Harrison," she cries out.

"Shhh," I murmur. "Heath is on the other side of that wall."

She nods and bites on her bottom lip. We stare at each other as I push my hand into her panties. Her flesh there is slick and smooth. One day, it's going to feel fucking amazing wrapped around my cock. I slide a finger to her wet hole and breach the opening. With her legs spread open, I easily push inside her tight channel. I work her juicy cunt until she's riding me like a pro.

"More," she breathes.

I know she wants my dick, but that'll have to wait until later. I'll give her something, though. Slipping my other finger inside, a crooked grin tugs one side of my lips up when she rasps out a husky moan.

"Baby, you're so damn tight," I rumble. "You know my dick is a helluva lot bigger than these two fingers."

I work her in and out, letting the heel of my palm rub against her clit until she's shaking. When she gets close, I urge a third finger into her slick heat. She whimpers as I stretch her, but it's necessary. My sweet girl is a virgin and she'll need a little prepping to take my cock.

"That's it," I praise. "Feel how fucking wet you are for me? It hurts because that little innocent part of you is getting broken away. I'm going to stretch you and get you ready because next time I have you naked like this, I'm going to fuck you, Cat. I'm going to fuck you so sweet and so nice that you'll crave me just like I crave you."

She moans again, her body shuddering in my grip. "Harrison, oh God!"

Her cunt clenches around my fingers as she orgasms. Slick juice coats my fingers as she shamelessly rides me. I keep slowly fucking her with my fingers until she sags against me, completely worn out and sated. Then, gently, I pull my fingers from her. She winces and looks down between us. Even in the blue light from the LCD lights, you can see the blood tinge on my wet fingers.

"Blood," she whispers.

"Better to get that over with now rather than later," I say with a grin.

"I want to make love to you. Right now."

I stroke her hair with my clean hand and kiss her pretty lips. "I do too, baby. But you'll thank me later. Let's put your gown back on and let me hold you for a bit before we go back to bed."

"What about you?" she asks, gesturing to my dick that's straining in my boxers.

"I'll be fine."

I kiss her again and then help her redress. Once she's clothed and curled up against me, I begin to realize something.

I'm happy.

Cat Lincoln has done what no one else ever could for me.

She's filled a hole inside me by filling it with herself.

And I don't think I'll ever get her out.

Hell, I don't fucking want to.

I drop the wrench in my hand with a loud clatter that has Lou howling with laughter at me when I hear the grinding of a clutch. Stepping away from the '89 Honda Accord with a fucked transmission, I swipe away the sweat on my brow with a filthy rag and seek out the sound of the asshole destroying his car. As soon as I step out of the garage bay and see a shiny, black Porsche, irritation burns in my gut. The car jerks and sputters to a halt. Through the glass, I can see Theo in the driver's seat scowling as Heath's hands move in the air. He's yelling at him.

That's about the only good goddamned thing about having Theo in that house.

Heath seems to forget I exist.

He's too busy spoiling his already rotten son.

When they step out of the car, I cross my arms over my chest and nod at the Porsche. "Fuck it up already, kid?"

Theo's face reddens as he glares. "No, I'm here to see about Cat's car."

"What about Cat's car?" I demand.

He shoots his father a helpless stare. Heath, with laser sharp focus, watches me for a long beat before speaking. I hate being under his scrutiny. As though he can look right through me and know everything about me. It's too early in the morning for this shit.

"He's here to handle it," he says in a bland tone.

"It's been taken care of," I snap.

Heath laughs, cruel and mocking. "Did it wipe out your meager savings or are you having to fix it yourself?"

I clench my jaw. "I'm taking care of it. It's none of your business."

"Everything okay?" Damian asks from behind me. When I glance at him, he's got the winning businessman smile as he sizes up his potential Porsche-driving clients. I can practically see the dollar signs in his eyes.

Heath nods at the Mustang in one of the open bays. "My son has come to pay for the repairs and pick up the Mustang."

Damian shoots me a confused look. I helped him gut his kitchen a few months ago and he said he'd return a favor if ever I needed one. And I called in my favor.

"I thought Harrison was taking care of it," Damian says slowly, shooting me a *I thought this was our trade* look.

"Harrison is off the hook," Heath says curtly.

Theo pulls out his wallet and opens it, flashing a wad of bills. He smirks at me. "How much, sir?"

Damian, rolling with the punches, shrugs. "Three grand."

He can be such a pain sometimes when it involves money.

Theo, without batting an eye, pulls out thirty one-hundred-dollar bills. "When will she be ready?"

Damian opens his mouth, but Heath shakes his head. "This afternoon. My son will be by later with his girlfriend to pick it up. Make it happen."

His girlfriend?

Fuck him.

"Sorry, man, no can do," Damian says. "I have a part on order, but it doesn't come in until later this week."

"Fine, but call us as soon as it's ready," Heath barks out. Then to me, he says, "And my son will pick her up from school. You're not needed anymore, orphan."

Theo flashes me a triumphant smile. "Yeah. She's taken care of."

I fist my hand and glower at Theo and Heath. "I've got shit to do."

Heath's laugh makes my hackles rise, but I ignore him. They can throw their money around all they want, but at the end of the day, Cat wants to be with me. Not Heath, who manipulated her into letting him touch her. Not Theo, who thinks he can buy his way into her heart.

Me.

And I'll continue to give her the shit money can't buy.

That's something they'll never be able to compete with.

CHAPTER THIRTY-THREE

UCKING HARRISON. THE GUY IS BECOMING A SERIOUS PAIN IN my ass. He is nothing more than a pathetic, uneducated grease monkey. He has no money and no future.

But he does have the one thing I want.

Cat.

"What the fuck does Cat even see in him?" My blood is boiling. That fucker needs to stop cock blocking me. Cat is mine. I've spent all summer softening her up. And just when I'm almost in, he shows up and thinks he can have her. If I thought I would win in a fight against him, I would beat that loser's ass.

"She's young and dumb. She wants the broke bad boy." Heath shrugs. "It's just a phase. A shiny new toy to play with. She'll get bored and move on. In the end, she will choose money. Every spoiled little bitch does."

"Are you speaking from experience?" I put the car into reverse and back out, flinching at the grinding sound it makes. It's hard to drive a stick shift. I don't even see the point. That's why they make automatics.

"Fuck, boy! Pay attention while you're driving." Heath hisses. "Take me home," he demands. "I have shit to do."

"I'm trying!" I cry out in frustration. "If you would just let me drive an automatic…"

"What the fuck did your mother do to you?" I feel his hard glare on me. "Men drive clutch. Fuck, this is why your mother should've told me I had a son. Then I could've raised you to be less of a pussy."

His words hit me right in the gut. I clench my jaw to keep my expression cool. I want to reach over and throttle him for talking shit about my mom's parenting. She tried. She did the best she could. I always felt loved and cared for. These last couple of weeks have been hard because I've felt anything but from Heath. Certainly don't think of him as a father in the same way Cat thinks of Elliot as hers. Our connection is from blood only. He's a closed off, cold asshole. I'm glad he didn't have a hand in raising me. Clutches be damned.

I shift into third and the car jerks forward. Heath's hand flies out to grab the dashboard to brace himself. Shit! I flinch.

"Pull over!" he shouts. "Now!"

I do as he says with a groan and kill the engine by mistake. He's already out of the car and stalking around to switch places. With a huff, I climb out and sit in the passenger seat defeated.

Effortlessly, he peels out and onto the street. I carefully watch as he drives us home, taking mental notes. Each shift change is flawless and fluid. I glance over at Heath and notice the tattoo peeking out from under the collar of his button-down shirt. He has several that cover his arms and chest. Harrison has tattoos as well. Maybe it's the tattoos Cat likes. She might not have wanted it, but when I walked in on Heath fingering her, she was definitely enjoying herself.

Hot, green jealousy flares up inside me.

I've seen the way she reacts to Harrison. I've done everything in my power to get her to notice me, but she won't give me the time of day. I even joined the football team because she's a cheerleader. I don't know what else to do.

I sigh and Heath groans. "What now?"

I don't know why I even bother telling him. Half the time he acts like he hates me too. But then he hands me a handful of cash, tosses me a wicked smile, and for a second I feel connected to him. Because I crave that fatherly attention, I find myself blabbing what's on my mind.

"What if she doesn't pick me?" He seems so sure Cat will choose me, but nothing she's done indicates she's going to choose me over the mechanic. He hasn't seen the way she smiles whenever Harrison's near. The way they kiss when they're together.

It's disgusting to watch. She was a virgin when I arrived this summer. Sweet and innocent. The last thing I want are the scraps from that blue-collared stray dog. It's only a matter of time until he convinces her to let him pop that cherry. "It's not fair."

"Stop whining like a little bitch," Heath snaps. "I said she'll pick you. End of story. Now pay attention to how I drive so you don't destroy this two-hundred-thousand-dollar car."

"I'm not whining," I say. "I'm just saying if she doesn't pick me soon, she's going to fuck him, and I don't want his leftovers." It's bad enough my dad has gone further with her than I have.

I feel Heath glaring daggers at me. "You're not giving up on her, are you?"

"No, I mean…I don't know."

He pulls up the driveway and slams on the brake. "Listen here, boy. If you want to be left anything in my fucking will. If you want that credit card and bank account. If you want me to pay for your pretty boy ass to go to Yale, you will get the girl." His face is nearly purple with rage and his brown eyes are flaring with fury. "You. Will. Get. The. Girl. Understood? Catrina Crenshaw should've been mine!"

I frown in confusion. "Don't you mean Lincoln?"

Heath seethes. "You know what I fucking mean! Man the fuck up and take what you want! Don't let that fucking orphan take what's yours. If he fucks her, it's only because you were too much of a fucking pussy to make her yours. And my son isn't a fucking pussy."

He slams the door and stalks inside. Sighing, I get out so I can go pick up Cat from school. I took the day off to go to the bank and sign some papers with my dad and handle Cat's car situation. She should be done with practice by now.

"Theo." I look up from my phone and see Anne standing there. I didn't notice her car is parked in the drive.

"What are you doing here?"

"I came by to talk to Cat." She rolls her eyes.

"Everything okay?" Cat should be at practice with Anne.

"Yeah." She shrugs. "Apparently she's considering quitting the cheer squad. She hasn't shown up to practice in a few days. I told the girls I would come over and talk to her, even though she totally doesn't deserve it after the way she went off on everyone on Monday."

"What happened?" This doesn't sound like the Cat I know. She spent the entire summer creating new cheers outside by the pool. Excited to teach them to her squad.

"It's that mechanic." Anne's nose scrunches up in disgust. "He showed up to practice to pick her up. A couple comments were made and she went crazy defending him."

"He's a bad influence on her." A lightbulb goes off. "Maybe you could convince her otherwise." I run my fingers down Anne's arm and she melts right here. Why the fuck can't Cat do that?

"I tried." She pouts. "Wanna show me your room?" She bats her lashes. I told myself I wouldn't fuck Anne anymore. I want Cat, and I can't chance her finding out I'm still fucking her friend.

"No." My goal is Cat.

Anne steps closer and grips my dick through my pants. "I'll let you call me Cat." She kisses the side of my neck and rubs up and down my erection. I groan at her touch. Maybe just once more.

"Help me break up Harrison and Cat."

"You told me the name calling was just a kink." Anne gives me a look of disgust. "You don't like want to date her, do you?"

"No!" I bark out. "We're family and I'm worried about her. The guy is a fucking loser. Cat deserves better."

"I don't know what you want me to do. I can ask my sister about him. She hooked up with him before."

"Really?"

"Yeah, Daddy calls it her rebel phase. She dropped out of school and started working at Tillie's." Anne sticks her finger in her throat and pretends to gag.

"What's Tillie's?"

"The strip club in town. We're not exactly close right now, but I could talk to her."

"Call her."

"What?" She gives me a confused look.

"Call your sister right now."

Anne pouts but does as I ask, handing me the phone.

"Is this Anne's sister?" I ask when she answers the phone.

"It is. This is Violet. Who's this?"

"I'm a friend of your sister's. How would you like to make five grand?"

"I'm listening."

I go through the details of what I want her to do and when I'm done, I give her my number so she can let me know when everything is in place. When I hang up, Anne's hand goes back to my dick.

"Let me please you, Theo. You seem very stressed."

She unbuttons my pants and pulls my dick out. Then, dropping onto her knees right here on the driveway, she swallows me whole. Fuck, her wet mouth feels so good. Gripping her hair,

I pump my dick in and out of her mouth. Closing my eyes, I imagine it's Cat's mouth on me, taking me down her throat. I imagine the noises are Cat enjoying the taste of my dick, and seconds later I'm shooting my load down her throat with a groan and my cousin's name on my lips.

Anne stands and wipes her mouth, and I zip my pants.

"I need to find out where Cat is. I'll let her know you came by."

"She's inside. I already told you I came by to see her. She had your maid pick her up from school. Guess her new boy toy must not have been available."

Shit! I glance around, checking to make sure Cat didn't just see Anne suck my dick. I don't need her coming up with another reason not to give us a chance.

"I'm going out of town," Heath announces. "I have some business in Jersey that needs my attention. Helen will be here if you need anything."

"Oh," Helen says, setting down the lasagna she made for dinner. "Did you forget to check the calendar? I leave tomorrow for the weekend."

"Cancel," Heath demands.

"No." Helen frowns. "I visit my family's graves, like I do every year."

Heath glares.

Helen smirks.

Heath groans.

Apparently Helen has the magic touch because she's the only one Heath doesn't treat like shit.

"Fucking great," Heath hisses.

My eyes dart down to my phone for the millionth time. Violet needs to hurry her ass up. I'm not sure what time Harrison gets off work and in order for my plan to be successful he needs to be there.

"I'm leaving you in charge. Anything gets fucked up and I'm holding you responsible."

I pull my gaze off my phone to see who Heath's speaking to. His eyes are trained on me.

"Me?" I question.

"Yes, you! Pay fucking attention." He reaches over and smacks the back of my head.

"Heath, language," Helen chides, and he scoffs.

Cat's eyes meet mine and she gives me a bright smile. Confused, I tilt my head to the side. She looks into her lap and a second later, my phone goes off.

Cat: Daddy's leaving! Party!

"I'm not sure what day I'll be back. Most likely Sunday. Think you can handle holding shit down here until then?"

"Yeah."

"Good. Don't fuck up."

I glance back down at my phone and there's another text from Cat.

Cat: Tomorrow night after the football game.

Shit! Well, he did tell me to get the fucking girl.

Me: Okay

Cat sends me a text right back.

Cat: Whoop! Thank you!

Before I can reply, my phone goes off again with a message from Violet.

Violet: On my way.

"Hey, Cat, we need to go." It's time to put my plan into motion. If everything goes the way I'm hoping for, soon enough Cat will be all mine.

"Where?" Cat gives me a perplexed look.

I stand and grab my keys from the counter. "Your car is ready. We need to go pick it up."

"Wow, that was fast," Cat says. "I thought it would take another week at least."

"Money talks," I quip.

"What about dinner?" Helen asks.

"We need to go now before the shop closes. Can you save it for us for when we get back?"

"Sure." Helen smiles softly.

Heath gives me a questioning look but remains silent. He knows there's no way the car is ready.

Cat stands and asks, "How much do I owe you? I'm looking into getting a job."

"You don't owe me anything," I insist. "I told you already I would take care of it. I'll take care of you."

She frowns but nods. "I appreciate that, but I want to pay you back."

Not wanting to argue, I say, "We'll figure it out."

We arrive at the auto shop, and I send a quick text to Violet to let her know we're here. I drive slowly to give her a second to get in place, being careful not to grind the gears so I don't tip off fuckboy. Instead of parking in the parking lot, I pull up right in front, giving us a perfect view of inside the shop.

And just as I planned, leaning against some piece-of-shit car with a hot woman pressing up against him, is none other than Harrison. Violet's in a skimpy as fuck pair of shorts with her ass cheeks hanging out. I can't see the front of her, but her shirt is so short, it must be showing the bottom of her tits. She's definitely earning that five grand. Maybe, I'll even give her an extra grand just to be nice. It's not like it's my money I'm spending.

Violet's arms are wrapped around Harrison's neck, and by the look on his face, I only have a few seconds before he shoves her away.

"Holy shit!" I yell and Cat looks up from her phone. I know when she sees the scene in front of her because her lips down-turn into a frown and her head tilts slightly to the side. Her beautiful green eyes squint like she can't believe what she's seeing and she needs to focus harder.

"What a fucking asshole!" I hiss dramatically. "Let me get you out of here." Putting the car into reverse, I start to back up. The gear grinds at the same moment Harrison finally shoves Violet off him. The timing couldn't have been better. His gaze hits the car and his eyes go wide like he's been caught doing something he shouldn't have been doing.

He starts stalking toward the car as I press the gas, peeling out and heading away from the shop.

"Wait! Turn around!" Cat begs, finally finding her voice. "I need to see who that was. I couldn't tell for sure from behind."

"Cat, that's Violet. Stripper Violet. As in Anne's sister."

Cat's forehead creases with a deep frown. "That's who I thought it was." She's quiet for a moment and then she says, "Wait! How do you know her?"

"I've seen her with her sister, Anne," I lie. "We hung out last week and she was stopping by to borrow an outfit from Anne."

"Why would Harrison be with her?" Cat shakes her head back and forth, not wanting to believe her precious Harrison would ever cheat on her.

"Cat, I thought you knew." I slow down the car to give us more time to talk. "Harrison and Violet fuck each other on the regular."

"No, that doesn't make sense. Anne told me it was only once." Cat pulls her vibrating cell phone out.

Shit! Thinking quick, I say, "Maybe he decided to give her another chance. You saw her body. I mean, she's fucking hot."

Cat glares daggers at me. Fuck! Wrong thing to say.

"I'm just saying from what I've heard, Harrison has fucked his way through the entire town. Is it so shocking that we would see him with Violet, a stripper he's fucked before?"

"I need to talk to him," she insists. "If he is fucking her then he needs to tell me to my face. Turn back around."

Shit. Fuck. Damn.

"I don't think that's a good idea. What if we go back there and they're fucking? Do you really want to see that?"

"Turn around or I'm going to get out and walk back there myself," she demands with her hand on the handle. Her phone vibrates and it's Harrison. Before she can answer the call, I snatch the phone out of her hand.

"What the hell!" she shrieks. "Give me my damn phone!" She starts attacking me for the phone and I have no choice but to pull over before we get into an accident.

"Cat, think about this," I plead. "You know what you saw. If you answer his call, he's just going to lie. Say it's not what it looked like. I've heard bad things about him. Trust me, please."

She freezes in her place for a moment and I think she's going to listen. But then she pulls the handle on the door and before I can hit the locks, she swings the door open and stumbles out.

"Cat, wait!" I yell, fumbling with the keys to turn the car off. "Where are you going?" I run after her.

"I told you I'm going to talk to Harrison!"

"Cat! Get back in the car!" I desperately beg. Fuck! I didn't see this coming. I thought she would be heartbroken. I'd take her home and she'd cry on my shoulder while I comforted her.

I would convince her to forget about that dumbass and give me a chance.

"Cat, please!"

"No!" She continues to trek down the road. I pick up my pace to catch up to her. I need to get her ass back in the car! If I have to drag her back, that's what I'll do. She can't talk to Harrison. It will fuck everything up! I just need some more time to convince her.

My hand grips her bicep and she flails her arm out. It smacks me right in my nose, and I stop and bring my hands up to my nose to see if I'm bleeding. Crimson liquid runs down my fingers.

"Cat! I think you broke my nose!" I cry out. I look up to see if she's stopped. The rumble of a motorcycle is heard first. And then I see him…her stupid mechanic hero on his metal horse coming to save *my* princess.

Fuck.

CHAPTER THIRTY-FOUR

"GET OUT OF THE FUCKING WAY," I ROAR AS THE MINIVAN IN front of me taps its brakes for the hundredth time since I pulled out onto the road.

They put on their blinker and I gas it, zipping past them. The wind is cold tonight and I didn't have time to grab my hoodie, but I don't care. I was a man on a mission. Hell, if Damian knew I left the shop wide-open to chase after them, I'd probably lose my job. At one time, I wouldn't have done such a thing to jeopardize the job I love so much.

But right now, all that matters is clearing shit up with Cat.

My gut churns at remembering the look on her face. Everything happened so fast. I was working on replacing the timing belt on a Volkswagen Bug when some chick I bagged one lonely night decided to waltz in and throw herself at me. Before I could tell her to back the fuck off, I saw Cat and Theo watching us. It was almost as if that little shit planned it.

I wouldn't put it past him.

He's Heath's son after all.

I'll figure out the whys later, but for now, I have to get my girl back.

My girl.

Possessiveness, hot and fiery like motherfucking lava, burns through my veins. Hell yes, she's mine. I've been with enough women to know what feels different and right and fucking real. Cat is all of those things. She's mine. I don't care if I have to chase her down, toss her over my shoulder, and yell it to the world. Now that I finally know what it feels like to be happy, I'll be damned if I let a misunderstanding steal it away from me.

Up ahead, I see brake lights on a vehicle that's pulled over on the side of the road. My chest tightens as I hold out hope it's Cat. That fucker can barely drive his car, so the odds are stacked in my favor that he's stalled out or some shit. As I near the vehicle and see my beautiful fucking girl stomping away from him, my heart stutters in my chest.

I hit the brakes as I pull off on the shoulder and my bike slips. I fishtail a bit on the gravel but manage to stop twenty feet in front of her.

"Cat," I call out, my voice strained.

She runs toward me, her stupid cousin calling after. I yank off my helmet and hand it to her. We can talk later. Away from this prick. She straddles the bike behind me and situates her helmet.

"Get me out of here," she orders, hugging my middle.

I gas it and whip back around the way we came. Theo calls out behind us, but the roar of my engine drowns him out. She hugs me tighter and some of the tension bleeds from me. If she thought something worse than what she saw, she wouldn't be here with me. Her palms wouldn't be rubbing my stomach as though she can't get enough of me.

We whip into the shop parking lot and I pull into the open bay. Thank fuck the chick from earlier is gone and nobody is trying to rob the place. I shut off the engine and before I can get a word out, she climbs off. I slide off and approach her. She looks so fucking cute with the helmet on her head. My little bobble head with the big, sweet lips I'm craving to kiss.

"Who was she?" she asks, her voice shaky.

"Nobody," I say, stepping closer.

She takes a step back and unlatches the helmet. Once she's

freed herself, she hands it to me, putting space between us. Her green eyes flicker with sadness and her pouty lips aren't smiling.

Fucking Theo.

I don't know what he did, but I know that asshole is responsible.

"Cat, listen," I say softly as I set the helmet down on the ground beside me. "Whatever you saw—"

"You," she snips, crossing her arms over her chest. "With a stripper. That's what I saw, so we're clear."

Scrubbing my palm over my face in frustration, I try to remind myself that she came to me. She didn't run. "I fucked her once. Months ago. You know my past is shitty."

Her brows furl together. "You don't stay with any of them. Just fuck and run."

Wincing at her words, I rub at the back of my neck and shrug. "No one was worth staying for."

"She's so pretty," she mutters.

I glower at her as I close the distance. My palms cradle her cheeks as I press a kiss to her nose. "Nobody is as pretty as you."

A smile tugs at her lips and she tilts her head up. "You're sucking up to me."

"I'm telling you the truth. You've consumed me, Cat. Completely fucking consumed me."

She unfolds her arms and her palms find my chest. "So you weren't trying to get with her again?"

"Fuck no," I growl. "One second I'm fiddling with the car I was working on and the next this chick is trying to get on my nuts. I yelled at her and told her to get the hell away. Then, I took off after you because the last thing I ever wanted you to think was that I'd choose someone like her when I had someone like you."

"Her name is Violet," she says primly, batting her lashes at me.

"All I saw was you, Cat. All I cared about was you."

I press my lips to hers and she grants me access to her sweet tongue. My mouth dominates hers as I kiss her with a vigorous apology. She seems to forgive me because her palms slide up my chest to my neck. I'm about to do something that might cost me my job if Damian sees on the video cameras, when her stomach grumbles loudly.

She giggles when I pull away and lift a brow at her. "Hungry?"

"Dinner was interrupted when Theo rushed me out the door," she says and then frowns. "It's like he knew."

I grip her jaw and press another kiss to her perfect lips. "Convenient, huh?" I release her and pull some bills from my wallet. "I have to close up the garage, but the sandwich shop next door is still open. Want to grab us dinner?"

She beams at me as she takes the money. "Is this a date?"

Reaching out, I snag her wrist and pull her before she can leave me. "Cat Lincoln, will you have dinner with me?"

"I will," she says, a silly grin on her face. "But you better wash up, mister."

I kiss her wrist and then release her. "You like it when I'm dirty."

"If you clean up, maybe I'll let you get dirty again," she throws back at me, her eyes flashing with mischief.

"Hurry and get back, woman. You don't give a man a hard-on with dirty talk and then leave for too long."

She wiggles her fingers in a wave and dances out the door.

It takes everything in me not to prowl after her.

Too close.

That asshole Theo is going to have to answer for his hand in nearly destroying my happiness.

"So my car's not ready?" she asks as she tosses our trash from dinner in the bin.

"Not quite."

She pouts but when I simply lift my brows at her, she laughs. "Fine. Well, are you going to show me around?"

I stiffen and cock my head to the side. "Around the shop?"

"Yeah, what? You don't want to show me?" Fuck, those pouty lips make me crazy.

"I'm just shocked you would want to see…you know…" I trail off, frowning.

Her nose scrunches. "I guess I *don't* know. You work here and love it. It makes you happy. And because I like you, I want to see all the parts of you, especially the ones you're proud of."

"Come here," I growl.

She throws her arms around me and I grab her ass, lifting her. Her legs wrap around my waist and she locks them behind me. Her eyes glimmer with joy as she grins at me.

"You're so beautiful," I tell her, kissing her lips. "So beautiful."

"And you're sweet, but you're not going to distract me, stallion."

I flash her a crooked grin. "Stallion, huh? And you haven't even taken a ride yet."

"I have an appointment soon," she tells me, her chin lifted. "I know what you're packing."

Leaning toward her, I nip at her jaw. "You can pet my stallion later if you're a good girl."

"Oh, I can be good," she says sweetly. "Now giddy-up! Show me the cool stuff."

We spend the next half hour walking around the shop while I explain stuff to her. She's a girl and I know car stuff isn't the most exciting thing, but she listens with rapt attention. After I've bored her long enough, I take her to the bay where her car sits. I open the door and sit inside with her settling on my lap. At least we're somewhat hidden from the cameras.

Her features grow serious as she runs her fingernails along my buzzed scalp. "It scares me how much I care."

My brows furrow and I brush her hair behind her ears so I can see her face better. "Me too."

"The way I feel when I'm around you…" she trails off.

"It's intense."

She nods. "It's like this strong pull and I want to give into it fully. But I'm afraid I'll never be able to pull back away."

"Why would you ever back away?" I growl, my palms roaming down her sides, desperate to touch her everywhere.

"Because what if it hurts? What if I let it pull me and then it hurts? How do you come back from something like that?" Her jade-colored orbs dart back and forth, studying my features.

"But what if it doesn't hurt?" I challenge, kissing the corner of her mouth, letting my lips linger on her skin. "What if it feels good?"

She kisses me deeply and then rocks her hips, making my cock ache for the attention she's giving it. "It feels good," she agrees, her voice breathy.

"So let it pull you," I rumble as I dig my fingers into her hips, helping her grind against me.

"Harrison," she murmurs.

Our kiss becomes hot and frantic. I slip a hand under her shirt and cup her breast over her bra. She moans and I nearly come right then.

"Fuck, Cat," I groan. "You feel too good."

"Too good, mmm?"

I nip at her bottom lip and slide my hand between her thighs. Through her jeans, I rub her sweet spot until she shudders in my arms. When she collapses against me, I chuckle against her hair.

"Too good," I reiterate.

She leans back and looks at me with a soft expression that makes my chest ache more than my fucking cock. "I want to make it too good for you too."

"Not here."

She caresses my cheek. "Then take me home."

I lie in bed staring up at the ceiling in the dark as frustration rattles my bones. We came home hours ago only for her bratty-ass cousin to throw himself at her fucking crying. He was so distraught, he couldn't get three words out. I could tell she wanted to lay into him but was softening to his wailing.

He's her cousin after all.

She knows where I am. When she gets done coddling the baby, she can come see her man. And she will come to me because of the pull. I feel it nonstop. I can't get her out of my head and when I'm around her, I can't get her out of my hands.

I'm fucking obsessed.

It reminds me of a love letter from Heath to Catrina I'd found once. The letter was a madman's rant of love and possession and obsession. At the time I'd thought it was fucked up that someone could be so into someone that they would rather cut open their veins and bleed out than spend one second without the other. It makes me wonder how he dealt with Catrina's death. Thank God I was too young to remember. I'm not sure I'd want to be a witness to that level of grief.

And I'm headed that way.

Overwhelming intensity for another person.

Just out of nowhere, it tackles you.

I don't want to get out from beneath her, though. It's like I finally understand those journals and love letters. It all makes sense now.

I'm not sure a feeling like this ever disappears. It's a beast, *the pull*. Furiously ravenous. Uncontrollable. Wild and uncaged.

I let it tug, tug, tug me so far from what I know that I'm practically on another plane of existence. Like all those sci-fi novels I'd read when I was a teenager. Foreign and different, but beautiful. It's something I want to explore and stake my claim on.

My bedroom door creaks open and the ache in my heart eases. The door closes with a click and then soft footsteps make it over to my bed. I scoot over toward the wall as she sits down and then slides beneath the covers with me.

"Hey," she murmurs. "I'm sorry." Her hand splays on my bare chest and I relax.

"Babies need coddling," I say in a flippant tone.

She lets out a quiet laugh. "He was upset that I ran off without giving him a chance to explain."

"And did he?"

"No. He cried himself to sleep," she says. "I snuck away."

I groan when her palm slides south.

"I promised to make it good for you." Her voice is a sexy, seductive purr that has my dick straining against my boxers. "I owe it to you."

She slides down the bed, tugging the covers with her. Her fingers dip past my waistband and she pulls my boxers down my thighs. She rids me of them completely. My dick bobs out, bouncing against my lower abs. When her small hand wraps around my length, I hiss in pleasure.

"Cat," I warn.

"Hmm?" She strokes me slowly, teasing me.

"You're headed down a dangerous path."

Her hot breath is near my cock and her hair tickles my stomach and hips. "Why is it dangerous?"

"Because you'll make me lose control. I want to be sweet with you, but teasing my cock is going to make me crazy," I growl.

"So this is bad?" she asks and then runs her tongue along the underside of my shaft.

My fingers blindly grab at her hair. "So bad."

Her breathy laugh against my skin has my hips bucking, searching for her sweet mouth.

"You're a tease," I groan. "If you're not going to put those plump lips on my dick, then let me put my lips on you. See how you like to be tormented."

Before I can taunt her anymore, she slides her mouth around the crown of my cock. I grit my teeth and tighten my grip on her hair. She's inexperienced, I know this, but the curious way she explores my cock drives me wilder than I've ever been. Nothing compares to this moment. Fucking nothing.

"Christ, Cat," I curse. "You're fucking perfect."

She hums around my dick at my praise and her tongue lashes out, tasting my underside. I can barely control myself. My hips are bucking, urging her on. Her drool leaks out, making a lubricant for her lips and she bobs up and down, getting the hang of it. With each second that passes—each hiss I make in pleasure—she grows more confident. Her hand wraps around the base of my cock and she strokes me. When she eases me toward the back of her throat and then gags, I nearly come right then.

"You perfect, goddamn girl." I want to spread her thighs and worship this woman from my knees. She's pulled me into her world, rocked my foundation, and placed herself on a pedestal.

I'm enamored—fucking obsessed with her. "Cat," I growl. "Cat, I'm going to come."

Her fist jerks at me faster and her bobbing becomes more determined. I can read her actions. She wants to taste me.

"Fuck, baby," I moan. "You want to taste it, well, it's coming. Hope you're thirsty, dirty girl."

She hums in appreciation, but then I'm coming. Without restraint. My hips buck toward her mouth and she gags as my cum douses my little flame. She's burning with lust—on fire for me—and I try to get her under control with my release.

But my sweet girl can't be contained.

No, she swallows and then pops off my dick like a fucking pro. Then, she crawls up my body and attacks my mouth. I love that my salty musk is what I taste in her mouth. It's like I've marked her as mine.

Flipping her onto her back, I slide my thigh between hers. She's wearing pajama pants and a tank top from what I can tell in the dark. I slide my palm beneath her shirt and grope her tit as my mouth finds her neck.

"Too good," I mutter, pinching her nipple. "You're too good."

"It was my first time," she says, a smile in her voice. "I had to impress you."

"Consider me fucking wowed."

She giggles and then it gives way to a yawn.

"You're tired." I kiss her neck. "You have school tomorrow. Better get your rest."

"I wanted to make love to you," she says with a pout.

"Soon, baby. I like taking my time with you."

She yawns again. "Can I sleep here with you tonight?"

"I'm never letting you go," I growl.

My words seem to soothe her because seconds later, she's

out. With her limbs tangled with mine and her scent all I can sense, I'm completely content. I tighten my hold on her.

Never.

I'm never letting her go.

I don't care if that makes me sound just as crazy as motherfucking Heath.

When a man knows, he knows.

And I fucking know.

Cat is mine.

CHAPTER THIRTY-FIVE

Harrison

"Y OU HAVE TO GO," I TELL HER, SLAPPING HER ASS.

She pouts, looking too fucking tempting in her school uniform. The knee-high socks are killing both me and my cock. "I could skip class," she suggests, her brow arching and her lips turning up wickedly.

"No, woman," I growl. "Get your sexy ass to class before I do something that'll get you suspended."

A few students walking past us do a double take.

"I hate that you get to have fun all day and I have to do boring stuff," she groans.

"One day, when I have my own shop, you can stay with me all day. Until then, I don't need you distracting me," I tell her, smirking.

She smiles shyly at me as she grips the front of my hoodie and stands on her toes to kiss me. "You're going to keep me that long?"

"I'm going to keep you forever."

Her eyes shine with happiness. "You should do it."

"Keep you?"

"That too," she teases. "I mean, you should get your own shop. You really love what you do. I could tell when you showed me around last night."

"One day."

"One day," she agrees. "Until then, I'll go do this boring

shit. Try not to miss me too much." Her palm grips my dick through my jeans. "I know your cock will."

I shake my head at her. "You're ten kinds of evil, Cat Lincoln. How's a man supposed to drive down the highway with a ten-inch boner in the way?"

She laughs. "Ten inches, hmmm? You think highly of yourself."

"You're testing me, woman."

Her smile lights up the world. "I like to keep you on your toes, *man*."

"Be good and when I get off work, I'm going to show you once again that I can back up my claims."

She pats my dick and steps away. "I mean, you're hung, stallion, but ten inches?"

Before I can argue, she wiggles those cute fingers at me and then blows me a kiss. I watch her ass bounce as she runs toward the building. The bell rings. She'll be late. And my girl doesn't care because she stops to wave from the doorway.

As soon as she's out of sight, my smile falls and my chest feels hollow. This girl fills my soul up with her. I'm falling so hard for her and I'm unable to stop it. I don't want to stop it.

A party.

Theo threw a fucking party.

"Seriously," I groan. "Nobody better fuck with my shit."

"I'm sorry. It was my idea, but then after all the crap that happened, I asked him to call it off. He didn't." Cat sighs into the phone. "He's too busy being king of the party. I told him to make everyone go home, but he ignored me. I couldn't handle him anymore tonight and bailed. I'm painting my toenails in my room." She yawns. "If I'm asleep when you get here, wake me up."

"I'll be home in an hour or so. I'm going to go talk to Violet."

She's silent for a beat. "Violet, huh? Stripper Violet?"

"That's the one."

"Tell her I said to keep her dirty claws away from you and we won't have a problem," she snips out.

"You're such a little badass, aren't you? Little Cat the cheerleader is gonna beat some stripper's ass to defend her boyfriend's honor?" I tease.

She laughs and I love the breathy sound of it. "I am a little badass. Glad you're finally learning. And she'll meet my kitty cat claws if she even thinks about throwing herself at you again." I can hear her shuffling around and then she says, "Boyfriend, hmmm?"

"Yep," I tell her.

"Good. I like it. A nice pretty label on what we're doing."

"I'm not pretty," I grumble.

"Oh, you're pretty. Super pretty," she says with amusement in her tone.

"I think you meant 'fuck hot.'"

"Potato, po-tah-toh," she sings.

"Bye, woman. I'll see you soon."

She laughs. "Bye!"

I hang up on her, otherwise we'll do this all day. I love verbally sparring with her. But I'd rather do it with my hands roaming all over her body. I exit the break room and snag my keys and helmet.

"Where you headed out so early?" Damian asks as I start for the door.

"To get answers," I grunt.

"This have to do with the woman I saw you all over in the video feed last night?"

"You're a fucking stalker," I tell him.

He shrugs. "I don't deny it. The girl with the Mustang? Is she the reason why you're at war with that skinny twerp who can't drive his Porsche?"

"You really are a stalker."

"Again, I don't deny it. Spill, boy. If I'm going to let you slack off and get out of here early, you have to indulge an old man." He scratches at his wiry beard. "Besides, I need to know she was worth blowing out of here and leaving my shop open with no one inside but a skanky stripper."

"She's worth it," I growl.

"I figured she was. Never seen you act this way before. You're in deep."

"My girl, Cat, has a dipshit cousin who thinks he can fuck with what we have," I grit out. "I'm going to find out for sure and then I'm going to deck his ass."

"Hope she's worth going to jail over," he says, laughing.

"She's worth everything."

He grows serious for a moment. "You don't remember Wanda because you were just a little kid, but she took a liking to you before she died. Miss Helen and she were close at church, before breast cancer took my wife. She told me to look after you. Said, 'He doesn't have a proper daddy and he needs a little love and guidance, Dame.' And hell if I didn't want to take you under my wing. It was like serenfuckingdipity when you came strutting in here when you were a fifteen-year-old grumpy bastard with one helluva chip on your shoulder. I did as Wanda asked and took you in, even though your attitude was rotten as hell. But I did and you got tolerable. You were a quick study too. Weren't a happy thing at all, but you loved any job I threw your way. So to see you finally smiling, I gotta tell you, she must have known something I didn't. I feel a little proud like I'm sure your dad would have if he were still around."

I playfully punch his arm. "Don't go getting soft on me, man."

"I'm just saying it's good to see you not be such an asshole. You're growing up. I've been waiting for this day for years, kid."

"Is that so?"

"Yeah," he says, grinning. "I was just about to give you a promotion, too, but you left my shop wide-open."

"She was worth it," I tell him with a wink.

"The good ones always are."

"I'm looking for Violet," I tell the bouncer as I enter the club I've been to more times than I'd like to count.

The fat guy laughs and his belly quivers. "A crowd favorite."

"I want to ask her some questions."

His brows furrow. "You a cop?"

"You've brought your piece of shit truck to me at the shop on the corner. You know I'm not a cop."

"Yeah, yeah," he grumbles. "She's working the bar tonight."

I give him a nod and stalk into the smoky club. Violet is bent across the bar with her cleavage hanging out talking to a balding old man. When she sees me, her eyes flare with appreciation until realization sets in. She groans when I take a seat on a barstool next to the old man.

"What can I get ya?" she asks, smacking her gum. The flirty act she put on me last night is gone.

"Answers."

"I guess it doesn't matter," she huffs. "It's not like he paid me anyway. I did my job. The asshole held out on me."

I arch a brow in question. "Who?"

"Heath's new kid. I guess he isn't new, but you know what I mean. Theo. He was supposed to give me five grand."

"Five grand?" I growl. "To do what? Fuck me?"

The old man chuckles. "Baby doll, get me another vodka tonic. I feel like there's a story here and I need another drink."

She smiles sweetly at him and shoots me the bird before setting off to make his drink. Once he's settled, she puts a hand on her hip and glares at me.

"Not to fuck you," she reveals. "To make her think we were fucking." Her brows furl together. "For the record, we did fuck. You don't even remember me?"

Vaguely.

Maybe I remember her voice. I don't fucking know. They all blend together.

"I know you're Violet," I say with a grunt.

She rolls her eyes. "You didn't last night. It doesn't matter. I failed, apparently. Theo's a dick like his dad. At least Heath tips well when I do my job." She pops her gum. "He certainly doesn't whine like a little bitch when we fuck." A fake smile forms on her lips. "And I'm at least memorable enough that he knows my name."

"Don't worry," I grumble. "I won't forget your name after this."

"Tell Theo I hope his dick rots off," she calls out after me.

"Gladly, Violet." I look over my shoulder and frown at her. "And if you know what's good for you, stay away from fucking Heath of all people. He's bad for the soul."

She smirks. "But he tips well."

Cars are everywhere and my blood boils. This idiot is going to get his ass handed to him when Heath gets back. But first, Theo and I are going to have words. I want to know why the fuck he thought he could throw an obscene amount of money at some chick to try and break up Cat and me. If he gives me any lip, I won't be in a talking mood. I'll be in a *I'm going to whip your scrawny ass* mood. He better tread lightly.

As soon as I open the door, the stench of marijuana assaults my senses. It grates on my nerves that he'd allow drugs in the house. His cousin is fairly innocent and I don't like the fact he exposed her to this shit. A couple of girls giggle when they see me and I tip my head at them before rushing to the stairwell. I reach the top of the stairs and start for her room when I see someone go into mine.

Oh fucking hell no.

I stalk down the hall and yank some blond asshole from my room, scaring the shit out of him. "Leave," I snarl.

His girl squeaks as she runs from my room after him. Thank God I got here before those two fucked on my bed. I smell like an ashtray from the club, so I hurry and take a quick shower. Once I'm clean and dry, I pull on a pair of loose sweats. I slip out of my room, run off a couple more people, and then make it to Cat's room. When I open the door, it's dark inside.

A small whimper makes me take pause.

A familiar whimper.

Fire explodes within me as I swat at the light switch. Light bursts around me, exposing the source of the moans. Cat is facing the wall and her fuckwad cousin is behind her, rutting against her like a fucking barn animal.

"What the fuck?" I roar, my hands curling into fists.

Cat jolts and swivels her head around. Her face goes from confused to horrified.

"You liked it," Theo slurs. "I heard you moan."

She shrieks and slaps away his hand from between her thighs. "Theo! You idiot!"

Stalking forward, I grab the twerp by the back of his neck and jerk him from the bed. I send him careening into the armoire. He cries out and holds his side.

"I thought it was you, Harrison," Cat cries out. "Ew! Theo, ew!"

He tries to stand, but he's drunk as shit. The kid can barely get up on his knees without swaying. I kick his chest and he falls back, knocking his head on the floor.

"Stop," he whines. "You fucking brute!"

"You touch what's mine," I snarl as I approach, "and I'll touch yours." I give him a swift kick to the balls and he howls. "Touch her again and I'll do a lot worse than that."

The little asshole is such a weak bastard that I don't even feel right about kicking his ass. Fuck him for being a pussy. If he were a real man—like his father—I'd take him out to the barn and go at him fist to fist. But this dickhead is so drunk, I'd probably kill him with one punch to the throat.

"Harrison," Cat says, gripping my elbow. "Get me out of here."

"Fucking gladly," I growl. I nudge Theo with my foot and glower down at him. "I want you to get your ass downstairs and send them home. Then, tomorrow, I want you to apologize to my goddamn girl for touching her."

"You're a bully," he cries, writhing on the floor, still grabbing his nuts.

"Me?" I seethe. "You tried to get my girlfriend—your cousin—to break up with me because you wanted to fuck her. If I were a bully, I'd tie you up and drag you behind my bike for acting like a damn idiot. Stay the fuck away from me and Cat. Got it?"

"Fucking fine," he snaps.

"I'm telling your dad," Cat says, digging her own knife in.

"Cat…" he pleads.

I grab her hand and haul her out of her room. From the top of the stairs, I yell down, "You have ten minutes to get the fuck out of my house or I'll call the cops."

We don't wait to see if they obey or not.

I take my girl to my room where she's safe and lock us inside.

CHAPTER THIRTY-SIX

CAT

I LIKE HARRISON'S ROOM. IT'S MORE SPACIOUS THAN MINE AND HE has quirky decorations. As though he's collected items over the years and somehow made a representation of himself through his décor. I turn over a particularly heavy hunk of metal and stare at it in confusion. It's clunky and I have no idea what it even is. But I guess art is that way. Beloved to the eye of the beholder and all that jazz.

My eyes drift to the window and I stare longingly at the house in the distance. I can see it beyond the fog that's starting to clear. It makes my chest ache.

My home.

Well, my old home.

I miss it.

And not just for the things in it. I miss the memories. The smell. My dad's always cheery disposition.

"It's an alternator." Harrison takes the clunky metal thing and places it back on the dresser. "A car part."

"I thought it was a decoration," I say, smiling.

He rubs at his eyes and I take a minute to admire him as he yawns. His gray sweatpants hang low on his narrow hips, revealing a very obvious bulge. Morning wood. I bite back a smile as I let my eyes roam up along his dark happy trail to his sexy belly button. Over his gloriously chiseled abs decorated in ink painting every inch of him. Up along his chest and between his pectoral muscles that are downright lickable. I slide my gaze up his strong neck that's corded with muscle. His Adam's apple protrudes and I find myself fixated on that lovely but unusual part of the human anatomy. Eventually, I let my eyes flit to his face. He's watching me, minus his usual knowing smirk. So serious this morning.

"Did you get your fill?" he asks, his voice still rough and gravelly from sleep.

"Not yet," I say, darting my gaze to his dick before meeting his eyes again. "Someone insisted on my sleeping last night."

His jaw clenches and his features harden. "Your cousin had just felt you up. Didn't exactly feel like the right time to fuck my girl for the first time."

I try to make light of it, but he's right. Last night, we came to his room and I burst into tears. I was pissed at Theo but also upset that he'd creep on me like that, pretending to be Harrison. It was disturbing. A shudder ripples through me.

"Hey," Harrison says, kneeling in front of me. He tips my chin up with his fingers so his blue eyes sear into mine. "You okay?"

I swallow down the emotion and smile. "Perfect."

"Liar," he says, smirking. "Talk to me, mustang girl."

Turning from him, I stare out the window again. "I was feeling homesick."

He takes my hand and brings it to his mouth. After giving each knuckle a sweet kiss, he bites my thumb.

"Hey!" I yelp.

He grins wickedly at me. "I was trying to cheer you up."

"By biting me?"

The asshole shrugs. "It was worth a try."

"Dumbest idea ever, Harrison." But I'm smiling stupidly at him.

"It worked," he says smugly. He bites me again and I swat

him in the head. His laughter fills my soul this morning, driving out any lingering depression.

"I guess I'll leave so you can get ready for work," I say in resignation.

He shakes his head. "I'm calling in sick today."

"You are?"

"You mentioned last night you missed riding Shorty. I thought we could take the horses out and you could take me to some of your spots," he says with a smile that makes my heart flutter.

"My spots belong to someone else now."

"The sweet spots are mine," he says with a wolfish grin. "But the secret spots at your old house, those are the ones I'm talking about. We'll pack a lunch and make a day of it."

"A day of breaking and entering?" I ask with an arched brow.

"Unless you have something better to do." He smirks as he rises to his feet, offering me his hand.

I allow him to pull me up and into his arms. "Nope, nothing better. Let's be bad together."

His lips press to my neck as he squeezes me. "You sure you're okay?"

"I'm perfect now."

"You always were."

We sneak away on the horses before Theo gets up. When I went to grab some clothes, I found him in my bed snoring. I hope he wakes up and regrets the way he behaved. Although, I'm not going to hold out hope. Heath is a bad influence on my cousin. He's turned into an ass since we've come to live here.

I'm so over this place.

Once Dad finds a new job, I'm leaving. I'll somehow convince Harrison to come with me. We can leave Windy Hills and never come back. Theo can spend the rest of his life trying to please an unhappy man.

I glance over at Harrison as he rides Heath's horse, Brontë. He's wearing a black Henley that hugs all his muscles and a baseball hat that's flipped backward on top of his head. A bad boy riding a horse. Yummy.

"Whoa there," I say to Shorty as I guide him around a large rock.

"The scenery is great and all, but don't kill yourself looking at it." He grins at me, his blue eyes glimmering. Smug ass.

We continue riding and I inhale the cool morning air. This is nice. Every moment I have with Harrison is nice. It makes me realize that for the first time in my entire life, I feel wholly a part of something. In this case, it's another person. Not cheerleading or my friends or my family or my future.

Just him.

"My boss Damian met his wife their senior year in high school," Harrison says as we clomp along on our horses. "He said they just knew."

"Oh yeah?"

"Yeah. Their folks had a shit fit when they ran off and got married."

"Sounds like a sweet story," I say, grinning.

"They met in first hour on a Monday and were married in the courthouse by Friday after school."

I let out a gasp. "What? No way!"

"He told me that one time when we were taking apart a bitch of an engine. I thought he was stupid, but they'd been married for a long-ass time before she died of cancer. Looking back, it was smart."

My heart squeezes in my chest. "Smart?"

He stops his horse and turns his intense stare my way. "They didn't waste a minute, Cat. They just knew and that was that." He pulls off his hat to run his palm over his head before putting it back on and pinning me with a penetrating stare. "You know, your mom and Heath…" He sighs. "What a fucking tragedy."

"They wasted it," I murmur. "They wasted their minute."

He nods. "Damian is happy. He runs his shop with a smile on his face. My boss lost his wife, but he remains happy because they stole every second together."

"And Heath is miserable because he and my mother wasted their time," I agree.

"I want to be happy," he says before trotting off, not waiting for my answer.

We're quiet until we get the horses put away in the barn. He shoulders his bag filled with our packed lunch and we walk up to the door. After a quick peek through the windows, it's clear to see no one has moved in, which frustrates me even more over the whole debacle. We didn't have to leave in such a rush. Heath is just a dick.

"Ready to break in?" he asks as though this is a regular, everyday task.

"Luckily, we don't have to." I kneel and lift a pot to reveal a key.

"Clever girl."

I grin as I pick up the key and unlock the door. The house is quiet and partially empty, but most of the furniture still remains. I spend the next half hour showing him all the nooks and crannies in the house. Eventually, I take him to my spot. The attic. When I was a girl, I was always hiding. Dad got tired of losing his mind when I'd disappear for hours and converted the attic to a hideout for me so he could always find me. It's the part I miss the most about this house.

"You have to climb," I say to Harrison as I point to a ladder on the wall at the end of the hallway.

"Maybe you should go first. To show me how," he flirts.

I swat at him. "You just want to check out my ass."

"You say that like it's a bad thing."

"Try not to get distracted and fall," I tease.

We climb up to the attic and I inhale the familiar scent. Dad packed up everything except here. I'd been too upset to even check. Now, I'm glad it remains untouched.

"Watch your head, big boy," I tell him as I hunch to avoid a rafter on the angled ceiling.

He grunts but mimics my actions. We make our way over to the mattress on the floor by the only window. It's covered with soft, chenille blankets and has a ton of pillows thrown on top. Stacks of books litter the floor around the bed. It's cozy and my heart warms at being here again.

"I love this place," I tell him sadly. "It's not mine anymore."

He kicks off his boots and sprawls out on the bed. "What makes this place so special?"

With a sigh, I pull off my shoes and curl up beside him. I run my fingers along his jaw and kiss his lips. "I love how I feel like I'm someplace far, far away from the world. A secret place. I love getting lost in my books and napping on rainy days. It's quiet and perfect."

"Like my spots," he agrees, his thumb running along the outside of my neck.

"Yeah." I smile. "Like yours."

He pulls me so I'm lying on top of him. "*You* make the spot, you know. This," he says, waving around us, "can be anywhere."

"It's much better with you in it," I admit.

"My spots were empty until you came along." His steel blue eyes sear into me, brimming with unspoken words and emotion.

I sit up and pull off my shirt. His stare burns a trail along my exposed flesh. When I reach back and unhook my bra, he lets out a hiss.

"Cat…"

I toss my bra at him, loving the way he turns from predatory to grinning wide. He sits up and peels off his own shirt, losing his hat along the way. I lick my lips as I admire his chest. Never gets old. The man is hotter than hell.

"Lie back, mustang girl," he says playfully.

I fall back on the pillows and watch him as he unbuttons my jeans. He efficiently undresses the rest of me. When he leaves my pink knee-high socks on, I lift my brows, trying to ignore the nerves flitting through me.

"I heard leaving socks on during sex was extremely unsexy," I whisper. My voice shakes and it embarrasses me.

"You heard wrong," he murmurs as he sits up on his knees. He grabs my foot and tickles it. I squeal at him. "These are very sexy." He bites my foot before letting it hit the pillows.

"Are you going to leave your socks on?" I curl my arms around me, suddenly uneasy.

He pushes down his jeans and boxers. His cock springs out, bouncing. I've had it in my mouth. I've had his fingers inside me. But…that thing seems pretty huge right now.

"Do you want me to leave my socks on?"

I nod and swallow. "Harrison," I choke out. "I'm freaking out right now."

His features soften as he prowls over me and kisses me. "Cat, baby, we don't have to do this."

"I want to," I breathe, digging my fingers into his back and pulling him against me. "I just, uh, I need a minute."

He settles his naked body against mine and rests on one elbow. His other hand strokes the hair from my face and he regards me tenderly. I melt under his attention.

"I don't want to waste a second," he murmurs, "but I'd wait an eternity for you."

Tears sting my eyes and I scratch my fingers along his head. "Don't waste any more seconds." I pull him to me and he kisses me deeply. His hand caresses my breast and then he slides it south. All it takes is for him to start sliding his finger along my slit, and all apprehension melts away. He rubs on my clit until I'm squirming and then he slides his longest finger between my pussy lips before pushing inside me. My back arches up off the mattress as I moan in appreciation.

"Right there," he growls against my mouth. "Feel that?"

I jolt at the pleasure that zings from within me. "Y-Yes, I feel it."

"That's my new favorite spot."

My eyes flutter closed when he rubs that tiny spot of pleasure inside me until I'm crying out in ecstasy. I kiss him frantically when he slips his wet finger out. My legs wrap around him and I urge him to me.

"I need you," I beg. "Please, Harrison."

"Cat, baby," he groans. His cock slides against my wet slit. "I want so many things from you."

"So take them," I encourage, my heels digging into his ass.

He nips at my bottom lip. "We should be careful—"

His words are cut short when I grip his throbbing cock and guide it to the part of me that practically weeps in need for him. We both hiss as he slides his thickness inside me. It stings as it stretches me, but I've never felt anything so unreal. So amazing. Like I'm connected to another person on a level that is not of this world—something of another plane of existence. It transcends anything I've ever known.

"Fuckfuckfuckfuck," he chants as he sinks all the way inside me. "I've never done this."

"You've had sex," I breathe.

"Not like this," he growls. "Not so…raw."

His mouth crashes against mine and he thrusts his hips. I'm dizzied at how maddeningly beautiful it feels to have him filling up every inch of me. We're connected. I love being with him this way. He slides out slightly only to drive back in. The stretching of his thickness inside me sort of hurts, but it's a pain I could get addicted to. And I'm feeling every single part of his supposed ten inches as he buries himself deep inside me.

"You okay, mustang girl?" he rasps against my mouth. I love how utterly out of control he sounds. Like I make him just as crazy as he makes me.

"Perfect, stallion."

He grins against my lips before kissing me hard. His hips buck harder. Wilder. I dig my fingers into his shoulders. My breasts bounce as he drives into me over and over again. When his hand slips between us to show my clit some attention, my pussy tightens around him. It causes some discomfort on my end, but he lets out a ragged moan that encourages me. I try to rock my hips with him, clenching my inner walls hoping it feels good for him, when he gives my clit a slight pinch. Stars glitter around me as an orgasm slices through me without warning.

"Fuck," he hisses, his body stilling as heat surges inside me. He starts to pull out, but I've never felt anything so satisfying in my entire life. The heat of his cum as he marks me from the inside. I dig my heels into his ass, imploring him to stay. I win out because he does a lazy grind of his hips before relaxing on top of me. I like that his cock remains inside of me despite the fact it has softened. His nose nuzzles my hair and he finds my ear with his lips. "Mine, Cat."

I rub his buzzed scalp and smile. "You're mine too."

After we get cleaned up and get dressed, we decide to eat our lunch down by the lake. We've been to Harrison's side of the lake, so it's only fitting while I'm showing him my secret spots, we visit my side.

Harrison unravels the blanket he packed and shakes it out across the grass a few feet from the water. We sit and I open the bag with our food, handing him a sandwich and keeping one for myself. I pull out a container of strawberries and set them down between us, then hand Harrison a bottle of water. For a few minutes, we eat in silence. My thoughts back with our conversation from earlier. After I had finished reading my mom's journals, I almost wished I could go back to being ignorant. For so long, I had put my parents' relationship on this imaginary pedestal. They were madly in love and created me. Then one horrific night, a storm came through and she went into labor. That night I was born and my mother died, and my father lost the love of his life. But after reading her thoughts and feelings, I'm no longer ignorant to the type of woman she really was, and I now know my mother wasn't capable of love. Not of loving my father. Or Heath. Or me. Or even herself for that matter.

But Heath loved her.

Enough to wreak havoc on my entire life just to get revenge on my dad.

It's sad that love could breed so much hate.

"What's got you so quiet?" Harrison asks, breaking me out of my thoughts. I stare into his questioning eyes for a moment and go for the truth.

"I was thinking about my mom's journals. Maybe they were left behind to serve a greater purpose. Like to be read as a cautionary tale."

"Like a warning?" he clarifies.

"Yeah, her entries all have one thing in common. She had two men who loved her, yet she never seemed truly happy—content. She seemed to always want more money, more materialistic possessions, more attention. More love. But it was never enough. That's not the kind of life I want to live. One where I'm always searching for more. Reading her thoughts have made me realize I don't want to be anything like my mother." I give him a sad smile.

Harrison sets his sandwich down and reaches his hand out for me to take. We link our fingers together and he pulls me toward him until I'm tucked between his legs. Keeping our fingers intertwined, he wraps his arms around me and nuzzles his scruffy face into the crook of my neck, his breath whispering across my skin. I sigh in contentment.

"Then don't be," he murmurs. "What is it you want, Cat? What will make you truly happy?"

I know the answer without having to even think about it. "You, Harrison. I want you."

"You have me," he breathes. His lips find their way to my neck and he trails soft kisses along my heated flesh, downward. He pulls the sleeve of my top down, peppering kisses across my shoulder.

His hands unlink from mine and come up to gently massage my breasts. My head falls back against his chest as I get lost in his touch. I can't imagine ever needing anything more than this man. The pull I feel toward him is stronger than anything I've ever felt in my life. Before Harrison, I might've been able to understand my mother's needs, but now, I don't comprehend how, if she felt even half for Heath what I feel for Harrison, she could choose anything or anyone over him.

Harrison's fingers pinch my nipples through my bra and shirt and I let out a breathy moan. He chuckles softly, knowing exactly what his touch does to me, as his lips make their way back up to my neck, landing on my earlobe. His tongue darts out as he licks the outer shell of my ear, eliciting a shiver down my spine.

"Are you sore, baby?" he rasps. I don't have to squeeze the

muscles between my legs to know I am. But I'm not in pain. It's more of a delicious kind of soreness. A reminder of what we shared. I know if I say I'm sore, he won't continue. It's one of the many things I love about Harrison. He always puts my needs first. Not wanting him to stop, but also not wanting to lie, I speak around the truth. "I want you. Please."

He grunts softly into my ear, then gripping my hips lifts me and flips me onto my back, so he's hovering above me. He pulls off my shoes and throws them to the side, once again leaving my socks on. Then he pulls my jeans down my legs at the same time I lift and remove my shirt. His eyes appreciatively roam down my body as I pull away my bra, and I'm almost positive it's not just lust but something more shining bright in his irises.

Needing to feel him skin to skin, I sit up and drag his shirt over his head. My gaze travels directly to the beautiful ink decorating his body. Almost his entire chest and biceps are covered with images and words. But one quote in particular catches my attention.

Years of love has been forgot, in the hatred of a minute.

My heart squeezes at the sadness embedded in the meaning of the words. Realization that Harrison hasn't just felt alone his entire life, but if that quote is anything to go by, he also felt unloved. The only woman who loved him, left him before he was old enough to have any real memory of her, and the only thing he knows is that she chose to leave him with his father, who chose to overdose and leave his son in the hands of a monster. The words across his chest have me vowing to spend the rest of my life showing him what true love feels like.

Harrison's eyes follow mine. "Edgar Allan Poe." He shrugs one shoulder self-consciously, and for the first time, I'm seeing a deeper, more vulnerable layer of Harrison, and it only has me falling even more in love with him.

"It's beautiful," I say.

My eyes continue their trail downward and I spot another quote on his ribs.

It does not do to dwell on dreams and forget to live.

"Poe?" I ask.

"No." He shakes his head and his cheeks turn slightly pink. "J.K. Rowling."

It takes me a second to think about who that author is, and when it hits me, I fall back onto the blanket in a fit of laughter. "Harry Potter?" I confirm. "How do you end up with quotes from both Poe and Rowling on your body?"

Harrison's hands drop down to either side of my head, caging me in. His mouth brushes up against mine once, twice, before he pulls back just enough to look into my eyes. "Don't make fun of Harry Potter. There are many lessons to be learned in those books." His voice is deadly serious, but his eyes are dancing with laughter.

"Can I just say how damn sexy it is that you know both Poe and Rowling?" I waggle my eyebrows.

"Oh yeah?" His face dips closer to mine, and his nose rubs against mine playfully. "How sexy?" he asks softly.

Before I can answer, one of his hands leaves the side of my head and glides down my front. He cups the material covering my sex. "Is it sexy enough to make you wet?" Harrison taunts, and I squirm at the thought.

"I don't know," I tease. "Why don't you find out?"

His eyes glimmer with lust as he pushes the material of my panties to the side and plunges two fingers into me, finding out what I already know. I'm drenched.

"Fuck, Cat," he rasps, and without another word, his mouth crashes against mine. He rips my panties from my body as I push his jeans and boxers down his thighs. My legs wrap around his waist and my hands grip around his neck. And with his lips never leaving mine, he pushes his hard length into me. Unlike the first time we made love just a couple short hours ago, this time isn't soft or gentle. It's fierce and passionate as he drives in and out of me with abandon.

My orgasm builds higher and higher as the head of his dick hits that special spot. The pain mixing deliciously with the pleasure. I'm almost there. I can feel my body tightening, ready to detonate. Just a few more thrusts will set me off. Harrison's lips leave mine and move to my shoulder. His thrusts turn frantic, unhinged, and just as I'm about to explode in pleasure, he bites down on my shoulder and stills. His warm seed filling me. He looks into my eyes, his breathing still erratic. Sweat dotting his forehead. I stay quiet, unsure if I should tell him I didn't get off. Maybe women don't orgasm every time. Not wanting to ruin the moment, I decide not to say anything.

Harrison bites down on his lip and gives me a boyish grin. "Fuck, I'm sorry," he says still out of breath. "You just felt too fucking good. Too fucking tight. The way your cunt chokes my cock." He shakes his head with a low chuckle. "You make me feel like a thirteen-year-old virgin all over again." I give him a questioning look and then it hits me. He knows I didn't get off. And what the hell? He lost his virginity at thirteen? I'm pretty sure I was still playing with Barbies at that age.

"It's okay," I say, not wanting to ruin the moment. All that matters to me is how I feel when he's inside of me. The closeness we share. The orgasm is just a bonus.

Harrison gives me a *what the fuck* look then pulls out of me. "No, Cat, it's not okay." His hard body glides down mine until he's on his stomach, between my legs with his mouth parallel with my pussy. "But I'm going to make it up to you." He shoots me a playful wink.

Remembering I'm full of his cum, I try to press my legs together, not wanting him down there, but he just scowls and forces my legs to part.

When his fingers slowly separate my folds, I close my eyes, embarrassed that he's down there in the broad daylight. "Open your eyes," he demands and my lids shoot open.

"I want you to watch as I eat your cunt. Let's see how many times I can make you come on my fingers and tongue." My pussy clenches at his dirty words and I let out a low groan.

His wet tongue hits my clit, and my eyes roll back, until I remember he told me to watch. Quickly, I open my eyes and dart them back down. I was already close before, so as I watch his tongue swirl around my clit with the perfect amount of pressure, it doesn't take more than a half a minute before he sets me off and my orgasm explodes around his tongue.

He glances up at me, his lips glistening with my juices. "That was one," he states matter-of-factly. He pushes his fingers into my soaked pussy. "Let's see how quickly I can make you come this way."

With his eyes never leaving mine, he fingers me slow and deep, hitting the same spot his dick was hitting earlier. His head dips slightly and he places soft, sensual kisses along the inside of my thigh. His hand moves up to my breast. His thumb and forefinger squeeze my sensitive nipple, rolling it between his fingers. Feeling overstimulated, my body begins to shake uncontrollably. I've only experienced less than a handful of orgasms—all at the hands of Harrison—but something is different this time. Something *feels* different. Harrison's fingers twist inside of me. His lips leave my thigh and land on my clit. He sucks on the sensitive nub. Instinctively, I try to push his head off me, but before I succeed, my body begins to convulse. My thighs begin to shake. And then the most powerful orgasm I've ever felt hits me with so much force, my back arches off the blanket. My eyes close of their own volition and stars hit the back of my lids as I come so hard, I'm almost positive I black out.

When I finally come to, Harrison is sitting up, still between my legs with a goofy grin splayed across his face. My butt drops back down and I feel wetness. *Oh my God! Did I pee myself?*

"That was so fucking hot," he says. "The way you came all over my fingers and tongue."

He climbs up my body. "I want you to taste it." He rubs the pads of his finger along my bottom lip then my top, coating me with our cum. "Taste what we created."

Curiously, my tongue darts out and I taste our mixed juices. Salty with a bit of tang mixed in. Harrison groans loudly before he melds his lips to mine. He sucks on my tongue for a few seconds, and I find myself wanting him again. He's like an addiction I can't get enough of. It doesn't matter that my body is spent and I probably couldn't even handle another orgasm.

I still want it.

I want him.

Need him.

Crave everything and anything that's him.

When his mouth leaves mine and he looks at me with the same intensity I'm feeling, the words are out of my mouth before I can stop them. "I love you."

His eyes widen at first then soften. I hold my breath, praying he doesn't reject me. I'm about to give him an out, tell him he doesn't have to say it back, when he opens his mouth and says the only two words that are crazier than the three I just spoke.

"Marry me."

CHAPTER THIRTY-SEVEN

The Present...

"OH MY GOD," I SHRIEK. "THEY DIDN'T USE PROTECTION!"

Mom gives me a soft, happy smile. "No, they didn't."

"When I think about them as a story, it's not that gross," I say, scrunching my nose. "But when I think about you and Dad..." I trail off. "Gross."

She laughs. Mom's laughs always soothe me. No matter what's going on in my life, she makes it all better. Her laughs are contagious and comforting. "I can assure you, nothing about my love story was gross."

"This is the most romantic story ever, Mom," I say with a sigh. "They're going to get married. A happily ever after. It's sweet and perfect."

Mom stiffens and drains her wine glass. "Nothing is perfect, baby." She turns her emerald eyes my way and they flicker with pain.

"But you got Dad. I know you won. I know the story ends happily," I argue.

She swallows and looks off into the distance. "Our story may end happily, but the story isn't over yet. You've seen chapters, but not all of them."

"Theo," I hiss with disdain.

"Theo was the least of our worries, honey."

My phone buzzes and I pick it up. Finn sent me a picture of

the two of us. Last summer at the lake. We're both eating popsicles and happy. Back then, I did foolishly wish for more than our friendship because at the lake in our swimsuits we weren't two people on different rungs of the social ladder. We were equals. But all it took was drying off and getting in his expensive-ass car to grab some burgers to remind me we're not equal at all. He goes to school with socialites and other rich kids.

And me?

I'm a normal girl who is seeing a normal guy. Porter is better matched for me. He's my true equal. It's who I should choose if I were smart.

But...

Apparently I'm being stupid. My heart is tugging me farther and farther away from Porter with each passing second. I'm not sure I'd ever even given it to him in the first place. A stubborn boy with blue eyes and a devilish grin, who just so happens to drive a Maserati, took it when I wasn't looking and never let it go. I thought it wasn't his to begin with, but he always does what he wants.

"Finn is a good man," Mom says, peering over my shoulder at the picture.

I let out a huff, trying to bite back the smile. "He's difficult."

"All the best ones are," she says. "Do you think your dad was easy? He drove me insane most days."

"Not like Finn. Finn infuriates me. A rich dick."

A rich dick who smells good. Who makes a good pillow. The man who tells the stupidest jokes that somehow always make me laugh.

My heart aches in my chest. The ache has been there for months while I've been trying this thing with Porter. I assumed it was because I wanted Porter to fall madly in love with me. Turns out, my heart ached because I missed my best friend.

"Finn is also the only person I've ever seen to make you

smile like that," she says softly. "Regardless of how much money he has."

A pang slices through my chest and I tap out a reply to him.

Me: Stop trying to butter me up. It's not working.

But it is working. It always works. He knows me better than anyone else and has always had the ability to make me happy with one of his handsome grins.

My heart does another little flutter and I try to ignore it. I want him to respond. Finn may be spoiled rich and gets his way a lot, but he's never once made me feel like I'm merely an option. He always puts me first. His interest in me never wavers. When I'm with Finn, we laugh and have fun. He doesn't try to get in my pants or push me away when I try to know more about him. Finn gives and gives.

What happens if I give back?

Nervous energy thrums through me. My mind drifts to images of Finn and I watching a movie on the couch like usual. But instead of just cuddling, what if we kissed instead? What if we did more? Heat, fiery and intense, burns through me. It's a foreign sensation and one I can't get out of my head now that it's been planted.

I can see the dots moving, but I set my phone down. "Tell me the rest," I tell my mother, taking her hand into mine. "Tell me what Heath did."

"You're so sure it was Heath?"

"Come on, Mom," I say in exasperation. "The whole story was about him. You were simply a character in it."

CHAPTER THIRTY-EIGHT

Harrison

Past...

"I'M GOING TO GET YOU A RING," I PROMISE AS WE WALK HAND IN hand from the barn to the house.

She flashes me a wide smile, her green eyes shining with happiness. "I don't need a ring."

"I know, but you deserve one," I tell her. "One day I'll be able to give you more and—"

Her arms fling around my neck and she kisses me silent. I grab her ass and lift her. If we weren't in the yard where anyone could see, I'd lay her in the grass and take her again. I'll never get tired of taking this girl.

When we've had our fill, she slides her legs down and pulls away to regard me with a tender expression. "I don't want more. I want this," she murmurs.

I'm about to kiss her again when we hear yelling coming from inside. She frowns at me and when something crashes, she jerks from my grip to run into the house. I stalk after her and nearly run into her once we reach the source of the sounds in the living room. The house is wrecked from the party. Red Solo cups litter every surface. Drinks have been spilled. Furniture overturned. Decorations broken. Theo is sitting on his knees, cowering as Heath towers over him.

"I'm sorry, Dad," Theo mutters lamely. "I fell asleep and it must have gotten out of hand."

Like an animal getting a whiff of his prey, Heath's head

slowly turns to regard us. Unbridled rage burns in his brown eyes and the vein in his neck is throbbing wildly. His hands are fisted and he seems seconds from unleashing a beast.

Hooking my arm around Cat's waist, I pull her to me, keeping her as far from the motherfucker as possible. His eyes home in on the way I hold her to me and his lip curls up in disgust.

"You," he sneers as he takes a predatory step my way. "This is all your doing."

Cat flinches and sinks against me. Her body trembles in fear. I tense, my muscles coiled and ready for a fight. I will bash his fucking face in if he so much as thinks about touching my girl.

"You've lost your damn mind," I spit out, slowly moving Cat to where she's standing behind me.

Heath's eyes narrow as he watches my movement. I'm slow as though anticipating him striking like the snake he is. Once she's safely behind me, I fist my hands and square my shoulders, meeting him dead in the eye.

A challenge.

Fucking try me, old man.

His head cocks to the side as he regards me, no doubt sizing up my ability to physically take him. When he rolls his neck and the bones crack, I'm sure he's going to attack. But then, in true Heath fashion, he uses his most vicious weapon.

His tongue.

"I want you out of my house," he snarls. "I kept you because you were a fucking tool to be used for my advantage. But now you're useless. Nothing more than an uneducated orphan with nothing going for him aside from his ability to fuck. Your services are no longer needed, boy. I want you and your shit out of my house in fifteen minutes."

"Gladly," I bite back. "Come on, Cat. Only grab what you need and then we're out of here."

Theo whimpers. "Don't let him take her."

Cat fists my shirt from behind, but I don't dare turn my attention from the monster in front of me to comfort her.

"We're going," I tell them both coolly.

Theo stands and grabs onto Heath's arm, but his father shakes him off and advances on me. When he's close enough for me to feel his wrath rolling off him in waves, but not close enough for me to clock the crazy bastard, his brown eyes gleam with wickedness as he darts his attention to Cat.

"She stays." His words are clipped and final. No room for argument.

"Over my dead fucking body," I challenge.

"If only that could be legally arranged," Heath sneers. "She stays and your worthless ass goes."

"I won't stay," Cat says, her voice shaking only slightly as she peers around me. "We're leaving. You've wreaked enough havoc on everyone's lives."

Heath barks out a harsh, cruel laugh. "You dumb girl. It's as though you forget who owns you. Who owns your father."

She tenses but shakes her head in protest. "I don't care if you fire him. Dad is brilliant. He'll find another job. My father only wants for me to be happy. Your blackmailing me won't work." She clutches my arm and gives me a squeeze. "I have everything I need right here."

Heath's fury melts away as legitimate confusion passes over his features. "What?"

"I'm leaving. Fire Dad if you must, but I'm not staying here any longer for you to try and control me." She lifts her chin and stares defiantly at him. "You. Don't. Own. Me."

Before Heath can argue, I grab Cat's hand and jerk her with me to the stairs. We make quick work at packing the essentials into one backpack and then we're rushing back down the stairs. Theo sits in a chair with his palms covering his face looking like shit while Heath paces the floor gripping at his hair in frustration. They've never looked so much alike as they do now.

Pathetic.

Ruined.

Broken.

"Let's go," I murmur to Cat as we head to the door.

But then Heath launches into action, a furious roar escaping him. I release her hand in time to swing my fist. Hard and without much thought. Pain explodes across my knuckles the moment it makes impact with his jaw. His head snaps to the side and his palm instantly goes to the spot I hit him. He gapes at me in shock at first, as though he couldn't believe I'd actually hit him, and then his features turn murderous.

"Back the fuck away from us," I growl before giving Cat a little push to the door.

I help Cat put on the heavy backpack and then straddle my bike. She quickly puts on her helmet when Heath stands in the doorway watching us. I flip him the bird before gunning it out of there. We fishtail a bit and she grips me tightly. It's not until we're miles away that I begin to feel a giant weight lifted from me.

We're free.

Free of Heath's revenge and hate and games.

Finally.

"Ridiculous," Elliot mutters as he sips his coffee. "He's always been unpredictable and violent." Elliot's gaze falls to where the bag of peas sits on my knuckles.

"I did what had to be done to protect her from him," I say curtly, hoping he's not insinuating that I'm violent too.

Cat snuggles against my side and smiles up at me. "Thank you. I was so scared."

Leaning forward, I kiss her forehead. "I'll always protect you." Then, I turn my gaze back to Elliot. "I'm going to marry your daughter." Not a question but a statement. I'm informing him of my intentions.

"W-What?" he stutters out. "She's barely eighteen."

"When did you know you loved Mom?" Cat challenges him.

He deflates and sips his coffee again. "From the moment I saw her so full of fire, I knew I wanted her right then."

"And she was a teenager," Cat probes.

Elliot nods. "We both were."

"What I feel for Cat is more than words can describe. I want to marry her and make her happy," I tell him, my gaze burning into him. "I'll do whatever it takes."

Elliot's gaze softens. "Love that intense can't be ignored." He rises from the sofa and disappears.

"What now?" Cat asks.

"We can't stay here. I'm not sleeping on a damn sofa. We'll get a room at a hotel tonight and then tomorrow we can look for apartments," I tell her. "I have a good bit of savings and Damian will let me pick up more shifts. We'll make it work, baby."

She beams at me. "I have no doubts."

Elliot returns and sits. "Cat, darling," he says softly. "I'm sorry I haven't been the best father."

"Dad, don't," she starts, but he waves her off.

"It's true. I wasn't a good husband, but I always tried to be the best father I could. I love you more than words can describe. And I'm sorry that you are tangled up in this mess with

Heath. He's a monster and I never imagined his hate would bleed on decade after decade." He sighs and regards his daughter sadly. "I loved her too. Maybe not the way he loved her, but I did. I'll never apologize for pursuing and marrying your mother. But while it pains me to admit it, she never loved me like she did him. I wished for it to have been differently, but it was not. She died loving that man."

Cat sniffles. "Oh, Dad. I'm so sorry."

"We had you, though," he says smiling. "Even if for a short while, I had your mother's love and affection. That is when you were conceived. The moment she died, I promised you I'd love and protect you until my dying breath. The love she and I shared may have paled in comparison to that of her and Heath, but the love I have for you is undeniable. You're my baby girl. I regret nothing."

Cat rises and rushes over to her dad. He pulls her to him and he hugs her tightly. Seeing them in such a loving embrace makes my heart ache. One day, I want to be like him. The dad I never had. I want to love and protect my child as he so clearly does his daughter.

"I'd be a fool to intervene in an intense love storm again," Elliot says, stroking Cat's silky brown hair. "Which is why I'm going to go with it."

Cat pulls away and regards her dad with tears in her eyes. "You approve of our getting married? You don't think we're being foolish?"

Elliot smirks. "I think you're both blind idiots." He grins and kisses her forehead. "Blind idiots hopelessly in love. I want you to embrace it and not deny yourself a second of it. You deserve all the love in the world, Cat. Just as she did. I'd been a selfish, jealous boy and didn't care back then. It almost cost me everything. It nearly cost me my relationship with you—the most important part of my entire life. I'll be damned if I try and stop something so powerful ever again."

He waves me over to them. I stand, dropping the bag of peas on the table, and walk their way. He holds out his fist and I take what he offers.

A ring.

Brilliant and bright.

Expensive as all hell.

"It was your mother's," he explains to Cat. "And if this is what you really want, I want you to take it. Wear it every day as a reminder that love doesn't pay the bills. You two will have to fight to keep this love and marriage afloat. If times get too tight, you can sell it. I'm sure it could buy a home with its value." He strokes her hair gently. "But I'd love for you to work hard enough to find a way to keep it. It's meaningful to me and I hope it is the same for you."

I kneel down in front of them and take Cat's hand. "Will you wear this ring forever and fight for love with me?" I ask, running my thumb along her knuckles.

"Every step of the way," she breathes, grinning as tears glisten in her eyes.

The ring slides on easily and glitters in the light.

I stand and pull her into my arms, kissing her much too desperately in front of her father. I don't care, though. I'm going to marry this girl and keep her forever.

"Let's go, mustang girl," I tell her, smiling against her lips. "Seems we ought to celebrate."

We spend the next day looking at apartments. I take her to some nicer ones—ones that'll wipe out my savings pretty quickly in order for us to move into, but she's not interested in those. There's one in the classified ad that she's circled. I'm certain she's circled it simply because it's the cheapest rent. All the other places, she's crossed off with an X, but she keeps running her thumb across the same one.

"It's an apartment over someone's garage," I tell her as I practically inhale my burger while we sit at a park bench.

"But all bills are included in the rent," she challenges, fire in her tone.

I grin over at her. "You sure you're not choosing it because it's the cheapest? I can pick up three jobs if need be, Cat. We can live wherever you want."

She tosses her trash in the bag and shrugs. "I don't care about living somewhere fancy. You know that. Something about this place just calls to me."

"Why?"

"I'm not sure, but I think we should check it out."

Fifteen minutes later, we're driving along a dirt road through a thicket of trees. We come to a clearing. A nice ranch-style home is situated on the property beside a sparkling lake. The garage detached from the house is a two-car garage and a set of stairs along the side of it lead up to the garage apartment in question. We shut the engine off and an older woman with white hair shuffles out of the house.

"Can I help you kids?" she calls out.

Cat walks over to her and smiles. "Hi, I'm Cat and this is my fiancé, Harrison. We're interested in the garage apartment."

The old woman looks us over. When she apparently senses our genuine interest, she nods. "The rent is so cheap because I need help around the house. I could use a strong fella to mow and keep the flowerbeds up. And I could use a young lady to dust and mop the floors a few times a week." She lifts her chin in challenge.

"It sounds negotiable," Cat says. "Do you mind if we check out the space before we commit?"

The old woman frowns. "I'm afraid I can't climb those stairs anymore. It's probably not in the best shape but nothing a little tender loving care can't fix."

"It's okay," I tell her. "I like fixing stuff up."

"Good," she says. "I'm Ethel Greene. When you're done looking, come on inside the house for some pie. It's been ages since I've had visitors."

She leaves to go back inside. Cat turns to look at me, her eyes wide with excitement.

"I love it here," she says breathily.

My chest feels as though it's expanding. "Me too. Come on. Let's go check out the apartment."

Hand in hand, we climb the stairs. The door isn't locked, so we step inside. Upon first inspection, the place is a dated shithole. Curtains from the seventies hang from the windows that overlook the lake. The brown shag carpet has seen better days. But it's furnished, much to my surprise. Cat walks over to the couch and pulls away the sheet.

"It's hideous," I remark.

Cat giggles. "I think it's kind of cute."

"The couch has pictures of lanterns on it, Cat. It's not cute."

She simply grins as she peels away more sheets over the furniture in the living room. Then, I follow her into the tiny kitchenette. She fiddles with the stove and then the refrigerator. All are in working order.

Next, we inspect the tiniest lime green bathroom and Cat screams when she sees a spider. Once that fucker is dead, I take her to the bedroom. All the furniture remains in this room as well. Covered and protected from dust. Cat makes quick work to remove it all. I lean against the doorframe, watching her get lost in her excitement. She stands on the bed and draws the blinds up. Then she settles on her knees to stare out at the sparkling lake.

"Harrison, come here. Hurry," she says, waving me to her.

I climb onto the bed, mimicking her action, and put my arm around her. Her palm splays over my chest and she looks up at me.

"It's our spot."

I kiss her forehead. "It's our spot."

She lets out a squeal when I twist with her on the bed and pin her to the old, lumpy mattress. Her smiles turn into breathy murmurs when I start peeling away her clothes. Once we're both naked, I spread her thighs and enter her wet, inviting body. Our eyes lock as I fuck her sweetly in our spot. When I get closer to losing control, I reach between us and strum her clit just the way she likes. Soon, she's crying out and quivering as an orgasm strikes her. Her cunt clenches my shaft and I groan as my release spurts from me, soaking her insides as I claim her as mine once more.

Falling against her, I bury my nose in her hair as my weight pins her to the bed.

"I love it here," I tell her honestly. "It feels like home."

She strokes her palms over my shoulders. "It feels like home because we make it that way."

"It's crazy, Cat, but I don't care. I love you. I have since the moment I laid eyes on you," I whisper, seeking out her earlobe to kiss it.

"I love you too, Harrison. When you know, you know. And I don't want to waste one second of it."

My cock begins to harden inside her and I nip at her ear.

"Good, then I'm not going to waste one second of fucking you again before we go have pie with our new landlord."

"Make it quick, stallion," she teases.

Gripping her wrists, I pin them to the bed and lift up so I can stare at her soft, pretty face. "Actually," I say as I slowly thrust in and out of her. "I'd like to take my time and do this for the rest of my life."

Her green eyes twinkle with love. "I'd like that too."

CHAPTER THIRTY-NINE

HEATH
One week later...

I WATCH THROUGH MY WINDSHIELD AS MY WEAK SON ATTEMPTS TO talk to his cousin. There, standing in her school uniform, she lifts her chin as she listens to what he has to say. He keeps reaching for her and she steps away each time.

Weak boy.

So fucking weak.

It's embarrassing that he comes from my flesh. That he, even with all the money he has access to, would allow these people to make him feel so small. It's ridiculous.

From what Theo tells me, Harrison has plans to marry Cat on Sunday. A small affair in a tiny church because those idiots can't afford anything more. Her mother is probably turning over in her grave knowing her daughter is settling for less.

Bile rises in my throat. I'm disgusted. Fury and hatred burn through me. I've been trying to think of a way to make them pay. Elliot was my first attempt. But before I could fire him, I found the letter of resignation sitting on his desk.

He quit.

The fool left my company knowing it was more than he could have ever deserved. I researched and discovered he works selling insurance. Fucking insurance. How that man who was born with a silver spoon in his mouth would ever willingly step down is beyond me. It's unimaginable. I'm infuriated trying to figure him out.

They all probably sit around at dinner discussing how they outsmarted poor old Mr. Heath. Fuck them. They only paused the game. I'm strategizing my next move while they gloat in their perceived win.

They have not won.

They will never win.

This game has always been mine. I make the rules. I dictate the plays. I say who wins. And that's me.

My eyes track Theo and Cat as they walk down the steps. She doesn't seem happy with him, but she's listening to what he has to say. Nothing like her mother. Catrina would have flayed the boy right there. Reminded him that you don't fuck with her.

Not Cat.

Too much Elliot Lincoln in her.

She's fucking soft.

And the moment she marries that good for nothing piece of shit orphan, this will all have been for nothing. Decade after wasted decade. It's almost as though she seems happy to run off with the worthless mechanic. As though he has more to offer than the likes of my son.

I roll my windows down and listen when they approach.

"I don't need a ride," she tells him, waving her keys in his face. "I have my own."

His shoulders hunch when she climbs into her Mustang and drives off. My idiot son runs to his own car, turns his engine over, and immediately kills it. I watch in horror as he just lets her get away.

Something clicks inside my mind and my engine roars to life. I see Theo's confused look when he realizes I was watching them. My car peels out as I fire out of the parking lot after her. She drives slow until she makes it to a stop sign and sees me in the rearview mirror. Then, she puts the muscles to the test on her Mustang and peels out. I'm in my Mercedes rather than Theo's Porsche he's damn near killed, so I'm not as fast as her Mustang.

But she's a girl who drives like an idiot. I easily catch up and ride alongside her, waving for her to pull over. She shakes her head and guns it again. We're on a two-way street and she flails and screams, pointing ahead where a big-ass semi-truck barrels toward us.

"Pull the fuck over," I roar, even though she can't hear me.

She shoots me a panicked look. At the last second, she brakes and pulls off on the shoulder. I whip back into my lane and jerk the wheel off onto the shoulder, blocking her car. Then, I jolt from the vehicle and rush over to hers. She scrambles for the lock, but I'm quicker. I yank the door open and reach for her. Her fingernails rake down my forearm, but my suit jacket protects me from her assault. I snag her neck and then unbuckle her seatbelt. Dragging her from the car, I kick the door shut and wrangle her toward my car.

"What are you doing?" she screams. "Let me go!"

"You should have never left," I snarl as I pop the trunk. "You should have never left!"

She fights me as I push her inside the trunk. Her hands slap at me and her feet kick out. We struggle against each other. The girl has fire in her. Definitely got that from her mother.

"You can't do this!" she bellows, her foot clocking me in my still-sore jaw.

I howl and grip her neck again, pinning her down. "I can and I will."

Jerking my hand back quickly, I shut the trunk down on her. She screams and pounds, but I ignore her as I climb back in my car. I punch on the gas and tear off down the road. Violent energy thrums through me.

I will win.

I just had to make my move.

She's not going anywhere.

Harrison and Elliot. They will pay for trying to make a fool out of me. I'll keep the girl like I should have kept her fucking mother.

Do you like her better than me?

The bitter voice in my mind is familiar. Feminine. Catrina. My heart stutters in my chest and I grind the heel of my hand into my temple. I fucking hate when I hear her voice. It's not real. It's my mind making a mess of my memories.

She's pretty. Admit it.

"Fuck you," I roar to nothing and no one. "She could never compare."

The crazed laughter in my head soothes me and my heart thrums in its cage. Just having her daughter in my clutches has me feeling closer to the woman I loved than I've felt since her death.

Are you going to keep her?

"Yes."

Fuck her?

"No." I crack my neck as I speed down the road. "She's nothing like you. She's too much like that motherfucking Elliot."

More cackles echo in my mind.

Good.

Gritting my teeth, I rub at my temple again. I hate when I rationalize my thoughts by using her voice. Her fucking memory. I'm not crazy, but this sure makes me feel that way.

They made you crazy, the voice in my head purrs.

Elliot. Harrison. My brother and his wife. Isabel.

Fury ravages through me at the thought of Isabel. Apparently my thoughts mimic that of my imagined Catrina. She hated her so fully.

You were always mine. I was always yours. Our souls are the same. Black and tarnished.

Ignoring my maddening thoughts, I pull into my driveway and exit the vehicle. When I pop the trunk, it flings open and she flies out like a wild animal. Her green eyes—identical to her mother's—are frantic. She's frightened but also furious. The fury in her green orbs reminds me so much of her mother. It makes me pounce on her. I easily pin the slight girl in my arms. My nose runs along the side of her neck as I inhale her. She squirms and screams, but I ignore it.

"I'm keeping you," I tell her. "It's what's owed to me."

"Noooo!"

She kicks out when I carry her over to the door and we're shoved back a few steps. With a growl, I turn and then push through sideways. When Helen drops the cup of coffee in her hands and it hits the floor with a shatter, I snarl at her.

"Mind your own business, woman."

Her eyes widen in horror. "Mr. Heath."

"So help me if you do anything other than your fucking job, which is to serve me until the day I die, I swear to you, I will drown you in the lake," I yell.

The older woman flinches and scurries away. I drag my unwilling captive to the basement door. As soon as I open it, she detonates in my arms. Her flailing gets stronger and I almost drop her to her death. One false move and she'd go stumbling down the steps. Break her pretty little neck with one quick pop.

I prefer a lifetime of agony.

"Not that easy," I growl against her hair as I force her into the darkness. We reach the bottom and it's pitch-black. I blindly reach out for the light and flip it on. The light flickers and sputters, acting as though it's about to go out. As I'm fumbling around looking for a box of lightbulbs to replace the dying one, she scrambles loose. I tackle her before she can get too far away. We hit the cold, hard dirty floor, knocking the wind out of us both.

"Help! Helen!" she screams. "Help!"

I manhandle her until her wrists are secured and my body pins her to the ground. Her sobs come next. I listen to each sound she makes and drink them in. The light flickers out. In the dark, she sounds like her.

"Heath," she pleads through her tears.

So much like her.

So. Much. Like. Her.

Leaning forward, I run my tongue along the side of her neck. Her entire body goes still.

"I like your taste, Catrina," I murmur.

"Heath," she whimpers. "I'm not her."

Pressing my lips to hers, I kiss her hard and dominating. She fights against my kiss and manages to nip my lip. Blood rushes out and I growl.

"No, you're nothing like her," I bite out. "But you're still mine."

Her terrified howls seem to sing to my vengeful, black heart.

I want all her screams.

I deserve them.

They're mine.

CHAPTER FORTY

EMILY

Present...

"Mom!" I cry out, horrified by the turn of the story. "This is awful! Why would he do such a thing?"

Her hand shakes as she pours another glass of wine. The ring that belonged to my grandmother catches the light and shines. She sips her wine and smiles at me. How could she be smiling after telling me this story? It's horrible.

"He was an awful man," she mutters. "That was an awful time."

My phone buzzes. She laughs lightly and nods at it.

"You better answer that so we can finish our story," she says.

With tears threatening, I snatch my phone up.

Finn has sent another picture. This one is of me. I'm asleep in the front seat of his car. My hair is a mess and my cheeks are sunburned. I have a book clutched to my chest. He wanted to fish a little longer, but I was beat after being at the lake all day. We argued and I told him I was going to sit in the car. He told me to have fun suffocating. It was hot, but I was determined to have the last word. I sat in the car until I fell asleep. He must have unknowingly taken my picture. When I woke, I found the car on and the air conditioning running.

Finn: I know you say you don't date guys like me, but I don't care. You're my heart, angel. You have been since we were twelve years old and I found you skipping rocks on the lake.

He doesn't mention how he pushed me in. I'd been so mad I pretended to drown. He dove in and saved me. I'd been smitten with the little asshole right then. We spent the next day, and every day after, teasing each other. Then, we were inseparable. It wasn't until two years later that I realized our financial differences were something that set us apart. He was a have and I was a have not. I hated the way his parents flaunted money like it made them better than people like my parents. My parents are the best people in the world. I hate money and all it implies. So, by default, Finn gets shoved into that category. And if he wasn't such an annoying, persistent brat, I would've stopped being friends with him long ago.

But he always shows up.

We don't go to school together, but he always shows up to pick me up and cart me around places. I let him know at every chance that his stupid money won't buy my affection and he just laughs at me.

"He loves you," Mom says softly. "I think he always has."

"Finn?" My entire body thrums.

Her smile widens. "Yes, Finn."

A smile of my own tugs at my lips, but then I deflate as reality sets in.

"Mom, you of all people know what money does to people. It makes them vile and horrible and selfish. Your entire life story proves that. Finn Browning is loaded and he's an asshole," I grumble.

But he's not. I know he's not.

I can't even lie to myself anymore.

Mom frowns. "Is that the message you're getting from all this? That money determines who a person is inside?"

"Yeah," I say. Duh.

Mom's lips purse together. "Sweetheart, love doesn't care

about money one way or the other. What matters is how a person makes you feel."

"Finn makes me feel angry sometimes," I argue. That's the truth.

"Your father makes me angry all the time." She shakes her head and then sips her wine. "But he makes me feel. All of the emotions. All the time. There isn't a dull moment with him. Just passion and fire always. I know you can't see it, but I see how Finn pokes at you to get a rise. It's because your eyes flare such a brilliant shade of green when you're angry."

I huff and gape at her.

"But when you're sad and he makes you laugh, your eyes that shine with tears grow soft. Or when you're frustrated and he helps you with something, relief and admiration shine in your gaze. Sweetie," Mom says with a sigh. "He wants all those moments. You just have to let him in."

I try not to think about how last week I was bummed about Porter ignoring my texts and Finn showed up in his ridiculous Maserati. He brought my favorite kind of pizza and some movies. While I brooded and pouted, he was quiet and allowed me to wallow in my rejection. But not alone. He was there. Like always.

Tears burn in my eyes and I feel a lump of emotion in my throat. I've been clinging to this thought that money was bad and it bred hate. All while ignoring my heart. That's what I've been doing after all. Hardening my heart and protecting myself from the stinging rejection of not being good enough. Not rich enough. I wanted to be a step ahead.

A shudder wracks through me because it reminds me of something Heath would do. Blinking away my tears, I reply to Finn.

Me: Sometimes the heart is confusing.

He replies immediately.

Finn: It's the mind that's confusing, angel. The heart always knows.

Speaking of hearts, mine patters in my chest.

Me: I'm sorry.

Before he can respond, Porter replies.

Porter: Panties? You never answered my question.

I cringe as I finally tap out a reply to him.

Me: Plans have changed. I can't hang out.

No response. I'm not surprised. He'll just call up some other girl instead. I used to let it bother me. Not tonight, though. Tonight, I'm excited for something different and familiar all at once. I'm excited to take a step. To see what happens. And if I screw it all up, I'll deal with it when it happens. Until then, I'll throw caution to the wind.

Finn: I'll be in our spot. Come find me.

My heart does a flop in my chest. Our spot is on the dock at the lake. The same spot he chose to throw me into the water. The same spot I pretended to be dead and he frantically tried to give me CPR, giving me my first taste of a boy. The same spot I'd give him all kinds of hell. The same spot we'd share popsicles and smiles and secrets.

Our spot.

Me: I'll be there. Just as soon as I finish talking to Mom.

Finn: I'll be waiting. I always will.

When I look up, Mom's smiling. "You ready to hear what happens next?"

Despite wanting to kick off my shoes and run all the way to the lake, I nod. I can't get this deep into the story and stop now.

"I need to know what happened," I tell her. "All the awful details. I can handle it."

She pats my hand. "You can handle anything, sweetheart. You're my daughter."

CHAPTER FORTY-ONE

Past...

HEATH HAS LOST HIS DAMN MIND. GONE. IT'S NOWHERE TO be found. The light flickers back on and bathes us in its eerie glow. As he pulls his mouth away from mine, crimson dripping down his bottom lip, he wears a manic smile that tells me what little bit of sanity he might've had left has vanished. His finger comes up to his lip and he swipes at the blood before he sticks the tip of his finger into his mouth and sucks on it.

I search his eyes for something, anything that will prove he's still human. But all I see is a crazed man who is so lost in his vengeance he can't see straight. He can't think clearly. There will be no negotiating with him. He's not in a state of mind to see reason. He's already kidnapped me. Broken the law. He's not just going to let me go. And it's clear Helen isn't going to save me.

Harrison will find me. He will see I never made it home. He will know Heath took me. He will save me. But what if he can't? What if Heath did something to him?

I can't wait for Harrison to find me. To save me. What if it's too late?

My eyes dart around to find something I can use against Heath. An object that will give me the upper hand. I just need to be able to get out of here so I can call for help. Then I remember my cell phone is still in my car. On the side of the road. I need a plan. If I escape but don't get away, Heath will drag me back, and then who's to say what he will do to me. As if fate is against me, the light flickers out once more.

The basement is dark again and Heath releases me to rummage through a box looking for something.

"Don't move," he commands. I can't see him, but I'm assuming he's replacing the bulb. This is my chance. Once the light is on, he's coming for me. I fumble around as I stand and my hands roam over several rakes and shovels hanging on the wall. On the other wall I know is a door, but I can't tell in the darkness if it will open. I can't chance it. My only option is to take him down and run up the stairs and through the house.

He's fumbling with the bulb. I hear it clanking against the ceiling. His attention is no longer on me and I know it's now or never. I grab the shovel from the wall, knocking several other tools onto the floor with a loud clatter. As I'm running over to Heath, the entire area illuminates and he's able to see what I'm doing. He jumps off the chair and comes at me. Bringing the shovel around behind me, I swing it like it's a baseball bat and Heath is the baseball. His eyes widen momentarily as the shovel hits the side of his body. It's not enough to immobilize him, but it's enough that he stumbles back in shock and I'm able to drop the shovel and run up the steps.

I can hear his heavy footfalls and know he's right behind me. I don't turn around. I keep running. I swing the door open and scream for Helen.

"Helen! Help!"

And that's when my body hits something…no, someone. I glance up slightly and see Theo standing there. His face is devoid of all emotion.

"Theo! Thank God! Please help me. Your dad kidnapped me!"

When he doesn't say anything, I start to run around him.

I can't chance Heath catching me. But just as I'm about to pass him, his fingers grip my wrist, halting me in place.

No. This can't be happening. Theo wouldn't…

I yank my arm away, but it doesn't budge.

"Good, you caught the little bitch," Heath hisses and then snatches me from Theo. "Maybe you are my son after all." He grins proudly at Theo and Theo visibly straightens, a small smile splaying upon his lips at his father's rare compliment. And my heart sinks. There's no getting away. It's two versus one.

Remembering Helen is still somewhere around here, I start screaming again. "Help! Someone help! Hel—"

Heath's hand covers my mouth with one hand, while his other hand wraps around my body, holding my arms down. He drags me back down into the basement. I kick and flail my body, but it's no use. Heath flings me onto an old wood chair then releases my mouth.

"Help!" I scream again as Heath starts to tie my hands up with rope.

"I saw Helen on my way in," Theo says. "I locked her in the pantry. She won't be helping you."

Heath smiles darkly and gives his son a nod of approval. "Good boy."

Theo's lips upturn into a sweet smile like a small boy who has just been praised for making his bed or cleaning his room. And suddenly I'm overtaken with fear.

"You're both going to rot in hell!" I yell and Heath shoves a piece of cloth into my mouth to silence me. I try to push it out, but without the use of my hands, I only gag myself.

I watch as Heath ties my ankles to the legs of the chair and when he's done, he stands back and grins cruelly. "My sweet Catrina. You are finally mine." He walks around behind me and I try to turn to keep my eyes on him, but I can't move. I'm tied up too tight. His fingers feather across my shoulder and he brushes my hair to the side. My gaze darts to Theo, who is still standing in place, his eyes furrowing in concern. He isn't lost yet, but soon he will be.

I groan as loud as I can to get Theo's attention. It's muffled, but he hears it and his eyes meet mine. I beg him with my eyes. Plead for him to do the right thing. And I think he might. His features turn sorrowful, almost remorseful as he watches from the sidelines.

Heath, on the other hand, mistakes my groaning as a moan, and his lips brush up against my earlobe. "I just want one touch, my sweet Catrina. It's your blood that runs through her veins."

My eyes widen in shock. In fear. He's not speaking to me. He's speaking to my mother! Theo must've heard him as well because he now looks worried, confused. He opens his mouth to speak, and I think he might tell his father to stop.

"Go find the orphan," Heath demands. "We must make him pay for trying to take my sweet Catrina away from me."

"You mean from me?" Theo clarifies.

"She is no longer yours! You don't deserve her," Heath lashes out. "You didn't fight!" He steps away from my chair and stalks toward Theo. "Prove you deserve her. Go handle the mangy mutt and then come back once you're done." He leaves no room for argument in his tone and Theo obeys.

When the basement door shuts, Heath turns and faces me. There's a sadistic glint in his eye that sends chills down my spine. He cuts across the room and my eyes squeeze shut in fear of what's to come. I feel the material leave my mouth and my body flying backward. My lids spring open and see his face only a breath away from mine. He's leaning me back in the chair. My feet still tied down and dangling off the ground. His fingers dig into my chin.

"I loved you, my sweet Catrina." His words come out in a choked sob. "I loved you and you betrayed my heart. You chose him over me. You chose to marry him. To have his baby." He blinks once and a single tear falls. My heart constricts at the reality of what my mother did to this man. She destroyed not only his heart but his mind. I read the events through her eyes, her words, her heart. But it isn't until now, looking into the worn out eyes of Heath that I'm able to see how muddled her view was.

"I have loved you my whole life," he continues, his voice strained with raw emotion. I don't even think he sees me anymore. "You've broken me, Catrina. But still I love you. I see you everywhere I go. In my room. In my bed. In the stables. I can't get your image out of my head. Everything around me is nothing more than a reminder that I'm forced to exist in this world without you. It is only you I see, my love."

His lips brush against mine and I stay frozen in place. I should bite him or head butt him, do something to hurt him, but I do nothing. Because he is already hurting. And my heart is aching for him.

"Heath," I whisper against his lips. "I'm sorry for what she did to you. You didn't deserve what she did. You deserved to be loved."

Heath backs up slightly and his eyes roam over my face. "She loved me," he croaks out. "She loved me the only way she knew how. Like crazy."

His eyes are filled with unshed tears. His face showing of defeat, of a man who has lost everything.

CHAPTER FORTY-TWO

Harrison

"*I* *THINK HE'S GOING TO HURT HER.*"

Those words play over and over in my head as I haul ass through town on a mission. A mission to save my girl from that fucking monster.

Helen called me bawling her eyes out. Said Heath dragged in a kicking and screaming Cat before hauling her downstairs into the basement. I'd been trying to figure out what the fuck she was going on about when I heard a scuffle and the line went dead.

"I think he's going to hurt her."

I roll through a stop sign once I realize no cars are coming and gas it again. As I drive, I see her Mustang abandoned on the side of the road. That motherfucker just took her. Right from her car.

"I think he's going to hurt her."

Why?

All because of some sick revenge plan?

I've lived with Heath my entire life. He's a dick of epic proportions. Plays games all the damn time. But, until Cat, I never assumed him to be so violently out of control. It's like her arrival detonated a bomb inside him. With us leaving last week, I thought that was the end of it. He'd move the hell on and go find someone else to terrorize. Instead, it's as though he's been lying low and biding his time. Waiting for the right moment to pounce.

But why Cat?

I get why he hates Elliot. Elliot stole the love of his life right from his grasp. I never really understood the obsession he had with Catrina. If she truly loved him, would she have left him to marry some other man in the first place? Love doesn't work like that. Love isn't selfish. Love is fierce and feral and out of control, but it's also wholesome and good. How is leaving the one you love for the affection of another considered good? I'm an outsider looking in, but it's clear as day to me that Catrina Lincoln didn't love Heath like he loved her.

Heath, on the other hand…

His love for her is his existence. His reason for being. His love for her dictates his every move. His every emotion. I read and memorized those journals. Everything he did was for her. Until death and thereafter. It's like his love for her became a beast. A beast hell-bent on destroying everything responsible for taking her away from him.

And Cat?

I suppose she took from him too. The moment she was born and her mother took her last breath, Cat was written into Heath's ultimate revenge plan. His beast is hungry to devour every last piece of what he thinks has wronged him.

If he kills her…

Surely not. Surely he wouldn't harm one hair on her head.

My stomach churns with worry. He's lost it. No longer the calculating, intelligent man. It's as though he's finally given in to the madness that's been edging on him more and more through the years. I should have taken her and run far away so we'd never have to see him again. But I thought it was over. That he'd admit defeat and move on.

I'll never assume again when it comes to my girl.

I slam on the brakes and am off the bike before the roar of the engine has stopped echoing through the air. Stalking inside, I make a beeline toward the kitchen. Someone slaps at the door inside the pantry. A chair is wedged under the door handle.

"Cat!" I call out and rush to the door, yanking the chair away.

But when I open the door, Helen falls into my arms, sobbing. I give her a squeeze before pulling away to inspect her.

"Are you okay?" I demand.

"Y-Yes, but get downstairs!"

I release her and stalk toward the basement door. Before I can reach it, Theo stands in my way. His chin is lifted in defiance and his brown eyes are hot with anger.

"Get out of my way," I growl.

"She belongs with us," he says, his voice shaking.

"Move."

He squares his shoulders as though it'll make him bigger and taller. A roar of anger rushes through me as I grab the prick by the throat. I sling my fist across his jaw and he crumples to the floor like a sack of potatoes. Pushing past him, I start down the stairs where I hear Cat's frantic crying.

As I reach the bottom, I halt my movements. Cat is sitting in a wooden chair. Her hands and legs both bound with rope. Heath is bent at the waist, his fingers holding her chin in place. His face only a breath away from hers. His body is coiled tight with fury. She's so small and fragile in his grip.

"Let her go," I command, my voice steady despite the chaotic storm of emotions brewing inside me.

He stiffens and cocks his head to the side to regard me. Gone is the shrewd, evil glare of a madman. In its place is someone lost. Broken and ravaged by grief. His wild eyes are glassy with unshed tears and his dark brows are furled together. He stares at me as though I'm a surprise he didn't see coming.

I was always coming.

My intentions with Cat have been clear from the start. She's mine and I would do anything to protect her. That's what love is. It's not revenge and hate and manipulation. Love is walking through fire, uncaring if you get burned, to get to where the other half of your heart is.

"She *chose* you," he says harshly, his voice catching with emotion. "Why?"

Stepping closer, I hold up a hand to calm him. "We chose each other. Love isn't one-sided, Heath."

He flinches at my words. "You don't know anything, orphan."

My gaze slides over to Cat's. Tears stream silently down her cheeks. Her green eyes practically glow with love and relief at seeing me.

"I know you spent your entire life letting one thing drive you. Revenge," I say softly.

"Because they deserved it!" he roars, shaking Cat in his grip.

Another step.

"Not her. Not Cat. She did nothing to you," I argue. "Just like I never did anything to you."

"You think life is fair, boy?" he bellows at me. "You think life is tit for tat? That if you're good and love someone it'll all just work the fuck out?" His brown eyes flame with malevolence. "It doesn't work the fuck out. No matter how much you love someone, money can just take them away. Fucking poof!"

I shake my head. "No."

"Don't tell me no," he snarls. "I've been around a lot fucking longer than you. I know how this world works."

"No, you know how your world works. But the rest of the world?" I say, taking another step closer. "We follow our hearts. Cat couldn't care less about money or things. She just wants to love and be loved back. I'm going to marry her and we're going to be happy, Heath. No one can stop us. Not even you or your ominous agendas or a lifetime of revenge."

His head snaps around and he shakes Cat again. "Why? Why did you choose him? Why didn't she choose me? She chose Elliot and I gave her everything that was ever important to me. I gave her so much fucking love, Cat. So why the fuck did she choose him?"

Cat sobs. "I-I don't know. I'm sorry." Her eyes meet mine as I approach. I'm seconds from whacking him over the head, but she gives me a look that says to chill.

"Your apologies mean nothing to me," Heath growls. "It can't be fixed. Nothing will bring her back."

"Heath," Cat whispers and he turns his attention back to her. "I miss her too," she admits softly. "I never even knew her, but I miss her so much."

Heath nods slowly, his eyes trained on Cat for several long seconds. Then, he shocks the hell out of both of us when he undoes the ropes that are tying her down to the chair. First, her legs and then her hands.

When he's done, he backs up slowly. But before he's out of her reach, Cat reaches up and grips his wrist. He allows the action. His shoulders hunch and his head hangs in defeat. In a surprising move, she stands up and hugs him. At first he's stiff. His body even shakes as though he'll toss her onto the floor. But then, his arms wrap around her and he squeezes her so tight I'm afraid he'll break her.

I watch, stunned, as the mean man who dictated every move my entire life trembles and a harsh, ragged sound escapes him. Not crying. No, it's far more sad and awful. Like his soul is thrashing and screaming, begging for escape from his throat. He clings to my girl as though their embrace answers questions for him—as though it forgives every terrible thing he's done.

Once the guttural sounds coming from him grow silent, I step forward and nudge his shoulder. He jerks away from her and steps back. She flings herself into my arms and I kiss her desperately.

Safe.

She's safe with me.

Safe and loved and adored and cherished.

I'll never let her go.

"You're mine until the end of time, Cat Lincoln."

"You're mine too," she sobs against my lips.

I possess her in another crushing kiss as my palms roam all over her, checking to make sure she's okay. Our kiss ends and I hug her to my chest. Heath watches us with a sullen expression. The heel of his hand is rubbing at his chest as he watches us with such longing. Not as though he wants her, but as though he wants what we have.

"It hurts," he rasps as he absently rubs at his chest. His eyes fall to the floor. "It hurts so bad. The emptiness claws at me. It shreds every part of me. Nothing ever stops it. I bleed every goddamn day, never drying up. This brutal cage of a body imprisons my soul—a dark, heavy soul who only wants his other half." His hand falls to his side as he looks up at us again. "I don't know what it feels like to not hurt."

I stroke my fingers through Cat's hair as I murmur, "I hope one day you will."

His lips press together and no more words come out. Heath isn't apologetic or remorseful. He's just Heath. What I do get from him is a look of resignation in his eyes. He's tired. Tired of trying so hard and never finding the peace he's looking for. Whatever he's looking for won't be found through us. We're not a part of his world, no matter how hard he tries to make it happen.

Scooping my soon-to-be bride into my arms, I carry her toward the steps. Together, we climb from hell and find our heaven.

And the sad, defeated devil stays where he belongs.

CHAPTER FORTY-THREE

EMILY

Present...

"You're crying, Mom," I say, my voice trembling with my own emotion.

She swipes away her tears. "Not all stories are happy. His certainly wasn't."

Leaning into her, I hug my mother tight and inhale her familiar scent. My mom has always been loving and fun and kind. Where the other mothers cared about money and status and achievements, my mom only cared about one thing.

Us.

Me, Dad, Helen, and Grandpa.

Her family.

"Your story was a happy one," I say, smiling through my tears. "Because eventually you got me, right? I was your happily ever after."

She laughs softly and pats my back. "You were. We didn't have to wait long either. Our love was something that couldn't be destroyed by fiery revenge and hate. Something strong and unbreakable was born from the ashes. Your father and I didn't take my father's words lightly. We fought for us every step of the way."

"Can you tell me what happened after? When I came along? Were you happy?" I ask, eager to hear more of the good stuff.

"We were beyond happy. You were our rainbow after the storm."

CHAPTER FORTY-FOUR

CAT

Past—One year later

I LOOK DOWN AT MY BEAUTIFUL SLEEPING DAUGHTER IN HER CRIB. Emily is six weeks old today. When I found out I was pregnant it wasn't much of a surprise. Not with all the times Harrison and I had unprotected sex. I would've been more surprised if I didn't wind up pregnant. I graduated from high school eight months pregnant with my dad, Harrison, and Helen cheering me on from the stands.

After the whole ordeal with Heath went down, Helen quit working for him and since she didn't need to work anymore, unofficially retired. A few weeks later, she came by to see our new home. She and Ethel hit it off and Helen is now living with Ethel as her roommate. Helping her around the house. She's also been invaluable these last several weeks with Emily. Every time I doubt myself, she's right there holding my hand.

I'm not quite sure what happened with Theo, but the rumor is Heath paid for him to finish his senior year back at his old boarding school and he spent the summer traveling through Europe. Nobody has heard from Heath since the day we walked out of his home. I often think about him, though. Wondering if he's lonely. Harrison thinks I'm crazy to even give the man a moment of my thoughts, but between my mother's journals and living with Heath for that short time, I can't help but feel sympathy toward him. He might be vindictive and malicious, but it's only because he gave my mother so much of his heart, there wasn't enough of it left for him to love anyone else. A love that powerful and all-consuming is so rare, and it breaks my heart that it was wasted on a woman who took it for granted.

"Hey," a baritone voice whispers into my ear. "You ready for bed, Mrs. Crenshaw?" Harrison's comforting arms snake around my waist and his chin rests on top of my shoulder. My body relaxes against his strong frame. We were married in a small church in town. Harrison offered to give me any kind of wedding I wanted, but every time I envisioned marrying him, all I could see was the two of us—with my dad and Helen as witnesses—in front of a minister, promising to love each other for the rest of our lives. And that's exactly what we did. I wore a pretty white dress and Harrison wore a suit. We had dinner with my dad and Helen and afterward he took me home and made love to me all night long. A few weeks later, I found out I was pregnant.

"I am," I answer him, but I don't move from the side of the crib. I've recently started at a local college, but I hate leaving my baby girl for ten minutes, let alone hours to go sit in class. Harrison wants me to get an education like I planned, though. He even offered to move to New Haven so I could attend Yale like I always dreamed, but I told him no. Yale might've been my dream, but that was before I became a mother. Now, my only aspiration is to be a good mother to our daughter and a good wife to my husband. When I found out a lot of my life was a lie, I wasn't sure where I belonged. But standing here with my daughter asleep and my husband holding me close, I know exactly where I belong. Right here.

Harrison laughs softly and the sound makes me smile. "She's sleeping, Cat. Safe and sound in her crib."

"I know. I was thinking, though…what if we moved her crib into our—"

Harrison cuts me off. "Not happening, mustang girl. For one, she would hate us for it."

"Why?" I ask, my eyes not leaving Emily's tiny little body.

"Because it's been six weeks since I've made love to my wife, and once I'm between those creamy thighs, I'm never leaving. And we both know how loud you can get." His shoulders shake with laughter and I roll my eyes.

"I'm not that loud," I huff.

"Yes, you are. And even if you weren't, I'm not having sex with you with our daughter in the room. If she wakes up, she'll be traumatized for life."

I snort loudly and Emily startles slightly.

"Let's go," Harrison insists. His arms leave my body and he comes around me. He bends over the side of the crib and gives our daughter a kiss on her forehead. "Good night, pony girl."

Taking my hand in his, he guides us out of the room and into ours. We're barely through the door and he's pinning me up against the wall. His lips trail soft kisses down my neck and my eyes flutter shut. The feeling of my husband's touch sends shockwaves straight to my core. He removes my shirt and his lips go to my hardened nipple. When I let out a sigh of pleasure, he chuckles knowingly. Okay, so maybe I am loud in the bedroom. But it's not my fault, he's good at pleasing me.

When I feel his hands grabbing my ass and lifting me up, my eyes spring open. My arms wrap around his neck. He carries me to our bed and lays me gently in the middle, situating himself between my legs. My eyes stay trained on him as he removes his shirt over his head, exposing his beautiful artwork. My gaze lands on his newest piece: a horse identical to mine that appears to be galloping through the fields. In the tail is mine and Emily's name. The artist worked it in around his other tattoos, making it seem as though the horse was jumping through them. When I asked him why the horse, he said he would never forget the moment he saw me on my horse that first day when Theo and I rode over to the Windy Hills Estate.

"I knew in that moment that one day you would become mine. There were no other options."

Harrison pulls his shorts and boxers down and throws his clothes to the floor. His blue eyes sparkle with lust and love and so much happiness. I could live the rest of my life staring into those eyes.

Dropping on top of me, both of his hands land on either side of my head. His mouth fuses with mine in a passionate kiss. Our bodies pressed tightly against one another's. My hands go to his back. Rubbing all over him, craving the connection. Harrison breaks the kiss to look into my eyes. Love and adoration shining brightly in those sapphire irises. Then he's kissing me again. My forehead, my cheeks, my neck. He kisses along my jaw. His lips find their way to my heavy breasts. He gives each one attention, licking and sucking gently on my pert nipples. Then he works his way down my soft belly to my pussy. He gives it a chaste kiss before he pushes a single finger into me to make sure I'm wet. I am. I always am for this man. He grins at the sound my pussy makes when it accepts his second and then third finger.

"Fuck, baby," he groans. "I'm never going to last inside this tight cunt."

"It's a good thing we have a few hours before Emily wakes up." I grip his biceps and pull him back up my body. His mouth plants kisses along my shoulder and then his lips are back on mine.

"All mine," he breathes against my lips as he pushes his hard length into me. My back bows at the sweet intrusion. It's been too long since I've felt him inside of me. His mouth makes love to mine while he makes love to me. All too soon, we're both finding our release. Too sated and exhausted to even clean up,

Harrison rolls me over onto my side, his warm, naked body snuggling against my own.

HARRISON

Twelve years later…

"She's nearly a teenager," I grumble from under the hood of Cat's old Mustang. This car's been around for as long as we've been together. And like the sentimental pair we are, we keep it alive and running.

Well, *I* do.

Cat continues to drive like a bat out of hell and hits curbs on the regular.

"I know," she says, offering me a bottle of water. "But I just worry about her."

I grab my grease rag that's hanging out of my jeans pocket and swipe the sweat off my face. Then, I pocket the rag and take the bottle. It's hot as fuck this late summer afternoon. I unscrew the lid and down the entire thing in a few quick gulps.

My wife bites down on her bottom lip and gives me the wicked look that leads to even more wicked acts.

"See something you like, mustang girl?" I rumble as I prowl over to her, tossing the plastic bottle into the grass.

She squeals when I pull her into my arms, my sweaty, bare chest soaking her thin tank top. "Harrison Crenshaw!"

I laugh and grab a handful of her ass. She's going to have a helluva time getting the grease off her shorts. Lifting her up, I'm happy when she settles where she belongs—with her legs spread around me and her lips fused to mine. We kiss lazily as I blindly walk us up the porch steps and over to the swing. It's bittersweet this place. *"Our friend Ethel was our fairy godmother. Every story has one,"* as Cat always says. Ethel passed away when Emily was only five. Our daughter loved the old woman and we were in complete shock when she left us her farm in her will.

I settle into the swing and hold my wife. She relaxes on my chest as I draw soft circles on her back over her shirt. Eventually, she lifts up and regards me with her bright green eyes that have been the light of my world since the day I looked at them.

"It's hard to let her go off on her own," Cat says, a frown tugging at her plump lips.

"It's just the other side of the lake." I wink at her. "I was doing much worse at twelve than exploring the property."

"I don't even want to know," she groans. "And I wasn't. My dad kept me on a tight leash. What if she drowns? What if someone kidnaps her?"

I smirk at her. "Our loud, sassy kid? They'd bring her right back."

She chuckles and runs her fingers over my buzzed head. "I was getting used to the long hair and beard this past winter. Now you're the young man I fell in love with again."

"It's too damn hot for all that hair."

"I should go check on her, but I need to start dinner," she huffs. All playfulness fades. "What if he comes back one day, Harrison?"

We both grow somber. We haven't spoken to Heath since that night he took Cat. I've seen him driving through town here and there, and once last year, he slowed down in front of my shop but never stopped. Thank fuck too, because I didn't want to give my company a bad name for beating someone's ass in the parking lot.

"He won't come back. He knows better," I assure her.

She nods and then changes the subject. "Did you ever look over those ads I texted you?"

Groaning, I shake my head. "Don't you have dinner to start, woman?"

"No way. You're not going to get off that easily. Those ads are important to our business. Keeps that dinner you're so eager for me to start on the table." Her brow arches in challenge.

Fuck, she's so cute when she sasses me.

"Fine," I grunt. "I'll look at them."

She beams at me. "Thank you. Now go check on our girl before I run off and embarrass her. You're better at this stuff than me." She climbs off my lap and I rake my gaze up her perfect, curvy body, admiring every inch of her. People say love fades, but they must not know real love. Our love gets more colorful and beautiful each day that passes.

I steal one more kiss and then walk down the steps of the porch toward the lake. On my way, I look at my phone to check the ad mockups Cat sent. C&H Automotive has been ours for two years now ever since Damian sold me his shop. We renamed it and rebranded it thanks to Cat. She's the brains of our operation—always up to date on the newest marketing and advertising trends. The customers adore her and the other guys at the shop like having a lady to help look after them. As for me, I'm the one who makes it all run smoothly. Cars are my life, and now, it's a huge part of Cat's life too. The fact she wanted to do this with me is a dream come true. Everything about her is more than I could have ever hoped for. I choose the second ad in the text and reply back before pocketing my phone.

When I hear shouting, I tense up, my eyes searching for my daughter. I see her standing on the dock talking—no, yelling—at a boy much taller than her. I'm unable to hear what she's saying, but she's wagging her finger at him and her other hand is on her hip. Looks and acts just like her mom, this kid.

As I approach the dock, the boy tears his gaze from her and his eyes widen upon seeing me. Emily lets out a growl of frustration and marches past him over to me. She throws her arms around me and hugs me tight. She's soaked to the bone from swimming. I squeeze her back. This kid and her mother are my entire world.

"Hey, pony girl. That boy giving you trouble?" I ask, tugging on her wet ponytail.

She pulls away and her finger points at the boy. "Finn tried to drown me."

I arch a brow at him and the poor kid trembles.

"N-No, sir, I didn't t-try to drown her," he stammers all over his words.

"Big liar," Emily huffs. "You pushed me right in."

Finn flinches and shakes his head. "I was only playing. I didn't know you didn't know how to swim."

She scoffs. "I nearly died."

I bite back a laugh. This girl of mine is a fish. Been swimming in this lake since she was a year old.

"But I saved you," the boy murmurs.

A smile tugs at her lips, but she quickly hides it. "Just barely."

"Sir," he says to me, taking a step toward us. "I swear, I didn't mean to hurt her. I know CPR. She was safe."

"CPR, hmm?" I say with a rumble.

Emily flashes me a look of embarrassment, her cheeks turning bright red. "It's fine, Dad. He saved me. I'm fine."

"I think there's been enough swimming for today," I grunt. "Em, get back to the house and help your mom with supper. I'm going to have a little chat with Finn."

"Don't kill him," she mouths to me. Then she turns to the boy. "He's probably going to kill you for trying to kill me." With that, she shrugs and skips off. The poor sap stares off after her with such longing in his eyes. When she's gone from sight, he swallows thickly and regards me with fear flashing in his eyes. His gaze peruses down my frame and a shudder ripples through him. I'm well over six feet and solid muscle. Covered in tats and glaring at this kid with a "you touch my daughter, you die" kind of stare.

He's probably going to piss his pants soon.

"She's not allowed to kiss," I tell him, my voice stern.

His eyes widen. "Kiss? I was saving her."

I don't let him in on the fact my daughter just stole her first kiss from a boy who tried to drown her.

"Come on," I tell him, nodding with my head to indicate he should follow me. "Let's chat man to man."

He falls into step beside me with his chin lifted. There's something in this kid's bright blue eyes that I akin to myself. Maybe it's the smitten look for the green-eyed fireball. Maybe it's the fearless way he goes off with a man who could fold him into a pretzel without breaking a sweat. Whatever it is, I feel something for the kid right away. Call it intuition.

We walk until we reach the woods. The grassy fields end along the edge of the trees and it's a dark thicket beyond that. I point to a tree that has C&H carved into it. Pulling my knife from my pocket, I revel in the sharp intake of breath coming from the kid. I deepen the grooves of our initials and then swipe away the shavings on the blade with my thumb.

"You like her?" I ask, eyeing the kid with an arched brow.

"Uh, yes, sir." He rubs at the back of his neck. "I mean like a friend, sir."

Smirking, I fold my knife up and slide it back into my pocket. "Good. You be a good friend to her. You want to know who my best friend is?"

He swallows and nods. "Yes, sir."

"Her mother."

A smile spreads across his face. "We just moved here." He points across the way to the big house down the road. "There."

"Nice place."

He shrugs. "I miss our townhouse in the city," he says, his features pulling into a frown. "Well, I did until I met her." Another smile on his face.

"Emily is a special girl. She deserves only the best," I tell him.

He nods quickly. "I can be the best friend to her. I swear. I was only playing with her. I only wanted to…" he trails off and his brows scrunch in confusion.

"Flirt?"

His cheeks blaze bright red. "N-No, sir."

"Good," I say, grinning. "But just so you stop beating yourself up about it, Emily can swim."

Relief flashes over his features and then his face turns bright red again. "How long will she be mad at me?" he asks.

Reaching forward, I tousle the kid's hair and walk past him. "She's stubborn and fiery. Knowing my daughter, forever."

He doesn't respond, so I look over my shoulder at him. Determination glints in his eyes as he stares at our house. "It's a good thing I'm patient," he says. "I'll convince her to be my friend. I'll wait until forever if I have to."

It's then I realize what I see in this kid that makes me like him so much. It's not myself or fearlessness or anything like that.

It's certainty.

The same certainty I had when I saw Cat.

When you know, you know.

I should be scared as hell that this kid looks at Emily the way I looked at Cat all those years ago, but I'm not.

"I think you have one helluva chance, kid," I tell him. "Don't fuck it up."

His wide, happy grin tells me everything I need to know.

He won't.

When you know, you know.

And Finn—the new kid who lives in the big-ass house down the road—knows. It's written all over his goofy face, and if he's anything like me, already written all over his heart too.

"See you around," I call out to him.

"You bet, sir."

CHAPTER FORTY-FIVE

EMILY

Present...

AFTER MOM GOES TO BED, I SLIDE ON MY FLIP-FLOPS AND HEAD toward the lake. Normally, Finn's over-the-top car is sitting near the dock, but not tonight. Apprehension bubbles up inside me. He said our spot. Surely he wouldn't stand me up.

A pang cuts through me.

What if I pushed him too far?

Now that I realize I have always wanted Finn and not allowed myself to have him, the very thought of losing him nearly guts me.

God, I am so stupid.

Every smile he's ever given me flips through my mind like a slide show. By the time I make it to the lake, my vision is blurred with tears. I kick off my shoes when I make it to the dock and walk out to the end. Closing my eyes, I let the hot tears roll down my cheeks.

I'd been so busy trying to mold someone like Porter into something better, that I lost sight of the perfect man right in front of me.

He has every right to want to move on. I've been awful to him. Since the day he pushed me into the lake. My heart aches for a redo. To rewind back to that summer day and change things. I'd been smitten with him, but then I'd been introduced to his parents, seen his giant home, and felt the coldness of what money does to people. It was so different from what I was used to with my own family that it spooked me.

But Finn?

He was never cold.

Finn Browning is fire and warmth and comfort.

I let out a sad sigh. Tomorrow, I'll go to his house and talk to him. It's not too late. Determination is just burning through me when two solid hands give me a push from behind. I barely have a chance to cry out and suck in a breath before I plunge into the cold, dark lake water. Kicking up, I rise to the surface in time to hear a splash but not see the culprit. Panic rises up inside me and then something grabs me from beneath the water.

The scream I let out gets muffled by the water as I'm pulled under. I thrash until I'm pulled into a familiar pair of strong, muscular arms. He kicks us to the surface and the moment I open my eyes, I start yelling.

"You little asshole!" I holler. "You scared the shit out of me!"

His laughter makes my heart catch as he swims us back over to the dock. As though I weigh nothing, he hoists me out of the water and lays me on my back. That smug grin of his is the last thing I see before his lips hover above mine.

"What are you doing?" I whisper, my fingers sliding up his muscular arms.

"What I should have done six years ago," Finn rumbles.

"Oh yeah?" I breathe. "What's that?"

"Claiming you."

His lips press to mine sweetly at first—reminiscent of that day when he thought he was giving me CPR. But then he urges my lips apart and his tongue seeks mine. This isn't like any kiss I've ever had. No kiss has tasted like fire and need and a bond only forged through years of friendship and love. His body pins mine to the wood planks and in desperation to be closer to him, my legs part. He settles between my thighs and I can feel how hard he is through our wet clothes. When he grinds against my center, I moan into his mouth and claw at his shoulders.

"I knew I'd eventually convince you, angel," he says in that smartass way that boils my blood. And tonight is no different. My blood is boiling, but I like the way he stokes my fires. I want him to burn me with this intensity he always directs my way.

"So sure of yourself," I say, nipping at his bottom lip. "You're going to have to work harder at convincing me."

A growl rumbles through him and straight to my core. He rocks his hips in such a way that he rubs against my clit each time. Stars of pleasure dance behind my lids. His tongue dances with mine as his hands rove over me in a reverent way.

I've never felt so wanted and adored in all my life.

My heart skips with joy. I'm an idiot for denying myself this man for so long.

"Emily," he rasps, lifting up to stare down at me. His blue eyes shine with such emotion that my heart seems to crack open.

"Finn."

He smiles. No smugness. Just pure happiness. Me. I make him smile this way. "I've loved you from the moment I saw you standing on the end of that dock. I always knew I'd make you mine one day."

My bottom lip trembles. "I'm sorry I pushed you away."

"It just makes the reward much sweeter," he says, pressing small kisses on my lips. "You are worth the wait."

His lips kiss down to my neck and then he rubs against me until I'm whimpering with a sudden orgasm. Before I can come down from my high, he stands up, stealing his warmth away from me.

"Don't look so sad, angel," he teases. "I'm going to take you somewhere where I can take my time with you." He offers his hand to me and then pulls me to my feet. Instead of letting go of my hand, he guides me over to the edge of the dock so I can put my shoes back on. Quietly, we walk over to my house to the garage. When I was a kid, after we moved into the main house, my parents would let me play in the garage apartment. Finn and I hang out up there a lot since it has a television and we can be as loud as we want without bothering anyone.

This time is different, though.

We're no longer best friends going there to have an innocent time.

Tonight, we're taking a new step. Breaking past the friendship barrier we've been stuck behind all this time.

He guides me up the stairs and we step into the apartment. Once inside, he walks over to the stereo and turns on some music. Then, he motions for me to follow him to the back. Nerves get the best of me and when I reach the doorway, I pause.

His eyes dart over to me and he stares at me with such an unguarded expression. Love and need and desire all burning in his blue eyes. But since it's just Finn, the apprehension bleeds away and I find myself slowly approaching. When I'm close, he wraps his arms around me and hugs me to him.

"We don't have to do this," he says, pulling away to stare at me. "I've waited this long. I can continue to wait until you're ready."

His earnest stare is my undoing.

Grabbing the hem of his soaked T-shirt, I start lifting it up. I peel his shirt off him and then admire his lean, cut physique. Finn has those V muscles that make girls like me stupid. Even when trying to keep him in the friend zone all these years, I've allowed myself to admire this god of a man. Tonight, though, I'm allowed to touch. And greedily, I roam my palms over his hard, tanned flesh on his lower stomach.

"Finn Browning," I whisper as I lean forward and kiss between his pectoral muscles. My lips linger there and I can feel his heart steadily thumping. "I've loved you from the moment you looked at me and pressed your lips to mine when we were twelve. And then I spent the next six years pushing you away. I'm sorry."

His palms slide into my wet hair and he tilts my head up. Intensity burns in his blue eyes and he bites on the inside corner of his bottom lip as he stares at me. "Waiting all those years just to hear that you love me was worth every second." His lips crash to mine and all sweetness fades as our need takes over like two feral animals. He's not gentle as he practically rips my dress from my body. My fingernails make him hiss when they claw at his hips in desperation to remove his basketball shorts. Soon, we're both naked and panting between kisses.

"God, you're beautiful," he groans as his palms find my ass. He lifts me, urging me to wrap my legs around him. His cock bounces against the crack of my ass as he carries us to the bed. As though I'm something fragile, he lowers us onto the bed with the utmost care. His cock slides between the lips of my pussy, but he doesn't enter me.

"I'm nervous," I squeak, my eyes darting all over his face.

He frowns. "This isn't your first time." His features grow stormy. "You've been with him."

"No," I rasp out. "He wanted to one night, but I was scared."

His cock teases me. Back and forth. "Why were you scared?" His voice is husky and raw.

Running my fingers into his hair, I pull him closer for a kiss. "I was scared I was about to make a big mistake."

"Are you scared now?"

The tip of his cock pokes against my entrance. A thrill of need shoots through me. "No, just nervous that it will hurt. But scared? Not with you. I trust you with my everything, Finn."

He crashes his lips to mine and then slides his hand between us. At first I think he's going to guide himself into me, but his fingers find my clit that's still buzzing from my last orgasm. When he starts strumming me so expertly, I moan into his mouth and tug at his hair.

"That's it, angel," he croons. "Let me take care of you."

He massages me until I'm crying out in ecstasy. I'm still trembling when he fists his cock and then wets the tip of it with the juices running out of me. His eyes are down between us where he's rubbing me and I truly appreciate how gorgeous he is. Strong nose and chiseled jaw. A dusting of facial hair and tousled light brown hair that sometimes takes on blond hues with too much sun. His lips are full and kissable. God, he's hot.

His blue eyes sear into mine, flashing with love and assurance as he pushes barely inside me. My breath hitches and his brows furrow together in concern.

"You okay?" he asks, his body stilling.

I dig my heels into his ass and urge him closer. "I've never been better."

He grins that crooked boyish grin I love so much before pouncing on me for a kiss. His cock stretches me to the point of pain as he pushes further inside me. I let out a mewl of fear, but then he's kissing me with such love and passion that I want everything with him. Pain. Pleasure. Forever.

His hips thrust into me hard. Just once. Enough that he breaks through any barrier separating us and is completely seated inside me. The burn is enough to bring tears to my eyes, but the way he kisses me in such a soothing way, I relax.

This feels right.

This feels like love.

For so long I've been an idiot, pushing away what's been right in front of me. All because I thought money and status mattered. My parents prove that it doesn't matter. Love matters. Love doesn't give one damn about how much money you make or where you come from. Love is a storm that decimates everything in its path with equal fierceness. Love is madness and it just doesn't care. It doesn't care about what school you go to or what kind of car you drive. Love does what it wants.

"God, I love you, Emily Crenshaw," he murmurs as his hips begin a seductive rhythm that sings to my soul.

I claw and kiss at him, desperate for more. Now that I've finally allowed myself a taste, I'm hungry for it all.

"I love you too, Finn Browning."

My words set him off and he bucks into me. I love how my sweet, funny, put together boy turns into a beast dead set on ravaging me. His teeth nip at me and his groans become growls. And then he's coming and marking me. Claiming me as his forever.

In this moment, we're not best friends or neighbors.

No, we're finally *here*.

Exactly where we should be.

This is our spot.

Together.

CHAPTER FORTY-SIX

FINN

Present...

"Mom says to come down for breakfast," Emily says, grinning at me from the doorway.

This morning, she's more beautiful than ever in a pair of cut off shorts and a black T-shirt. Her brown hair has been freshly washed and dried and pulled into a high ponytail. I take a moment to admire her full, pouty lips and her mischievous green eyes. My cock aches to take her again—as if three times last night wasn't enough.

"She knows I spent the night?" I ask, lifting a challenging brow.

She smirks and saunters into the room looking too fucking sexy. My morning wood is begging to take this cowgirl for a ride. As if cued into my thoughts, she rakes her eyes over the sheet barely covering me and lingers her stare at where my dick tents the sheet. "Someone's happy to see me." Then, she waggles her finger at me. "But there will be none of that right now. Mom will send Dad up here if we don't get into the kitchen soon and I doubt you want my dad knowing you just deflowered his little girl."

My dick lurches at the mention of her big-ass dad. "Then stop looking so hot," I grumble.

Her laughter is music to my ears. "You're so grumpy in the mornings." She tosses my boxers and shorts at me. They're still damp, but I'll live. I pull on the wet clothes and then snag her wrist.

"I love you," I blurt out, hating that I sound like a lovesick fool. It's the truth, though. I've loved her for so long. No other girl compared to her. There was only one girl I ever wanted. And now that I have her, it feels unreal.

She smiles sweetly at me and her green eyes shine with an adoration I've craved for so long. "I love you too."

I kiss the top of her head before stepping into the bathroom to piss and brush my teeth with one of the extras in the cabinet. My hair has that just-fucked look, which won't do in front of her parents, so I wet it down and try to tame it some.

"You done primping yet?" she sasses from the bathroom doorway.

A growl rumbles from me as I pounce on her. I kiss her hard and without apology against the doorframe. "I could use thirty more minutes," I rumble.

"Thirty?" she teases. "More like three."

I snort. "Three? You know I fuck you much slower than that because I like to savor you, angel."

"Maybe we should time it next time," she breathes. "Because I'm pretty sure it was three."

She starts squealing when I tug at her shorts button. But her squeals turn to moans when I get them down her hips and shove her panties down as well. I push her into the bathroom over the counter and tease her pussy from behind. She moans and squirms as I rub at her clit from behind until she's coming with my name—oh, how fucking sweet it sounds—on her lips. Our eyes meet in the old, dingy mirror as I enter her swiftly from behind. I palm her perfect tits as I thrust into her hard. She braces herself against the mirror, pushing against my dick, eager for every inch of me. My palm abandons one tit to massage her clit some more. I love how wild she gets when she comes. How her pussy clenches around me like a fucking vise when she's losing control.

"Finn!" she cries out, slamming her palm against the mirror. Her cunt squeezes me and I lose it. A feral grunt escapes me as I drain my release into her tiny, sweet little body. With a grin, I pull out and slap her cute ass.

"I guess you were right. Three minutes."

"Smartass," she says with a giggle.

We clean up and then walk hand in hand to the house. The house smells like bacon when we enter. Her dad, Harrison, is hugging her mom from behind, whispering things into her ear. My parents act like business partners. There is no love and passion in their relationship. What Emily's parents have is what I want with my girl.

Yeah, she's fucking mine.

She always was…she just didn't know it yet.

"Morning," I greet as I break away from Emily to steal some fresh bacon. Cat swats at me but smiles. Something different shines in her eyes this morning. Something I can't quite put my finger on.

"Morning, Finn," Cat says.

"You look like hell, kid." Harrison smirks at me.

I chuckle and chomp on the bacon. Then, I wrap my arm around Emily. "She thinks I look hotter than hell," I correct.

Harrison grunts. "Mouthy is what you are."

"You love me," I joke.

It's true. I've worked my way into everyone's hearts over the years. They're the family I felt more connected to than my own.

The doorbell rings and the door swings open just as Harrison yells, "Come in!"

"Good morning!" Helen says when she enters the kitchen a moment later. She makes her way around the room, giving everyone a hug. When she stops at me with my arm still around

Emily, she gives me a knowing smile. "Good morning, Finn." She winks. "Good morning, Emily."

"Morning, Nanny," Emily says back. "I think you've met Finn…my *boyfriend*." I chuckle at how adorable she is. I've known Helen as long as I've known Emily. The woman is like a second grandmother to me.

Helen's smile turns into a full-blown grin. "Nice to meet you, Emily's *boyfriend*." She laughs.

"Morning, everyone," Elliot announces, walking into the kitchen and setting down some bags on the counter. He steals a piece of bacon, then, as he walks out of the kitchen, he pops Helen on the ass before sitting in his chair.

"Elliot!" she admonishes. "Not here." She swats at him playfully before taking the seat next to him.

"Time to eat," Cat announces and everyone else finds their seat at the table.

Breakfast goes like it does any other time I eat over here, except this time, instead of getting Emily's eye rolls, she flashes me sweet smiles. It has pride thumping in my chest.

"Whatever happened to Heath?" Emily asks her mom.

I tense because I don't know who this Heath is. My eyes automatically dart to Harrison for support. It's like he's always looked after me all these years. He winks at me and I relax.

"He still lives at Windy Hills Estate," Cat says, her eyes darting over to Helen, who grimaces. "Still trying to get a glimpse of your grandmother's ghost, I'm sure."

Emily frowns. "That's sad. Even after all he did, I feel sorry for him."

I listen raptly, curious about her grandmother and the man who loved her. I'm always eager to hear little pieces of Emily's life. She's mine and I want to know everything about her.

"Some stories are sad," Cat agrees. "And some are happy." She reaches over and takes her husband's hand.

"Will he ever get his happily ever after?" Emily asks.

This time it's Helen who answers her. "With Heath, his happily ever after will come the day he's reunited with the love of his life." She looks over at her husband, who takes her hand in his and gives it a soft kiss.

"In death," Emily says sadly. "Seems like a long time he's had to wait to be with her."

"Your soulmate is worth waiting for," I murmur, locking eyes with Emily. "No matter how long you have to wait."

Everyone around the table smiles at me.

They get it.

EPILOGUE

HEATH
The Dark Place...

"C ATRINA!"

Dark. Dark. So dark.

"Catrina!"

Frantically, I search for her. I can feel her. I can smell her. So close...

"Catrina!"

Why the fuck is it so cold here?

I fumble through the darkness, seeking a bit of warmth. A dull glimmer of light. I can really feel her now. Closer. So close.

"Catrina, my love!"

Heath.

Was that whisper my imagination or was it real?

"Heath..."

Warmer and warmer and warmer.

I can feel her smile. It's sunshine and happiness and delight.

"Catrina!"

"Heath!"

Hot. So hot. So close. And fuck, it's bright.

I'm knocked over by love. It saturates my soul. It puts me back together again.

"You came for me," she whispers. "It took so long, but you came for me."

"I'm here now, my heart."

I hold her close and don't let her go.

Not ever again.

"Where are we going?" she asks.

"We're going home."

"And where's that?"

"Together."

The End

NIKKI ASH'S PLAYLIST

Love the Way you Lie—Eminem featuring Rihanna
The Monster—Eminem featuring Rihanna
So Good—Zara Larsson featuring Ty Dolla $ign
Heavy—Lincoln Park featuring Kiiara
Love Like This—Natasha Bedingfield featuring Sean Kingston
Over Now—Post Malone
Remind Me to Forget—Kygo and Miguel
Tattoo—Jordin Sparks
Best Thing I Ever Had—Beyoncé
Stay—Rihanna featuring Mikky Ekko
Meant To Be—Bebe Rexha and Florida Georgia Line
Lips of an Angel—Hinder
Him & I-G—Eazy and Halsey
Take It All Back—Judah & the Lion
Strip That Down—Liam Payne Featuring Quavo
Bad Blood—Taylor Swift featuring Kendrick Lamar
God Gave Me You—Blake Shelton
Closer—The Chainsmokers featuring Halsey
Over—Drake
The Hills—The Weeknd featuring Eminem (Remix)
I'm a Mess—Ed Sheeran
Red—Taylor Swift
Wildest Dreams—Taylor Swift
Come Back—Usher
Better Now—Post Malone
Look What We've Become—Grace Potter
The Scientist—Coldplay
Your Love is My Drug—Kei$ha
Unfaithful—Rihanna
Please Don't Leave Me—P!nk
Somebody That I Used to Know—Gotye featuring Kimbra
Beautiful Trauma—P!nk

K WEBSTER'S PLAYLIST

"Shark" by Oh Wonder

"Meet Me in the Hallway" by Harry Styles

"Love The Way You Lie" by Eminem, Rihanna

"Love on the Brain" by Cold War Kids, Bishop Briggs

"Lips of an Angel" by Hinder

"Bad at Love" by Halsey

"Don't Walk Away" by The Mayfield Four

"How's It Going To Be" by Third Eye Blind

"Fade Into You" by Mazzy Star

"Dancing With Your Ghost" by No Resolve

"I Found" by Amber Run

"Wild Horses" by Bishop Briggs

"Last Goodbye" by Jeff Buckley

"To Be Alone" by Hozier

"Say Hello 2 Heaven" by Temple of the Dog

"Crazy" by Gnarls Barkley

"Cupid Carries A Gun" by Marilyn Manson

"If You Want Love" by NF

"Stubborn Love" by The Lumineers

"I Will Possess Your Heart" by Death Cab for Kutie

"No One's Gonna Love You" by Band of Horses

"Love is a Bitch" by Two Feet

"Codex" by Radiohead

NIKKI ASH ACKNOWLEDGEMENTS

Kristi, without you giving Wuthering Heights a chance, this book wouldn't even exist. Thank you for falling in love with Heathcliff and showing me even the blackest of hearts are capable of loving and breaking. To everybody who contributed to this book in some way, whether it was beta reading, editing, proofreading, formatting, making teasers, or simply posting about this book, thank you! To the bloggers, thank you for sharing and taking a chance on Heath. To my children, thank you for simply being you. And to the readers, you are the reason why I'm able to continue to write. Your love and passion for my books never seizes to amaze me. Thank you.

K WEBSTER ACKNOWLEDGMENTS

A big, happy thank you to Nikki Ash. Thank you for making me read *Wuthering Heights*. Had you not expressed your undying love for that book, I may never have picked it up. I enjoyed nerding out with you late into the night over that story. And what was even better than that was when you didn't call me crazy when I suggested we do a modern retelling. Our mutual love for Heathcliff and Cathy drove us to tell our own tale, and I'll be forever grateful you went along that path with me. It was a blast…and for that, I dedicate this book to you, Nikki Ash. Until next time, friend. There will definitely be a next time! Love ya bunches, even when you try to micromanage me!

Thank you to my husband. You'll always be my Heath and I'll be better than your Catrina! I love you bunches!

A huge thank you to my Krazy for K Webster's Books reader group. You all are insanely supportive and I can't thank you enough.

A gigantic thank you to those who always help me out. Elizabeth Clinton, Ella Stewart, Misty Walker, Holly Sparks, Jillian Ruize, and Gina Behrends—you ladies are my rock!

Thanks so much to Misty. You go THERE with me all the time, no matter where THERE is. Even if it's far out into space, or under the sea with mermaids, or in fairy lands, or the barn, or the 1800s. No matter where THERE is, THERE you are. I absolutely love the fact that you go out of your comfort zones

for me. You're a dedicated friend and I love you to pieces.…
totally in the creepiest way imaginable.

A big thank you to my author friends who have given me your
friendship and your support. You have no idea how much that
means to me.

Thank you to all of my blogger friends both big and small that
go above and beyond to always share my stuff. You all rock!
#AllBlogsMatter

Emily A. Lawrence, thank you SO much for editing this book.
You're amazing and I can't thank you enough! Love you!

Thank you Stacey Blake for being amazing as always when
formatting my books and in general. I love you! I love you! I
love you!

A big thanks to my PR gal, Nicole Blanchard. You are fabulous
at what you do and keep me on track!

Lastly but certainly not least of all, thank you to all of the
wonderful readers out there who are willing to hear my story
and enjoy my characters like I do. It means the world to me!

ABOUT AUTHOR NIKKI ASH

Nikki Ash is a *USA Today* Bestselling author of contemporary romance, focusing on single parent, secret baby, and surprise pregnancy romances. She spends her days and nights getting lost in words. When she's not writing, she's reading. From the Boxcar Children, to Wuthering Heights, to the latest single parent romance, she has lived and breathed every type of book.

Nikki resides in South Florida with her husband, two children, and dog that she considers to be one of her kids. When she's not reading or writing, she's traveling the world with her family—in search of inspiration.

Contact Nikki Ash
Facebook: facebook.com/authornikkiash
Twitter: twitter.com/authornikkiash
Instagram: instagram.com/authornikkiash
Amazon: amazon.com/author/nikkiash
Website: www.authornikkiash.com

Nikki Ash's reader group:
www.facebook.com/groups/booksbynikkiash

Subscribe to Nikki Ash's newsletter:
bit.ly/NikkiAshNewsletter

ABOUT AUTHOR K WEBSTER

K Webster is a *USA Today* Bestselling author. Her titles have claimed many bestseller tags in numerous categories, are translated in multiple languages, and have been adapted into audiobooks. She lives in "Tornado Alley" with her husband, two children, and her baby dog named Blue. When she's not writing, she's reading, drinking copious amounts of coffee, and researching aliens.

Download at
books.bookfunnel.com/k_webster_short_story_bundle

JOIN MY NEWSLETTER
at authorkwebster.com/newsletter

JOIN MY PRIVATE GROUP
at reamstories.com/authorkwebster

Follow K Webster here!

Facebook: www.facebook.com/authorkwebster

Readers Group:
www.facebook.com/groups/krazyforkwebstersbooks

Patreon: patreon.com/authorkwebster

Twitter: twitter.com/KristiWebster

Goodreads:
www.goodreads.com/author/show/7741564.K_Webster

Instagram: www.instagram.com/authorkwebster

BookBub: www.bookbub.com/authors/k-webster

Wattpad: www.wattpad.com/user/kwebster-wildromance

TikTok: www.tiktok.com/@authorkwebster

Pinterest: www.pinterest.com/kwebsterwildromance

LinkedIn: www.linkedin.com/in/k-webster-396b7021

9 781963 654608